# Praise for the novels of Richard Montanari

"Richard Montanari has amped up the fictional world of suspense with his powerful Philly crime series."
—*The Madison County Herald*, on *Merciless*

"This thriller has it all. It's fast paced, laced with red herrings, descriptively terrifying and leads to an electrifying conclusion. Bravo."
—*Winnipeg Free Press*, on *Merciless*

"What makes *The Skin Gods* engrossing isn't just the sustained suspense but the adept rendering of the characters."
—*Rocky Mountain News*, on *The Skin Gods*

"A page-turner."
—*The Philadelphia Inquirer*, on *The Skin Gods*

"A relentlessly suspenseful, soul-chilling thriller that will hook you instantly."
—Tess Gerritsen, on *The Rosary Girls*

"Readers of this terrifying page-turner are in the hands of a master storyteller. Be prepared to stay up all night."
—James Ellroy, on *The Rosary Girls*

# MERCILESS

A NOVEL OF SUSPENSE

# RICHARD
# MONTANARI

BALLANTINE BOOKS • NEW YORK

2008 Ballantine Books Mass Market Edition

Copyright © 2007 by Richard Montanari
Excerpt from *Badlands* copyright © 2008 by Richard Montanari

Published in the United States by Ballantine Books, an imprint of The Random House Publishing Group, a division of Random House, Inc., New York.

BALLANTINE and colophon are registered trademarks of Random House, Inc.

This book contains an excerpt from the forthcoming hardcover edition of *Badlands* by Richard Montanari. This excerpt has been set for this edition only and may not reflect the final content of the forthcoming edition.

Originally published in hardcover in the United States by Ballantine Books, an imprint of The Random House Publishing Group, a division of Random House, Inc., in 2007.

ISBN 978-0-345-49241-8

Cover design: Derek Walls
Cover photograph: Richard T. Nowitz/Corbis

Printed in the United States of America

www.ballantinebooks.com

OPM 9 8 7 6 5 4 3 2 1

To Ajani
*Anchi konjo nesh*

# PROLOGUE

In his dream they are still alive. In his dream they have blossomed into beautiful young women with careers and homes and families of their own. In his dream they shimmer beneath a golden sun.

Detective Walter Brigham opened his eyes, his heart a cold and bitter stone in his chest. He glanced at the clock, although it was unnecessary. He knew what time it was: 3:50 AM. It was the exact moment he had gotten the call six years earlier, the dividing line by which he had measured every day prior, and every day since.

Seconds earlier, in the dream, he had been standing at the edge of the forest, the spring rain an icy shroud over his world. Now he lay awake in his bedroom in West Philadelphia, a layer of sweat covering his body, the only sound his wife's rhythmic breathing.

In his time, Walt Brigham had seen many things. He had once seen a drug case defendant try to eat his own flesh in a courtroom. Another time he'd found the body of a monstrous man named Joseph Barber—pedophile, rapist, murderer—lashed to a steam pipe in a North Philly tenement, a decomposing corpse with thirteen knives in its chest. He had once seen a veteran homicide detective sitting on a curb in Brewerytown, quiet tears etching his face, a bloodied baby shoe in his hand. That man was John Longo, Walt Brigham's partner. That case was Johnny's.

All cops had an unsolved case, a crime that haunted their every waking moment, stalked their dreams. If you dodged the bullet, the bottle, the cancer, God gave you a case.

For Walt Brigham, his case began in April 1995, the day two young girls walked into the woods in Fairmount Park and never walked out. It was the dark fable that dwelt at the foothill of every parent's nightmare.

Brigham closed his eyes, smelled the dank brew of loam and compost and wet leaves. Annemarie and Charlotte had worn matching white dresses. They were nine years old.

The Homicide Unit had interviewed a hundred people who had been in the park that day, had collected and sifted through twenty full bags of trash from the area. Brigham himself found the torn page of a children's book nearby. Since that moment the verse had been a terrible echo in his brain:

*Here are maidens, young and fair,*
*Dancing in the summer air,*
*Like two spinning wheels at play,*
*Pretty maidens dance away.*

Brigham stared at the ceiling. He kissed his wife's shoulder, sat up, glanced out the open window. In the moonlight, beyond the night-bound city, beyond the iron and glass and stone, was the dense canopy of trees. A shadow moved through those pines. Behind the shadow, a killer.

Detective Walter Brigham would face this killer one day. One day.

Maybe even today.

# PART ONE

# IN THE FOREST

# 1

He is Moon, and he believes in magic.

Not the magic of trapdoors, and false bottoms, and sleights of hand. Not the magic that comes in the form of a pill or a potion. But rather the magic that can grow a beanstalk to the sky, or spin straw into gold, or turn a pumpkin into a carriage.

Moon believes in the pretty girl who loves to dance.

He had watched her for a long time. She is in her twenties, slender, above average in height, possessed of great refinement. Moon knows she lived for the moment, but for all that she was, for all she was going to be, she still seemed quite sad. Yet he is certain she understood, as does he, that there is an enchantment that lives within all things, an elegance unseen and unappreciated by the passing pageant—the curve of an orchid's petal, the symmetry of a butterfly's wings, the breathtaking geometry of the heavens.

A day earlier he had stood in shadows, across the street from the Laundromat, watching as she loaded clothes into the dryer, marveling at the graceful way she encountered the earth. The night was clear, terribly cold, the sky a seamless black fresco above the City of Brotherly Love.

He watched her step through the frosty glass doors,

onto the sidewalk, her bag of laundry over her shoulder. She crossed the street, stood at the SEPTA stop, stamped her feet against the chill. She had never been more beautiful. When she turned to see him, she knew, and he was filled with magic.

Now, as Moon stands on the bank of the Schuylkill River, the magic fills him again.

He looks at the black water. Philadelphia is a city of two rivers, twin tributaries of the same heart. The Delaware River is muscular, broad of back, unyielding. The Schuylkill River is crafty and cunning and serpentine. It is the hidden river. It is *his* river.

Not unlike the city itself, Moon has many faces. Over the next two weeks he will keep this face unseen, as he must, just another dull daub on a gray winter canvas.

He gently places the dead girl on the bank of the Schuylkill, kisses her cold lips one last time. As beautiful as she is, she is not his princess. He will meet his princess soon.

Thus the tale is spun.

She is Karen. He is Moon.

And this is what the moon saw . . .

# 2

The city hadn't changed. He'd been away only a week, and hadn't expected miracles, but after more than two decades on the police force of one of the toughest cities in the nation, one could always hope. On the way into town he had seen two accidents and five arguments, along with a trio of fistfights outside three different taverns.

*Ah, the holiday season in Philly,* he thought. *Warms the heart.*

Detective Kevin Francis Byrne sat at the counter of the Crystal Diner, a small, clean coffee shop on Eighteenth Street. Since the Silk City Diner had closed, this had become his favorite late night haunt. The speakers offered "Silver Bells." The chalkboard overhead heralded the holiday message of the day. The multicolored lights on the street spoke of Christmas and joy and merriment and love. All well and good and *fa-la-la-la-la*. Right now Kevin Byrne needed food, a shower, and sleep. His tour started at 8 AM.

And then there was Gretchen. After a week of looking at deer droppings and shivering squirrels, he needed to look at something beautiful.

Gretchen upended Byrne's cup, poured coffee. She may not have poured the best cup in town, but nobody ever looked better doing it. "Haven't seen you in a while," she said.

"Just got back," Byrne replied. "Took a week in the Poconos."

"Must be nice."

"It was," Byrne said. "Funny thing though, for the first three days I couldn't sleep. It was too damned quiet."

Gretchen shook her head. "You city boys."

"City boy? *Me?*" He caught a glimpse of himself in the night-blackened window—seven-day growth of beard, L.L.Bean jacket, flannel shirt, Timberland boots. "What are you talking about? I thought I looked like Jeremiah Johnson."

"You look like a city boy with a vacation beard," she said.

It was true. Byrne was born and bred a Two-Streeter. And he'd die one.

"I remember when my mama moved us here from Somerset," Gretchen added, her perfume maddeningly sexy, her lips a deep burgundy. Now in her mid-thirties, Gretchen Wilde's teenaged beauty had softened into something far more striking. "I couldn't sleep either. Way too noisy."

"How's Brittany?" Byrne asked.

Gretchen's daughter Brittany was fifteen, going on twenty-five. She had gotten busted a year earlier at a rave in West Philly, caught with enough Ecstasy to pull a charge of possession with intent. Gretchen had called Byrne that night, at wit's end, not really realizing the walls that existed between the divisions in the police department. Byrne had reached out to a detective who owed him a favor. The charge was reduced to simple possession by the time it got to municipal court, and Brittany had gotten community service.

"I think she's gonna be okay," Gretchen said. "Her grades are up, she's getting home at a respectable hour. At least on weeknights."

Gretchen had been married and divorced twice. Both of her exes were drug-addled, violent losers. But somehow, against the odds, Gretchen had managed to keep her head up through it all. There was no individual on earth Kevin Byrne admired more than the single mother. It was, hands down, the hardest job in the world.

"And how's Colleen?" Gretchen asked.

Byrne's daughter Colleen was the lighthouse at the end of his soul. "She's amazing," he said. "Absolutely amazing. A brand-new world every day."

Gretchen smiled. They were two parents who, for the moment, had no worries. Give it another minute. Everything could change.

"I've been eating cold sandwiches for a week," Byrne said. "And *lousy* cold sandwiches at that. What do you have that's warm and sweet?"

"Present company excluded?"

"Never."

She laughed. "I'll see what we've got."

She sashayed into the back room. Byrne watched. In her tight pink tricot uniform, it was impossible not to.

It was good to be back. The country was for other people: *country* people. The closer he got to retirement, the more he thought about leaving the city. But where would he go? The past week had all but ruled out the mountains. Florida? He wasn't big on hurricanes either. The southwest? Didn't they have Gila monsters there? He'd have to give this more thought.

Byrne glanced at his watch, a huge chronograph with a thousand dials. It seemed to do everything but tell the time. It had been a present from Victoria.

He had known Victoria Lindstrom for more than fifteen years, ever since they'd met during a vice raid at a massage parlor where she had been working. At the time she was a confused and stunningly beautiful seventeen-year-old, not long from her home in Meadville, Pennsylvania. She had continued in the life until one day a man attacked her, viciously cutting her face with a box cutter. She had endured a number of painful surgeries to repair the muscles and tissue. No surgeries could repair the damage inside.

They had recently found each other again. This time with no expectations.

Victoria was spending time with her ailing mother in Meadville. Byrne had been meaning to call. He missed her.

Byrne glanced around the restaurant. There were only a handful of other diners. A middle-aged couple in a booth. A pair of college girls sitting together, both on cell phones. A man at the booth nearest the door, reading a newspaper.

Byrne stirred his coffee. He was ready to get back to

work. He had never been one to flourish in the down times between jobs, or on those rare occasions when he took his vacation time. He wondered what new cases had come into the unit, what progress had been made in ongoing investigations, what arrests, if any, had been made. The truth was, he'd thought about these things the entire time he'd been away. It was one of the reasons he hadn't brought his cell phone with him. He would have been on the horn to the unit twice a day.

The older he got, the more he came to terms with the fact that we are all here for a very short time. If he'd made even the slightest difference as a police officer, then it was worth it. He sipped his coffee, content with his dime-store philosophies. For the moment.

Then it hit him. His heart picked up a beat. His right hand involuntarily formed a pistol grip. That was never good news.

He knew the man sitting by the door, a man named Anton Krotz. A few years older than the last time Byrne had seen him, a few pounds heavier, a little more muscular, but there was no doubt it was Krotz. Byrne recognized the elaborate scarab tattoo on the man's right hand. He recognized the mad-dog eyes.

Anton Krotz was a cold-blooded killer. His first documented murder had come as a result of a botched robbery at a variety store in South Philly. He had shot the cashier point-blank for thirty-seven dollars. They had brought him in for questioning on that case, but had to let him go. Two days later he robbed a jewelry store in Center City and shot the man and woman who owned the store—execution style. It was caught on video. A massive manhunt nearly shut down the city that day, but somehow Krotz slipped through.

As Gretchen made her way back with a full Dutch apple pie, Byrne slowly reached over to his duffel on the adjoining stool, casually unzipped it, watching Krotz out of the corner of his eye. Byrne eased his weapon out, slipped it onto his lap. He had no two-way radio, no cell phone. For the moment, he was on his own. And you didn't want to take down a man like Anton Krotz on your own.

"You have a phone in the back?" Byrne asked Gretchen softly.

Gretchen stopped slicing the pie. "Sure, there's one in the office."

Byrne grabbed her pen, wrote a note on her check pad:

*Call 911. Tell them I need assistance at this address. Suspect is Anton Krotz. Send SWAT. Back entrance. After you read this, laugh.*

Gretchen read the note, laughed. "Good one," she said. "I knew you'd like it."

She looked into Byrne's eyes. "I forgot the whipped cream," she said, loud enough, no louder. "Hang on."

Gretchen walked away, betraying no urgency in her stride. Byrne sipped his coffee. Krotz had not moved. Byrne wasn't sure if the man had made him or not. Byrne had interrogated Krotz for more than four hours the day they'd brought him in, trading a lot of venom with the man. It had even gotten physical. Neither party tended to forget the other after something like that.

Whatever, there was no way Byrne could let Krotz out that door. If Krotz left the restaurant he would disappear again, and they might never get another shot at him.

Thirty seconds later, Byrne looked to his right, saw Gretchen in the pass-through to the kitchen. Her look said she had made the call. Byrne grabbed his weapon and eased it down, and to his right, away from Krotz.

At that moment, one of the college girls shrieked. At first Byrne thought it was a cry of distress. He spun on his stool, looked over. The girl was still on her cell phone, reacting to some unbelievable college-girl news. When Byrne glanced back around, Krotz was out of his booth.

He had a hostage.

The hostage was the woman from the booth behind Krotz's booth. Krotz stood behind her, one arm around her waist. He held a six-inch knife to her neck. The woman was petite, pretty, perhaps forty. She wore a navy sweater, jeans, suede boots. She wore a wedding band. Her face was a mask of terror.

The man with whom she had been sitting was still in the booth, paralyzed with fear. Somewhere in the diner a glass or a cup crashed to the floor.

Time slowed as Byrne slid off his stool, weapon drawn and raised.

"Good to see you again, Detective," Krotz said to Byrne. "You look different. Going mountain on us?"

Krotz's eyes were glassy. *Meth,* Byrne thought. He recalled that Krotz was a user.

"Just take it easy, Anton," Byrne said.

*"Matt!"* the woman screamed.

Krotz angled the knife closer to the woman's jugular. "Shut the fuck *up*."

Krotz and the woman began to edge toward the door. Byrne noticed the sweat beading on Krotz's forehead.

"There's no reason for anyone to get hurt today," Byrne said. "Just be cool."

"No one's gonna get hurt?"

"No."

"Then why are you pointing that gun at me, hoss?"

"You know the drill, Anton."

Krotz looked over his shoulder, then back at Byrne. The moment drew out. "Gonna shoot a cute little citizen in front of the whole city?" He fondled the woman's breasts. "I don't think so."

Byrne turned his head. A handful of horrified people

were now looking in the front window of the diner. They were horrified, but not too terrified to leave, apparently. Somehow they had stumbled onto reality TV. Two of them were on cell phones. This would soon become a bona fide media event.

Byrne squared himself in front of the suspect and the hostage. He did not lower his weapon. "Talk to me, Anton. What do you want to do?"

"What, like, when I grow up?" Krotz laughed, high and loud. His gray teeth were shiny, black at the roots. The woman began to sob.

"I mean, what would you like to happen right now?" Byrne asked.

"I want to walk out of here."

"But you know that can't happen."

Krotz tightened his grip on the woman. Byrne saw the keen edge of the knife writing a thin red line on the woman's skin.

"I'm not seeing your bargaining chip, Detective," Krotz said. "I'm thinking *I* have control of this situation."

"There's no question about that, Anton."

"Say it."

"What? Say what?"

"Say 'You are in control, sir.' "

The words were bilious in Byrne's throat, but he had no choice. "You are in control, sir."

"Sucks to grovel, doesn't it?" Krotz said. Another few inches toward the door. "Been doing it my whole fucking *life*."

"Well, we can talk about that later," Byrne said. "Right now we have a state of affairs, don't we?"

"Oh, we most definitely have a state of affairs."

"So let's see if we can't find a way to end it so no one gets hurt. Work with me, Anton."

Krotz was six feet or so from the door. Though he was

not a big man, he was a head taller than the woman. Byrne had a clear shot. His finger caressed the trigger. He could take Krotz out. One round, dead center to the forehead, brains on the wall. It would break every rule of engagement, every departmental regulation, but the woman with the knife at her throat probably wouldn't mind. And that's all that really mattered.

*Where the hell is my backup?*

Krotz said, "You know as well as I do that if I give it up I'm gonna ride the needle for those other things."

"That's not necessarily true."

"Yes it *is*!" Krotz yelled. He pulled the woman closer. "Don't fucking lie to me."

"It's not a lie, Anton. Anything can happen."

"Yeah? Like what? Like maybe the judge is gonna see my inner child?"

"Come on, man. You know the system. Witnesses have memory lapses. Shit gets thrown out of court. Happens all the time. The hot shot is *never* a sure thing."

At that moment a shadow caught Byrne's peripheral vision. Left side. A SWAT officer was edging up the back hallway, his AR-15 rifle raised. He was out of Krotz's line of sight. The officer made eye contact with Byrne.

If a SWAT officer was on scene, a perimeter was being established. If Krotz made it out of the restaurant, he wouldn't get far. Byrne had to get that woman out of Krotz's grasp, and that knife out of his hand.

"Tell you what, Anton," Byrne said. "I'm going to put my weapon down, okay?"

"*That's* what I'm talkin' about. Put it on the floor and kick it over to me."

"I can't do that," Byrne said. "But I'm going to put it down, then I'm going to raise my hands over my head."

Byrne saw the SWAT officer get into position. Cap reversed. Eye to the scope. Dialed in.

Krotz slid another few inches toward the door. "I'm listening."

"Once I do that, you let the woman go."

"Then what?"

"Then you and I will walk out of here." Byrne lowered his weapon. He placed it on the floor, put his foot on top of it "We'll talk. Okay?"

For a moment, it appeared as if Krotz was considering it. Then it all went to hell just as quickly as it had begun.

"Nah," Krotz said. "Where's the fun in that?"

Krotz grabbed the woman by the hair, yanked back her head, and ran the blade across her throat. Her blood jetted halfway across the room.

*"No!"* Byrne screamed.

The woman folded to the floor, her neck a grotesque red smile. For a moment, Byrne felt weightless, immobilized, as if everything he had ever learned and done was pointless, as if his whole career on the street was a lie.

Krotz winked. "Don't you love this fucking *city*?"

Anton Krotz lunged at Byrne, but before he could take a single step the SWAT officer at the back of the diner fired. Two rounds slammed into Krotz's chest, propelling him back into the window, exploding his torso in a dense crimson burst. The blasts were deafening in the confined space of the small diner. Krotz tumbled backward through the shattered glass onto the sidewalk in front of the restaurant. Onlookers scattered. A pair of SWAT officers deployed in front of the diner rushed over to Krotz's supine form, putting heavy boots to his flesh, rifles aimed at his head.

Krotz's chest heaved once, twice, then fell still, steaming in the frigid night air. A third SWAT officer arrived, took his pulse. He signaled. The suspect was dead.

Detective Kevin Byrne's senses went into overdrive. He smelled the cordite in the air, mixed with smells of coffee and onions. He saw the bright blood spread on the tile. He heard the last shard of glass shattering on the floor, coupled with someone's soft crying. He felt the sweat on his back turn to sleet with the rush of freezing air from the street.

*Don't you love this fucking city?*

Moments later an EMS van screeched to a halt, bringing the world back into focus. Two paramedics sprinted into the diner and began to treat the woman on the floor. They tried to stem the bleeding, but it was too late. The woman and her killer were both dead.

Nick Palladino and Eric Chavez—two detectives from the Homicide Unit—ran into the diner, weapons drawn. They saw Byrne and the carnage. They holstered. Chavez spoke into his two-way. Nick Palladino began to set up a crime scene.

Byrne looked over at the man who had been sitting in the booth with the victim. The man stared at the woman on the floor as if she were sleeping, as if she could stand up, as if they might finish their meal, pay the check, and walk out into the night, gazing at the Christmas decorations on the street. Byrne saw a half-opened individual creamer next to the woman's coffee. She was going to put cream in her coffee, then five minutes later she was dead.

Byrne had witnessed the grief dealt by homicide many times, but rarely this soon after the act. This man had just seen his wife brutally murdered. He had been only a few feet away. The man glanced up at Byrne. In his eyes was an anguish far deeper, and darker, than Byrne had ever known.

"I'm sorry," Byrne said. The moment the words left his lips, he wondered why he'd said them. He wondered what he *meant*.

"You killed her," the man said.

Byrne was incredulous. He felt gut-punched. He couldn't begin to process what he was hearing. "Sir, I—"

"You . . . you could have shot him, but you hesitated. I *saw*. You could have shot him and you didn't."

The man slid from the booth. He took a moment, steadied himself, and slowly approached Byrne. Nick Palladino made a move to get between them. Byrne waved Nick off. The man got closer. Just a few feet away now.

"Isn't that your job?" the man asked.

"I'm sorry?"

"To *protect* us? Isn't that your *job*?"

Byrne wanted to tell the man that there *was* a blue line, yes, but when evil stepped into the light, there was nothing any of them could do. He wanted to tell the man that he had stayed his trigger *because* of his wife. For the life of him, he couldn't think of a single word to begin to express any of this.

"Laura," the man said.

"Pardon me?"

"Her name was Laura."

Before Byrne could say another word, the man swung his fist. It was a wild shot, poorly thrown, inexpertly leveraged. Byrne saw it coming at the last instant, and managed to sidestep it with ease. But the look in the man's eyes was so full of rage and hurt and sorrow, Byrne almost wished he had taken the hit. It may have, for the moment, filled a need in both of them.

Before the man could take another swing, Nick Palladino and Eric Chavez grabbed him, held him. The man did not struggle, but began to sob. He went limp in their grasp.

"Let him go," Byrne said. "Just . . . let him go."

THE SHOOTING TEAM wrapped up around 3 AM. A half dozen detectives from the Homicide Unit had shown up for support. In a loose circle they stood around Byrne, protecting him from the media, even from the brass.

Byrne gave his statement and was debriefed. He was

free to go. For a while, he didn't know where *to* go, where he wanted to be. The idea of getting drunk wasn't even appealing, though it just might blot out the horrible events of the evening.

Just twenty-four hours earlier he had been sitting on the cold, comfortable porch of a cabin in the Poconos, feet up, and a few inches of Old Forester in a plastic mug. Now two people were dead. It seemed as if he brought death with him.

The man's name was Matthew Clarke. He was forty-one. He had three daughters—Felicity, Tammy, and Michele. He worked as an insurance broker for a large national firm. He and his wife had been in the city to see their oldest daughter, a freshman at Temple University. They had stopped at the diner for coffee and lemon pudding, his wife's favorite.

*Her name was Laura.*

She had hazel eyes.

Kevin Byrne had a feeling he would see those eyes for a long time to come.

# 3

TWO DAYS LATER

The book sat on the table. It was constructed out of harmless cardboard, benign paper, nontoxic ink. It had a dust jacket, an ISBN number, blurbs on the back, a title along the spine. It was similar in all ways to just about every other book in the world.

Except it was different.

Detective Jessica Balzano, a ten-year veteran of the Philadelphia Police Department, sipped her coffee and stared at the terrifying object. In her time she had squared off with killers, muggers, rapists, Peeping Toms, burglars, other model citizens; had once looked down the barrel of a 9mm weapon, aimed point-blank at her forehead. She had punched and been punched by a select group of thugs, creeps, whackos, punks, and gangsters; had chased psychopaths down dark alleys; had once been threatened by a man wielding a cordless drill.

And yet the book on her dining room table scared her more than all of that combined.

Jessica had nothing against books. Nothing at all. As a rule, she loved books. In fact, rare was the day she didn't have a paperback in her purse for those down times on the job. Books were great. Except this book— the bright, cheerful, yellow and red book on her dining room table, the book with a menagerie of grinning cartoon animals on the front—belonged to her daughter, Sophie.

Which meant that her daughter was going to school.

Not preschool, which to Jessica had seemed like a glorified day-care center. Regular school. *Kindergarten.* Granted, it was only a get-acquainted day for the real thing that began next fall, but all the trappings were there. On the table. In front of her. Book, lunch, coat, mittens, pencil case.

*School.*

Sophie came out of her bedroom dressed and primed for her first official day of academe. She wore a navy blue accordion-pleat skirt and crewneck sweater, a pair of lace-up shoes, and a wool beret-and-scarf set. She looked like a miniature Audrey Hepburn.

Jessica felt sick.

"You okay, Mom?" Sophie asked. She slid onto her chair.

"Of course, sweetie," Jessica lied. "Why wouldn't I be okay?"

Sophie shrugged. "You've been sad all week."

"Sad? What have I been sad about?"

"You've been sad about me going to school."

*My God,* Jessica thought. *I have a five-year-old Dr. Phil living in my house.* "I'm not sad, honey."

"Kids go to school, Mom. We talked about it."

*Yes we did, my darling daughter. Except I didn't hear a word. I didn't hear a word because you are just a baby. My baby. A tiny, helpless, pink-fingered little soul who needs her mommy for everything.*

Sophie poured herself some cereal, added milk. She dug in.

"Morning, my lovely ladies," Vincent said, walking into the kitchen, tying his tie. He planted a kiss on Jessica's cheek, and one on top of Sophie's beret.

Jessica's husband was always cheerful in the morning. He brooded almost all the rest of the time, but in the morning he was a ray of sunshine. Exactly the opposite of his wife.

Vincent Balzano was a detective working out of Narcotics Field Unit North. He was trim and muscular, still the most devastatingly sexy man Jessica had ever known—dark hair, caramel eyes, long lashes. This morning his hair was still damp, swept back from his broad forehead. He wore a dark blue suit.

During six years of marriage, they'd hit a few rough patches—had been separated for nearly six months—but they were back together and making a go of it. Two-badge marriages were an extremely rare commodity. Successful ones, that is.

Vincent poured himself a cup of coffee, sat at the table. "Let me look at you," he said to Sophie.

Sophie jumped up from her chair, standing at rigid attention in front of her father.

"Turn around," he said.

Sophie spun in place, vamped, giggled, hand on hip.

"Va-va-voom," Vincent said.

"Va-va-*voom*," Sophie echoed.

"So, tell me something, young lady."

"What?"

"How did you get so pretty?"

"My *mom's* pretty." They both looked at Jessica. This was their routine when she was feeling a little down.

*Oh God,* Jessica thought. Her chest felt like it was going to rumble right off her body. Her lower lip quivered.

"Yes, she is," Vincent said. "One of the two prettiest girls in the world."

"Who's the other girl?" Sophie asked.

Vincent winked.

"*Dad,*" Sophie said.

"Let's finish our breakfast."

Sophie sat back down.

Vincent sipped his coffee. "Are you looking forward to visiting the school?"

"Oh, yes." Sophie spooned a blob of milk-sodden Cheerios into her mouth.

"Where's your backpack?"

Sophie stopped chewing. How could she get through the day without her backpack? It all but defined her as a person. Two weeks earlier she had tried on more than a dozen, finally settling on a Strawberry Shortcake model. For Jessica it had been like watching Paris Hilton at a Jean Paul Gaultier trunk show. A minute later Sophie finished eating, brought her bowl to the sink, and rocketed back to her room.

Vincent then turned his attention to his suddenly fragile wife, the same woman who once punched out a thug in a Port Richmond bar for putting his arm around her waist, the woman who once went four full victorious rounds on ESPN2 with a monstrous gal from Cleveland, Ohio, a heavily muscled nineteen-year-old nicknamed "Cinder Block" Jackson.

"Come here, you big baby," he said.

Jessica crossed the room. Vincent patted his lap. Jessica sat. "What?" she asked.

"You're not dealing with this too well, are you?"

"No." Jessica felt the emotions well up again, a hot coal burning behind her breastbone. Big brute of a Philly homicide detective was she.

"It's only an orientation thing, I thought," Vincent said.

"It is. But it's going to orient her to *school*."

"I thought that was the point."

"She's not ready for school."

"News flash, Jess."

"What?"

"She *is* ready for school."

"Yeah but . . . but that means she'll be ready to wear makeup, and get her license, and start dating, and—"

"What, in first grade?"

"You know what I mean."

It was obvious. God help her and save the republic she wanted another baby. Ever since she had rolled the odometer to thirty, she'd thought about it. Most of her friends were on bundle number three. Every time she saw a swaddled baby in a stroller, or in a papoose, or in a car seat, or even in a stupid television commercial for Pampers, she felt the pang.

"Hold me tight," she said.

Vincent did. As tough as Jessica thought she was—in addition to her life as a police officer, she was also a professional boxer, not to mention a South Philly girl, born and raised at Sixth and Catharine—she never felt safer than at moments like this.

She pulled back, looked into her husband's eyes. She kissed him. Deep and serious and let's-make-a-baby big-time.

"Wow," Vincent said, his lips smeared with lipstick. "We should send her to school more often."

"There's a lot more where that came from, Detective," she said, probably a little too seductively for seven in the morning. Vincent was, after all, Italian. She slid off his lap. He pulled her right back. He kissed her again, and then they both looked at the wall clock.

The bus was coming for Sophie in five minutes. After that Jessica didn't have to meet her partner for almost an hour.

Plenty of time.


KEVIN BYRNE HAD been off for a week, and although Jessica had had enough on her plate to keep her busy, the week without him had dragged. Byrne had been scheduled to return three days ago, but there had been that horrible incident at the diner. She'd read the accounts in the *Inquirer* and *Daily News,* read the official reports. A nightmare scenario for a police officer.

Byrne had been put on a brief administrative leave. There would be a review in the next day or two. They hadn't talked about the episode in depth yet.

They would.


WHEN SHE TURNED the corner, she saw him standing in front of the coffee shop, two cups in hand. Their first stop of the day would be to visit a ten-year-old crime scene in Juniata Park, the location of a 1997 double drug-homicide, followed by an interview with an elderly gentleman who had been a potential witness. It was day one of a cold case to which they had been assigned.

There were three sections in the homicide unit—the Line Squad, which handled new cases; the Fugitive Squad, which tracked down wanted suspects; and SIU, the Special Investigation Unit, which, among other things, handled cold cases. The roster of detectives was generally set in stone, but sometimes when all hell broke loose, which happened all too often in Philly, detectives on any given shift could work the line.

"Excuse me, I was supposed to meet my partner here," Jessica said. "Tall, clean-shaven guy. Looks like a cop. Have you seen him?"

"What, you don't like the beard?" Byrne handed her a cup. "I spent an hour shaping it."

"Shaping?"

"Well, you know, trimming around the edges so it doesn't look ragged."

"Ah."

"What do you think?"

Jessica leaned back, scrutinized his face. "Well, to be honest, I think it makes you look . . ."

"Distinguished?"

She was going to say homeless. "Yeah. That."

Byrne stroked his beard. It hadn't grown fully in, but Jessica could see that when it did it would be mostly gray. As long as he didn't go Just For Men on her, she could probably handle it.

As they headed to the Taurus, Byrne's cell phone rang. He flipped it open, listened, pulled out his notebook, made a few notes. He glanced at his watch. "Twenty minutes." He folded his phone, pocketed it.

"Job?" Jessica asked.

"Job."

The cold case would stay cold a while longer. They

continued up the street. After a full block, Jessica broke the silence.

"You okay?" she asked.

"Me? *Oh*, yeah," Byrne said. "Never better. Sciatica's acting up a little, but other than that."

"Kevin."

"I'm telling you, I'm a hundred percent," Byrne said. "Hand to God."

He was lying, but that's what friends did for each other when they wanted you to know the truth.

"We'll talk later?" Jessica asked.

"We'll talk," Byrne said. "By the way, why are *you* so happy?"

"I look happy?"

"Let me put it this way. Your face could open a smile outlet in Jersey."

"Just glad to see my partner."

"Right," Byrne said, slipping into the car.

Jessica had to laugh, recalling the unbridled marital passion of her morning. Her partner knew her well.

# 4

The crime scene was a boarded-up commercial property in Manayunk, an area in the northwest section of Philly, just on the eastern bank of the Schuylkill River. For some time now the neighborhood seemed in a constant state of redevelopment and gentrification, evolving from what was once a quarter for those working in the mills and factories, to an upper middle-class section of the city. The name Manayunk was a Lenape Indian term meaning "our place for drinking," and in the past decade or so, the neighborhood's lively Main Street strip of pubs, restaurants, and night clubs—essentially Philadelphia's answer to Bourbon Street—had tried mightily to live up to that long-ago bestowed name.

When Jessica and Byrne rolled up on Flat Rock Road there were two sector cars securing the site. The detectives pulled into the parking lot, exited the vehicle. The uniformed officer on the scene was Patrol Officer Michael Calabro.

"Good morning, detectives," Calabro said, handing them the crime scene log. They both signed in.

"What do we have, Mike?" Byrne asked.

Calabro was as pale as the December sky. In his late thirties, stocky and solid, he was a veteran patrol officer whom Jessica had known almost ten years. He didn't rattle easily. In fact, he usually had a smile for everyone, even the knuckleheads he met on the street. If he was this shaken, it wasn't good.

He cleared his throat. "Female DOA."

Jessica walked back to the road, surveyed the exterior of the large two-story building and the immediate vicinity: a vacant lot across the street, a tavern next to that, a warehouse next door. The crime scene building was square, blocky, clad in a dirty brown brick and patched with waterlogged plywood. Graffiti tagged every available inch of the wood. The front door was secured with rusted chains and padlocks. At the roofline was a huge For Sale or Lease sign. Delaware Investment Properties, Inc. Jessica wrote down the telephone number, walked back to the rear of the property. The wind cut across the lot in sharp little knives.

"Any idea what kind of business used to be here?" she asked Calabro.

"A few different things," Calabro said. "When I was a teenager it was an auto parts wholesaler. My sister's boyfriend worked here. He used to sell us parts under the counter."

"What were you driving in those days?" Byrne asked.

Jessica saw a smile grace Calabro's lips. It always happened when men talked about the cars of their youth. "Seventy-six TransAm."

"No," Byrne replied.

"Yep. Friend of my cousin wrecked it in '85. Got it for a song when I was eighteen. Took me fours years to restore."

"The 455?"

"Oh, yeah," Calabro said. "Starlite Black with the T-top."

"Sweet," Byrne said. "So how soon after you got married did she make you sell it?"

Calabro laughed. "Right around the 'You may kiss the bride' part."

Jessica saw Mike Calabro brighten considerably. She had never met anyone better than Kevin Byrne when it came to putting people at ease, at taking minds off the horrors that can haunt people in their line of work. Mike Calabro had seen a lot in his day, but that didn't mean the next one wouldn't get to him. Or the one after that. That was the existence of a uniform cop. Every time you turned a corner your life could change forever. Jessica wasn't sure what they were about to confront at this crime scene, but she knew that Kevin Byrne had just made the day a little easier for this man.

The building had an L-shaped parking lot that ran behind the structure, then down a slight slope to the river; a parking lot at one time fully fenced off with chain link. The fence had long ago been clipped and bent and tortured. Huge sections were missing. Trash bags, tires, and street litter were strewn everywhere.

Before Jessica could inquire about the DOA, a black Ford Taurus, identical to the departmental car Jessica and Byrne were driving, pulled into the lot, parked. Jessica did not recognize the man behind the wheel. Moments later the man emerged, approached them.

"Are you Detective Byrne?" he asked.

"I am," Byrne said. "And you are?"

The man reached into his back pocket, pulled out a gold shield. "Detective Joshua Bontrager," he said. "Homicide." He proffered a big smile, the color rising in his cheeks.

Bontrager was probably thirty or so, but he looked much younger. A slim five ten, his hair was summer blond gone December dull, cropped relatively short; spiky, but not in a GQ way. It looked like it may have been a homemade haircut. His eyes were mint green. He had about him the air of scrubbed country, of rural Pennsylvania that spoke of state college on an academic scholarship. He pumped Byrne's hand, then Jessica's. "You must be Detective Balzano," he said.

"Nice to meet you," Jessica said.

Bontrager looked between them, back and forth. "This is just, just, just . . . great."

If nothing else, Detective Joshua Bontrager was full of energy and enthusiasm. With all the cutbacks, retirements, and injuries to detectives—not to mention the spiking homicide rate—it was good to have another warm body in the unit. Even if that body looked like it just stepped out of a high school production of Our Town.

"Sergeant Buchanan sent me out," Bontrager said. "Did he call you?"

Ike Buchanan was their boss, the day watch commander of the homicide unit. "Uh, no," Byrne said. "You've been assigned to homicide?"

"Temporarily," Bontrager said. "I'll be working with

you and two other teams, rotating tours. At least until things, you know, calm *down* a bit."

Jessica looked closely at Bontrager's clothing. His suit coat was a dark blue, and his slacks were black, as if he had cobbled together an ensemble from two different weddings, or had gotten dressed while it was still dark. His striped rayon tie was from sometime around the Carter administration. His shoes were scuffed but sturdy, recently resoled, tightly laced.

"Where do you want me?" Bontrager asked.

The look on Byrne's face fairly screamed the answer. *Back at the Roundhouse.*

"If you don't mind me asking, where were you before you got assigned to Homicide?" Byrne asked.

"I was in the Traffic Unit," Bontrager said.

"How long were you there?"

Chest out, chin high. "Eight years."

Jessica thought about looking at Byrne, but she couldn't. She just couldn't.

"So," Bontrager said, rubbing his hands together for warmth, "what can I do?"

"For now we want to make sure the scene is secure," Byrne said. He pointed to the far side of the building, to the short driveway on the north side of the property. "If you could secure that entry point, it would be a great help. We don't want folks coming onto the property and disturbing the evidence."

For a second, Jessica thought Bontrager was going to salute.

"I am *so* on it," he said.

With this, Detective Joshua Bontrager all but ran across the grounds.

Byrne turned to Jessica. "What is he, about seventeen?"

"He'll *be* seventeen."

"Did you notice he's not wearing a coat?"

"I did."

Byrne glanced at Officer Calabro. Both men shrugged. Byrne pointed at the building. "Is the DOA on the first floor?"

"No, sir," Calabro said. He turned and pointed to the river.

"The victim is in the river?" Byrne asked.

"On the bank."

Jessica glanced toward the river. The angle sloped away from them, so she could not yet see the bank. Through the few barren trees on this side she could see the opposite side of the river, the cars on the Schuylkill Expressway. She turned back to Calabro. "Have you cleared the immediate area?"

"Yes," Calabro said.

"Who found her?" Jessica asked.

"Anonymous 911 call."

"When?"

Calabro looked at the log. "About an hour and fifteen minutes ago."

"Has the ME's office been notified?" Byrne asked.

"On the way."

"Good work, Mike."

Before heading down to the river, Jessica took a number of photographs of the exterior of the building. She also photographed the two abandoned vehicles in the lot. One, a twenty-year-old midsize Chevy; the other, a rusted out Ford van. Neither had plates. She walked over, felt the hoods of both vehicles. Stone cold. On any given day there were hundreds of derelict cars in Philadelphia. Sometimes it seemed like thousands. Every time someone ran for mayor or council, one of the planks in their platform was always the promise to get rid of the abandoned vehicles and tear down the abandoned buildings. It never seemed to happen.

She took a few more photographs. When she was finished, she and Byrne snapped on latex gloves.

"Ready?" he asked.

"Let's do it."

They walked to the end of the lot. From there, the ground gently sloped down toward the soft riverbank. Because the Schuylkill was not a working river—almost all commercial traffic navigated the Delaware River—there were few docks as such, but occasionally there were small stone jetties, the infrequent narrow floating pier. As they reached the end of the asphalt, they saw the victim's head, then her shoulders, then her body.

"Ah, God," Byrne said.

She was a young blond woman, perhaps in her mid-twenties. Perched on a short stone dock, her eyes were wide open. It looked like she was just sitting at the river's edge, watching it flow.

In life there was no doubt she had been very pretty. Now her face was a ghastly and pallid gray, her bloodless skin already beginning to split and crack from the ravages of the wind. Her nearly black tongue lolled to the side of her mouth. She wore no coat, no gloves, no hat, only a long dusty-rose-colored dress. It looked to be very old, suggesting a time long gone. It hung below her feet, nearly touching the water. It appeared that she had been there for a while. There was some decomposition, but not nearly as much as there would have been if the weather had been warm. Still, the smell of decaying flesh hung heavy in the air, even ten feet away.

Around the young woman's neck was a nylon belt, knotted in the back.

Jessica could see that some exposed parts of the victim's body were covered in a thin layer of ice, giving the corpse a surreal, artificial gloss. It had rained the day before, then the temperature had plummeted.

Jessica took a few more photographs, stepped closer.

She would not disturb the body until the medical examiner cleared the scene, but the sooner they got a better look, the sooner they could begin their investigation. While Byrne walked the perimeter of the parking lot, Jessica knelt next to the body.

The victim's dress was clearly a few sizes too large for her slender frame. It was long-sleeved, had a removable lace collar, as well as knife pleats at the cuff. Unless Jessica had missed a new fashion trend—and that was a possibility—she didn't see why this woman had been walking around Philadelphia, in winter, in such an outfit.

She looked at the woman's hands. No rings. There were no obvious calluses either, no scars or healing cuts. This woman did not work with her hands, not in the manual labor sense. She had no visible tattoos.

Jessica moved a few steps back and took a picture of the victim in relation to the river. It was then that she noticed what looked like a drop of blood near the hem of the dress. A single drop. She crouched down, took out her pen, and lifted the front edge of the dress. What she saw caught her completely off guard.

"Oh, God."

Jessica fell back on her heels, nearly toppling into the water. She grabbed at the earth, found purchase, sat down hard.

Having heard her cry out, Byrne and Calabro came running over.

"What is it?" Byrne asked.

Jessica wanted to tell them, but the words were logjammed in her throat. She had seen a lot in her time on the force—in fact, she really believed she could look at anything—and she was usually braced for the special horrors that came with working homicides. The sight of this dead young woman, her flesh already giving way to the elements, was bad enough. What Jessica saw when she lifted the victim's dress was a geometric progression of the revulsion she felt.

Jessica took a moment, leaned forward, and once again picked up the dress's hem. Byrne crouched down, angled his head. He immediately looked away. "Shit," he said, standing up. *"Shit."*

In addition to having been strangled and left on a frozen riverbank, the victim's feet had been amputated. And it looked to have been done recently. It was a precise and surgical amputation, just above the ankles. The wounds had been crudely cauterized, but the black and blue trauma from the excisions ran halfway up the victim's pale, frozen legs.

Jessica glanced at the icy water below, then a few yards downstream. There were no body parts visible. She looked at Mike Calabro. He put his hands in his pockets, walked slowly back to the entrance of the crime scene. He was not a detective. He didn't have to stay. Jessica thought she had seen tears welling in his eyes.

"Let me see if I can redline the ME's office and CSU," Byrne said. He pulled out his cell, took a few steps away. Jessica knew that every second that went by before the Crime Scene Unit secured the scene, precious evidence might be slipping away.

Jessica looked closely at what was most likely the murder weapon. The belt around the victim's neck was about three inches wide, and appeared to be made of tightly woven nylon, not unlike the material used to manufacture a seat belt. She took a close-up photograph of the knot.

The wind churned, bringing a bitter chill. Jessica braced herself, waited it out. Before stepping away, she forced herself to look closely at the woman's legs one more time. The cuts looked clean, as if done with a very sharp saw. For the young woman's sake, Jessica hoped that it had been done postmortem. She looked back at the victim's face. They were now linked, she and the dead woman. Jessica had worked a number of cases in her time in homicide, and she was forever connected to each of them. There would not come a time in her life when she would forget the way death fashioned them, the way they silently asked for justice.

Just after nine o'clock Dr. Thomas Weyrich arrived with his photographer, who immediately began snapping away. A few minutes later, Weyrich pronounced the young woman dead. The detectives were cleared to begin their investigation. They met at the top of the slope.

"Christ," Weyrich said. "Merry Christmas, eh?"

"Yeah," Byrne said.

Weyrich lit a Marlboro, hit it hard. He was a seasoned veteran of the Philadelphia medical examiner's office. Even for him this was not a daily occurrence.

"She was strangled?" Jessica asked.

"At the very least," Weyrich replied. He would not remove the nylon belt until he got the body back to the city. "There's evidence of petechial hemorrhaging of the eyes. I won't know more until I get her on the table."

"How long has she been out here?" Byrne asked.

"I'd say at least forty-eight hours or so."

"And her feet? Pre- or post?"

"I won't know until I can examine the wounds, but based on how little blood there is on scene, I believe she was dead when she got here, and the amputation took place elsewhere. If she had been alive, she would've had to have been tied down, and I'm not seeing ligature marks on her legs."

Jessica walked back to the riverbank. There were no footprints on the frozen ground near the river's edge, no blood splatter or trail. A slight trickle of blood from the victim's legs etched the mossy stone wall in a pair of thin, deep scarlet tendrils. Jessica looked directly across the river. The jetty was partially obscured from the expressway, which might explain why no one had called in a report of a woman sitting motionless on the frigid riverbank for two full days. The victim had gone unnoticed—or that was the truth Jessica wanted to believe. She *didn't* want to believe the people of her city saw a woman sitting in the freezing cold and did nothing about it.

They needed to ID the young woman as soon as possible. They would begin a thorough grid search of the parking lot, the riverbank, and the area surrounding the structure—along with a canvass of nearby businesses and residences on both sides of the river—but with a carefully constructed crime scene such as this, it was unlikely they were going to find a discarded pocketbook with any ID in the vicinity.

Jessica crouched behind the victim. The way the body was positioned reminded her of a marionette whose strings had been cut, causing the puppet to simply collapse to the floor—arms and legs waiting to be reconnected, reanimated, brought back to life.

Jessica examined the woman's fingernails. They were short, but clean and painted with a clear lacquer. They would examine the nails to see if there was any material beneath them, but with the naked eye it didn't appear so. What it did tell the detectives was that this woman was not homeless, not indigent. Her skin and hair looked clean and well-groomed.

Which meant that there was somewhere this young woman was supposed to be. It meant that she was missed. It meant that there was a puzzle out there in Philadelphia, or beyond, to which this woman was the missing piece.

Mother. Daughter. Sister. Friend.

Victim.

# 5

The wind swirls off the river, curling along the frozen banks, bringing with it the deep secrets of the forest. In his mind, Moon draws the memory of this moment. He knows that, in the end, a memory is all you were left with.

Moon stands nearby, watching the man and the woman. They probe, they calculate, they write in their journals. The man is big and powerful. The woman is slender and pretty and clever.

Moon is clever, too.

The man and the woman may witness a great deal, but they cannot see what the moon sees. Each night the moon returns and tells Moon of its travels. Each night Moon paints a mind-picture. Each night a new story is told.

Moon glances up at the sky. The cold sun hides behind the clouds. He is invisible, too.

The man and woman go about their business—quick and clocklike and precise. They have found Karen. Soon they will find the red shoes, and this tale will be spun.

There are many more tales.

# 6

Jessica and Byrne stood near the road, waiting for the CSU van. Though only a few feet apart, each was adrift in their own thoughts about what they had just seen. Detective Bontrager was still dutifully guarding the north entrance to the property. Mike Calabro stood near the river, his back to the victim.

For the most part, the life of a homicide detective in a major urban area was about the investigation of garden-variety murders—gang slayings, domestics, bar fights that went one punch too far, robbery-homicides. Of course, these crimes were very personal and unique to the victims and their families, and a detective had to constantly remind himself of that fact. If you got complacent about the job, if you failed to take into account a person's sense of grief or loss, it was time to quit. In Philadelphia, there were no divisional homicide squads. All suspicious deaths were investigated out of one office, the homicide unit at the Roundhouse. Eighty detectives, three shifts, seven days a week. Philly had more than one hundred neighborhoods, and many times, based on where the victim was found, an experienced detective could all but predict the circumstance, the motive, sometimes even the weapon. There was always a revelation, but very few surprises.

This day was different. It spoke of a special evil, a

depth of brutality that Jessica and Byrne had rarely experienced.

Parked in the vacant lot across the road from the crime scene was a food-service truck. There was only one customer. The two detectives crossed Flat Rock Road, retrieving their notebooks. While Byrne interviewed the driver, Jessica spoke to the customer. He was in his twenties, dressed in jeans and a hooded sweatshirt, a black knit cap.

Jessica introduced herself, showed her badge. "I'd like to ask you a few questions if you don't mind."

"Sure." Pulling off his cap, his dark hair fell into his eyes. He brushed it aside.

"What's your name?"

"Will," he said. "Will Pedersen."

"Where do you live?"

"Plymouth Valley."

"Wow," Jessica said. "Long way from home."

He shrugged. "You go where the work is."

"What do you do?"

"I'm a brick mason." He pointed over Jessica's shoulder, at the new condominiums being constructed along the river about a block away. A few moments later Byrne finished with the driver. Jessica introduced Pedersen to him, continued.

"Do you work down here a lot?" Jessica asked.

"Almost every day."

"Were you here yesterday?"

"No," he said. "Too cold to mix. Boss called early and said bag it."

"What about the day before yesterday?" Byrne asked.

"Yeah. We were here."

"Did you get coffee about this time?"

"No," Pedersen said. "It was earlier. Maybe seven o'clock or so."

Byrne gestured to the crime scene. "Did you see anyone in this parking lot?"

Pedersen looked across the street, thought for a few moments. "Yeah. I did see someone."

"Where?"

"Back by the end of the parking lot."

"Man? Woman?"

"Man, I think. It was still kind of dark."

"There was just the one person?"

"Yes."

"Did you see a vehicle?"

"No. No cars," he said. "None I noticed, anyway."

The two abandoned vehicles were behind the building. They were not visible from the road. A third vehicle could have been back there.

"Where was he standing?" Byrne asked.

Pedersen pointed to a spot at the end of the lot, just above where the victim was found. "Right to the right of those trees."

"Closer to the river, or closer to the building?"

"Closer to the river."

"Can you describe this person you saw?"

"Not really. Like I said, it was still kind of dark and I couldn't see too well. I wasn't wearing my glasses."

"Exactly where were you when you first saw him?" Jessica asked.

Pedersen pointed to an area a few feet away from where they stood.

"Did you get any closer?" Jessica asked.

"No."

Jessica glanced toward the river. You could not see the victim from that vantage point. "How long were you here?" she asked.

Pedersen shrugged. "I don't know. A minute or two. Had my Danish and coffee, walked back to the site to set up."

"What was this person doing?" Byrne asked.

"Nothing, really."

"He didn't move from where you saw him? He didn't walk down toward the river?"

"No," Pedersen said. "But now that I think about it, it was a little weird."

"Weird?" Jessica asked. "Weird how?"

"He was just standing there," Pedersen said. "I think he was staring up at the moon."

# 7

As they headed back to Center City, Jessica scrolled through the photographs on her digital camera, looking at each one on the small LCD screen. At that size, the young woman on the bank of the river looked like a doll posed in a miniature setting.

A *doll*, Jessica thought. It was the first image she'd had when she saw the victim. The young woman looked like a porcelain doll on a shelf.

Jessica had given Will Pedersen a business card. The young man promised to call if he remembered anything else.

"What did you get from the driver?" Jessica asked.

Byrne glanced at his notebook. "The driver is one Reese Harris. Mr. Harris is thirty-three, lives in Queen Village. He said he hits Flat Rock Road three or four mornings a week, now that those condos are going up. He said he always parks with the open side of the truck facing away from the river. Keeps the wind off the merchandise. He said he didn't see anything."

Detective Joshua Bontrager, late of the Traffic Unit, armed with Vehicle Identification Numbers, was off to check on the two abandoned vehicles parked in the lot.

Jessica scrolled through a few more pictures, looked up at Byrne. "What do you think?"

Byrne ran a hand over his beard. "I think we have a sick son of a bitch running around Philly. I think we have to shut this fucker down fast."

Leave it to Kevin Byrne to break the case down to the essentials, Jessica thought. "Full-blown nut job?" she asked.

"Oh, yeah. With icing."

"Why do you think she was posed on the bank? Why not just dump her in the river?"

"Good question. Maybe she's supposed to be looking at something. Maybe it's a 'special place.' "

Jessica could hear the acid in Byrne's voice. She understood. There were times, in their job, when you wanted to take the unique cases—the sociopaths some people in the medical community wanted to preserve and study and quantify—and throw them off the nearest bridge. *Fuck* your psychosis. *Fuck* your rotten childhood and your chemical imbalance. *Fuck* your whack-job mother who put dead spiders and rancid mayonnaise in your underwear. If you're a PPD homicide cop and somebody kills a citizen on your beat, you're going down—horizontal or vertical, it didn't much matter.

"Have you run across this amputation MO before?" Jessica asked.

"I've seen it," Byrne said, "but not as an MO. We'll run it, see if anything flags."

She looked back at her camera's screen, at the victim's outfit. "What do you make of the dress? I suppose the doer dressed her like that."

"I don't want to think about that yet," Byrne said. "I really don't. Not before lunch."

Jessica knew what he meant. She didn't want to think about it either, but of course they both knew they would have to.

DELAWARE INVESTMENT PROPERTIES, Inc. was in a freestanding building on Arch Street, a three-story steel and glass box with mirrored windows, and something resembling modern sculpture out front. The company employed about thirty-five people. Their main focus was buying and selling real estate, but in the past few years they had branched out into riverfront development. At the moment, the prize in Philadelphia was the carrot of casino development, and it seemed that anyone with a Realtor's license was rolling the dice.

The man in charge of the Manayunk property was David Hornstrom. They met in his second-floor office. The walls were covered with pictures of Hornstrom on various mountaintops around the world, sunglasses in place, climbing gear in hand. One picture frame bore an MBA from Penn State.

Hornstrom was in his late twenties, dark hair and eyes, well dressed and a little too confident, the poster boy for energetic junior executive types. He wore a two-button charcoal suit, expertly tailored, white shirt, blue silk tie. His office was small, but well appointed with contemporary furniture and furnishings. In one corner was a rather expensive-looking telescope. Hornstrom sat on the edge of his sleek metal desk.

"Thanks for taking the time to see us," Byrne said.

"Always happy to help Philly's finest."

*Philly's finest?* Jessica thought. She didn't know anyone under fifty who used that phrase.

"When was the last time you were at the Manayunk property?" Byrne asked.

Hornstrom reached over to a desk calendar. Considering the wide-screen monitor and desktop computer, you'd think he wouldn't be using a paper calendar, Jessica mused. He looked the BlackBerry type.

"About a week ago," he said.

"And you haven't been back?"

"No."

"Not even just to drive by and check on things?"

"No."

Hornstrom's answers were coming a little too fast and a little too pat, not to mention curt. Most people were at least somewhat rattled by a visit from the homicide police. Jessica wondered why this man was not.

"The last time you were there, was there anything out of the ordinary?" Byrne asked.

"Not that I noticed."

"Were those three abandoned vehicles on the lot?"

"Three?" Hornstrom asked. "I remember two. Is there another one?"

Byrne flipped back his notes, for effect. Old trick. This time it didn't work. "You're right. My mistake. Were the two vehicles there last week?"

"Yes," he said. "I've been meaning to make the call to get them towed. Is that something you guys can take care of for me? That would be super."

*Super.*

Byrne glanced at Jessica, back. "We're with the police department," Byrne said. "I may have mentioned that earlier."

"Ah, okay." Hornstrom leaned over, made a note on his calendar. "No problem at all."

*Cocky little bastard,* Jessica thought.

"How long have the cars been there?" Byrne asked.

"I really don't know," Hornstrom said. "The man who was handling that property recently left the company. I've only had the listing for a month or so."

"Is he still in the city?"

"No," Hornstrom said. "He's in Boston."

"We'll need his name and contact information."

Hornstrom hesitated a second. Jessica knew that if someone was going to start to resist this early in an interview, and over something seemingly minor, they might be in for a battle. On the other hand, Hornstrom did not look stupid. The MBA on his wall confirmed his education. Common sense? Another story.

"That's doable," Hornstrom finally said.

"Has anyone else from your company visited the property in the past week?" Byrne asked.

"I doubt it," Hornstrom said. "We have ten agents and over one hundred commercial sites in the city alone. If another agent had shown the property I would know about it."

"Have *you* shown the property recently?"

"Yes."

Awkward moment number two. Byrne sat, pen poised, waiting for more information. He was the Irish Buddha. No one Jessica had ever met could outlast him. Hornstrom tried to match his gaze, failed.

"I showed it last week," Hornstrom finally said. "A commercial plumbing company out of Chicago."

"Do you think anyone from that company has been back?"

"Probably not. They weren't too interested. Besides, they would have called me."

*Not if they were dumping a mutilated body,* Jessica thought.

"We'll also need their contact information," Byrne said.

Hornstrom sighed, nodded. Whatever cool he may have projected at Center City happy hours, whatever Sporting Club macho he floated with the Brasserie Perrier crowd, he was no match for Kevin Byrne.

"Who has keys to the building?" Byrne asked.

"There are two sets. I have one, the other set is kept in a safe here."

"And everyone here has access?"

"Yes, but like I said—"

"When was the last time that building was operational?" Byrne asked, interrupting him.

"Not for a few years."

"And all the locks were changed since then?"

"Yes."

"We'll need to look inside."

"That shouldn't be a problem."

Byrne pointed to one of the photographs on the wall. "You're a climber?"

"Yeah."

In the photograph, Hornstrom stood alone on a mountaintop, with a bright blue sky behind him.

"I've always wondered, is all this gear heavy?" Byrne asked.

"Depends on what you bring," Hornstrom said. "If it's a one-day climb you can get away with the minimum. If you're camping at base camps, it can get cumbersome. Tents, cooking gear, et cetera. But, for the most part, it's designed to be as lightweight as possible."

"What do you call this?" Byrne pointed at the photograph, to a beltlike loop hanging from Hornstrom's jacket.

"That's called a dogbone sling."

"It's made out of nylon?"

"I believe it's called Dynex."

"Strong?"

"*Very* strong," Hornstrom said.

Jessica knew where Byrne was headed with this line of apparently innocent, conversational questioning, even though the belt around the victim's neck had been a light gray, and the sling in the photograph was a vibrant yellow.

"Thinking about climbing, Detective?" Hornstrom asked.

"*God,* no," Byrne said with his most winning smile. "I have enough trouble with the stairs."

"You should try it sometime," Hornstrom said. "It's good for the soul."

"Maybe one of these days," Byrne said. "If you can find me a mountain with an Applebee's halfway up."

Hornstrom laughed his corporate laugh.

"Now," Byrne said, standing, buttoning his coat. "About getting into the building."

"Sure." Hornstrom shot his cuff, looked at his watch. "I can meet you out there, say, around two o'clock. Would that be okay?"

"Actually, *now* would be much better."

"Now?"

"Yeah," Byrne said. "Is that something you can take care of for us? That would be *super.*"

Jessica stifled a laugh. Hornstrom, clueless, looked to her for help. He found none.

"Can I ask what this is all about?" he asked.

"Give me a ride, Dave," Byrne said. "We'll talk on the way."

BY THE TIME they reached the crime scene the victim had been moved to the medical examiner's office on University Avenue. Tape circled the parking lot, down to the riverbank. Cars slowed, drivers gawked, were waved on by Mike Calabro. The food-service truck across the street was gone.

Jessica watched Hornstrom closely as they ducked under the crime scene tape. If he was in any way involved in the crime, or had any knowledge of it whatsoever, there would almost certainly be a tell, a behavioral tic that would give him away. She saw nothing. He was either good or innocent.

David Hornstrom unlocked the back door of the building. They stepped inside.

"We can take it from here," Byrne said.

David Hornstrom held up a hand as if to say, "Whatever." He pulled out his cell phone and dialed.

THE LARGE FRIGID space was all but empty. A few fifty-gallon drums were scattered about, a few stacks of wooden pallets. Cold daylight peered in through the cracks in the plywood over the windows. Byrne and Jessica roamed the floor with their Maglites, the thin shafts of light being swallowed by the darkness. Because the space had been secure, there was no evidence of break-ins or squatting, no telltale signs of drug use—needles, foil, crack vials. Moreover, there was nothing to indicate a woman had been murdered in this building. In fact, there was little evidence that any sort of human activity had *ever* taken place in this building.

Satisfied, at least for the moment, they met at the rear entrance. Hornstrom was just outside, still on his cell. They waited until he clicked off.

"We may need to get back inside," Byrne said. "And we're going to have to seal the building for the next few days."

Hornstrom shrugged. "It's not like the tenants are lining up," he said. He glanced at his watch. "If there's anything else I can do, please don't hesitate to call."

*The standard crock,* Jessica thought. She wondered how cocky he would be if they dragged him down to the Roundhouse for a more detailed interview.

Byrne gave David Hornstrom a business card and repeated his request for contact information for the previous agent. Hornstrom grabbed the card, jumped into his car, and sped away.

The last image Jessica had of David Hornstrom was the license plate on his BMW as he turned onto Flat Rock Road.

HORNEE1.

Byrne and Jessica saw it at the same moment, looked at each other, then shook their heads and headed back to the office.

BACK AT THE Roundhouse—the police administration building at Eighth and Race streets, where the homicide unit occupied part of the first floor—Jessica ran an NCIC and PDCH check on David Hornstrom. Clean as an operating room. Not even a moving violation in the past ten years. Hard to believe, considering his taste in fast cars.

She then entered the victim's information into the Missing Person database. She didn't expect much.

Unlike television cop shows, there was no twenty-four-to-forty-eight-hour waiting period when it came to missing persons. Usually, in Philadelphia, a person called 911 and an officer went to the house to take the report. If the missing person was ten years old or under, police immediately began what was called a "tender age search." The officer directly searched the residence and any other residence at which the child lived, in the event of shared custody. Then each sector patrol car would be given the description of the child and began a grid method search for him or her.

If the missing child was eleven to seventeen years old, a report with description and photo was taken by the first officer, and that report was taken back to the district to be put into the computer and sent to a national registry. If a missing adult was mentally challenged, the report was also quickly put into the computer, and sector searches were done.

If the person was a regular Joe or Jane and just didn't

come home—as was probably the case with the young woman found on the riverbank—the report was taken, given to the detective division and the case was looked at again in five days, then again in seven days.

And sometimes you got lucky. Before Jessica could pour herself a cup of coffee, there was a hit.

"Kevin."

Byrne hadn't even gotten his coat off yet. Jessica held the digital camera's LCD screen next to the computer screen. On the computer screen was a missing person report with a photograph of a pretty blond woman. The picture was a little fuzzy, a driver's license or state ID photo. On Jessica's camera was a close-up of the victim's face. "Is that her?"

Byrne looked closely, from the computer screen to the camera, back. "Yeah," he said. He pointed to the small beauty mark above the right side of the young woman's upper lip. "That's her."

Jessica scanned the report. The woman's name was Kristina Jakos.

# 8

Natalya Jakos was a tall, athletic woman in her early thirties. She had dove gray eyes, smooth skin, and long, elegant fingers. Her dark hair was tipped with silver, cut into a pageboy style. She wore pale tangerine sweats and new Nikes. She had just returned from a run.

Natalya lived in an older, well-kept brick twin row house on Bustleton Avenue in the Northeast.

Kristina and Natalya were sisters, born eight years apart in Odessa, the coastal city in the Ukraine.

Natalya had filed the missing person report.

THEY MET IN the living room. On the mantel over the bricked-in fireplace was a number of small, framed pictures, mostly slightly out of focus, black-and-white snapshots of a family, posed in snow, on a sad-looking beach, around a dining table. One was of a pretty blond girl in a black-and-white checked sunsuit and white sandals. The girl was clearly Kristina Jakos.

Byrne showed Natalya a close-up photograph of the victim's face. The ligature was not visible. Natalya calmly identified her as her sister.

"Again, we are terribly sorry for your loss," Byrne said.

"She was killed."

"Yes," Byrne said.

Natalya nodded, as if she had been expecting the news. The lack of passion in her reaction was not lost on either detective. They had given her a bare minimum of information on the phone. They had not told her about the mutilation.

"When was the last time you saw your sister?" Byrne asked.

Natalya thought for a few moments. "It was four days ago."

"Where did you see her?"

"Right where you are standing. We argued. As we often did."

"May I ask what about?" Byrne asked.

Natalya shrugged. "Money. I had lent her five hundred dollars as part of what she needed for security deposits with the utility companies for her new apartment.

I think she may have spent it on clothes. She always bought clothes. I got mad. We argued."

"She was moving out?"

Natalya nodded. "We were not getting along. She moved out weeks ago." She reached for a tissue from the box on the end table. She was not as tough as she wanted them to believe she was. No tears, but it was clear that the dam was about to burst.

Jessica began to amend her timeline. "You saw her four days ago?"

"Yes."

"When?"

"It was late. She was here to pick up a few things, then she said she was going to do laundry."

"How late?"

"Ten or ten thirty. Perhaps later."

"Where did she do laundry?"

"I don't know. Near her new apartment."

"Have you been to her new place?" Byrne asked.

"No," Natalya said. "She never asked me."

"Did Kristina have a car?"

"No. Her friend would drive her usually. Or she would take SEPTA."

"What is her friend's name?"

"Sonja."

"Do you know Sonja's last name?"

Natalya shook her head.

"And you didn't see Kristina again that night?"

"No. I went to sleep. It was late."

"Can you remember anything else about that day? Where else she might have been? Who she saw?"

"I'm sorry. She did not share these things with me."

"Did she call you the next day? Maybe leave a message on the answering machine or voice mail?"

"No," Natalya said, "but we were supposed to meet the next afternoon. When she did not come, I called the police. The police said there was not much they could do, but they would put it in the system. My sister and I may not have been getting along, but she was always punctual. And she was not the type to just . . ."

The tears came. Jessica and Byrne gave the woman a moment. When she began to compose herself they continued.

"Where did Kristina work?" Byrne asked.

"I'm not sure exactly where. It was a new job. A *receptionist* job."

The way Natalya said the word *receptionist* was curious, Jessica thought. That was not lost on Byrne, either.

"Did Kristina have a boyfriend? Someone she was seeing?"

Natalya shook her head. "No one steady that I know of. But there were always men around her. Even when we were small. In school, at church. Always."

"Is there an ex-boyfriend? Someone who might be carrying a torch?"

"There is one, but he no longer lives here."

"Where does he live?"

"He went back to the Ukraine."

"Did Kristina have any outside interests? Hobbies?"

"She had it in her mind to be a dancer. It was her dream. Kristina had many dreams."

*A dancer*, Jessica thought. She flashed on the woman and her amputated feet. She moved on. "What about your parents?"

"They are long in their graves."

"Any other brothers or sisters?"

"One brother. Kostya."

"Where is he?"

Natalya grimaced, waved a hand, as if swatting away a bad memory. "He is *tvaryna*."

Jessica waited for a translation. Nothing. "Ma'am?"

"An animal. Kostya is a wild animal. He is where he belongs. In prison."

Byrne and Jessica exchanged a glance. This news opened a whole new set of possibilities. Maybe someone wanted to get to Kostya Jakos through his sister.

"May I ask where he is incarcerated?" Jessica asked.

"Graterford."

Jessica was going to ask why the man was in jail, but all of that information would be on the record. No need to open that wound now, so soon after another tragedy. She made a note to look it up.

"Do you know of anyone who might want to do your brother harm?" Jessica asked.

Natalya laughed, but it was without humor. "I don't know anyone who *doesn't*."

"Do you have a recent picture of Kristina?"

Natalya reached onto the top shelf of a bookcase. She retrieved a wooden box. She shuffled the contents, produced a photograph, a shot of Kristina that looked to be a head shot from a modeling agency—slightly soft focus, provocatively posed, lips parted. Jessica again thought the young woman was very pretty. Perhaps not model-gorgeous, but striking.

"Can we borrow this photograph?" Jessica asked. "We will return it."

"No need to return," Natalya said.

Jessica made a mental note to return the picture anyway. She knew from personal experience that as time passed the tectonic plates of grief, however thin, tended to shift.

Natalya stood, reached into a desk drawer. "As I said, Kristina was moving into a new place. Here is the extra key to her new apartment. Maybe this will help."

There was a white tag attached to the key. Jessica glanced at it. It bore an address on North Lawrence.

Byrne took out his card case. "If you think of anything

else that might help us, please give me a call." He handed a card to Natalya.

Natalya took the card, then handed Byrne a card of her own. It seemed to come from nowhere, as if she already had it palmed and ready to produce. As it turned out, "palmed" was probably the right word. Jessica glanced at the card. It read: Madame Natalya—Cartomancy, Fortune-Telling, Tarot.

"I think you have a great deal of sadness within you," she said to Byrne. "A great many unresolved issues."

Jessica glanced at Byrne. He looked a little rattled, a rare state for him. She sensed her partner wanted to continue the interview alone.

"I'll get the car," Jessica said.

THEY STOOD IN the too-warm front room, silent for a few moments. Byrne glanced inside a small space off the parlor—round mahogany table, two chairs, a credenza, tapestries on the walls. There were candles burning in all four corners. He looked back at Natalya. She was studying him.

"Have you ever had a reading?" Natalya asked.

"A reading?"

"A palm reading."

"I'm not exactly sure what that is."

"The art is called chiromancy," she said. "It is an ancient practice in which the lines and markings of your hand are studied."

"Uh, no," Byrne said. "Never."

Natalya reached out, took his hand in hers. Immediately Byrne felt a slight electrical charge. Not necessarily a sexual charge, although he could not deny that was a component.

She closed her eyes briefly, opened them. "You have a sense," she said.

"Excuse me?"

"Sometimes you know things you should not know. Things that are not seen by others. Things that turn out to be true."

Byrne wanted to take his hand back and run out of there as fast as he could, but for some reason he couldn't seem to move. "Sometimes."

"You were born with a veil?"

"A veil? I'm afraid I don't know anything about that."

"You came very close to dying?"

Byrne was a little spooked by this, but he didn't let on. "Yes."

"Twice."

"Yes."

Natalya let go of his hand, looked deep into his eyes. Somehow, in the past few minutes, her eyes seemed to have changed from a soft gray to a glossy black.

"The white flower," she said.

"I'm sorry?"

"The white flower, Detective Byrne," she repeated. "Take the shot."

Now he really *was* spooked.

Byrne put his notebook away, buttoned his coat. He thought about shaking hands with Natalya Jakos, but decided against it. "Once again, we're very sorry for your loss," he said. "We'll be in touch."

Natalya opened the door. An icy blast of air greeted Byrne. Walking down the steps, he felt physically drained.

*Take the shot,* he thought. *What the hell was that about?*

When Byrne reached the car he glanced back at the house. The front door was closed, but every window now had a glowing candle in it.

Had the candles been there when they arrived?

# 9

Kristina Jakos's new apartment was not an apartment at all, but rather a two-bedroom brick townhome on North Lawrence. As Jessica and Byrne approached, one thing was clear. No young woman who worked as a receptionist could afford the rent, or even half the rent if she was sharing. These were pricey digs.

They knocked, rang the bell. Twice. They waited, cupped their hands on the windows. Sheer curtains. Nothing visible. Byrne rang one more time, then inserted the key in the lock, opened the door. "Philly PD!" he said. No answer. They stepped inside.

If the outside was attractive, the inside was immaculate—heartwood pine floors, maple cabinets in the kitchen, brass fixtures. There was no furniture.

"I think I'm going to see if there are any receptionist jobs open," Jessica said.

"Me too," Byrne replied.

"You can work a switchboard?"

"I'll learn."

Jessica ran a hand over the raised paneling. "So, what do you think? Rich roommate or sugar daddy?"

"Two distinct possibilities."

"Maybe an insanely jealous psycho*pathic* sugar daddy?"

"A *definite* possibility."

They called out again. The house appeared to be

empty. They checked the basement, found a washer and dryer, still in the boxes, waiting to be installed. They checked the second floor. One bedroom held a folded futon; the other had a rollaway bed in the corner, a steamer trunk next to it.

Jessica returned to the foyer, picked up the pile of mail on the floor in front of the door. She sorted through the stack. One of the bills was addressed to a Sonja Kedrova. There was also a pair of magazines addressed to Kristina Jakos—*Dance* and *Architectural Digest*. There were no personal letters or postcards.

They stepped into the kitchen, opened a few drawers. Most were empty. Ditto on the lower cabinets. The cabinet beneath the sink held a collection of new apartment staples—sponges, Windex, paper towels, cleanser, bug spray. Young women always had a supply of bug spray.

She was just about to close the last cupboard door when they heard the creak of the floorboards. Before they could turn around they heard something that was far more ominous, far more lethal. The click of a revolver being cocked behind them.

"Don't . . . fucking . . . move," came a voice from the other side of the room. It was a woman's voice. Eastern European accent and cadence. It was the roommate.

Jessica and Byrne froze, hands out to their sides. "We're police officers," Byrne said.

"And I'm Angelina Jolie. Now put your hands up."

Jessica and Byrne both raised their hands.

"You must be Sonja Kedrova," Byrne said.

Silence. Then, "How do you know my name?"

"Like I said. We're police officers. I'm going to reach into my coat now, very slowly, and pull out my ID. Okay?"

A long pause. Too long.

"Sonja?" Byrne asked. "You with me?"

"Okay," she said. "Slow."

Byrne complied. "Here we go," he said. Without turning around, he plucked his ID out of his pocket, held it out.

A few more seconds passed. "Okay. So you are police. What's this about?"

"Can we put our hands down?" Byrne asked.

"Yes."

Jessica and Byrne put down their hands, turned around.

Sonja Kedrova was about twenty-five. She had teardrop eyes, full lips, deep auburn hair. Where Kristina had been pretty, Sonja was glamorous. She wore a long tan coat, black leather boots, a plum silk scarf.

"What is that you're holding?" Byrne asked, pointing at the gun.

"It's a gun."

"It's a starter's pistol. It fires blanks."

"My father gave it to me to protect myself."

"That gun is about as deadly as a squirt gun."

"And yet you put your hands up."

*Touché,* Jessica thought. Byrne wasn't amused.

"We need to ask you a few questions," Jessica said.

"And this could not wait until I arrived home? You had to break into my house?"

"I'm afraid it can't wait," Jessica replied. She held up the key. "And we didn't break in."

Sonja looked confused for a moment, then shrugged. She put the starter's pistol into a drawer, closed it. "Okay," she said. "Ask your 'questions.'"

"Do you know a woman named Kristina Jakos?"

"Yes," she said. Wary now. Her eyes danced between them. "I know Kristina. We are roommates."

"How long have you known her?"

"Maybe three months."

"I'm afraid we have some bad news," Jessica said.

Sonja's brow narrowed. "What happened?"

"Kristina is dead."

"Oh my God." Her face drained of color. She grabbed the counter. "How did this . . . what happened?"

"We're not sure," Jessica said. "Her body was found this morning in Manayunk."

Any second Sonja was going to topple. There were no chairs in the dining area. Byrne retrieved a wooden crate from the corner of the kitchen, set it down. He eased the woman onto it.

"Are you familiar with Manayunk?" Jessica asked.

Sonja took a few deep breaths, puffing out her cheeks. She remained silent.

"Sonja? Are you familiar with that neighborhood?"

"I'm sorry," she said. "No."

"Did Kristina ever talk about going there? Or if she knew someone who lived in Manayunk?"

Sonja shook her head.

Jessica made a few notes. "When was the last time you saw Kristina?"

For a moment, it appeared as if Sonja might be ready to do the floor-kiss. She weaved in that special way that indicated a fainting spell on the rise. In a moment it seemed to pass. "Not for maybe a week," she said. "I have been out of town."

"Where were you?"

"In New York."

"City?"

Sonja nodded.

"Do you know where Kristina worked?"

"All I know is that it was in Center City. A receptionist job for an important company."

"And she never told you the name of the firm?"

Sonja dabbed her eyes with a Kleenex, shook her head. "She did not tell me everything," she said. "She was sometimes very secretive."

"How so?"

Sonja frowned. "Sometimes she would come home

late. I would ask her where she was and she would get quiet. It was as if she was doing something about which she was ashamed maybe."

Jessica thought of the vintage dress. "Was Kristina an actress?"

"Actress?"

"Yes. Either professionally, or maybe in community theater?"

"Well, she liked to dance. I think she wanted to dance professionally. I don't know if she was that good, but maybe."

Jessica consulted her notes. "Is there anything else you know about her that you think would help?"

"She sometimes worked with the kids at St. Seraphim."

"The Russian Orthodox church?" Jessica asked.

"Yes."

Sonja stood, picked up a glass on the counter, then opened the freezer, extracted a frosty bottle of Stoli, and poured herself a few ounces. There was hardly anything to eat in the house, but there was vodka in the fridge. When you are in your twenties, Jessica thought—a demographic she had just recently, grudgingly, left behind—there are priorities.

"If you could just hold off on that for a minute, I'd appreciate it," Byrne said. He had a way about him that made his commands sound like polite requests.

Sonja nodded, put down the glass and the bottle, retrieved the Kleenex from her pocket, dabbed her eyes.

"Do you know where Kristina did her laundry?" Byrne asked.

"No," Sonja said. "But she would often do it late at night."

"How late?"

"Eleven o'clock. Maybe midnight."

"What about boyfriends? Did she have someone she was seeing?"

"Not that I know of, no," she said.

Jessica pointed toward the stairs. "The bedrooms are upstairs?" She said this as amiably as she could. She knew that Sonja was well within her rights to ask them to leave.

"Yes."

"Do you mind if I have a quick look?"

Sonja thought about it briefly. "No," she said. "It's okay."

Jessica mounted the stairs, stopped. "Which bedroom was Kristina's?"

"The one at the back."

Sonja turned to Byrne, held up her glass. Byrne nodded. Sonja let herself down to the floor, took a huge gulp of icy vodka. She immediately poured herself another.

Jessica continued upstairs, walked down the short hallway, entered the back bedroom.

Next to the rolled futon in the corner was a small box with an alarm clock on it. A white terry-cloth bathrobe hung on a hook on the back of the door. This was a young woman's apartment, early days. There were no pictures on the walls, no posters. There were none of the frilly accoutrements one might expect in the bedroom of a young woman.

Jessica thought about Kristina, standing right where she was standing. Kristina, considering her new life in her new home, all the possibilities that are yours when you are twenty-four. Kristina, imagining a room full of Thomasville or Henredon furniture. New rugs, new lamps, new bedclothes. New life.

Jessica crossed the room, opened the closet door. There were just a few dresses and sweaters in garment bags, all fairly new, all good quality. There was certainly nothing like the dress Kristina wore when she was found on the riverbank. Nor were there any baskets or bags of just laundered clothes.

Jessica took a step back, trying to catch the vibe. As a detective, how many closets had she looked in? How many drawers? How many glove compartments and trunks and hope chests and purses? How many lives had Jessica run through like a trespasser?

On the floor of the closet was a cardboard box. She opened it. There were tissue-wrapped figurines of glass animals—turtles mostly, squirrels, a few birds. There were also Hummels: miniatures of rosy-cheeked children playing the violin, the flute, the piano. At the bottom was a beautiful wooden music box. It looked to be walnut, and had a pink and white ballerina inlaid on top. Jessica took it out, opened it. There was no jewelry in the box, but the song it played was "The Sleeping Beauty Waltz." The notes echoed in the nearly empty room, a sad melody charting the end of a young life.

THE DETECTIVES MET back at the Roundhouse, compared notes.

"The van belonged to a man named Harold Sima," Josh Bontrager said. He had spent the afternoon tracking down information on the vehicles at the Manayunk crime scene. "Mr. Sima lived in Glenwood, but unfortunately met an untimely death by way of a fall down the stairs in September of this year. He was eighty-six. His son confessed to leaving the van in that lot a month ago. He said he couldn't afford to have it towed and junked. The Chevrolet was the property of a woman named Estelle Jesperson, late of Powelton."

"Late as in deceased?" Jessica asked.

"Late as in deceased," Bontrager said. "She died of a massive coronary three weeks ago. Her son-in-law left the car in that lot. He works in East Falls."

"Did you run checks on everyone?" Byrne asked.

"I did," Bontrager said. "Nothing."

Byrne briefed Ike Buchanan on what they had so far,

and the possible direction of further inquiries. As they prepared to leave for the day, Byrne asked Bontrager a question that had probably circled him all day.

"So where are you from, Josh?" Byrne asked. "Originally."

"I'm from a small town near Bechtelsville," he said.

Byrne nodded. "You grew up on a farm?"

"*Oh,* yeah. My family is Amish."

The word slammed around the duty room like a ricocheting .22 bullet. At least ten detectives heard it, and got immediately interested in whatever piece of paper was in front of them. It took every ounce of her power for Jessica not to look at Byrne. *An Amish homicide cop.* She'd been down the shore and back, as they say, but this was a new one.

"Your family is Amish?" Byrne asked.

"They are," Bontrager said. "I decided a long time ago not to join the church, though."

Byrne just nodded.

"You've never had Bontrager Special Preserves?" Bontrager asked.

"Never had the pleasure."

"It's very good. Damson plum, strawberry rhubarb. We even make a great peanut butter *schmier.*"

More silence. The room became a morgue full of tight-lipped corpses in suits.

"Nothing like a good *schmier,*" Byrne said. "My motto."

Bontrager laughed. "Yeah, yeah. Don't worry, I've heard all the jokes. I can take it."

"There are Amish jokes?" Byrne asked.

"Tonight we're gonna party like it's 1699," Bontrager said. "You just might be Amish if you ask, 'Does this shade of black make me look fat?' "

Byrne smiled. "Not bad."

"And then there's the Amish pickup lines," Bontrager

said. "Are thee at barn-raisings often? Can I buy thee a buttermilk colada? Are thee up for some plowing?"

Jessica laughed. Byrne laughed.

"Yeah, yuck it up," Bontrager said, reddening at his own off-color humor. "Like I said. I've heard them all."

Jessica glanced around the room. She knew the people in the homicide unit. She had the feeling that, before too long, Detective Joshua Bontrager would hear a few new ones.

# 10

Midnight. The river was black and silent.

Byrne stood on the riverbank in Manayunk. He looked back, toward the road. No streetlights. The parking lot was dim, long-shadowed by moonlight. If someone pulled in at that moment, even to turn around, Byrne would not be seen. The only illumination came from the headlights of the cars on the expressway, glimmering on the other side of the river.

A madman could pose his victim on the riverbank, take his time, compelled by whatever madness ruled his world.

Philadelphia had two rivers. Where the Delaware was the working soul of the city, the Schuylkill, and its winding course, always held a dark fascination for Byrne.

Byrne's father Padraig had been a longshoreman his entire working life. Byrne owed his childhood, his education, his life to the water. He had learned in grade school that Schuylkill meant "hidden river." In all his years in Philadelphia—which, except for his time in the service, had been Kevin Byrne's whole life—he had looked at the river as an enigma. It was more than one hundred miles long, and he honestly had no idea where it led. From the oil refineries in southwest Philly to Shawmont and beyond, he had worked its banks as a police officer, but never really followed it out of his jurisdiction, an authority that ended where Philadelphia County became Montgomery County.

He stared down into the dark water. In it he saw the face of Anton Krotz. He saw Krotz's *eyes*.

*Good to see you again, Detective.*

For what was probably the thousandth time in the past few days, Byrne second-guessed himself. *Had* he hesitated out of fear? *Was* he responsible for Laura Clarke's death? He realized that, for the past year or so, he had begun to question himself more than he ever had, had seen the architecture of his indecision. When he was a young cocky street cop he had known—*known*—that every decision he made had been right.

He closed his eyes.

The good news was that the visions were gone. For the most part. For many years he had been plagued and blessed with a vague sort of second sight, the ability to sometimes see things at a crime scene that no one else could see, an ability that began years earlier when he had been pronounced dead after plunging into the icy Delaware River. The visions were tied to migraine headaches—or so he had convinced himself—and when he had taken a bullet to the brain from the gun of a psychopath, the headaches stopped. He'd thought the visions were gone, too. But now and then they came back with a vengeance, sometimes for only a vivid split second. He'd learned to accept it. Sometimes it was just a glimpse of a face, a sliver of sound, a rippled vision not unlike something seen in a fun-house mirror.

The premonitions came less often these days, and that was a good thing. But Byrne knew that at any moment he might put his hand on a victim's hand, or brush up against something at a crime scene, and he would feel that terrible surge, the fearsome knowledge that would take him to the dark recess of a killer's mind.

*How had Natalya Jakos known this about him?*

When Byrne opened his eyes, Anton Krotz's image was gone. Now there was another pair of eyes. Byrne thought about the man who had carried Kristina Jakos to this place, the raging storm of madness that compelled someone to do what he had done to her. Byrne stepped onto the edge of the dock, the very spot where they had discovered Kristina's body. He felt a dark exhilaration knowing he was in the same place where the killer had stood just a few days earlier. He felt the images seep into his consciousness, saw the man—

—*cutting through skin and muscle and flesh and bone . . . taking a blowtorch to the wounds . . . dressing Kristina Jakos in that strange dress . . . slipping one arm into a sleeve, then the other, like you would dress a sleeping child, her cold flesh unresponsive to his touch . . . carrying Kristina Jakos down to the riverbank under cover of night . . . getting his twisted scenario just right as he—*

—heard something.

Footsteps?

Byrne's peripheral vision caught a shape, just a few feet away, a hulking black silhouette stepping from the deep shadows—

He turned toward the figure, his pulse thrumming in his ears, his hand on his weapon.

There was no one there.

He needed sleep.

Byrne drove home to his two-room apartment in South Philly.

*She wanted to be a dancer.*

Byrne thought of his daughter, Colleen. She had been deaf since birth, but it had never stopped her, never even slowed her down. She was a straight-A student, a terrific athlete. Byrne wondered what her dreams were. When she was small she had wanted to be a cop like him. He had talked her out of that one pronto. Then there was the obligatory ballerina stage, launched when he took her to see a hearing-impaired staging of *The Nutcracker*. Over the last few years she had talked quite a bit about becoming a teacher. Had that changed? Had he asked her lately? He made a mental note to do so. She would, of course, roll her eyes, flash a sign telling him he was *so* queer. He'd do it anyway.

He wondered if Kristina's father had ever asked his little girl about her dreams.

BYRNE FOUND A spot on the street and parked. He locked the car, entered his building, pulled himself up the steps. Either he was getting older, or the steps were getting steeper.

Had to be the latter, he thought.

He was still in his prime.

FROM THE DARKNESS of the vacant lot across the street, a man watched Byrne. He saw the light come on in the detective's second-floor window, watched his big shadow ripple across the blinds. From his perspective he witnessed a man coming home to a life that was in all ways the same as it had been the day before, and the day before that. A man who found reason and meaning and purpose in his life.

He envied Byrne as much as hated him.

The man was slight of build, with small hands and feet, thinning brown hair. He wore a dark coat, was ordinary in every manner, except for his facility for mourning, an unexpected and unwanted aptitude he never would have believed possible at this point in his life.

For Matthew Clarke the substance of grief had settled into the pit of his stomach like a dead weight. His nightmare had started the moment Anton Krotz took his wife from that booth. He would never forget his wife's hand on the back of the booth, her pale skin and painted nails. The terrifying glimmer of the knife at her throat. The hellish roar of the SWAT officer's rifle. The blood.

Matthew Clarke's world was in a tailspin. He did not know what the next day would bring, or how he would be able to go on. He did not know how he would bring himself to do the simplest of things: order breakfast, make a phone call, pay a bill, pick up the dry cleaning.

Laura had a dress at the cleaners.

*Nice to see you,* they would say. *How is Laura?*

Dead.

*Murdered.*

He didn't know how he would react in these inevitable situations. Who could possibly know? What was the training for this? Would he find a face brave enough to respond? It wasn't as if she had died from breast cancer, or leukemia, or a brain tumor. It wasn't as if he'd had a moment to prepare. She'd had her throat cut in a diner, the most degrading, public death possible. All under the watchful eye of the ever-vigilant Philadelphia Police Department. And now her children would live out their lives without her. Their mother was gone. His best *friend* was gone. How does one go about accepting all that?

Despite all these uncertainties, Matthew Clarke was sure of one thing. One fact was as apparent to him as the knowledge that rivers ran to the sea, as clear as the crystal dagger of sorrow in his heart.

Detective Kevin Francis Byrne's nightmare was just beginning.

PART TWO

# THE
# NIGHTINGALE

# 11

"Rats and cats."

"Huh?"

Roland Hannah closed his eyes for a moment. Whenever Charles said *huh,* it was the spoken equivalent of fingernails on a blackboard. It had been this way for a long time, ever since they'd been children. Charles was his stepbrother, slow to the world, sunny in his outlook and demeanor. Roland loved the man as much as he had ever loved anyone in his life.

Charles was younger than Roland, preternaturally strong and fiercely loyal. More than once he had proven that he would lay down his life for Roland. Instead of admonishing his stepbrother for the thousandth time, Roland continued. There was no dividend to reprimand, and Charles hurt very easily. "That's all there is," Roland said. "You're either a rat or a cat. There is nothing else."

"No," Charles said in full agreement. This was his way. "Nothing else."

"Remind me to make a note of that."

Charles nodded, adrift on the concept, as if Roland had just decoded the Rosetta Stone.

They were driving south on Route 299, nearing the Millington Wildlife Management Area in Maryland. The weather in Philadelphia had been brutally cold, but here the winter was a little milder. This was good. It meant the soil would not yet be deeply frozen.

And while this was good news for the two men in the front of the van, it was probably the worst news of all for the man lying facedown in the back, a man whose day had not been going all that well to begin with.

ROLAND HANNAH WAS tall and lithely muscular, precise in his language, although he'd never been formally educated. He wore no jewelry, kept his hair short, his body clean, his clothes modest and well pressed. He was of Appalachian descent, the child of a Letcher County, Kentucky, mother and a father whose ancestry and criminal past could be traced to the hollows of Helvetia Mountain, no further. When Roland had been four years old his mother had left Jubal Hannah—a brutal, violent man who had on many occasions taken the strap to his wife and child—and moved her son to North Philadelphia. Specifically, to an area known derisively, but quite accurately, as the Badlands.

Within a year Artemisia Hannah married a man far worse than her first husband, a man who controlled every aspect of her life, a man who gave her two damaged children. When Walton Lee Waite was killed in a botched robbery in Northern Liberties, Artemisia—a woman of fragile mental health to begin with, a woman who looked at the world through the prism of burgeoning madness—sank into the bottle, into self-harm of all manners, into the devil's own caress. By the age of twelve Roland was fending for his family, doing odd jobs of various natures, many of them criminal, dodging the police, the welfare services, the gangs. Somehow, he survived them all.

At fifteen, through no choice of his own, Roland Hannah found a new path.

\* \* \*

THE MAN WHOM Roland and Charles had transported from Philadelphia was named Basil Spencer. He had molested a young girl.

Spencer was forty-four, grossly overweight and equally overeducated, a Bala Cynwyd estate lawyer with a client list comprising mostly elderly and wealthy Main Line widows. His taste for young girls went back many years. Roland had no idea how many times Spencer had done this profane and defiling thing, but it really didn't matter. On this day, at this time, they were meeting in the name of one particular innocent.

By nine o'clock that morning the sun had breached the tops of the trees. Spencer knelt next to a freshly dug grave, a hole perhaps four feet deep, three feet wide, six feet long. His hands were tied behind his back with strong twine. Despite the chill, his clothes were soaked with sweat.

"Do you know who I am, Mr. Spencer?" Roland asked.

Spencer looked up, around, clearly wary of his own answer. The truth was, he didn't know *precisely* who Roland was—he had never laid eyes on him until the blindfold had come off half an hour earlier. In the end Spencer said, "No."

"I am the other shadow," Roland replied. His voice bore the slightest trace of his mother's Kentucky idiom, although he had long ago surrendered her accent to the streets of North Philadelphia.

"The . . . the *what*?" Spencer asked.

"I am the spot on the other man's X-ray, Mr. Spencer. I am the car that runs the red light just after you pass through the intersection. I am the rudder that fails on the earlier flight. You have never seen my face because, until today, I have been that which happens to everyone else."

"You don't under*stand*," Spencer said.

"Enlighten me," Roland replied, wondering what elaborate story would be coming his way this time. He glanced at his watch. "You have one minute."

"She was eighteen," Spencer said.

"She is not yet *thir*teen."

"That's crazy! Have you seen her?"

"I have."

"She was willing. I didn't force her to do anything."

"This is not what I have heard. I heard you took her to the crawlspace in your house. I heard you kept her in the dark, fed her drugs. Was it amyl nitrite? Poppers, as you call them?"

"You can't *do* this," Spencer said. "You don't know who I am."

"I know precisely who you are. What is more important is *where* you are. Look around. You are in the middle of a field, your hands are tied behind your back, you are begging for your life. Do you feel the choices you have made in this life have served you well?"

No answer. None was expected.

"Tell me about Fairmount Park," Roland said. "April 1995. The two girls."

"What?"

"Admit what you did, Mr. Spencer. Confess to what you did back then and you may survive this day."

Spencer looked from Roland, to Charles, back. "I don't know what you're talking about."

Roland nodded at Charles. Charles picked up the shovel. Basil Spencer began to cry.

"What are you going to do with me?" Spencer asked.

Without a word, Roland kicked Basil Spencer in the chest, knocking the man back into the grave. As Roland stepped forward he could smell the feces. Basil Spencer had soiled himself. They all did.

"Here's what I will do for you," Roland said. "I will speak to the girl. If indeed she was a willing participant,

I'll come back and get you, and you will take with you from this experience the greatest lesson of your life. If not, well, perhaps you can work your way out. Perhaps not."

Roland reached into his gym bag, held forth a long hose made of PVC. The plastic tube was corrugated, of the gooseneck variety, one inch in diameter and four feet in length. On one end was a fitted mouthpiece like those used for pulmonary testing. Roland held the tube over Basil Spencer's face. "Grip it between your teeth."

Spencer turned his head, the reality of the moment too great to bear.

"Suit yourself," Roland said. He took the hose away.

"No!" Spencer screamed. "I want it!"

Roland hesitated, then dangled the hose over Spencer's face again. This time Spencer gripped the mouthpiece tightly between his teeth.

Roland nodded at Charles, who placed the lavender gloves on the man's chest, then began to shovel the dirt into the hole. When he was finished, the conduit was sticking out of the ground about five or six inches. Roland could hear the frantic, wet inhale and exhale of air through the narrow pipe, the sound not unlike that of a suction tube at a dentist's office. Charles tamped the dirt. He and Roland walked over to the van.

A few minutes later, Roland backed the vehicle over to the grave and left the motor running. He got out, retrieved a long rubber hose from the back, this one of a greater diameter than the gooseneck plastic tube. He walked around to the back of the van and fitted one end over the exhaust. He put the other end over the pipe sticking out of the ground.

Roland listened, waited until the sucking sounds began to fade, his mind traveling, for the moment, to a place where two young girls had skipped along the banks of the Wissahickon, many years ago, the eye of God a golden sun above them.

THE CONGREGATION WAS dressed in its finest: eighty-one people sardined into the small storefront church on Allegheny Avenue. The air was thick with the smells of floral perfume, tobacco, and no small amount of boardinghouse whiskey.

The pastor came out of the back room to the strains of "This Is the Day That the Lord Hath Made" from the five-member choir. His deacon soon followed. Wilma Goodloe took the lead vocal; her big voice a true blessing from above.

At the sight of the pastor, the congregation leapt to its feet. The good Lord reigned.

After a few moments the pastor stepped to the rostrum, held up a hand. He waited until the music subsided, until his flock was seated, until the spirit moved him. As always, it did. He began slowly. He constructed his message as a builder might erect a house—an excavation of sin, a foundation of scripture, rigid walls of praise, topped by a crowning roof of glorious tribute. After twenty minutes, he brought it home.

"But make no mistake about it, there is much darkness in the world," the pastor said.

"*Darkness,*" someone echoed.

"Oh yes," the pastor continued. "Oh my, yes. This is a dark and *terrible* time."

"*Yes sir.*"

"But the darkness is not darkness to the Lord."

"*No sir.*"

"Not darkness at all."

"*No.*"

The pastor came around the pulpit. He clasped his hands in prayer. Some of the congregation stood. "Ephe-

sians 5:11 sayeth: 'Do not participate in the fruitless do-
ings of darkness but rather *expose* them.' "

"*Yes sir.*"

"Paul sayeth: 'Everything that is exposed by the light
is made visible, and where everything is visible there *is*
light.' "

"*Light.*"

Moments later, by the time the sermon was over, the
congregation had worked itself into a tumult. Tam-
bourines sang.

Pastor Roland Hannah and Deacon Charles Waite
were on fire. News was made in heaven this day, and the
New Page Church of the Divine Flame was the story.

The pastor considered his assembly. He thought about
Basil Spencer, about how he had learned of Spencer's
terrible deeds. People will tell their pastor many things.
Including children. He had heard many truths from the
mouths of children. And he would address them all. In
time. But there was a matter that had been a stagnant
black water in his soul for more than a decade, something that consumed every ounce of joy in his life, something that woke with him, walked with him, slept with
him, and prayed with him. There was a man out there
who had stolen his spirit. Roland was getting close to
him. He could feel it. Soon he would find the right one.
Until then, as he had in the past, he would do God's
work.

The voices of the choir rose in united praise. The raf-
ters shook with homage. Brimstone *would* spark and
flash on this day, Roland Hannah thought.

Oh my, yes.

A day that the Lord indeed hath made.

# 12

St. Seraphim was a tall, narrow structure on Sixth Street in North Philadelphia. With its cream stucco front, tall turrets, and golden onion domes above, the church—founded in 1897—was an imposing edifice, one of the oldest Russian Orthodox churches in Philadelphia. Jessica, having been raised Roman Catholic, didn't know much about the Orthodox Christian religions. She knew there were similarities in the practices of confession and communion, but that was about it.

Byrne was attending a review board and press conference regarding the incident in the diner. The review board was mandatory; the press conference was not. But Jessica had never known Byrne to shy away from his actions. He would be there, front and center, badge polished, shoes shined. It seemed that the families of both Laura Clarke and Anton Krotz felt the police should have handled the fraught situation differently. The press was all over it. Jessica had wanted to be there as a show of support, but her orders were to continue the investigation. Kristina Jakos deserved a timely inquiry. To say nothing of the very real concern that her killer was still on the loose.

Jessica and Byrne would meet up later in the day and she would brief him on any developments. If it got late they would meet at Finnigan's Wake. There was going to be a retirement party for a detective that night. Cops never miss a retirement party.

Jessica had called the church and made an appointment with Father Gregory Panov. While Jessica conducted the interview, Josh Bontrager canvassed the immediate area surrounding the church.

JESSICA PEGGED THE young priest at twenty-five or so. He was jovial, clean-shaven, dressed in black slacks and black shirt. She handed him a card, introduced herself. They shook hands. He had a sparkle in his eyes, suggesting a bit of the mischief.

"What should I call you?" Jessica asked.

"Father Greg will be fine."

Ever since she could remember, Jessica had been fawningly reverential around men of the cloth. Priests, rabbis, ministers. In her line of work it was a hazard—the clergy could certainly be as guilty of a crime as anyone—but she couldn't seem to help it. The Catholic school mentality had been implanted deeply. More like hammered in.

Jessica took out her notebook.

"I understand Kristina Jakos was a volunteer here," Jessica said.

"Yes. I believe she still is." Father Greg had dark, intelligent eyes, slight laugh lines. His expression told Jessica that the tense of her verb was not lost on him. He crossed the room to the door, opened it. He called out to someone. A few seconds later, a pretty, light-haired girl of fourteen or so arrived, spoke to him softly in Ukrainian. Jessica heard Kristina's name mentioned. The girl left. Father Greg returned.

"Kristina is not here today."

Jessica summoned her courage to say what she had to say. It was tougher to say it in a church. "I'm afraid I have bad news, Father. Kristina was killed."

Father Greg paled. He was an inner-city priest, in a tough area of North Philly, and thus probably braced for such news, but that didn't mean it ever came easy. He looked down at Jessica's business card. "You are with the homicide division."

"Yes."

"Are you saying she was murdered?"

"Yes."

Father Greg glanced at the floor for a moment, closed his eyes. He brought a hand to his heart. After a deep breath he looked up and asked, "How can I help?"

Jessica held up her notebook. "I just have a few questions."

"Whatever you need." He gestured to a pair of chairs. "Please." They sat.

"What can you tell me about Kristina?" Jessica asked.

Father Greg took a few moments. "I did not know her that well, but I can tell you she was very outgoing," he said. "Very giving. The children here really liked her."

"What did she do here exactly?"

"She helped out at the Sunday-school classes. Mostly in the role of assistant. But she was willing to do just about anything."

"For instance."

"Well, in preparation for our Christmas concert, like many volunteers, she painted backdrops, sewed costumes, helped nail together the sets."

"A Christmas concert?"

"Yes."

"And that concert is this week?"

Father Greg shook his head. "No. Our Holy Day Divine Liturgies are celebrated according to the Julian calendar."

The Julian calendar sort of rang a bell for Jessica, but she couldn't remember what it was. "I'm afraid I'm not familiar with that."

"The Julian calendar was begun by Julius Caesar in 46

BC. It is sometimes designated by OS, meaning Old Style. Unfortunately, for many of our younger parishioners, OS means Operating System. I'm afraid the Julian calendar is woefully outdated in a world of computers, cell phones, and DirecTV."

"So you don't celebrate Christmas on December twenty-fifth?"

"No," he said. "I'm not a scholar in these matters, but it is my understanding that, as opposed to the Gregorian calendar, due to solstices and equinoxes, the Julian calendar has picked up a full day every 134 years or so. Thus we celebrate Christmas January seventh."

"Ah," Jessica said. "Good way to pick up on the after-Christmas sales." She was trying to lighten the mood. She hoped she wasn't being disrespectful.

Father Greg's smile lit up his face. He really was a handsome young man. "And Easter candy, as well."

"Can you find out when Kristina was last here?" Jessica asked.

"Certainly." He stood, walked over to a huge calendar tacked to the wall behind his desk. He scanned the dates. "It would have been a week ago today."

"And you haven't seen her since?"

"I have not."

Jessica had to get to the hard part. She wasn't sure how to go about it, so she dove right in. "Do you know of anyone who may have wanted to harm her? A spurned suitor, ex-boyfriend, something like that? Perhaps someone here at the church?"

Father Greg narrowed his brow. It was clear that he did not want to think of anyone in his flock as a potential killer. But there seemed to be an air of ancient wisdom about him, tempered by a strong sense of the street. Jessica was sure he was wise to the ways of the city, the dark motives of the heart. He circled the far side of his desk, sat back down. "I did not know her all that well, but people talk, yes?"

"Of course."

"I understand that, as fun loving as she may have been, there was a sadness about her."

"How so?"

"It seemed as if she might have been a penitent. Perhaps there was something in her life that filled her with guilt."

*It was as if she was doing something about which she was ashamed,* Sonja had said.

"Any idea what that might be?" Jessica asked.

"No," he said. "I am sorry. But I must tell you that sadness is a common thing among Ukrainians. We are a gregarious people, but we've had a hard history."

"Are you saying she may have had the potential to harm herself?"

Father Greg shook his head. "I cannot say for sure, but I don't think so."

"Do you think she was the sort of person to intentionally put herself in harm's way? To take chances?"

"Again, I do not know. It's just that she—"

He stopped himself abruptly, ran a hand over his jaw. Jessica gave him an opportunity to continue. He did not.

"What were you about to say?" she asked.

"Do you have a few moments?"

"Absolutely."

"There is something you should see."

Father Greg rose from his chair, crossed the small room. In one corner was a metal cart holding a nineteen-inch television. Beneath it was a VHS machine. Father Greg flipped on the TV, then walked over to a glass-front cabinet full of books and tapes. He searched for a moment, extracted a VHS tape. He inserted the tape into the VCR, hit PLAY.

A few moments later an image appeared. It was handheld footage, sparsely lit. The image on the screen quickly resolved to Father Greg. He had shorter hair, wore a plain white shirt. He was seated on a chair, surrounded by young children. He was reading them some sort of fable, a story regarding an old couple and their granddaughter, a little girl who was able to fly. Behind him stood Kristina Jakos.

Onscreen Kristina wore faded jeans and a black Temple University sweatshirt. When Father Greg was finished with the story, he stood, removed his chair. The children gathered around Kristina. It appeared that she was teaching them a folk dance. Her students were about a dozen five- and six-year-old girls, adorable in their red and green Christmas outfits. Some wore traditional Ukrainian costumes. The girls all looked at Kristina as if she were a fairy princess. The camera panned left, found Father Greg at a battered spinet piano. He began to play. The camera turned back to Kristina and the children.

Jessica glanced at the priest. Father Greg watched the videotape, rapt. Jessica could see that his eyes were getting shiny.

On the videotape the children all followed Kristina's slow, deliberate movements, miming her actions. Jessica didn't know all that much about dance, but Kristina Jakos seemed to move with a gentle grace. Jessica couldn't help but see Sophie in that little group. She thought about the way Sophie often followed Jessica around the house, mimicking her movements.

Onscreen, when the music finally stopped, the little girls ran around in a circle, eventually crashing into each other and falling into a giggling, brightly colored pile. Kristina Jakos laughed as she helped them to their feet.

Father Greg hit PAUSE, freezing Kristina's smiling, slightly blurred image on the screen. He turned back to Jessica. His face was a collage of joy and confusion and bereavement. "As you can see, she will be missed."

Jessica nodded, at a loss for words. She had just recently seen Kristina Jakos, posed in death, horribly mutilated. Now the young woman was smiling at her. Father Greg broke the awkward silence.

"You were raised Catholic," he said.

It seemed to be a statement, not a question. "What makes you think that?"

He held up her card. "Detective Balzano."

"It's my married name."

"Ah," he said.

"But yes, I was. *Am*." She laughed. "What I mean is, I'm still Catholic."

"Practicing?"

Jessica was right in her assumptions. Orthodox priests and Catholic priests *do* have a lot in common. They both had a way of making you feel like a heathen. "I try."

"As do we all."

Jessica scanned her notes. "Is there anything else you can think of that might help us?"

"Nothing comes readily to mind. But I will ask among the people here who knew Kristina better," Father Greg said. "Perhaps someone will know something."

"I'd appreciate it." Jessica said. "Thank you for your time."

"You are most welcome. I am sorry it had to be on such a tragic day."

As Jessica put her coat on at the door, she glanced back into the small office. A somber gray light sifted through the leaded glass windows. Her last image from St. Seraphim was of Father Greg, his arms crossed, his face brooding, watching the freeze-framed image of Kristina Jakos.

# 13

The press conference was a zoo. It was held in front of the Roundhouse, near the statue of the police officer holding the child. This entrance was closed to the public.

Today there were twenty or so reporters—print, radio, and television. On the tabloid menu: roasted police officer. The media was a slavering horde.

Whenever a police officer was involved in a controversial shooting—or a shooting made controversial by a special interest group, a reporter with a dull axe, or for any number of headline-generating reasons—it was incumbent upon the police department to respond. Depending on the circumstances, a variety of respondents might take on the task. Sometimes it was Internal Affairs, sometimes the commanding officer of a particular district, sometimes even the commissioner himself if the situation, and the city politics, warranted. Press conferences were as necessary as they were annoying. It was a time for the department to pull together for one of their own.

This conference was run by Andrea Churchill, the Public Affairs Inspector. In her mid-forties, a former patrol officer in the Twenty-sixth District, Andrea Churchill was a scrapper, and more than once Byrne had seen her shut down an inappropriate line of questioning with a stare from her ice blue eyes. In her time on the street she had received sixteen merit awards, fifteen citations, six Fraternal Order of Police awards and the Danny Boyle Award. To Andrea Churchill, a pack of clamoring, bloodthirsty reporters was a Tastykake for breakfast.

Byrne stood behind her. To his right was Ike Buchanan. Behind him, in a loose semicircle, were seven other detectives, street faces in place, jaws firm, badges out front. The temperature was around fifteen degrees. They could have held the conference in the lobby of the Roundhouse. The decision to make a bunch of reporters wait around in the cold was not lost on anyone. The conference was mercifully winding down.

"We are confident that Detective Byrne followed procedure to the letter of the law on that terrible night," Churchill said.

"What *is* the procedure for a situation like that?" This from the *Daily News*.

"There are specific rules of engagement. The officer must consider the life of the hostage first."

"Was Detective Byrne on duty?"

"He was off duty at the time."

"Will there be charges filed against Detective Byrne?"

"As you know, this is up to the district attorney's office. But at this time they have informed us that there will be no charges."

Byrne knew exactly how it was going to go from here. The media had already begun the public rehabilitation of Anton Krotz—his terrible childhood, his mistreatment by the system. There had also been an article on Laura Clarke. Byrne was sure she was a fine woman, but the piece had made her out to be a saint. She worked at a local hospice, she helped save greyhounds, she had done a year in the Peace Corps.

"Is it true that Mr. Krotz was once in police custody and then let go?" a reporter for *City Paper* asked.

"Mr. Krotz was questioned by police two years ago in

connection with a homicide, but was released due to insufficient evidence." Andrea Churchill glanced at her watch. "If there are no more questions at this time—"

"She didn't have to die." The words came from the back of the crowd. It was a plaintive voice, hoarse with exhaustion.

All heads turned. Cameras followed. Matthew Clarke stood at the back of the throng. His hair was unkempt, he sported a few days' growth of beard, he wore no overcoat, no gloves, just a suit in which it appeared he had slept. He looked pitiful. Or, more accurately, *pitiable*.

"He gets to go about his life as if nothing happened." Clarke pointed an accusatory finger at Kevin Byrne. "What do *I* get? What do my *children* get?"

For the press this was fresh chum in the water.

A reporter for *The Report,* a weekly tabloid rag with which Byrne had a not so amicable history yelled, "Detective Byrne, how do you feel about the fact that a woman was killed right in front of you?"

Byrne felt the Irish rise, his fists clench. Flashbulbs flashed. "How do I *feel*?" Byrne asked. Ike Buchanan put a hand on his arm. There was more Byrne wanted to say, much more, but Ike's grasp tightened, and he knew what it meant.

Be cool.

When Clarke moved to approach Byrne, a pair of uniformed officers grabbed him and hustled him away from the building. More flashbulbs.

"Tell us Detective! How do you *feeeeeel*?" Clarke shouted.

Clarke was drunk. Everyone knew it, but who could blame him? He had just lost his wife to violence. The officers took him to the corner of Eighth and Race and let him go. Clarke tried to smooth his hair, his clothing, find a little dignity in the moment. The officers—a pair of big kids in their twenties—blocked his path back.

A few seconds later Clarke disappeared around the corner. The last thing any of them heard was Matthew Clarke screaming "This . . . isn't . . . *over!*"

A stunned silence held the crowd for a moment, then the reporters and cameras all turned to Byrne. Beneath a blitzkrieg of flashing bulbs, the questions rang out.

"—could've prevented this?"

"—anything to say to the victim's daughters?"

"—would you do if you had to do it all over?"

Shielded by a wall of blue, Detective Kevin Byrne headed back into the building.

# 14

They met in the church basement every week. Some weeks there were as few as three people attending, other times there were upwards of a dozen. Some people came back over and over again. Some came once, unburdened their sorrows, and never returned. The New Page Ministry asked for no fee, no donations. The door was always open—sometimes a knock came in the middle of the night, often on holidays—and there were always pastries and coffee for all. Smoking was definitely permitted.

They would not be meeting in the church basement for much longer. Contributions had been coming in steadily for a bright, airy space on Second Street. They were currently renovating the building—in the drywall stage at the moment, paint next. With any luck they would be able to meet there around the first of the year.

For now the basement of the church was a refuge, as it had been for years, a familiar place where tears were shed, outlooks renewed, and lives mended. For Pastor Roland Hannah it was a portal to the souls of his flock, the source of a river running deep into their hearts.

They had all been victims of a violent crime. Or were related to someone who had. Robberies, assault, burglary, rape, murder. Kensington was a hard part of the city, and hardly anyone walking the streets was untouched by wrongdoing. These people were the ones who wanted to talk about it, the folks who had been altered by the experience, the ones whose souls cried out for answers, for sense, for salvation.

Today six people sat in a semicircle on unfolded chairs.

"I didn't hear him," Sadie said. "He was quiet. He come up behind me, hit me over the head, stole my pocketbook, and ran."

Sadie Pierce was in her mid-seventies. She was a slight, skeletal woman with hands long knotted by arthritis, a head full of henna-dyed hair. She always dressed in bright red, head to toe. She had once been a singer, working the Catskill circuit in the fifties, known as the Scarlet Thrush.

"Have they recovered your belongings?" Roland asked.

Sadie glared, all the answer anyone needed. Everyone knew the police were neither inclined nor motivated to track down some old lady's taped and patched and frayed pocketbook, regardless of its contents.

"How are you faring?" Roland asked.

"Just so," she said. "There wasn't much money, but it was the personal items, you know? Pictures of my

Henry. And then all my papers. You can't hardly buy a cup of coffee without your ID these days."

"Tell Charles what you need and we'll make sure you get bus fare to the appropriate agencies."

"Thank you, Pastor," Sadie said. "Bless you."

The meetings of the New Page Ministry were informal, but they always moved forward in a clockwise direction. If you wanted to speak, but needed the time to organize your thoughts, you sat to Pastor Roland's right. And so it went. Next to Sadie Pierce sat a man they all knew only by his first name, Sean.

In his twenties, quiet and respectful and unassuming, Sean had drifted into the group a year or so earlier, attending more than ten times. At first, not unlike the actions of someone entering a twelve-step program like Alcoholics or Gamblers Anonymous—unsure of his need for the group or the group's usefulness—Sean had hung around the periphery, hugging the walls, staying some days for just a few minutes. Eventually he got closer and closer. These days he sat with the group. He always left a small donation in the jar. He still had not told his story.

"Welcome back, Brother Sean," Roland said.

Sean reddened slightly, smiled. "Hi."

"How are you feeling?" Roland asked.

Sean cleared his throat. "Okay, I suppose."

Many months earlier Roland had given Sean a brochure for CBH, the Community Behavioral Health organization. He did not think Sean had made an appointment. Asking about it might make things worse, so Roland stayed his tongue.

"Is there anything you would like to share today?" Roland asked.

Sean hesitated. He wrung his hands. "No, I'm fine, thanks. I think I'll just listen."

"The good Lord loves a listener," Roland said. "Bless you, Brother Sean."

Roland turned to the woman next to Sean. Her name was Evelyn Reyes. She was a large woman, in her late forties, a diabetic who walked with the aid of a cane most days. She had never spoken before. Roland could tell that it was time. "Let us all welcome back Sister Evelyn."

"Welcome," they all said.

Evelyn looked up, from face to face. "I don't know if I can."

"You are in the house of the Lord, Sister Evelyn. You are among friends. Nothing can harm you here," Roland said. "Do you believe this to be true?"

She nodded.

"Please unburden your sorrows. When you are ready."

Tentatively, she began her story. "It started a long time ago." Her eyes welled with tears. Charles brought over a box of Kleenex, retreated, sat in his chair by the door. Evelyn grabbed a tissue, dabbed her eyes, mouthed a thank you to Charles. She took another long moment, continued. "We were a large family back then," she said. "Ten brothers and sisters. Twenty or so cousins. Over the years we all married, had children. We would have picnics every year, big family get-togethers."

"Where did you meet?" Roland asked.

"Sometimes in spring and summer we would meet at Belmont Plateau. But mostly we would meet at my house. You know, over on Jasper Street?"

Roland nodded. "Please go on."

"Well, my daughter Dina was just a little girl in those days. She had the biggest brown eyes. A shy smile. Kind of a tomboy, you know? *Loved* to play the boys' games."

Evelyn's brow furrowed. She took a deep breath.

"We didn't know it at the time," she continued, "but

at some of these family gatherings she had . . . trouble with someone."

"With whom did she have trouble?" Roland asked.

"It was her uncle Edgar. Edgar Luna. My sister's husband. *Ex*-husband now. They would play together. Or at least that was what we thought at the time. He was an adult, but we didn't give it much mind. He was family, right?"

"Yes," Roland said.

"Over the years Dina got quieter and quieter. All through her young teenage years she didn't play much with friends, didn't go to the movies or the mall. We all thought it was a shy phase she was going through. You know how children can be."

"Oh my, yes," Roland said.

"Well, time passed. Dina grew up. Then, just a few years ago, she had a breakdown. Like a nervous condition. She couldn't work. She couldn't do much of anything. We couldn't afford any professional help for her, so we did the best we could."

"Of course you did."

"Then one day, not long ago, I found this. It was hidden on the top shelf of Dina's closet." Evelyn reached into her purse. She produced a letter written on bright pink paper, a child's stationery with sculpted edges. At the top were festive, brightly colored balloons. She unfolded the letter, handed it to Roland. It was addressed to God.

"She wrote this when she was only eight years old," Evelyn said.

Roland read the letter from start to finish. It was written in a child's innocent hand. It told a horrifying tale of repeated sexual abuse. Paragraph after paragraph detailed what Uncle Edgar had done to Dina in the basement of her own house. Roland felt the rage rise within. He asked the Lord for calm.

"This went on for *years*," Evelyn said.

"Which years were these?" Roland asked. He folded the letter, slipping it into his shirt pocket.

Evelyn thought for a moment. "Through the mid-nineties. Right until my daughter was thirteen. We never knew any of this. She had always been a quiet girl, even before the problems, you know? She kept her feelings to herself."

"What happened to Edgar?"

"My sister divorced him. He moved back to Winterton, New Jersey, where he was originally from. His parents passed a few years back, but he still lives there."

"You haven't seen him since?"

"No."

"Did Dina ever speak to you of these things?"

"No, Pastor. Never."

"How is your daughter faring of late?"

Evelyn's hands began to tremble. For a moment, the words seemed locked in her throat. Then: "My baby is dead, Pastor Roland. Last week she took pills. She took her life, as if it were hers to take. We put her in the ground over in York, where I'm from."

The shock that went around the room was tangible. No one spoke.

Roland reached out, held the woman, putting his arms around her big shoulders, embracing her as she unabashedly wept. Charles stood and left the room. In addition to the possibility of his emotions overcoming him, there was much to do now, much to prepare.

Roland sat back in his chair, gathered his thoughts. He held out his hands and they all linked together in a circle. "Let us entreat the Lord for the soul of Dina Reyes, and the souls of all who loved her," Roland said.

Everyone closed their eyes, began to silently pray.

When they were finished, Roland stood. "He has sent me to bind up the brokenhearted."

"Amen," someone said.

Charles returned, stood in the doorway. Roland met his gaze. Of the many things with which Charles had trouble in this life—some of them simple tasks, many of them things most take for granted—working on a computer was not among them. The Lord had blessed Charles with the ability to navigate the deep mysteries of the Internet, an ability with which Roland had not been graced. Roland could tell that Charles had already found Winterton, New Jersey and printed out a map.

They would leave soon.

# 15

Jessica and Byrne spent the afternoon canvassing the Laundromats that were either in walking distance or within reasonable SEPTA distance from Kristina Jakos's house on North Lawrence. In all, there were five coin-op laundries on their list; only two of which were open past 11 PM. As they approached a twenty-four-hour laundry called the All-City Launderette, unable to resist any longer, Jessica asked the question.

"Was the press conference as bad as it looked on TV?" After leaving St. Seraphim she had stopped for a take-out coffee at a mom-and-pop on Fourth Street. She had caught the replay of the press conference on the TV behind the counter.

"Nah," Byrne said. "It was much, much worse."

Jessica should have figured. "Are we ever going to talk about it?"

"We'll talk."

As frustrating as it was, Jessica let it go. Sometimes Kevin Byrne put up walls impossible to scale.

"By the way, where is our boy detective?" Byrne asked.

"Josh is shuttling witnesses for Ted Campos. He's going to hook up with us later."

"What did we get from the church?"

"Only that Kristina was a wonderful person. That the kids all loved her. That she was dedicated. That she was working on the Christmas play."

"Of course," Byrne said. "There are ten thousand gangbangers going to bed tonight perfectly healthy, and a well-loved young woman who worked with kids at her church is on the marble."

Jessica knew what he meant. Life was far from fair. It was up to them to exact whatever justice was available. And that was all they could ever do.

"I think she had a secret life," Jessica said.

This got Byrne's undivided attention. "A secret life? What do you mean?"

Jessica lowered her voice. There was no reason to. She just seemed to do it out of habit. "Not sure, but her sister hinted at it, her roommate almost came out and said so, and the priest at St. Seraphim mentioned that she had a sadness about her."

"Sadness?"

"His word."

"Hell, everybody's sad, Jess. That doesn't mean they're up to something illegal. Or even unsavory."

"No, but I'm going to take another run at the roommate. Maybe poke around Kristina's things a little more closely."

"Sounds like a plan."

\* \* \*

THE ALL-CITY LAUNDERETTE was the third establishment they visited. The managers of the first two laundries had no recollection of ever seeing the pretty, slender blond woman in their place of business before.

All-City had forty washers, twenty dryers. Plastic plants hung from the rust-stained acoustic tile ceiling. At the front was a pair of laundry-detergent vending machines—SUDS N SUCH! Between them was a sign that made an interesting request: PLEASE DO NOT VANDALIZE MACHINES. Jessica wondered how many vandals would see that sign, follow the rules, and simply move on. Probably about the same percentage of people who obeyed the speed limit. Along the back wall were a pair of soda machines, and a change dispenser. On either side of the center row of back-to-back washers was a line of salmon-colored plastic chairs and tables.

It had been a while since Jessica had been in a coin-op laundry. The experience took her back to her college days. The boredom, the five-year-old magazines, the smell of powdered soaps and bleach and fabric softeners, the clank of the loose change in the dryers. She hadn't missed it all that much.

Behind the counter was a Vietnamese woman in her sixties. She was petite and bristly, wore a flower-print change vest, along with what looked like five or six different brightly colored nylon fanny packs. On the floor of her small alcove was a pair of toddlers working on coloring books. The television on the shelf showed a Vietnamese action film. Behind the woman sat an Asian man who might have been anywhere from eighty to a hundred years old. It was impossible to tell.

A sign next to the register proclaimed MRS. V. TRAN, PROP. Jessica showed the woman her ID. She introduced herself and Byrne. Jessica then held up the photograph they had gotten from Natalya Jakos, the glamour shot of Kristina. "Do you recognize this woman?" Jessica asked.

The Vietnamese woman slipped on a pair of glasses, glanced at the photograph. She held it at arm's length, brought it closer. "Yes," she said. "She's been in here a few times."

Jessica glanced at Byrne. They shared that charge of adrenaline that always trails the first lead.

"Do you remember the last time you saw her?" Jessica asked.

The woman looked at the back of the photograph, as if there might be a date there to help her answer the question. She then showed it to the old man. He answered her in Vietnamese.

"My father says five days ago."

"Does he recall what time?"

The woman turned again to the old man. He answered, at length, seemingly annoyed at having his movie interrupted.

"It was after eleven PM," the woman said. She hooked a thumb at the old man. "My father. He can't hear too well, but he remembers everything. He says he stopped here after eleven to empty the change machines. While he was doing it, she came in."

"Does he recall if anyone else was here at that time?"

She spoke to her father again. He answered, his response more like a bark. "He says no. No other customers at that time."

"Does he recall if she came in with anyone?"

She asked her father the new question. The man shook his head. He was clearly ready to blow.

"No," the woman said.

Jessica was almost afraid to ask. She glanced at Byrne. He was smiling, looking out the window. She wasn't going to get any help from him. *Thanks, partner.* "I'm sorry. Does that mean he doesn't recall, or that she didn't come in with anyone?"

She spoke to the old man again. He answered with a burst of high-decibel, high-octave Vietnamese. Jessica didn't speak Vietnamese, but she was willing to bet there were a few swear words in there. She figured the old man said Kristina came in alone, and that everyone should leave *him* alone.

Jessica handed the woman a card, along with the standard request to call if she remembered anything. She turned to face the room. There were currently twenty or so people in the Laundromat—washing, loading, fluffing, folding. The surfaces of the folding tables were covered with clothing, magazines, soft drinks, baby carriers. Trying to lift any fingerprints from any of the myriad surfaces would be a complete waste of time.

But they had their victim, alive, at a particular place and a particular time. From here they would begin a canvass of the immediate area, as well as determine the SEPTA route that stopped across the street. The laundry was a good ten blocks from Kristina Jakos's new house, so there was no way she would have walked that distance in the cold, with her laundry. Unless she got a ride from someone, or took a cab, she would have taken the bus. Or would have intended to. Maybe the SEPTA driver would remember her.

It wasn't much, but it was a start.

JOSH BONTRAGER CAUGHT up with them across from the Laundromat.

The three detectives worked both sides of the street, showing Kristina's picture to the street vendors, the shop owners, the local bike boys, the corner rats. The reaction, from both men and women alike, was the same. *Pretty girl.* Unfortunately, no one remembered seeing her coming out of the Laundromat a few days earlier, or any other day for that matter. By midafternoon they had spoken to everyone available—residents, store merchants, cabbies.

Directly across from the Laundromat was a pair of row houses. They had spoken to the woman who lived in the row house on the left. She had been out of town for two weeks, had seen nothing. They had knocked on the door of the other row house, had gotten no answer. On the way back to the car Jessica noticed the curtains part slightly, then immediately close. They returned.

Byrne knocked on the window. Hard. Eventually, a teenaged girl opened the door. Byrne showed her his ID.

The girl was thin and pale, about seventeen; very nervous, it seemed, about talking to the police. Her sandy hair was lifeless. She wore a pair of well-worn brown corduroy overalls and scuffed beige sandals, pilled white socks. Her fingernails were chewed raw.

"We'd like to ask you a few questions," Byrne said. "We promise not to take up too much of your time."

Nothing. No response whatsoever.

"Miss?"

The girl looked at her feet. Her lips trembled slightly, but she said nothing. The moment drew out into discomfort.

Josh Bontrager caught Byrne's eye, lifted an eyebrow as if to ask if he could take a shot at this. Byrne nodded. Bontrager stepped forward.

"Hi," Bontrager said to the girl.

The girl lifted her head slightly, but remained aloof and silent.

Bontrager glanced beyond the girl, into the front room of the row house, then back. *"Kannscht du Pennsilfaanisch Deitsch schwetzer?"*

The girl appeared stunned for a moment. She looked Josh Bontrager up and down, then smiled a thin smile and nodded.

"English okay?" Bontrager asked.

The girl put her hair behind her ears, suddenly conscious of her appearance. She leaned on the doorjamb. "Okay."

"What's your name?"

"Emily," she said softly. "Emily Miller."

Bontrager held out a picture of Kristina Jakos. "Have you ever seen this lady, Emily?"

The girl scrutinized the picture for a few moments. "Yes. I've seen her."

"Where have you seen her?"

Emily pointed. "She washes her clothes across the street. Sometimes she gets on the bus right here."

"When was the last time you saw her?"

Emily shrugged. She chewed on a fingernail.

Bontrager waited until the girl met his gaze once again. "It's really important, Emily," he said. "*Really* important. And there's no rush here. You take your time."

A few seconds later: "I think it was maybe four or five days ago."

"At night?"

"Yes," she said. "It was late." She pointed toward the ceiling. "My room is right up there, overlooking the street."

"Was she with anyone?"

"I don't think so."

"Did you see anyone else hanging around, see anyone watching her?"

Emily thought for a few more moments. "I did see somebody. A man."

"Where was he?"

Emily gestured to the sidewalk just in front of her house. "He walked past the window a few times. Back and forth."

"Did he wait right here at the bus stop?" Bontrager asked.

"No," she said, pointing to her left. "I think he stood in the alley. I figured he was trying to stay out of the wind. A couple of buses came and went. I don't think he was waiting for the bus."

"Can you describe him?"

"White man," she said. "At least, I think so."

Bontrager waited. "You're not sure?"

Emily Miller put her hands out, palms up. "It was in the dark. I couldn't see too much."

"Did you notice if there were any vehicles parked close to the bus stop?" Bontrager asked.

"There are always cars in the street. I didn't notice."

"That's okay," Bontrager said with his big farm-boy smile. It worked magic on the girl. "That's all we need for now. You did great."

Emily Miller colored slightly, remained silent. She wiggled her toes in her sandals.

"I may need to speak to you again," Bontrager added. "Would that be okay?"

The girl nodded.

"On behalf of my colleagues, and the entire Philadelphia Police Department, I would like to thank you very much for your time," Bontrager said.

Emily glanced from Jessica to Byrne, back to Bontrager. "You're welcome."

*"Ich winsch dir en hallich, frehlich, glicklich Nei Yaahr,"* Bontrager said.

Emily smiled, smoothed her hair. To Jessica, she looked rather smitten with Detective Joshua Bontrager. *"Gott segen eich,"* Emily replied.

The girl closed the door. Bontrager put away his notebook, smoothed his tie. "Well," he said. "Where to next?"

"What language was that?" Jessica asked.

"It was Pennsylvania Dutch. Which is mostly German."

"Why did you speak to her in Pennsylvania Dutch?" Byrne asked.

"Well, for one thing, that girl was Amish."

Jessica glanced up at the front window. Emily Miller was watching them through the parted curtains. Somehow she had managed to quickly run a brush through her hair. So she *was* smitten after all.

"How could you tell?" Byrne asked.

Bontrager thought about his answer for a moment. "You know how you can look at someone on the street and just *know* they're wrong?"

Both Jessica and Byrne knew what he meant. It was a sixth sense wired into police officers worldwide. "Yeah."

"Same thing with Amish folks. You just *know.* Besides, I saw a pineapple quilt on the couch in the living room. I know Amish quilting."

"What is she doing in Philly?" Jessica asked.

"Hard to say. She was wearing English clothes. She's either left the church, or she's on *rumspringa.*"

"What is *rumspringa*?" Byrne asked.

"Long story," Bontrager said. "We'll get to it later. Maybe over a buttermilk colada."

He winked and smiled. Jessica looked at Byrne.

Score one for the Amish kid.

AS THEY WALKED back to the car, Jessica ran the questions. Besides the obvious—who killed Kristina Jakos and why, three others loomed.

One: Where was she between the time she left the All-City Launderette and the time she was placed on that riverbank?

Two: Who called 911?

Three: Who was standing across the street from the Laundromat?

# 16

The medical examiner's office was on University Avenue. When Jessica and Byrne returned to the Roundhouse they had a message from Dr. Tom Weyrich. It was marked *Urgent*.

They met in the main autopsy theater. It was Josh Bontrager's first time. His face was the color of cigar ash.

TOM WEYRICH WAS on the phone when Jessica, Byrne, and Bontrager arrived. He handed Jessica a folder, held up a finger. The folder contained the preliminary autopsy findings. Jessica scanned the report:

> The body is that of a normally developed white female measuring sixty-six inches and weighing 112 pounds. Her general appearance is consistent with the recorded age of twenty-four years. Livor mortis is present. Eyes are open. The irises are blue and corneas are cloudy. Petechial hemorrhaging is present in the conjuctiva bilaterally. There is a ligature mark on the neck below the mandible.

Weyrich hung up the phone. Jessica handed him back the report. "So she was strangled," she said.

"Yes."

"And that was the cause of death?"

"Yes," Weyrich said. "But she was not strangled with the nylon belt found around her neck."

"So what was it?"

"She was strangled by a much narrower ligature. A polypropylene rope. Definitely from behind." Weyrich pointed to a photograph of the V-shaped ligature mark made at the back of the victim's neck. "This is not high enough to indicate hanging. I believe it was done manually. The killer stood behind her as she sat, wrapped the ligature once around, and pulled up."

"What about the rope itself?"

"At first I thought it was a standard three-strand polypropylene. But the lab has pulled a pair of fibers. One blue, one white. Presumptively it was of a type that has been treated to resist chemicals, probably floatable. There's a good chance it is a swim-lane-type rope."

Jessica had never heard the term. "You mean the kind of rope they use in pools to separate the lanes?" she asked.

"Yes," Weyrich said. "It's strong, made of a low-stretch fiber."

"So why was there another belt tied around her neck?" Jessica asked.

"Can't help you there. Perhaps to conceal the ligature mark for aesthetic reasons. Perhaps it means something. The lab has the belt now."

"Any word on it?"

"It's old."

"How old?"

"Maybe forty or fifty years or so. The composition of the fibers has begun to break down due to use and age and weather. They are getting a lot of different substances from the fiber."

"Like what?

"Sweat, blood, sugar, salt."

Byrne flicked a glance at Jessica.

"Her nails are in pretty good shape," Weyrich continued. "We've swabbed them anyway. No scratches or bruises."

"What about her feet?" Byrne asked. As of that morning, the missing body parts had not been recovered. The marine unit would be diving in the river near the crime scene later that day, but even with their sophisticated gear, it would be slow going. The water in the Schuylkill was frigid.

"Her feet were amputated postmortem with a sharp serrated instrument. There is some shattering of the bone, so I don't believe it was a surgical saw." He pointed to an extreme close-up of the cut. "It's more likely to have been a carpenter's saw. We pulled some trace from the area. Lab believes it was wood fragments. Mahogany perhaps."

"So you're saying that the saw was used in some sort of woodworking project before it was used on the victim?"

"All preliminary, but that sounds about right."

"And none of this was done at the scene?"

"Presumptively, no," Weyrich said. "But she was definitely dead when it happened. Thank God."

Jessica made her notes, a little taken aback. A carpenter's saw.

"There's more," Weyrich said.

*There's always more,* Jessica thought. *Whenever you step into the world of a psychopath, there is always more.*

Tom Weyrich pulled down the sheet. Kristina Jakos's body was colorless. Her musculature was already breaking down. Jessica remembered how graceful and strong she had looked on the videotape at the church. How alive.

"Look at this." Weyrich indicated a spot on the

victim's abdomen, a glossy whitish area about the size of a fifty-cent piece.

He flipped off the bright overhead light, picked up a handheld UV lamp, and switched it on. Jessica and Byrne immediately saw what he was talking about. There was a circle on the victim's lower stomach, measuring about two inches in diameter. From her vantage point of a few feet away, it looked to Jessica to be an almost perfect disk.

"What's this?" Jessica asked.

"It's a mixture of semen and blood."

This changed everything. Byrne looked at Jessica; Jessica at Josh Bontrager. Bontrager's face remained a bloodless gray.

"She was sexually assaulted?" Jessica asked.

"No," Weyrich said. "There was no recent vaginal or anal penetration."

"You ran a rape kit?"

Weyrich nodded. "It was negative."

"The killer ejaculated onto her?"

"No again." He picked up a lighted magnifying glass, handed it to Jessica. She leaned in, looked at the circle. And felt her stomach drop.

"Oh Jesus."

While the image was an almost perfect circle, it was much more than that. So much more. The image was a highly detailed drawing of the moon.

"This is a drawing?" Jessica asked.

"Yes."

"Painted with semen and blood?"

"Yes," Weyrich said. "And the blood doesn't belong to the victim."

"Oh this is just getting better and better," Byrne said.

"From the detail, it looks like it probably took hours to do," Weyrich said. "We have a DNA report coming.

It's on the fast track. Find the guy, and we'll match him to this and nail it shut."

"So this was *painted* painted? Like with a brush?" Jessica asked.

"Yes. We lifted a few fibers from the area. The doer used an expensive sable brush. Our boy is an accomplished artist."

"A woodworking, swimming, psychopathic, *masturbating* artist," Byrne offered, more or less to himself.

"Lab has the fibers?"

"Yes."

This was good. They would get the report on the brush hairs and perhaps trace the brush used.

"Do we know if this 'painting' was done pre- or post?" Jessica asked.

"I would say post," Weyrich said, "but there's no way to know for sure. That it's so detailed, that there were no barbiturates in the victim's system, leads me to believe it was done postmortem. She wasn't drugged. No one can or would sit that still if they were conscious."

Jessica looked more closely at the drawing. It was a classic rendering of the man in the moon, similar to an old woodcut of a benevolent face staring down at the earth. She considered the process of painting this on a corpse. The painter posed his victim, more or less, in plain sight. He was bold. And clearly insane.

JESSICA AND BYRNE sat in the parking lot, more than a little stunned.

"Please tell me this is a first for you," Jessica said.

"It's a first."

"We're looking for a guy who takes a woman off the street, strangles her, cuts off her feet, then takes hours to draw the moon on her stomach."

"Yep."

"In his own semen and blood."

"We don't know for sure whose blood and semen it is yet," Byrne said.

"Thanks," Jessica said. "I was just starting to think I had a handle on it. I was kind of hoping he jacked off, cut his own wrists, and eventually bled out."

"No such luck."

As they pulled out onto the street, four words ran through Jessica's mind:

*Sweat, blood, sugar, salt.*

BACK AT THE Roundhouse, Jessica called SEPTA. After running a series of bureaucratic gauntlets, she finally spoke to the man who drove the night route that passed in front of the All-City Launderette. He confirmed that he had driven his route the night Kristina Jakos did her laundry, the last night anyone to whom they had spoken recalled seeing her alive. The driver specifically remembered *not* picking anyone up at that stop all week.

Kristina Jakos had never made it onto the bus that night.

While Byrne put together a list of thrift shops and secondhand clothing stores, Jessica scanned the preliminary lab reports. There were no fingerprints on Kristina Jakos's neck. There was no blood on the scene other than the trace evidence found on the riverbank and on her clothing.

*Blood evidence,* Jessica thought. Her mind went back to the moon "painting" on Kristina's stomach. It gave her an idea. It was a long shot, but it was better than no shot. She picked up the phone and called the rectory at St. Seraphim. In short order she had Father Greg on the line.

"How can I help you, Detective?" he asked.

"I have a quick question," she said. "Do you have a moment?"

"Of course."

"I'm afraid it might sound a little strange."

"I am an inner-city priest," Father Greg said. "Strange is pretty much my business."

"I have a question about the moon."

Silence. Jessica expected as much. Then: "The moon?"

"Yes. When we spoke, you mentioned the Julian calendar," Jessica said. "I was wondering if the Julian calendar addressed any issues relating to the moon, the lunar cycle, anything like that."

"I see," Father Greg said. "Like I said, I'm not particularly scholarly on these matters, but I can tell you that, like the Gregorian calendar, which is also divided into months of irregular lengths, the Julian calendar is no longer synchronized to the phases of the moon. In fact, the Julian calendar is a purely solar calendar."

"So there is no particular significance given to the moon in Russian Orthodoxy or by the Russian people?"

"I didn't say that. There are many Russian folk tales and much Russian lore that address both the sun and the moon, but nothing I can think of regarding the *phases* of the moon."

"What sorts of folk tales?"

"Well, one story in particular, one that is widely known, is the story called 'The Sun Maiden and the Crescent Moon.'"

"What is that?"

"It is a Siberian folk tale, I believe. Maybe a Ket fable. Rather grotesque according to some."

"I'm an inner-city cop, Father. Grotesque is pretty much my business."

Father Greg laughed. "Well, 'The Sun Maiden and the Crescent Moon' is the story of a man who becomes the crescent moon, beloved of the Sun Maiden. Unfortunately—and this is the grotesque part—he is torn in half by the Sun Maiden and an evil sorceress as they fight over him."

"He's torn in half?"

"Yes," Father Greg said. "And, as it turns out, the Sun Maiden got the half without the hero's heart, and can only revive him for a week at a time."

"Sounds cheerful," Jessica said. "This is a children's story?"

"Not all folk tales are for children," the priest said. "I am sure there are other stories. I would be happy to ask around. We have many elderly parishioners. They will undoubtedly know much more than I do about these matters."

"I would really appreciate it," Jessica said, mostly out of courtesy. She couldn't imagine how any of this could be relevant.

They said their good-byes. Jessica hung up the phone. She made a note to visit the Free Library and look up the story, as well as try to find a book of woodcuts or books dedicated to renderings of the moon.

Her desk was covered with the photographs she had printed out from her digital camera, photographs taken at the Manayunk crime scene. Three dozen medium and close-up shots—the ligature, the crime scene itself, the building, the river, the victim.

Jessica grabbed the pictures and stuffed them into her shoulder bag. She would look at them later. She had seen enough for today. She needed a drink. Or six.

She glanced out the window. It was getting dark already. Jessica wondered if there would be a crescent moon this night.

# 17

There once lived a brave tin soldier, and he and all his brethren were cast from the same spoon. They dressed in blue. They marched in a line. They were feared and respected.

Moon stands across the street from the alehouse, waiting for his tin soldier, patient as ice. The lights of the city, the lights of the season, sparkle in the distance. Moon idles in darkness, watching the tin soldiers come and go from the alehouse, thinking of the fire that would reduce them to tinsel.

But this is not about the full box of soldiers—stacked and rigid and set at attention, tin bayonets fixed—just one. He is an aging warrior, still strong. It will not be easy.

At midnight this tin soldier will open the snuffbox and meet his goblin. At that time, in that concluding moment, there will be just be him and Moon. There will be no other soldiers to help, no paper lady to grieve. The fire will be terrible and he will shed his tin tears.

Will it be the fire of love?

Moon holds the matches in his hand.

And waits.

# 18

The crowd on the second floor of Finnigan's Wake was fearsome. Assemble fifty or so cops in one room and you had the potential for serious mayhem. Finnigan's Wake was a venerable institution on Third and Spring Garden streets, a celebrated Irish pub that drew officers from all districts, all parts of town. When you retired from the PPD there was a good a chance that your party would be held there. As well as your wedding reception. The catering at Finnigan's Wake was as good as anywhere in the city.

This night it was a retirement party for Detective Walter Brigham. After nearly four decades in law enforcement, he was turning in his papers.

JESSICA SIPPED HER beer, glanced around the room. She had been a police officer for ten years, the daughter of one of the most renowned detectives in the past three decades, and the sound of dozens of cops swapping war stories in a bar had become a lullaby of sorts. More and more she was beginning to accept the fact that, regardless of what she thought, her friends were, and would probably always be, fellow officers.

Sure, she still talked to her old classmates from the Nazarene Academy, and sometimes some of the girls from her old South Philly neighborhood—at least, those who had moved to the Northeast like she had. But for the most part, everyone she relied upon carried a gun and a badge. Including her husband.

Even though it was a party for one of their own, there was not necessarily a sense of unity in the room. The space was dotted with clusters of officers talking amongst themselves, the largest being a faction of gold-badge detectives. And although Jessica had certainly paid her entrance fee into that group, she was not quite *there* yet. As in any other large organization there were always internal cliques, subgroups that banded together for a variety of reasons: race, gender, experience, discipline, neighborhood.

The detectives were gathered at the far end of the bar.

Byrne showed up at just after nine. And even though he knew just about every detective in the room, had come up the ranks with half of them, when he walked in the room he chose to stake the near end of the bar with Jessica. She appreciated it, but she still sensed that he would rather be in with that pack of wolves—old and young alike.

BY MIDNIGHT, WALT Brigham's party had entered the serious drinking stage. Which meant it had entered the serious storytelling stage. Twelve PPD detectives bunched around the end of the bar.

"Okay," Richie DiCillo began. "I'm in a sector car with Rocco Testa." Richie was a lifer out of North Detectives. Now in his fifties, he had been one of Byrne's rabbis early on.

"This is 1979, right around the time those little battery-operated portable televisions came out. We're up in Kensington, *Monday Night Football* is on, Eagles and Falcons. Close game, back and forth. About eleven o'clock we get this knock on the window. I look up. Chubby transvestite, full regalia—wig, nails, false eyelashes, spangle dress, high heels. Name was Charlise,

Chartreuse, Charmoose, something like that. Used to call him Charlie Rainbow on the street."

"I remember him," Ray Torrance said. "He went about five seven, two-forty? Different wig for every night of the week?"

"That's him," Richie said. "You could tell what day it was by the color of his hair. Anyway, he has a busted lip, a black eye. Says his pimp beat the shit out of him, and he wants us to personally strap the asshole in the electric chair. *After* we cut off his nuts. Rocco and me look at each other, at the TV. The game is right at the two-minute warning. With the ads and shit we've got maybe three minutes, right? Rocco is out of the car like a shot. He brings Charlie around the back of the car, tells him we've got a brand-new system. Real high-tech. Says you can tell the judge your story, right from the street, and the judge will send a special squad to pick up the evildoer."

Jessica glanced at Byrne, who shrugged, even though they both had a pretty good idea where this was going.

"Of course Charlie *loves* this idea," Richie said. "So Rocco takes the TV out of the car, finds a dead channel with just snow and wavy lines on it, puts it on the trunk. He tells Charlie to look right at the screen and talk. Charlie fixes his hair, makeup, like he's going on the *Tonight Show,* right? He gets up really close to the screen, tells all the sordid details. When he's done, he leans back, like all of a sudden a hundred sector cars are gonna come screaming down the street. Except, right at that second, the TV speaker crackles, like it's picking up another station. Which it is. Except there's a commercial on."

"Uh-oh," somebody said.

"A commercial for StarKist Tuna."

"*No,*" somebody else said.

"*Oh,* yes," Richie said. "Outta nowhere the TV says, loud as hell, 'Sorry, Charlie.' "

Roars around the room.

"He thought it was the fuckin' *judge*. Off like a shot down Frankford. Wigs and high heels and sequins flying. Never saw him again."

"I can top that story!" someone said, shouting over the laughter. "We're running this sting in Glenwood . . ."

And so the stories ran.

Byrne glanced at Jessica. Jessica shook her head. She had a few stories of her own, but it was getting late. Byrne pointed at her nearly empty glass. "One more?"

Jessica glanced at her watch. "Nah. I'm out," she said.

"Lightweight," Byrne replied. He drained his glass, motioned to the barmaid.

"What can I say? A girl needs her beauty sleep."

Byrne remained silent, rocked on his heels, bopped a bit to the music.

*"Hey!"* Jessica yelled. She rammed a fist into his shoulder.

Byrne jumped. Although he tried to mask the pain, his face betrayed him. Jessica knew how to throw a punch. *"What?"*

"This is the part where you say, 'Beauty sleep? You don't need beauty sleep, Jess.' "

"Beauty sleep? You don't need beauty sleep, Jess."

"Jesus." Jessica slipped on her leather coat.

"I thought that was, you know, *understood*," Byrne added, treading water, his expression a caricature of virtue. He rubbed his shoulder.

"Nice try, Detective. You good to drive?" It was a rhetorical question.

"Oh, yeah," Byrne answered by rote. "I'm good."

*Cops,* Jessica thought. Cops could always drive.

Jessica crossed the room, said her good-byes and good-lucks. As she neared the door, she caught Josh Bontrager, standing by himself, smiling. His tie was askew; one pants pocket was turned out. He looked a little wobbly. When he saw Jessica, he extended a hand. They shook. Again.

"You doing okay?" she asked.

Bontrager nodded a little too forcefully, perhaps trying to convince himself. "Oh yeah. Fine. Fine. Fine."

For some reason Jessica was already feeling motherly about Josh. "Okay, then."

"Remember how I said I had heard all the jokes already?"

"Yes."

Bontrager waved an inebriated hand. "Not even close."

"What do you mean?"

Bontrager stood at attention. He saluted. More or less. "I'll have you know that I have the distinct honor of being the very first *Amishide* detective in the history of the PPD."

Jessica laughed. "See you tomorrow, Josh."

On the way out she saw a detective she knew from South showing a picture of his infant grandson to another cop. *Babies,* Jessica thought.

There were babies *everywhere*.

# 19

Byrne made himself a plate from the small buffet, put the food on the bar. Before he could take a bite, he felt a hand on his shoulder. He turned, saw the boozy eyes, the damp lips. Before Byrne knew it, Walt Brigham had

him in a bear hug. Byrne found the gesture a little
strange because they had never been that close. On the
other hand, this was a special night for the man.

They finally broke, did the manly, postemotional
things: cleared throats, straightened hair, smoothed ties.
Both men stepped back, scanned the room.

"Thanks for coming, Kevin."

"Wouldn't have missed it."

Walt Brigham was as tall as Byrne, a little round-
shouldered. He had a thicket of pewter gray hair, a
neatly trimmed mustache, big nicked hands. His ocean
blue eyes had seen a lot, and all of it floated there.

"Can you believe this collection of thugs?" Brigham
asked.

Byrne looked around. Richie DiCillo, Ray Torrance,
Tommy Capretta, Joey Trese, Naldo Lopez, Mickey
Nunziata. All longtimers.

"How many sets of brass knuckles you figure there
are in this room?" Byrne asked.

"Counting mine?"

Both men laughed. Byrne ordered a round for the two
of them. The barmaid, Margaret, brought over a pair of
drinks Byrne didn't recognize.

"What are these?" Byrne asked.

"These are from the two young ladies at the end of
the bar."

Byrne and Walt Brigham looked over. Two female patrol officers—fit and pretty and still in uniform, somewhere in their mid-twenties—stood at the end of the bar.
They each raised a glass.

Byrne looked back at Margaret. "You sure they
meant us?"

"Positive."

Both men looked at the concoction in front of them.
"I give up," Brigham said. "What are they?"

"Jager Bombs," Margaret said with a smile, the one

that always signaled a challenge in an Irish pub. "Part Red Bull, part Jägermeister."

"Who the hell drinks this?"

"All the kids," Margaret said. "Gives them a boost so they can keep partying."

Byrne and Brigham looked at each other, mugged. They were Philly detectives, which meant they were nothing if not game. The two men raised their glasses in thanks. They both downed a few inches of the drink.

"Holy *shit*," Byrne said.

"*Slainte,*" Margaret said. She laughed as she made her way back to the taps.

Byrne glanced at Walt Brigham. He was handling the strange potion with a little more ease. Of course, he was knee-shot drunk already. Maybe the Jager Bomb would help.

"Can't believe you're putting in your papers," Byrne said.

"It's time," Brigham said. "The street is no place for an old man."

"Old man? What are you talking about? Two twenty-somethings just bought you a drink. *Pretty* twenty-somethings, at that. Girls with guns."

Brigham smiled, but it sank fast. He got that remote look all retiring cops get. The look that all but shouted *I'm never going to saddle up again.* He spun his drink a few times. He started to say something, checked himself. Finally he said, "You never get them all, you know?"

Byrne knew exactly what he meant.

"There's always that one case," Brigham continued. "The one that won't let you be." He nodded across the room. At Richie DiCillo.

"You're talking about Richie's daughter?" Byrne asked.

"Yeah," Brigham said. "I was the primary. Worked that case for two straight years."

"Oh, man," Byrne said. "I didn't know that."

Richie DiCillo's nine-year-old daughter Annemarie had been found murdered in Fairmount Park in 1995. She had been attending a birthday party with a friend, who was also killed. The brutal case had made headlines in the city for weeks. The file was never closed.

"Hard to believe all these years have passed," Brigham said. "I'll never forget that day."

Byrne glanced over at Richie DiCillo. He was telling another of his stories. When Byrne had met Richie, back in the Stone Age, Richie was a monster, a street legend, a drug cop to be feared. You said the name DiCillo on the streets of North Philadelphia with a hushed reverence. After his daughter was killed he got smaller somehow, an abridged version of his former self. These days, he was just going through the motions.

"Ever catch a lead?" Byrne asked.

Brigham shook his head. "Got close a few times. I think we interviewed everyone in the park that day. Must have got a hundred statements. No one ever came forward."

"What happened to the other girl's family?"

Brigham shrugged. "Moved away. Tried to track them down a few times. No luck."

"What about the forensics?"

"Nothing. But that was back in the day. Plus there was that storm. It rained like crazy. Whatever might have been there was washed away."

Byrne saw the deep pain and regret in Walt Brigham's eyes. He understood, having a folder of the bad ones tucked away on the blind side of his heart himself. He waited a minute or so, tried to change the subject. "So, what's in the fire for you, Walt?"

Brigham looked up, fixed Byrne with a stare he found a little unsettling. "I'm gonna get my license, Kevin."

"Your license?" Byrne asked. "Your private investigator license?"

Brigham nodded. "I'm gonna start working the case on my own," he said. He lowered his voice. "In fact, between you, me, and the barmaid, I've been working it off the books for a while now."

"Annemarie's case?" Byrne had not expected this. He'd thought he was going to hear about some fishing boat, some RV plans, or maybe that standard setup that all cops have about one day buying a bar somewhere tropical—somewhere bikini-clad nineteen-year-old girls went to party on spring break—the plan on which no one ever seemed to pull the pin.

"Yeah," Brigham said. "I owe Richie. Hell, the city owes him. Think about it. His little girl is murdered on our beat and we don't close it?" He slammed his glass on the bar, raised an accusatory finger to the world, to himself. "I mean, every year we pull the file, make a few notes, put it back. It ain't fair, man. It ain't fucking *fair*. She was just a kid."

"Does Richie know your plans?" Byrne asked.

"No. I'll tell him when the time is right."

For a minute or so they fell silent, listening to the chatter, the music. When Byrne looked back at Brigham, he saw that far-off look again, the shine in his eyes.

"Ah, Christ," Brigham said. "They were the prettiest little girls you've ever seen."

All Kevin Byrne could do was put a hand on the man's shoulder.

They stood that way for a long time.

BYRNE LEFT THE bar, turned onto Third Street. He thought about Richie DiCillo. He wondered how many times Richie had held his service weapon in his hand, consumed by anger and rage and grief. Byrne wondered how close the man had come, knowing that if someone took his own daughter away, he would have to search far and wide for a reason to go on.

As he reached his car he asked himself how long he was going to pretend it hadn't happened. He had been lying to himself about it a lot lately. This night, the feelings had been strong.

He had felt something when Walt Brigham hugged him. He saw dark things, had even smelled something. He would never admit any of this to anyone, not even to Jessica, with whom he had shared just about everything over the past few years. He had never smelled anything before, not as a component of his vague prescience.

When he'd hugged Walt Brigham he smelled pine needles. And smoke.

Byrne slipped behind the wheel, strapped in, put a Robert Johnson disk into the CD player, and drove into the night.

*Jesus,* he thought.

*Pine needles and smoke.*

# 20

Edgar Luna stumbled out of the Old House Tavern on Station Road, his gut full of Yuengling, his head full of bullshit. The same kind of refried bullshit his mother force-fed him the first eighteen years of his life: He was a loser. He'd never amount to anything. He was stupid. Just like his father.

Every time he got within one lager of the limit, it all came flooding back.

The wind pinwheeled up the nearly empty street, flapping his trousers, making his eyes water, giving him pause. He bunched his scarf around his face, and headed north into the gale.

Edgar Luna was a small balding man, acne-scarred, long since delivered unto every malady of middle age—colitis, eczema, fungal toenails, gingivitis. He had just turned fifty-five.

He was not drunk, but he was not all that far from it either. The new barmaid, Alyssa or Alicia or whatever the fuck her name was had shut him down for the tenth time. Who gave a shit? She was too old for him anyway. Edgar liked them younger. *Much* younger. Always had.

The youngest—and the best—had been his niece Dina. Hell, she had to be, what, twenty-*four* now? Too old. By plenty.

Edgar rounded the corner, onto Sycamore Street. His shabby bungalow greeted him. Before he could get his keys out of his pocket he heard a noise. He spun around a little unsteadily, rocking a bit on his heels. Behind him two figures stood silhouetted against the glow of the Christmas lights across the street. A tall man and a short man, both dressed in black. The tall one looked like a freak—close-cropped blond hair, clean-shaven, a little sissy looking if you asked Edgar Luna. The short one was built like a tank. One thing Edgar was sure of, they weren't from Winterton. He'd never seen them before.

"Who the fuck are *you*?" Edgar asked.

"I am Malachi," the tall man said.

THEY HAD MADE the fifty-mile ride in less than one hour. They were now in the basement of an empty row house in North Philadelphia, in the center of a block of derelict row houses. There wasn't a light for nearly a hundred feet in any direction. They had parked the van in an alley-way behind the block of houses.

Roland had carefully selected the site. These struc-tures were set for rehabilitation soon, and he knew that as soon as the weather allowed they would be pouring concrete in these basements. One of his flock worked for the construction company that was in charge of the con-crete work.

In the middle of the frigid basement room, Edgar Luna was naked, his clothes already burned, bound to an old wooden chair with duct tape. The floor was packed dirt, cold, but unfrozen. In the corner of the room, a pair of long handled shovels waited. Three kerosene lanterns lit the space.

"Tell me about Fairmount Park," Roland said.

Luna glared at him.

"Tell me about Fairmount Park," Roland repeated. "April 1995."

It looked as though Edgar Luna was trying frantically to poke around his memory. There was no doubt that he had done many bad things in his life—reprehensible things for which he had known there might one day be a dark reckoning. That time had come.

"Whatever the fuck you're talking about, what . . . whatever this is about, you got the wrong man. I'm in-nocent."

"You are many things, Mr. Luna," Roland said. "Inno-cent is not one of them. Confess your sins and the Lord will show you mercy."

"I swear I don't know—"

"I, however, cannot."

"You're *crazy*."

"Admit what you did to those girls in Fairmount Park in April 1995. The day it rained."

*"Girls?"* Edgar Luna asked. *"1995? Rain?"*

"Surely you remember Dina Reyes."

The name shook him. He remembered. "What did she tell you?"

Roland produced Dina's letter. The sight of it made Edgar shrink.

"She liked pink, Mr. Luna. But I expect you knew that."

"It was her mother, wasn't it? That fucking *bitch*. What did she say?"

"Dina Reyes ate a handful of pills and ended her sad and sorrowful existence, an existence you destroyed."

Edgar Luna suddenly seemed to realize that he would never leave this room. He struggled mightily against his bindings. The chair rocked, creaked, then fell over, crashing into a lamp. The lamp tipped and splashed kerosene onto Luna's head, which suddenly caught fire. Flames slapped and licked up the right side of the man's face. Luna screamed and slammed his head against the cold, packed dirt. Charles calmly walked over, struck out the fire. The acrid smell of kerosene and burned flesh and melted hair filled the confined space.

Braving the stench, Roland got close to Edgar Luna's ear.

"How does it feel to be a captive, Mr. Luna?" he whispered. "To be at the mercy of someone? Isn't this what you did to Dina Reyes? Brought her to the basement? Just like this?"

It was important to Roland that these men understood exactly what they'd done, experienced the moment the way their victims had. Roland went to considerable lengths to re-create the fear.

Charles righted the chair. Edgar Luna's forehead, along with the right side of his scalp, was blistered and bubbled. A wide swath of hair was gone, replaced by a blackened, open sore.

"He shall wash his feet in the blood of the wicked," Roland began.

"You can't fucking *do* this, man," Edgar hysterically screamed.

Roland did not hear the words of anyone mortal. "He shall triumph over them. They shall be so utterly vanquished that their overthrow shall be final and fatal, and his deliverance complete and crowning."

"Wait!" Luna struggled against the tape. Charles took out the lavender handkerchief, and tied it around the man's neck. He held him from behind.

Roland Hannah set upon the man. Screams rose high into the night.

Philadelphia slept.

# 21

Jessica lay in bed, her eyes wide open. Vincent was enjoying the sleep of the dead, as usual. She'd never known anybody who slept more deeply than her husband. For someone who saw just about every depravity a city had to offer, every night around midnight, he reconciled himself with the world, and drifted right off to sleep.

Jessica had never been able to do that.

She couldn't sleep, and knew why. Actually, there were two reasons. One, the image in the story Father Greg had told her kept galloping around her mind: a man being torn in half by the Sun Maiden and the sorceress. *Thanks for that one, Father Greg.*

The competing image was of Kristina Jakos, sitting on the riverbank like a battered doll on a little girl's shelf.

Twenty minutes later Jessica was at the dining room table, a mug of cocoa in front of her. She knew that chocolate contained caffeine, and that it would probably keep her up a few more hours. She also knew that chocolate contained chocolate.

She spread the Kristina Jakos crime-scene photographs on the table, put them in order, top to bottom: photographs of the road, the driveway, the front of the building, the abandoned cars, the back of the building, the slope to the riverbank, then poor Kristina herself. Looking at them top to bottom Jessica approximated the view of the scene as seen by the killer. She retraced his steps.

Had it been dark when he posed the body? It must have been. Seeing as the man who had taken Kristina's life did not commit suicide at the crime scene, or turn himself in, he had wanted to get away with his twisted crime.

SUV? Truck? Van? A van would certainly make things easier for him.

But why Kristina? Why the odd clothing and mutilation? Why the "moon" on her stomach?

Jessica looked out the window at the ink-black night.

What kind of life is this? she wondered. She sat not fifteen feet from where her sweet little girl was sleeping, from where her beloved husband was sleeping, and she was looking at pictures of a dead woman in the middle of the night.

Still, for all the danger and ugliness Jessica encountered, she couldn't imagine doing anything else. From the moment she'd entered the academy, all she had ever wanted to do was work homicides. And now she was. But the job began to eat you alive the moment you stepped onto the first floor of the Roundhouse.

In Philadelphia, you got a job on Monday. You

worked it, chasing down witnesses, interviewing suspects, compiling forensics. Just when you started to make progress, it was Thursday and you were up on the wheel again and another body fell. You had to move on it, because if you didn't make an arrest within forty-eight hours, there was a good chance you might never make an arrest. Or so the theory went. So you dropped what you were doing—while still keeping an ear to all the calls you had out—and worked the new case. The next thing you knew it was next Tuesday, and another bloody corpse landed at your feet.

If you made your living as an investigator—any kind of investigator—you lived for the *gotcha*. For Jessica, as well as every detective she knew, the sun rose and set on *gotcha*. At times, *gotcha* was your hot meal, your good night's sleep, your long passionate kiss. No one understood the need but a fellow investigator. If junkies could be detectives for one second, they would toss away that needle forever. There was no high like *gotcha*.

Jessica wrapped her hand around her cup. The cocoa was cold. She looked back at the photographs.

*Was the* gotcha *in one of these pictures?*

# 22

Walt Brigham pulled onto the shoulder on Lincoln Drive, cut the engine, the headlights, still reeling from his farewell party at Finnigan's Wake, still a bit overwhelmed at the big turnout.

This section of Fairmount Park was dark at this hour. Traffic was sparse. He rolled down his window, the frigid air somewhat reviving him. He could hear the water of the Wissahickon Creek flowing nearby.

Brigham had mailed the envelope before he had gotten on the road. He felt underhanded, almost criminal, sending it anonymously. He'd had no choice. It had taken him weeks to make the decision, and now he had. All of it—thirty-eight years as a cop—was behind him now. He was someone else.

He thought about the Annemarie DiCillo case. It seemed like only yesterday when he had gotten the call. He remembered pulling up to the stormy scene—right at this spot—getting out his umbrella, walking into the forest . . .

Within hours they had rounded up the usual suspects, the peepers, the pedophiles, the men who had recently been released from prison after having served time for violence against children, especially against young girls. No one stood out from the crowd. No one cracked, or rolled over on another suspect. Given their nature, their heightened fear of prison life, pedophiles were notoriously easy to turn. No one did.

A particularly vile miscreant named Joseph Barber had looked good for a while, but he had an alibi—albeit a *shaky* alibi—for the day of the murders in Fairmount Park. When Barber himself was murdered—stabbed to death with thirteen steak knives—Brigham had figured it was the story of a man being visited by his sins.

But something nagged Walt Brigham about the circumstances of Barber's demise. Over the next five years, Brigham had tracked a number of suspected pedophiles, both in Pennsylvania and New Jersey. Six of those men had been murdered, all with extreme prejudice, none of their cases solved. Granted, no one in any homicide unit anywhere really busted his hump trying to close a murder case when the victim was a scumbag who hurt children, but still the forensic data was collected and analyzed, the witness statements taken, the fingerprints run, the reports filed. Not a single suspect materialized.

*Lavender,* he thought. *What was it about lavender?*

In all, Walt Brigham found sixteen men murdered, all of them molesters, all of them questioned and released—or at least suspected—in a case involving a young girl.

It was crazy, but possible.

*Someone was killing the suspects.*

His theory never really gained any traction in the unit, so Walt Brigham had dropped it. Officially speaking. He had made highly detailed notes about it anyway. As little as he might have cared about these men, there was something about the job, the nature of being a homicide detective that compelled him to do so. Murder was murder. It was up to God to judge the victims, not Walter J. Brigham.

He turned his thoughts to Annemarie and Charlotte. They had stopped running through his dreams just a short time ago, but that didn't mean the images didn't haunt him. These days, when the calendar flipped from March to April, when he saw young girls in their springtime dresses, it all came back to him in a brutish, sensory overload—the smell of the woods, the sound of the rain, the way it looked like those two little girls were sleeping. Eyes closed, heads bowed. And then the nest.

The sick son of a bitch who did it had built a *nest* around them.

Walt Brigham felt the anger wrench inside him, a barbwire fist in his chest. He was getting close. He could feel it. Off the record, he had already been to Odense, a small town in Berks County. He'd gone several times. He had made inquiries, taken pictures, spoken to people. The trail to Annemarie and Charlotte's killer led to Odense, Pennsylvania. Brigham had tasted the evil the moment he crossed into the village, like a bitter potion on his tongue.

Brigham got out of the car, walked across Lincoln Drive, continued through the barren trees until he reached the Wissahickon. The cold wind howled. He flipped up his collar, bunched his wool scarf.

This was where they had been found.

"I'm back, girls," he said.

Brigham glanced up at the sky, at the raw gray moon in the blackness. He felt the undressed emotion of that night so long ago. He saw their white dresses in the police lights. He saw the sad, empty expressions on their faces.

"I just wanted you to know, you have me now," he said. "Full time. Twenty-four seven. We're gonna get him."

He watched the water flow for a while, then walked back to the car, a sudden spring in his step, as if a great weight had been lifted from his shoulders, as if the rest of his life had been suddenly mapped. He slipped inside, started the engine, cranked up the heater. He was just about to angle onto Lincoln Drive when he heard . . . *singing?*

No.

It wasn't singing. It was more like a nursery rhyme. A nursery rhyme he knew very well. His blood froze in his veins.

*"Here are maidens, young and fair,*
*Dancing in the summer air . . ."*

Brigham looked into the rearview mirror. When he saw the eyes of the man in the backseat, he knew. This was the man for whom he had been searching a very long time.

*"Like two spinning wheels at play . . ."*

Fear lurched up Brigham's spine. His weapon was under the seat. He'd had too much to drink. He'd never make it.

*"Pretty maidens dance away."*

In those last moments many things became apparent to Detective Walter James Brigham. They settled upon him with a heightened clarity, like in those seconds before an electrical storm. He knew that Marjorie Morrison was indeed the love of his life. He knew that his father had been a good man, and that he had raised decent kids. He knew that Annemarie DiCillo and Charlotte Waite had been visited by true evil, that they had been followed into the forest and delivered unto the devil.

And Walt Brigham also knew that he had been right all along.

It had always been about the water.

# 23

The Health Harbor was a small gym and workout spa in Northern Liberties. Run by a former police sergeant out of the Twenty-fourth District, it had a limited membership, mostly cops, which meant you generally didn't have to put up with the usual gym games. Plus, it had a boxing ring.

Jessica got there about 6 AM, did her stretches, ran five miles on the treadmill while listening to Christmas music on her iPod.

At 7 AM, her great uncle Vittorio arrived. Vittorio Giovanni was eighty-one, but still had the clear brown eyes Jessica remembered from her youth, the kind and knowing eyes that had swept Vittorio's late wife Carmella off her feet one hot August night at the Feast of the Assumption festival. Even today those sparkling eyes said there was a much younger man still inside. Vittorio had once been a professional prizefighter. To this day he could not watch a televised boxing match sitting down.

For the past few years Vittorio had been Jessica's manager and trainer. As a professional, Jessica had a record of 5-0, with four knockouts, her last bout televised on ESPN2. Vittorio had always said that whenever Jessica was ready to quit, he would support the decision and they would both walk away. Jessica wasn't sure yet. What got her into the sport to begin with—the desire to lose weight after Sophie was born, along with the desire to be able to hold her own with the occasional violent suspect when necessary—had grown into something else: the need to fight the aging process with what was, hands down, the most brutal discipline there was.

Vittorio grabbed the pads, slowly slipped between the ropes. "You do your roadwork?" he asked. He refused to call it "cardio."

"Yeah," Jessica said. She was supposed to do six miles, but her over-thirty muscles were tired. Uncle Vittorio saw right through her.

"Tomorrow you do seven," he said.

Jessica didn't bother to deny it or to argue.

"Ready?" Vittorio slapped the pads together, held them up.

Jessica started slowly, jabbing at the pads, crossing with her right. As always, she fell into a rhythm, finding the zone. Her mind traveled from the sweaty confines of the gym, across town to the bank of the Schuylkill River, to the image of a dead young woman ceremoniously placed on the river's edge.

As she picked up the pace, her anger built. She thought of the smiling Kristina Jakos, the trust the young woman might have had in her killer, the faith that she would not be harmed in any way, that the next morning would dawn and she would be that much closer to her dreams. Jessica's anger ignited and blossomed as she thought of the arrogance and brutality of the person they sought, the act of strangling a young woman and mutilating her body—

"Jess!"

Her uncle was shouting. Jessica stopped, the sweat pouring off her. She pawed it out of her eyes with the back of her glove, took a few steps back. The handful of other people in the gym stared at them.

*"Time,"* her uncle said softly. He'd been here with her before.

*How long had she been gone?*

"Sorry," Jessica said. She walked over to one corner, then another, then another, circling the ring, catching her breath. When she stopped, Vittorio made his way over to her. He dropped the pads, helped Jessica wiggle out of her gloves.

"Tough case?" he asked.

Her family knew her well. "Yeah," she said. "Tough case."

JESSICA SPENT THE morning working the computers. She put a number of search strings into the various search engines. The results regarding amputation were meager, if incredibly gruesome. In medieval times it was not uncommon for a thief to lose a hand, or a Peeping Tom to lose an eye. Some religious sects still engaged in the practice. The Italian mob had been cutting up people for years, but they generally didn't leave the bodies in public and in broad daylight. They usually hacked folks up in order to fit them into a bag or a box or a suitcase so they could dump them in a landfill. Usually in Jersey.

She ran across nothing like what was done to Kristina Jakos on that riverbank.

The swim-lane rope was available from a number of online merchants. From what she could determine, it was similar to standard polypropylene stranded rope, but treated to resist chemicals such as chlorine. It was used primarily to hold together a line of floats. The lab had not detected any trace of chlorine.

Locally, between marine-supply and pool-supply retailers in Philadelphia, New Jersey, and Delaware, there were dozens of dealers who carried this type of rope. The minute Jessica had the final report from the lab, detailing a type and model, she would get on the phone.

At just after eleven, Byrne came into the duty room. He had the 911 tape of the call-in of Kristina's body.

THE AUDIO VISUAL Unit of the PPD was located in the basement of the Roundhouse. Its main purview was to supply AV equipment to the department as needed—cameras, video equipment, recording and surveillance devices—as well as monitor the local television and radio channels for important information the department could use.

The unit also aided in investigating surveillance tapes and audiovisual evidence.

Officer Mateo Fuentes was a veteran of the unit. He had been instrumental in cracking a recent case where a psychopath with a movie fetish had been terrorizing the city. In his thirties, precise and meticulous in his work, strangely scrupulous with his grammar, nobody in the AV Unit was better at finding the hidden truth in an electronic recording.

Jessica and Byrne entered the control room.

"What do we have, Detectives?" Mateo asked.

"Anonymous 911 call," Byrne said. He handed Mateo the audiocassette.

"No such thing," Mateo replied. He slipped the cassette into a machine. "I take it there was no caller ID?"

"No," Byrne said. "It looks like it was a terminated cell."

In most states, whenever a citizen calls 911 they give up their proprietary right to privacy. Even if you have a block on your phone—which prevents most people who receive your calls from seeing your number on their caller ID—the police department radio unit and dispatchers can still see your number. With a few exceptions. One of them is a 911 call from a terminated cell. When cell phones are turned off—for nonpayment, or perhaps because the subscriber has moved to a new number—the 911 capabilities remain. Unfortunately for investigators, the ability to trace the number does not.

Mateo hit PLAY on the tape machine.

*"Philadelphia Police, Operator 204, how can I help you?"* answered the operator.

*"There's . . . there's a dead body. It's behind the old auto parts warehouse on Flat Rock Road."*

Click. That was the extent of the recording.

"Hmmm," Mateo said. "Not exactly long-winded." He hit STOP. Then REWIND. He played it again. When it was finished, he rewound the tape and played it a third time, cocking his head to the speakers. He hit STOP.

"Man or woman?" Byrne asked.

"Man," Mateo replied.

"Are you sure?"

Mateo turned, glared.

"Okay," Byrne said.

"He's in a car or a small space. No echo, good acoustics, no background hiss."

Mateo played the tape again. He adjusted a few dials. "Hear that?"

There was music in the background. Very faint, but there. "I hear something," Byrne said.

Rewind. A few more adjustments. Less hiss. A melody emerged.

"Radio?" Jessica asked.

"Maybe," Mateo said. "Or a CD."

"Play it again," Byrne said.

Mateo rewound the tape, fed it into another deck. "Let me digitize it."

The AV Unit had an ever-expanding arsenal of audio forensic software with which they could not only clean up the sound of an existing audio file, but also separate the tracks of a recording, thereby isolating them for closer scrutiny.

A few minutes later Mateo was on a laptop. The 911 audio files were now a series of green and black spikes on the screen. Mateo clicked PLAY, adjusted the volume. This time the melody in the background was clearer, more distinct.

"I know this song," Mateo said. He played it again, adjusting slide controls, bringing the voice down to a barely audible level. Mateo then plugged in a pair of headphones, slipped them on. He closed his eyes, listened. He played the file again. "Got it." He opened his eyes, pulled off the headphones. "The name of the song is 'I Want You.' By Savage Garden."

Jessica and Byrne exchanged a glance. "Who?" Byrne asked.

"Savage Garden. Australian pop duo. They were big

in the late nineties. Well, medium-big. That song is from 1997 or 1998. Fair-sized hit then."

"How do you know all this?" Byrne asked.

Mateo glared again. "My life is not all Channel 6 Action News and McGruff videos, Detective. I happen to be a very social individual."

"What's your take on the caller?" Jessica asked.

"I'll need to run it some more, but I can tell you that this Savage Garden song doesn't get much airplay anymore, so it probably wasn't the radio," Mateo said. "Unless it was an oldies station."

"Ninety-seven is oldies?" Byrne asked.

"Deal with it, pops."

"Man."

"If the person who made the call has the CD, and is still playing it, they are probably under forty," Mateo said. "I'd guess thirty, maybe even twenty-five, give or take."

"Anything else?"

"Well, you can tell by the way he says the word 'there's' twice that he was nervous about calling. He probably rehearsed it a bunch of times."

"You're a genius, Mateo," Jessica said. "We owe you."

"And here it is, almost Christmas, with only a day or so left to shop for me."

JESSICA, BYRNE, AND Josh Bontrager stood outside the control room.

"Whoever called knows it was once an auto parts warehouse," Jessica said.

"Which means he is probably from the area," Bontrager said.

"Which narrows it down to about thirty thousand people."

"Yeah, but how many of them listen to Savage Garbage?" Byrne asked.

"Garden," Bontrager said.

"Whatever."

"Why don't I hit some of the bigger stores—Best Buy, Borders?" Bontrager asked. "Maybe this guy asked for the CD recently. Maybe someone will remember."

"Good idea," Byrne said.

Bontrager beamed. He grabbed his coat. "I'm working with Detectives Shepherd and Palladino today. If something breaks, I'll call you later."

A minute after Bontrager left, an officer poked his head into the room. "Detective Byrne?"

"Yeah."

"There's someone upstairs to see you."

WHEN JESSICA AND Byrne walked into the lobby of the Roundhouse they saw a diminutive Asian woman, clearly out of her element. She wore a visitor's ID badge. As they got closer Jessica recognized the woman as Mrs. Tran, the woman from the All-City Launderette.

"Mrs. Tran," Byrne said. "What can we do for you?"

"My father found this," she said.

She reached into her tote bag, held up a magazine. It was last month's issue of *Dance Magazine*. "He says she left it. She was reading it that night."

"By 'she' you mean Kristina Jakos? The woman we asked you about?"

"Yes," she said. "That blond lady. Maybe this will help you."

Jessica gripped the magazine by its edges. They'd brush it for prints. "Where did he find this?" Jessica asked.

"It was on top of dryers."

Jessica carefully flipped through the pages, making her way to the back of the magazine. On one of the pages—a full-page ad for Volkswagen, an ad made up of mostly white space—there was an elaborate web of doodles: phrases, words, drawings, names, symbols. It appeared that Kristina, or whoever had done the drawings, had doodled for hours.

"Your father is sure that Kristina Jakos was reading this magazine?" Jessica asked.

"Yes," Mrs. Tran said. "You want me to get him? He's in the car. You could ask again."

"No," Jessica said. "That's okay."

UPSTAIRS, IN THE duty room of the Homicide Unit, Byrne pored over the magazine page with the drawings. Many of the words were written in the Cyrillic alphabet, in what he figured was Ukrainian. He already had a call in to a detective he knew from Northeast, a young guy named Nathan Bykovsky whose parents came from Russia. In addition to the words and phrases, there were drawings of small houses, three-dimensional hearts, pyramids. There were also a few sketches of dresses, although nothing resembling the vintage-style dress Kristina Jakos wore in death.

Byrne got the call from Nate Bykovsky, then faxed the page. Nate called him back immediately.

"What is this about?" Nate asked.

Detectives never had a problem with another cop reaching out. Still, by nature, they liked to know the play. Byrne told him.

"I believe this is Ukrainian," Nate said.

"Can you read it?"

"Mostly. My family is from Belarus. The Cyrillic alphabet is shared by many languages—Russian, Ukrainian, Bulgarian. They are similar, but some symbols are not used by the others."

"Any idea what this says?"

"Well, two of the words—the two written above the hood of the car in the photograph—are illegible," Nate said. "Below them she has written the word 'love' twice.

At the bottom, the most legible words on the page, she has written a phrase."

"What's that?"

" 'I am sorry.' "

"I am sorry?"

"Yes."

*Sorry,* Byrne wondered. *Sorry for what?*

"The rest are individual letters."

"They don't spell anything out?" Byrne asked.

"Not that I can see," Nate said. "I will write them out in order, top to bottom, and fax them back to you. Maybe they add up to something."

"Thanks, Nate."

"Any time."

Byrne scanned the page again.

*Love.*

*I'm sorry.*

In addition to the words and letters and drawings there was one recurring image, a succession of numbers that were drawn in an ever-decreasing spiral. It looked to be a series of ten numbers. The drawing was on the page three times. Byrne took the page over to the copy machine. He positioned it on the glass, adjusted the settings to increase the size to three times that of the original. When the page emerged he saw that he had been right. The first three numbers were 215. It was a local phone number. He picked up a phone, dialed the number. When someone answered, Byrne apologized for dialing wrong. He hung up, his pulse quickening. They had a direction.

"Jess," he said. He grabbed his coat.

"What's up?"

"Let's take a ride."

"Where to?"

Byrne was nearly out the door. "A club called Stiletto."

"Want me to get an address?" Jessica asked, grabbing a two-way radio, hurrying to keep up.

"No. I know where it is."

"*Okay.* Why are we going there?"

They reached the elevators. Byrne punched the button, paced. "It's owned by a guy named Callum Blackburn."

"Never heard of him."

"Kristina Jakos doodled his phone number in that magazine three times."

"And you know this guy?"

"Yeah."

"How so?" Jessica asked.

Byrne stepped into the elevator car, held the door. "I helped put him in prison nearly twenty years ago."

# 24

There was an emperor of China and he lived in the most magnificent palace in the world. A nightingale lived nearby, in the great forest that ran to the sea, and people came from all over the world to hear it sing. Everyone marveled at the bird's beautiful song. The bird became so famous that when people met each other on the street one would say "nightin" and the other would say "gale."

Moon has heard the nightingale's song. He has watched her for many days. Not long ago he sat in the dark, surrounded by others, lost in the wonder of the *music. Her voice had been pure and magical and lilting, the sound of tiny glass bells.*

*Now the nightingale is silent.*

*Today Moon waits for her underground, the sweet fragrance of the emperor's garden dizzying his head. He feels like a nervous suitor. His palms sweat, his heart beats. He has never felt quite like this before.*

*If she had not been his nightingale, she might have become his princess.*

*Today it is time for her to sing again.*

# 25

Stiletto was an upscale—upscale for a Philly strip joint—"gentlemen's club" on Thirteenth Street. Two levels of jiggling flesh, short skirts, and glossy lipstick catering to the horny businessman. One floor was a live strip club, one level was a noisy bar and restaurant with scantily clad barmaids and waitresses. Stiletto had a liquor license, so the dancing wasn't full nude, but it was everything but.

On the way to the club, Byrne filled Jessica in. On paper, Stiletto was owned by a well-known former nose tackle for the Philadelphia Eagles, a high-profile, personable sports star who had made the Pro Bowl three times. The truth was there were four partners in all, including Callum Blackburn. The hidden partners were most likely the mob.

Mob. Dead girl. Mutilation.

*I am sorry,* Kristina wrote.

Jessica thought: *Promising.*

JESSICA AND BYRNE walked into the bar.

"I've got to hit the bathroom," Byrne said. "You going to be okay?"

Jessica stared at him for a moment, unblinking. She was a veteran police officer, a professional boxer, and she was armed. Still, it was kind of sweet. "I'll be fine."

Byrne went to the men's room. Jessica took the last stool at the bar, the one next to the pass-through, the one in front of the lemon wedges, pimiento olives, and maraschino cherries. The room was decorated like a Moroccan brothel, all gold paint, red flocking, and velvet furniture with pinwheel cushions.

The place did a brisk business. Not surprising. The club was located close to the convention center. The sound system blared George Thorogood's "Bad to the Bone."

The stool next to her was empty, but the one beyond that was occupied. Jessica glanced over. The guy sitting there was right out of strip-club-creep central casting— fortyish, shiny flowered shirt, tight navy blue double-knit slacks, scuffed loafers, gold-plated ID bracelets on both wrists. His two front teeth overlapped, giving him a sort of clueless, chipmunk look. He smoked Salem Light 100s with the filters busted off. He was staring at her.

Jessica met his gaze, held it.

"Something I can do for you?" she asked.

"I'm the assistant bar manager here." He slithered onto the stool next to her. He smelled like Old Spice stick deodorant and pork rinds. "Well, I will be in three months."

"Congratulations."

"You look familiar," he said.

"Do I?"

"Have we met before?"

"I don't think so."

"I'm sure we have."

"Well, it's certainly possible," Jessica said. "I'm just not remembering it."

"No?"

He said this like it was hard to believe. "No," she said. "But you know what? I'm okay with that."

Thick as a batter-dipped brick, he pressed on. "Have you ever danced? I mean, you know, professionally."

*Here we go,* Jessica thought. "Oh, sure."

The guy snapped his fingers. "I *knew* it," he said. "I never forget a beautiful face. Or a great body. Where did you dance?"

"Well, I was with the Bolshoi for a couple of years. But the commute was killing me."

The guy cocked his head at a ten-degree angle, thinking—or whatever he did as a substitute for thinking—that the Bolshoi might have been a strip club in Newark. "I'm not familiar with that place."

"I'm stunned."

"Was that full nude?"

"No. They make you dress like a swan."

"Wow," he said. "Sounds hot."

"Oh, it is."

"What's your name?"

"Isadora."

"I'm Chester. My friends call me Chet."

"Well, Chester, it was great chatting with you."

"You leaving?" He made a slight move toward her. Spidery. Like maybe he was thinking about keeping her on the stool.

"Yeah, unfortunately. Duty calls." She slipped her badge onto the bar. Chet's face went drab. It was like showing a cross to a vampire. He backed off.

Byrne returned from the men's room, locked stares with Chet.

"Hey, how ya doin'?" Chet asked.

"Never better," Byrne said. To Jessica: "Ready?"

"Let's do it."

"See you around," Chet said to her. Cool now, for some reason.

"I'll count the minutes."

ON THE SECOND floor the two detectives, led by a pair of massive bodyguards, traversed a maze of hallways, the journey ending at a reinforced steel door, above which, encased in thick security plastic, was a CCTV camera. A pair of electronic locks graced the wall next to the hardware-free door. Thug One spoke into a handheld radio. A moment later the door inched open. Thug Two pulled it wide. Byrne and Jessica entered.

The large room was sparsely lighted with indirect spots, deep-orange sconces, pin-light cans recessed into the ceiling. An authentic-looking Tiffany lamp graced the colossal oak desk, behind which sat a man who, based on Byrne's description, could only have been Callum Blackburn.

The man's face lit up when he saw Byrne. "I don't be-*lieve* it," he said. He arose, put both hands in front of him, handcuff-style. Byrne laughed. The men hugged, clapped each other on the back. Callum took a half step backward, did a second inventory of Byrne, hands on his hips. "You look well."

"You too."

"I cannae complain," he said. "I was sorry to hear of your troubles." His accent was broad Scots, tempered by a number of years in eastern Pennsylvania.

"Thank you," Byrne said.

Callum Blackburn was a vigorous sixty. He had chiseled features, dark lively eyes, a pure silver goatee, salt-and-pepper hair swept back. He wore a well-tailored charcoal suit, white shirt, open collar, and a small hoop earring.

"This is my partner, Detective Balzano," Byrne said.

Callum straightened, turned fully toward Jessica, dipped his chin in greeting. Jessica had no idea what to do. Was she supposed to curtsy? She stuck her hand out. "Nice to meet you."

Callum took her hand, smiled. For a white-collar criminal, he *was* kind of charming. Byrne had filled her in on Callum Blackburn. His stretch had been for credit-card fraud.

"The pleasure is mine," Callum said. "If I knew that detectives were so beautiful these days, I would nae have given up my life of crime."

"Have you?" Byrne asked.

"I am just a humble businessman from Glasgow," he said with a glimmer of a smile. "Soon to be an auld father, at that."

One of the first lessons Jessica had learned on the street was that there was always subtext in conversations with criminals, an almost certain inversion of the truth. *I never met him* generally meant *We grew up together. I was never there* usually meant *It happened at my house. I am innocent* almost always meant *I did it.* When Jessica had first joined the force, she'd felt as if she needed a Criminal-to-English dictionary. Now, after nearly a decade, she could probably have taught Criminalese.

Byrne and Callum went way back, it seemed, which meant that the conversation would probably ring a little closer to the truth. Once someone puts you in handcuffs and watches you walk into a prison cell, it's harder to play tough guy.

Still, they were here to get information from Callum

Blackburn. For the time being, they had to play his game. Small talk before big talk.

"How is your bonny wife?" Callum asked.

"Still bonny," Byrne said, "but no longer my wife."

"This is such sad news," Callum said, looking genuinely surprised and disheartened. "What did you do?"

Byrne sat back, crossed his arms. Defensive. "What makes you think *I* screwed it up?"

Callum lifted one eyebrow.

"Okay," Byrne said. "You're right. It was the job."

Callum nodded, perhaps accepting that he himself—and those of his ilk and criminal persuasion—had been part of "the job," and therefore partly responsible. "We have a saying in Scotland. 'Clippet sheep will growe again.'"

Byrne looked at Jessica, back at Callum. Did the man just call him a sheep? "Truer words, eh?" Byrne said, hoping to move on.

Callum smiled, winked at Jessica, knitted his fingers. "So," he said. "To what do I owe this visit?"

"A woman named Kristina Jakos was found murdered yesterday," Byrne said. "Did you know her?"

Callum Blackburn's face was unreadable. "I'm sorry, what is her name again?"

"Kristina Jakos."

Byrne put the photograph of Kristina on the desk. Both detectives watched Callum as he glanced at it. He knew they were watching him, and he betrayed nothing.

"Do you recognize her?" Byrne asked.

"Aye."

"How so?" Byrne asked.

"She recently came into my employ," Callum said.

"You hired her?"

"My son Alex does all the hiring."

"She worked as a receptionist?" Jessica asked.

"I will let Alex explain." Callum stepped away, took

out a cell phone, made a call, clicked off. He turned back to the detectives. "He will be here shortly."

Jessica glanced around the office. It was well appointed, if not a little gaudy: faux-suede wallpaper, gold filigreed-framed oils of landscapes and hunting scenes, a fountain in the corner that looked like a trio of golden swans. Talk about your irony, she thought.

The wall to the left of Callum's desk was the most impressive. On it were ten flat-screen monitors hooked into closed-circuit cameras, showing various angles on the bars, the stages, the front door, the parking lot, the cash room. On six of the screens were dancing girls in varying stages of undress.

While they waited, Byrne stood in front of the display, transfixed. Jessica wondered if he was aware that his mouth hung open.

Jessica walked over to the monitors. Six sets of breasts jiggled, some more than others. Jessica counted them off. "Fake, fake, real, fake, real, fake."

Byrne was horrified. He looked like a five-year-old boy who had just learned the cold hard truth about the Easter Bunny. He pointed to the last monitor, one showing a dancer, an impossibly leggy brunette. "Those are fake?"

"Those are fake."

While Byrne gawked, Jessica perused the books on the shelves, mostly by Scottish writers—Robert Burns, Walter Scott, J. M. Barrie. She then noticed a single widescreen monitor on its own, built into the wall behind Callum's desk. It showed a screensaver of sorts, a small golden box that continually opened to reveal a rainbow.

"What's this?" Jessica asked Callum.

"That is a closed-circuit feed to an unusual club," Callum said. "It is on the third floor. It is called the Pandora Lounge."

"Unusual how?"

"Alex will explain."

"What goes on up there?" Byrne asked.

Callum smiled. "The Pandora Lounge is a special place for special girls."

# 26

For once Tara Lynn Greene had made it on time. She had risked a speeding ticket—one more and her license would definitely be suspended—and she had parked in the expensive lot down the street from the Walnut Street Theater. These were two things she couldn't afford.

On the other hand, this was a casting call for *Carousel* and Marc Balfour was directing. The coveted role was Julie Jordan. Shirley Jones had played the part in the 1956 film and she had parlayed the role into a lifelong career.

Tara had just come off a successful run of *Nine* at the Centre Theater in Norristown. A local reviewer had called her "fetching." For Tara, "fetching" was about as good as it was going to get. She caught her reflection in the front window of the theater lobby. At twenty-seven, she was no newcomer, and hardly the ingenue. *Okay, twenty-eight,* she thought. *But who's counting?*

She walked the two blocks back to the indoor parking lot. A freezing wind whistled down Walnut. Tara rounded the corner, looked at the sign on the small kiosk and calculated her parking fee. She owed sixteen dollars. *Sixteen frickin' dollars.* She had a single twenty in her wallet.

Ah, well. It looked like Ramen noodles again tonight. Tara took the steps down to the basement level, slipped into her car, waited until it warmed up. While she waited, she turned up the CD—Kay Starr singing *"C'est Magnifique."*

When the car was finally warm, she put it in reverse, backed up, her mind a clutter of hopes, opening-night jitters, stellar reviews, wild applause.

Then she felt the bump.

*Oh my God,* she thought. Had she run over something? She put the car in park, pulled the hand brake, and got out. She walked behind the vehicle, looked beneath. Nothing. She hadn't run over anything or anybody. Thank God.

Then Tara saw it: she had a flat. On top of everything else, she had a *flat.* And she had less than twenty minutes to get to her job. Like every other actress in Philly, probably the world, Tara waited tables.

She glanced around the parking level. No one. Thirty cars or so, a few vans. No people. *Shit.*

She tried to combat the anger, the tears. She didn't even know if there was a spare tire in the trunk. The car was a two-year-old compact and she hadn't ever had to change one of its tires before.

"Having a problem?"

Tara wheeled around, a little startled. A man was getting out of the white van a few spaces down from her car. He carried a bouquet of flowers.

"Hi," she said.

"Hi." He pointed at her tire. "Doesn't look too good."

"It's only flat on the bottom," she said. "Ha-ha."

"I'm really good at these things," he said. "I'd be happy to help."

She looked at her reflection in the car window. She was wearing her white wool coat. Her best. She could just imagine the grease on the front. And the dry-cleaning bill. More expense. Of course, she had long ago let her AAA dues lapse. She had never once used it when she was paying for it. And now, of course, she needed it.

"I couldn't ask you to do that," she said.

"It's no big deal," he said. "You're not exactly dressed for automotive repair."

Tara saw him sneak a covert glance at his watch. If she was going to snag him for the task, it had better be soon. "Sure it wouldn't be too much trouble?" she asked.

"No trouble at all." He held up the bouquet. "I have to deliver these by four o'clock, and then I'm done for the day. I have plenty of time."

She looked around the parking level. It was all but deserted. As much as she hated to play the helpless female—she knew how to change a tire, after all—she could use the help.

"You're going to have to let me pay you for this," she said.

He held up a hand. "I wouldn't hear of it. Besides, it's Christmas."

*Good thing, too,* she thought. After she'd paid for her parking she'd have a grand total of four dollars and seventeen cents. "This is very nice of you."

"Pop the trunk," he said. "I'll be done in a minute."

Tara reached in the window, flipped the trunk lever. She walked to the back of the car. The man grabbed the jack, pulled it out. He looked around for somewhere to put down the flowers. It was an enormous bouquet of gladiolas wrapped in bright white paper.

"Do you think you could you put these back in my van for me?" he asked. "My boss would *kill* me if I got them dirty."

"Sure," she said. She took the flowers from him, turned toward the van.

"—gale," he said.

She spun around. "I'm sorry?"

"You could just put them in the back."

"Oh," she said. "Okay."

Tara walked over to the van, thinking that it was things like this—little kindnesses from total strangers—that all but restored her faith in people. Philly could be a tough town, but sometimes you wouldn't know it. She opened the back door of the van. She expected to see boxes, paper, greenery, florist foam, ribbons, maybe a bunch of those little cards and envelopes. Instead she saw . . . nothing. The interior of the van was immaculate. Except for the exercise mat on the floor. And the coil of blue and white rope.

Before she could put the flowers down she sensed a presence. A close presence. *Too* close. She smelled cinnamon mouthwash; saw a shadow just inches away.

When Tara turned toward the shadow, the man swung the jack handle at the back of her neck. It connected with a dull thud. Her head rattled. Black circles ringed with a supernova of bright orange fire presented themselves behind her eyes. He brought the steel bar down again, not hard enough to knock her cold, just to stun her. Her legs gave way beneath her and Tara collapsed into strong arms.

The next thing she knew she was on her back, on the exercise mat. She was warm. It smelled like paint thinner. She heard the doors slam, heard the engine start.

When she opened her eyes again there was gray daylight coming through the windshield. They were in motion.

When she tried to sit up he reached over, a white cloth in his hand. He placed it over her face. The medicine smell was strong. Soon she drifted away on a beam of dazzling light. But right before the world went away, Tara Lynn Greene—the *fetching* Tara Lynn Greene— suddenly realized what the man had said back at the parking garage:

*You are my nightingale.*

# 27

Alasdair Blackburn was a taller version of his father, around thirty, broad-shouldered, athletic. He was dressed casually, wore his hair a little long. He spoke with a slight brogue. They met in Callum's office.

"I'm sorry to keep you waiting," he said. "I had an errand." He shook hands with Jessica and Byrne. "Please call me Alex."

Byrne explained why they were there. He showed the man Kristina's photograph. Alex confirmed that Kristina Jakos had worked at Stiletto.

"What is your position here?" Byrne asked.

"I'm the general manager," Alex said.

"And you do most of the hiring?"

"I do all of it—performers, waitstaff, kitchen staff, security, cleaning, parking attendants."

Jessica wondered whatever had possessed him to hire her friend Chet downstairs.

"How long was Kristina Jakos an employee here?" Byrne asked.

Alex thought for a moment. "Perhaps three weeks or so."

"In what capacity?"

Alex glanced at his father. Out of the corner of her eye, Jessica saw the slightest nod of Callum's head. Alex might do the hiring, but Callum pulled the strings.

"She was a performer," Alex said. For a moment his eyes shone. Jessica wondered if his relationship with Kristina Jakos had gone beyond the professional.

"A dancer?" Byrne asked.

"Yes and no."

Byrne stared at Alex for a moment, expecting clarification. None was offered. He pressed harder. "And what exactly would be the *no* part?"

Alex sat on the edge of his father's massive desk. "She was a dancer, but not like these other girls." He waved a dismissive hand at the monitors.

"What do you mean?"

"I'll show you," Alex said. "Let's go up to the third floor. To the Pandora Lounge."

"What's on the third floor?" Byrne asked. "Lap dancing?"

Alex smiled. "No," he said. "This is different."

"Different?"

"Aye," he said, crossing the room, opening the door for them. "The young ladies who work in the Pandora Lounge are performance artists."

THE PANDORA LOUNGE on the third floor of Stiletto was a series of eight rooms, divided by a long, dimly lit hallway. On the walls were crystal sconces, fleur-de-lis velveteen wallpaper. The carpeting was deep blue shag. A table and gold-veined mirror stood at the end. Each door had a tarnished brass number.

"This is a private floor," Alex said. "Private dancers. Very exclusive. It is dark now because it does not open until midnight."

"This is where Kristina Jakos worked?" Byrne asked.

"Yes."

"Her sister said she worked as a receptionist."

"Some young ladies are a bit reluctant to admit that they are exotic dancers," Alex said. "We put whatever they choose on the forms."

As they walked down the hall, Alex opened doors. Each room was dedicated to a different theme. One had an Old West motif, complete with sawdust on the hardwood floor and a brass spittoon. One was a replica of a 1950s diner. Yet another had a *Star Wars* theme. It was like walking into that old movie *Westworld,* Jessica thought, the one about the exotic resort in which Yul Brynner played the robot gunslinger who went haywire. A closer look, in brighter light, would have revealed that these rooms were a bit shabby, and that the illusion of the various historical settings was just that, an illusion.

Each room had a single comfortable chair and a slightly elevated stage. There were no windows. The ceilings held an elaborate network of track lighting.

"So, men pay a premium price to get a private performance in these rooms?" Byrne asked.

"Sometimes women, but not often," Alex replied.

"Can I ask how much?"

"It varies from girl to girl," he said. "But the average is about two hundred dollars. Plus tips."

"For how long?"

Alex smiled, perhaps anticipating the next question. "Forty-five minutes."

"And dancing is all that goes on in these rooms?"

"Aye, Detective. This is not a bordello."

"Kristina Jakos never worked the stages downstairs?" Byrne asked.

"No," Alex said. "She worked up here exclusively. She had just begun a few weeks ago, but she was very good, very popular."

To Jessica, it was becoming clear how Kristina intended

to pay her half of the rent on that pricey town home on North Lawrence.

"How are the girls selected?" Byrne asked.

Alex walked down the hallway. At the end was a table bearing a crystal vase full of fresh gladiolas. Alex reached into a drawer, retrieved a leatherette portfolio. He opened the book to a page with four photographs of Kristina. One was Kristina in an Old West dance-hall costume; one was of her in a toga.

Jessica produced a photograph of the dress that Kristina had worn in death. "Did she ever wear a dress like this?"

Alex looked at the photo. "No," he said. "This is not one of our themes."

"How do your clients get up here?" Jessica asked.

"There is an unmarked entrance at the rear of the building. Clients enter, pay, and then they are escorted up by a hostess."

"Do you have a list of Kristina's clients?" Byrne asked.

"I am afraid we do not. This is not something that men generally put on their Visa cards. As you might imagine and understand, this is a cash business."

"Is there someone who might have paid more than once to see her dance? Someone who may have been obsessed with her?"

"This I do not know. But I will ask the other girls."

Before heading downstairs, Jessica opened the door to the last room on the left. Inside was a replica of a tropical paradise, complete with sand, beach chairs, and plastic palm trees.

There was an entire Philadelphia beneath the Philadelphia she thought she knew.

THEY WALKED TO their car on Locust Street. A light snow fell.

"You were right," Byrne said.

Jessica stopped walking. Byrne stopped with her. Jessica cupped a hand to her ear. "I'm sorry, I didn't quite hear that," she said. "Could you repeat that for me please?"

Byrne smiled. "You were right. Kristina Jakos had a secret life."

They continued up the street. "Do you think she might have picked up a suitor, refused his advances and he went off on her?" Jessica asked.

"It's certainly possible. But it sure seems like one hell of an extreme reaction."

"There are some pretty extreme people out there." Jessica thought about Kristina, or any dancer, up on a stage, with someone sitting in the dark, watching, planning the girl's death.

"True," Byrne said. "And anyone who would pay two hundred dollars for a private dance in an Old West saloon probably lives in a fairy-tale world to begin with."

"Plus tips."

"Plus tips."

"Did it strike you that Alex might have had a thing for Kristina?"

"Oh yeah," Byrne said. "He kind of glazed over when he was talking about her."

"Maybe *you* should interview some of the other Stiletto girls," Jessica said, tongue planted firmly in cheek. "See if they have anything to add."

"It's dirty work," Byrne said. "The things I do for the department."

They got in the car, buckled up. Byrne's cell phone rang. He answered, listened. Without a word, he clicked off. He turned his head, stared out the driver's side window for a while.

"What is it?" Jessica asked.

Byrne was silent for a few additional moments, as if he had not heard her. Then: "That was John."

Byrne meant John Shepherd, a fellow detective in the Homicide Unit. Byrne started the car, put a blue light on the dash, hit the gas, roared out into traffic. He remained silent.

"*Kevin.*"

Byrne slammed his fist into the dashboard. Twice. He then took a deep breath, exhaled, turned to her and said the last thing she expected to hear: "Walt Brigham is dead."

# 28

When Jessica and Byrne arrived on the scene on Lincoln Drive—a section of Fairmount Park near the Wissahickon Creek—there were two CSU vans, three sector cars, and five detectives already there. Crime-scene tape spanned the road. Traffic was being routed to two slow-moving lanes.

For the police, the site was charged with anger, determination, and a singular kind of rage. This was one of their own.

The sight of the body was beyond revolting.

Walt Brigham lay on the ground in front of his car, on the shoulder of the road. He was on his back, his arms were spread out to his sides, his palms were upturned in supplication. He had been burned to death. The smell of immolated flesh and crisped skin and flash-fried bone filled the air. His corpse was a blackened husk. His gold detective's badge had been delicately placed on his forehead.

Jessica nearly gagged. She had to turn away from the appalling spectacle. She thought back to the previous night, the way Walt had looked. She had only met him once before, but he had a stellar reputation in the department, and many friends.

Now he was dead.

Detectives Nicci Malone and Eric Chavez would be working the case.

Nicci Malone, thirty-one, was one of the newest detectives in the homicide unit, the only other female besides Jessica. Nicci had spent four years in narcotics. At just under five four, 110 pounds—blond, blue-eyed, and fair on top of it—she had a lot to prove, in addition to all the gender issues. Nicci and Jessica had worked a detail a year earlier and had instantly bonded. They had even worked out together a few times. Nicci practiced tae kwon do.

Eric Chavez was a veteran detective, and the unit's fashion plate. Chavez had never successfully passed a mirror without looking into it. His file drawers were stacked with *GQ, Esquire,* and *Vitals* magazines. A fashion trend did not emerge without his knowledge, but that same attention to detail made him a good investigator.

Byrne's role would be that of a witness—having been one of the last people to talk to Walt Brigham at Finnigan's Wake—although no one expected him to sit on the sidelines during the investigation. Whenever a police officer is murdered, there were about 6,500 men and women on the case.

Every cop in Philly.

\*　\*　\*

MARJORIE BRIGHAM WAS a slight woman in her late fifties. She had small, crisp features, close-cropped silvery hair, the raw clean hands of a middle-class woman who had never delegated a single household chore. She wore tan slacks and a chocolate cable-knit sweater, a simple gold band on her left hand.

Her living room was decorated in an Early American style, the wallpaper a cheerful beige gingham. In front of the window overlooking the street was a maple table bearing an assortment of healthy houseplants. In the corner of the dining room was an aluminum Christmas tree with white lights and red ornaments.

When Byrne and Jessica arrived, Marjorie was sitting on a wingback chair across from the TV. In her hand was a black Teflon spatula. She held it as she might a dead flower. This day, for the first time in decades, there was no one to cook for. She seemed unable to put the utensil down. Putting it down meant that Walt wasn't coming back. If you were married to a police officer, you were afraid every day. You were afraid of the telephone, the knock on the door, the sound of a car pulling into your driveway. You were afraid every time there was a "special report" on television. Then one day the unthinkable happened, and there was no longer anything to fear. You suddenly realized that, all that time, for all those years, fear had been your friend. Fear meant that there was life. Fear was *hope*.

Kevin Byrne was not there in an official capacity. He was there as a friend, a brother officer. Still, it was impossible not to ask the questions. He sat on the arm of the couch, took one of Marjorie's hands in his.

"Are you up for a few questions?" Byrne asked, as softly and gently as possible.

Marjorie nodded.

"Did Walt have any debts? Anyone he might have been having problems with?"

Marjorie thought for a few seconds. "No," she said. "Nothing like that."

"Did he ever mention any specific threats? Anyone who might have had a vendetta against him?"

Marjorie shook her head. Byrne had to try this line of inquiry, even though it was unlikely that Walt Brigham would have shared something like that with his wife. For a fleeting moment, the voice of Matthew Clarke echoed in Byrne's mind.

*This is not over.*

"Is this your case?" Marjorie asked.

"No," Byrne said. "Detective Malone and Detective Chavez are investigating. They'll come by a little later today."

"Are they good?"

"*Very* good," Byrne replied. "Now, you know they'll want to go through some of Walt's things. Are you all right with that?"

Marjorie Brigham just nodded, numb.

"Now remember, if there are any problems or questions, or if you just want to talk, you call me first, okay? Anytime. Day or night. I'll come right over."

"Thanks, Kevin."

Byrne rose, buttoned his coat. Marjorie stood up. Finally she put the spatula down, then hugged the big man in front of her, burying her face in his broad chest.

THE STORY WAS already all over the city, the region. News crews were setting up shop on Lincoln Drive. They had a potentially sensational story. Fifty or sixty cops convene at a tavern, and one of them leaves and is murdered along a remote section of Lincoln Drive. What was he doing there? Drugs? Sex? A payoff? For a police department that was constantly under scrutiny from every civil-rights group, every review board, every citizen-action committee, not to mention the local and often national media, it didn't look good. The pressure from the big bosses to solve this and solve it fast was already enormous, and growing by the hour.

# 29

"What time did Walt leave the bar?" Nicci asked. They were gathered around the assignment desk in the Homicide Unit, Nicci Malone, Eric Chavez, Kevin Byrne, Jessica Balzano, and Ike Buchanan.

"Not sure," Byrne said. "Maybe two."

"I've talked to a dozen detectives already. No one seems to have seen him leave. It was his party. Does that really sound *right* to you?" Nicci asked.

It didn't. But Byrne shrugged. "It is what it is. We were all pretty loaded. Especially Walt."

"Okay," Nicci said. She flipped a few pages back in her notebook. "Walt Brigham shows up at Finnigan's Wake at about 8 PM last night, where he proceeds to drink half the top shelf. Did you know him as a drinker?"

"He was a homicide cop. And this was his retirement party."

"Point taken," Nicci said. "Did you see him argue with anybody?"

"No," Byrne said.

"Did you see him leave for a while, come back?"

"I did not," Byrne replied.

"Did you see him make any phone calls?"

"No."

"Did you recognize most of the people at the party?" Nicci asked.

"Just about everybody," Byrne said. "I came up with a lot of those guys."

"Any long-standing feuds, anything that goes back?"

"Nothing I know of."

"So, you talked to the victim at the bar around one thirty, and you didn't see him after that?"

Byrne shook his head. He thought about all the times he had done exactly what Nicci Malone was doing, how many times he had used the word "victim" instead of the person's name. He had never really realized how it sounded. Until now. "No," Byrne said, suddenly feeling completely useless. This was a new experience for him—that of being a witness—and he didn't like it much. He didn't like it at all.

"Anything to add, Jess?" Nicci asked.

"Not really," Jessica said. "I was out of there around midnight."

"Where did you park?"

"On Third."

"Near the lot?"

Jessica shook her head. "Closer to Green Street."

"Did you see anyone hanging around the lot behind Finnigan's?"

"No."

"Anyone walking up the street as you were leaving?"

"No one."

A canvass had been conducted in a two-block radius. No one had seen Walt Brigham leave the bar, walk up Third Street, enter the lot, or drive away.

JESSICA AND BYRNE had an early dinner at the Standard Tap at Second and Poplar. They ate in a stunned silence over the news of Walt Brigham's murder. The first report had come in. Brigham had suffered blunt-force trauma to the back of the head, and had then been doused with gasoline and set ablaze. A gas can was found in the woods near the crime scene, an ordinary two-gallon plastic model, available everywhere, no prints. The ME's office would consult with a forensic odontologist, perform a dental ID on the body, but there was little doubt in anyone's mind that the charred corpse was that of Walter Brigham.

"So, what's up for Christmas Eve?" Byrne finally asked, trying to lighten the mood.

"My father's coming over," Jessica said. "It'll just be him, me, Vincent, and Sophie. Christmas Day we're going to my aunt's house. Been that way forever. How about you?"

"I'm going to stop at my father's, help him start to pack."

"How's your father doing?" Jessica had been meaning to ask. When Byrne had been shot, and was lying in an induced coma, she had visited the hospital every day for weeks. Sometimes she couldn't make it until well after midnight, but as a rule, when a police officer was hurt in the line of duty, there were no formal visiting hours. Regardless of the time, Padraig Byrne had been there. He had not been emotionally able to sit in the ICU with his son, so they had put a chair in the hallway for him, where he sat vigil—plaid Thermos at his side, newspaper in hand— around the clock. Jessica had never spoken to the man at length, but the ritual of her rounding the corner, seeing him sitting there with his rosary, nodding a good morning, good afternoon, or good evening, had been a constant she came to look forward to during those shaky weeks, the bedrock on which she built the foundation of her hopes.

"He's good," Byrne said. "I told you that he's moving to the Northeast, right?"

"Yeah," Jessica said. "Can't believe he's leaving South Philly."

"Neither can he. Later in the evening I'm having dinner with Colleen. Victoria was going to join us, but she's still in Meadville. Her mother's not well."

"You know, you and Colleen are welcome to come over after dinner," Jessica said. "I make one hell of a tiramisu. Fresh mascarpone from DiBruno's. Trust me, it's been known to make grown men weep uncontrollably. Plus, my Uncle Vittorio always sends a case of his homemade *vino di tavola*. We play the Bing Crosby Christmas album. It's a wild time."

"Thanks," Byrne said. "Let me see what's up."

Kevin Byrne was as gracious at accepting invitations as he was at avoiding them. Jessica decided not to push. They fell silent again as their thoughts, like those of everyone else in the PPD this day, went to Walt Brigham.

"Thirty-eight years on the job," Byrne said. "Walt put a *lot* of people away."

"You think it was someone he sent up?" Jessica asked.

"That's where I'd start."

"When you talked to him before you left, did he give you any indication that something was wrong?"

"Not at all. I mean, I got the sense that he was a little depressed about retirement. But he seemed upbeat about the fact that he was going for his license."

"License?"

"PI license," Byrne said. "He said he was going to look into Richie DiCillo's daughter's case."

"Richie DiCillo's daughter? I don't know what you mean."

Byrne gave Jessica a quick rundown on the 1995 murder of Annemarie DiCillo. The story gave Jessica chills. She'd had no idea.

AS THEY DROVE across town, Jessica thought about how small Marjorie Brigham had looked in Byrne's embrace. She wondered how many times Kevin Byrne had found himself in that position. He was intimidating as hell if you were on the wrong side of things. But when he brought you into his orbit, when he looked at you with those deep emerald eyes, he made you feel like you were the only other person in the world, and that your problems had just become his problems.

The hard reality was, the job went on.

There was a dead woman named Kristina Jakos to think about.

# 30

*Moon stands naked in the moonlight. It is late. It is his favorite time.*

*When he was seven, and his grandfather was taken ill for the first time, he thought he would never see the man again. He had cried for days, until his grandmother relented and took him to the hospital for a visit. On that long and confusing night, Moon stole a glass vial of his grandfather's blood. He sealed it tightly and hid it in the basement of his house.*

*On his eighth birthday, his grandfather died. It was the worst thing that ever happened to him. His grandfather had taught him many things, reading to him in the evenings, telling him stories of ogres and fairies and kings. Moon remembers long summer days when families would visit. Real families. Music played, and children laughed.*

*Then the children stopped coming.*

*His grandmother lived in silence after that, until the day she took Moon to the forest, where he watched the girls play. With their long necks and smooth white skin they were like the swans in the story. That day there was a terrible storm, thunder and lightning crashed over the forest, filling the world. Moon tried to protect the swans. He built them a nest.*

*When his grandmother learned of what he had done in the forest she took him to a dark and frightening place, a place where other children like himself lived.*

*Moon looked out the window for many years. The moon came to him every night, telling him of its travels. Moon learned of Paris and Munich and Upsala. He learned of the Deluge and the Street of Tombs.*

*When his grandmother took ill, they let him come home. He returned to a quiet and empty place. A place of ghosts.*

*His grandmother is gone now. Soon the king will tear everything down.*

*Moon makes his seed in the soft blue light of the moon. He thinks about his nightingale. She sits in the boat-house, waiting, her voice stilled for the moment. He mixes his seed with a single drop of blood. He arranges his brushes.*

*Later he will dress in his finery, cut a length of rope, and make his way to the boathouse.*

*He will show the nightingale his world.*

# 31

Byrne sat in his car on Eleventh Street, near Walnut. He'd had every intention of making it an early night, but his car had brought him here.

He was restless, and he knew why.

All he could think about was Walt Brigham. He thought about Brigham's face as he talked about the Annemarie DiCillo case. There had been real passion there.

*Pine needles. Smoke.*

Byrne got out of his car. He was going to head into Moriarty's for a quick one. Halfway to the door he decided against it. He walked back to his car in a sort of fugue state. He had always been a man of instant decision, of lightning reaction, but now he seemed to be walking in circles. Maybe the murder of Walt Brigham had gotten to him more than he realized.

As he opened the car he heard someone approaching. He turned around. It was Matthew Clarke. Clarke looked agitated, red-eyed, on edge. Byrne watched the man's hands.

"What are you doing here, Mr. Clarke?"

Clarke shrugged his shoulders. "This is a free country. I can go where I want."

"Yes, you can," Byrne said. "However, I'd prefer it if those places were not around me."

Clarke reached slowly into his pocket, pulled out a camera phone. He turned the screen toward Byrne. "I can even go to the twelve hundred block of Spruce Street if I feel like it."

At first Byrne thought he had heard wrong. Then he looked closely at the picture on the cell phone's small screen. His heart sank. The photograph was of his wife's house. The house where his daughter *slept*.

Byrne slapped the phone from Clarke's hand, grabbed the man by his lapels, slammed him into the bricks of the wall behind him. "Listen to me," he said. "Can you hear me?"

Clarke just stared, his lips trembling. He had planned for this moment, but now that it had arrived he was completely unprepared for the immediacy, the violence of it.

"I'm going to say this once," Byrne said. "If you ever go near that house again I will hunt you down and I will put a fucking bullet in your head. Do you understand?"

"I guess you don't—"

"Don't talk. *Listen.* If you have a problem with me, it is with *me*, not with my family. You do not *fuck* with my family. You want to settle this now? Tonight? We settle it."

Byrne let go of the man's coat. He backed up. He tried to control himself. That would be all he needed: a citizen complaint against him.

The truth was Matthew Clarke was not a criminal. Not yet. For the moment Clarke was just an ordinary man riding a terrible, soul-shredding wave of grief. He was lashing out at Byrne, at the system, at the injustice of it all. As misplaced as it was, Byrne understood.

"Walk away," Byrne said. "Now."

Clarke straightened his clothes, made an attempt to restore his dignity. "You can't tell me what to do."

"Walk away, Mr. Clarke. Get help."

"It's not that easy."

"What do you want?"

"I want you to own up to what you've done," Clarke said.

"What I've *done*?" Byrne took a deep breath, tried to calm down. "You don't know anything about me. When you've seen the things I've seen, and been the places I've been, we'll talk."

Clarke glared at him. He wasn't going to let it go.

"Look, I'm sorry for your loss, Mr. Clarke. I truly am. But there isn't—"

"You didn't know her."

"Yes I did."

Clarke looked stunned. "What are you talking about?"

"You think I didn't know who she was? You think I don't see it every day of my life? The man who walks into the bank during a robbery? The elderly woman walking home from church? The kid on a North Philly playground? The girl whose only crime was being Catholic? You think I don't understand *innocence*?"

Clarke continued to stare at Byrne, speechless.

"It makes me sick," Byrne said. "But there's nothing you or I or anybody else can do about it. Innocent people get hurt. You have my condolences, but as callous as it may sound, that's all I'm going to give you. That's all I *can* give you."

Instead of accepting this and leaving, it appeared that Matthew Clarke wanted to take matters to the next level. Byrne resigned himself to the inevitable.

"You took a swing at me in that diner," Byrne said. "A sucker punch. You missed. You want a free shot now? Take it. Last chance."

"You have a gun," Clarke said. "I'm not a stupid man."

Byrne reached into his holster, took out his weapon, tossed it into his car. His badge and ID followed. "Unarmed," he said. "I'm a civilian now."

Matthew Clarke looked at the ground for a moment. In Byrne's mind it could still go either way. Then Clarke reared back and hit Byrne in the face as hard as he could. Byrne staggered, saw stars for a moment. He tasted blood in his mouth, warm and metallic. Clarke was five inches shorter and at least fifty pounds lighter. Byrne did not raise his hands in defense or anger.

"That's *it*?" Byrne asked. He spit. "Twenty years of marriage and that's the best you can do?" Byrne was baiting Clarke, insulting him. He couldn't seem to stop himself. Maybe he didn't want to. "*Hit* me."

This time it was a glancing blow off Byrne's forehead. Knuckle on bone. It stung.

"Again."

Clarke ran at him again, this time catching Byrne on the right temple. He came back around with a hook to Byrne's chest. And then another. Clarke nearly came off the ground with the effort.

Byrne reeled back a foot or so, held his ground. "I don't think your heart is in this, Matt. I really don't."

Clarke screamed with rage—a crazed, animal sound. He swung his fist again, catching Byrne on the left side of his jaw. But it was clear that his passion, and strength, were waning. He swung again, this time a glancing blow that continued past Byrne's face and into the wall. Clarke screamed in pain.

Byrne spit blood, waited. Clarke slumped against the wall, spent for the moment, physically and emotionally, his knuckles bleeding. The two men looked at each other. They both knew this battle was winding down, the way men have known for centuries that a fight was over. For the moment.

"Done?" Byrne asked.

"Fuck . . . you."

Byrne wiped the blood from his face. "You're never going to have this opportunity again, Mr. Clarke. If this happens again, if you ever approach me again in anger, I will fight back. And as hard as it may be for you to understand, I'm as mad about your wife's death as you are. You don't want me to fight back."

Clarke began to cry.

"Look, believe this, or don't believe it," Byrne said. He knew he was reaching. He had been here before, but for some reason it had never been this hard. "I'm sorry about what happened. You'll never *know* how sorry. Anton Krotz was a fucking animal, and now he's dead. If there was something I could do, I would do it."

Clarke glared at him, his anger subsiding, his breathing returning to normal, his rage falling back into the dominion of grief and pain. He wiped the tears from his face. "Oh, there is, Detective," he said. "There is."

They stared at each other, five feet between them, worlds apart. Byrne could tell the man was not going to say anything else. Not this night.

Clarke picked up his cell phone, backed his way to his car, slipped inside, and sped off, fishtailing for a moment on the ice.

Byrne glanced down. There were long streaks of blood on his white dress shirt. It wasn't the first time. It was the first time in a *long* time, though. He rubbed his jaw. He had been punched in the face enough in his life, starting with Sal Pecchio when he was about eight years old. That time it had been over a water ice.

*If there was something I could do, I would do it.*

Byrne wondered what he'd meant by that.

*There is.*

Byrne wondered what Clarke had meant.

He got on his cell. His first call was to his ex-wife, Donna, under the pretense of saying "Merry Christmas." Everything was fine there. Clarke had not paid a visit. Byrne's next call reached out to a sergeant in the district where Donna and Colleen lived. He gave a description of Clarke and the car's plates. They would dispatch a sector car. Byrne knew he could have a warrant issued, have Clarke picked up, could probably have a charge of assault and battery stick. But he couldn't bring himself to do it.

Byrne opened the car door, retrieved his weapon and ID, headed for the pub. As he stepped into the welcoming warmth of the familiar bar, he had a feeling that the next time he confronted Matthew Clarke it was going to turn bad.

*Very* bad.

# 32

From her new world of total darkness, layers of sound and touch peeled away slowly—the echo of moving water, the feel of cold wood against her skin—but it was the sense of smell that beckoned first.

For Tara Lynn Greene, it had always been about smell. The scent of sweet basil, the redolence of diesel fumes, the aroma of a baking fruit pie in her grandmother's kitchen. All these things held the power to transport her to another place and time in her life. Coppertone was the shore.

This scent was familiar too. Decaying meat. Rotting wood.

*Where was she?*

Tara knew they had traveled, but she had no idea how far. Or how long it had been. She had dozed off, been rattled awake a few times. She felt wet and cold. She could hear wind whispering through stone. She was indoors, but that was about all she knew.

As her thoughts became clearer, her terror grew. The flat tire. The man with the flowers. The searing pain at the back of her neck.

Suddenly a light came on overhead. The low-watt bulb glowed through a layer of grime. She could now see that she was in a small room. To the right, a wrought-iron daybed. A dresser. A chair. All vintage, all very tidy, the room almost monastic in its precise order. Ahead was a passageway of some sort, an arched stone duct leading into blackness. Her eye was drawn back to the bed. There was something white on it. A dress? No. It looked like a winter coat.

It was *her* coat.

Tara looked down. She was now wearing a long dress. And she was in a boat, a small red boat in a canal that ran through this peculiar room. The boat was brightly colored with glossy enamel paint. Around her waist was a nylon seat belt, holding her snugly into a worn vinyl seat. Her hands were tied to the belt.

She felt something sour rise in her throat. She had read a newspaper story about the woman found murdered in Manayunk. The woman dressed in an old costume. She knew what this was all about. The knowledge squeezed the air from her lungs.

Sounds: metal on metal. Then a new sound. It sounded like . . . a bird? Yes, a bird was singing. The bird's song was beautiful, rich and melodic. Tara had never heard anything like it. Within moments she heard footsteps. Someone approached from behind, but Tara dared not try to turn around.

After a long silence, he spoke.

"Sing for me," he said.

*Had she heard correctly?* "I'm . . . I'm sorry?"

"Sing, nightingale."

Tara's throat was parched nearly shut. She tried to swallow. The only chance of getting out of this was with her wits. "What do you want me to sing?" she managed.

"A song about the moon."

*The moon the moon the moon the moon.* What does he mean? What is he talking about? "I don't think I know any songs about the moon," she said.

"Sure you do. Everybody knows a song about the moon. 'Fly Me to the Moon,' 'Paper Moon,' 'How High the Moon,' 'Blue Moon,' 'Moon River.' I especially like 'Moon River.' Do you know it?"

Tara knew that song. *Everyone* knew that song, right? But right then it would not come to her. "Yes," she said, buying time. "I know it."

He stepped in front of her.

*Oh my God,* she thought. She averted her eyes.

"Sing, nightingale," he said.

This time it was a command. She sang "Moon River." The lyrics came to her, if not the precise melody. Her theatrical training took over. She knew if she stopped, or even hesitated, something terrible would happen.

He sang with her as he untied the boat, walked to the rear, and gave it a shove. He turned off the light.

Tara moved through the darkness now. The small boat tapped and clacked against the sides of the narrow channel. She strained to see, but still her world was almost pitch-black. From time to time she noticed a glistening of icy moisture on shiny rock walls. The walls were closer now. The boat rocked. It was *so* cold.

She could no longer hear him, but Tara continued to sing, her voice rebounding off the walls and low ceiling. It sounded thin and shaky, but she couldn't stop.

Light ahead—consommé-thin daylight sneaking through cracks in what looked to be old wooden doors.

The boat hit the doors and they sprang open. She was outdoors. It looked to be just after dawn. A soft snow was falling. Above her, dead tree branches blackly fingered a mother-of-pearl sky. She tried to raise her arms, but could not.

The boat drifted into a clearing. Tara was floating down one of a series of narrow canals that snaked through the trees. The water was cluttered with leaves, branches, debris. On either side of the canals were tall, rotting structures, their supporting spines like diseased ribs in a decaying chest. One appeared to be a skewed and ramshackle gingerbread house. Another display looked like a castle. Yet another resembled a giant seashell.

The boat banged around a bend in the river and the view of the trees was now blocked out by a large display, perhaps twenty feet tall, fifteen feet wide. Tara tried to focus on what it might be. It looked like a child's storybook, open to the center, with a long-faded, paint-flaked red ribbon down the right side. Next to it sat a large rock, like something you might see in a breakwall. Something sat on top of the rock.

The wind kicked up at that moment, rocking the boat, stinging Tara's face, making her eyes water. The bitterly cold gust brought with it a fetid, animal smell that turned her stomach. A few moments later, when the motion settled and her vision cleared, Tara found herself directly in front of the huge storybook. She read a few words at the upper left.

*Far out in the ocean, where the water is as blue as the prettiest cornflower . . .*

Tara looked beyond the book. Her tormentor stood at the end of the canal, near a small building that looked like an old schoolhouse. He held a length of rope in his hands. He was waiting for her.

Her song became a scream.

# 33

By 6 AM, Byrne had all but given up on sleep. He drifted in and out of consciousness, the nightmares creeping, the faces accusing.

Kristina Jakos. Walt Brigham. Laura Clarke.

At seven thirty the phone rang. Somehow he had drifted off. The sound jolted him upright. *Not another body,* he thought. *Please. Not another body.*

He answered. "Byrne."

"Did I wake you up?"

Victoria's voice brought a burst of sunshine to his heart. "No," he said. It was marginally true. He had been on the rock-face of sleep.

"Merry Christmas," she said.

"Merry Christmas, Tori. How's your mom?"

Her slight hesitation told him a lot. Marta Lindstrom was only sixty-six, but she suffered from early-stage dementia.

"Good days and bad days," Victoria said. A long pause. Byrne read it. "I think I have to move back home," she added.

There it was. While both had wanted to deny it, they knew it was coming. Victoria had already taken an extended leave from her job at the Passage House, a runaway shelter on Lombard Street.

"Hey. Meadville isn't all that far away," she said. "It's

kind of nice here. Kind of quaint. You could look at it as a vacation. We could do a B and B."

"I've never actually been in a bed and breakfast," Byrne said.

"We probably wouldn't get to the breakfast part. We could have an illicit assignation."

Victoria could turn her mood on a dime. It was one of the many things Byrne loved about her. No matter how down she was, she could make him feel better.

Byrne glanced around his apartment. Although they had never officially moved in together—neither was ready for that step, each for their own reasons—in the time Byrne had been seeing Victoria she had transformed his apartment from the prototype bachelor pizza box into something resembling a home. He hadn't been ready for lace curtains, but she had talked him into honeycomb window blinds, their pastel gold color amplifying the morning sunlight.

There was an area rug on the floor, end tables where they were supposed to be: at the ends of the couch. Victoria had even managed to sneak in two houseplants that, miraculously, had not only survived, but grown.

Meadville, Byrne thought. Meadville was only 285 miles from Philadelphia.

It seemed like the other side of the world.

BECAUSE IT WAS Christmas Eve, Jessica and Byrne were both on duty for only half a day. They probably could have fudged it out on the street, but there was always something to wrap up, some report to read or file.

By the time Byrne entered the duty room, Josh Bontrager was already there. He had gotten three pastries and three coffees for them. Two creams, two sugars, a napkin, and a stirrer each—all laid out on the desk with geometric precision.

"Good morning, Detective," Bontrager said, smiling.

His brow narrowed when he saw Byrne's swollen face. "Are you all right, sir?"

"I'm fine." Byrne slipped off his coat. He was bone weary. "And it's Kevin," he said. "Please." Byrne uncapped his coffee. He held it up. "Thanks."

"Sure," Bontrager said. All business now. He flipped open his notebook. "I'm afraid I struck out with the Savage Garden CDs. The big stores carry it, but no one remembers anyone specifically asking for it in the last few months."

"It was worth a shot," Byrne said. He took a bite of the pastry Josh Bontrager had bought. It was a nut roll. Very fresh.

Bontrager nodded. "I'm not done yet. There are still the independent stores."

At that moment Jessica stormed into the duty room, sparks in her wake. Her eyes were blazing, her color was high. It wasn't from the weather. She was not a happy detective.

"What's up?" Byrne asked.

Jessica paced back and forth, the Italian invectives just beneath her breath. She finally slammed down her purse. Heads popped up over partitions around the duty room. "Channel Six caught me in the *fucking* parking lot."

"What did they ask?"

"The usual fucking bullshit."

"What did you tell them?"

"The usual fucking bullshit."

Jessica related how they had cornered her before she could even get out of her car. Cameras shouldered, lights on, questions flying. The department really didn't like detectives getting on camera unscheduled, but it always looked much worse seeing footage of a detective shielding their eyes and yelling "No comment." It didn't really inspire confidence. So she'd stopped and done her bit.

"How does my hair look?" Jessica asked.

Byrne took a step back. "Um, good."

Jessica threw both hands out. "*God*, what a silver-tongued devil you are! I swear I'm going to faint."

"What'd I say?" Byrne looked at Bontrager. Both men shrugged.

"However my hair looks, I'll bet it looks better than your face," Jessica said. "Gonna tell me about it?"

Byrne had iced his face down, cleaned it up. Nothing broken. It was slightly swollen, but the swelling was already starting to go down. He related the story of Matthew Clarke and their confrontation.

"How far do you think he might take this?" Jessica asked.

"I have no idea. Donna and Colleen are heading out of town for a week. At least that will be off my mind."

"Anything I can do?" Jessica and Bontrager said simultaneously.

"I don't think so," Byrne said, looking at both of them, "but thanks."

Jessica picked up her messages, moved toward the door.

"Where are you headed?" Byrne asked.

"I'm off to the library," Jessica said. "See if I can find this moon drawing."

"I'll finish the list of secondhand clothes stores," Byrne said. "Maybe we can find where he bought that dress."

Jessica held up her cell phone. "I'm mobile."

"Detective Balzano?" Bontrager asked.

Jessica turned around, her face a twist of impatience. "*What?*"

"Your hair looks very nice."

Jessica's anger slid away. She smiled. "Thank you, Josh."

# 34

The Free Library had a great number of books on the subject of the moon. Far too many to make any immediate sense of in a way that might help with the investigation.

Before leaving the Roundhouse Jessica ran "moon" through NCIC, VICAP, and the other national law-enforcement databases. The bad news was that perps who used the moon as the basis for their MO tended to be compulsive killers. She had teamed the word with others—specifically "blood" and "semen"—and gotten nothing of use.

With the help of a librarian Jessica selected a sampling of moon-related books from each section.

Jessica sat behind two stacks in a private room on the first floor. First she browsed through the books that dealt with the moon in a scientific sense. There were books about how to observe the moon, books about exploring the moon, books about the physical characteristics of the moon, amateur astronomy, the Apollo missions, maps and atlases of the moon. Jessica had never been all that good with the sciences. She felt her attention waning, her eyes glazing over.

She turned to the other stack. This one held more promise. These were books that dealt with the moon and folklore, as well as the iconology of the heavens.

After skimming some of the introductions, and making

notes, Jessica discovered that the moon seemed to be represented in folklore in five different phases: new, full, crescent, half, and gibbous, a state between half and full. The moon was prominent in tales from every country and culture, for as long as literature was recorded—Chinese, Egyptian, Arabic, Hindu, Nordic, African, Native American, European. Where there was myth and faith, there were tales about the moon.

In religious folklore, some pictures of the Assumption of the Virgin Mary showed the moon as a crescent under her feet. In stories that present the crucifixion, it is shown as an eclipse placed on one side of the cross, while the sun is placed on the other.

There were also a great number of Biblical references. In Revelations there was "a woman clothed with the sun, standing on the moon, and with the twelve stars on her head for a crown." In Genesis: "God made the two great lights: the greater light to govern the day, the smaller light to govern the night, and the stars."

There were tales where the moon was feminine, tales where the moon was masculine. In Lithuanian folklore, the moon was the husband, the sun was the wife, and the Earth was their child. One tale from British folklore held that if you were robbed three days after a full moon, the thief would be quickly caught.

Jessica's head spun with the images and the concepts. Within two hours, she had five pages of notes.

The last book she opened was dedicated to illustrations of the moon. Woodcuts, etchings, watercolors, oils, charcoal. She found illustrations by Galileo from *Sidereus Nuncius*. There were a number of tarot illustrations.

Nothing looked like the drawing found on Kristina Jakos.

Still, something told Jessica that there was a distinct possibility that the pathology of the man they sought was rooted in some kind of folklore, perhaps the type Father Greg had described to her.

Jessica checked out a half dozen books.

As she exited the library she glanced at the winter sky. She wondered if Kristina Jakos's killer was waiting for the moon.

AS JESSICA CROSSED the parking lot, her mind alive with images of witches, goblins, fairy princesses, and ogres, she found it hard to believe that this stuff hadn't scared the living hell out of her when she'd been small. She remembered reading some of the shorter fairy tales to Sophie when her daughter had been three and four, but none of them seemed as bizarre and violent as some of the stories she had run across in these books. She had never given it much thought, but some of the tales were downright lurid.

Halfway across the parking lot, before she reached her car, she sensed someone approaching from her right. *Fast.* Her instincts told her it was trouble. She spun quickly, her right hand instinctively throwing back the hem of her coat.

It was Father Greg.

*Calm down, Jess. It's not the big, bad wolf. Just an orthodox priest.*

"Well, *hello,*" he said. "Fancy meeting you here and all that."

"Hello there."

"I hope I didn't scare you."

"You didn't," she lied.

Jessica glanced down. Father Greg had a book in his hands. Incredibly, it looked like a volume of fairy tales.

"Actually, I was going to call you later today," he said.

"Really? Why is that?"

"Well, since we spoke, I kind of got the bug about all this," he said. He held up the book. "As you might imagine, folk tales and fables aren't really big in the church. We have a whole lot of hard-to-believe stuff already."

Jessica smiled. "Roman Catholics have their share."

"I was going to search through these stories and see if I could find a 'moon' reference for you."

"That's kind of you, but it's not necessary."

"It's really no problem at all," Father Greg said. "I love to read." He nodded at a vehicle, a late-model van parked nearby. "Can I give you a lift somewhere?"

"No, thanks," she said. "I've got my car."

He glanced at his watch. "Well, I'm off to the world of snowmen and ugly ducklings," he said. "I'll let you know if I find anything."

"That would be good," Jessica said. "Thanks."

He walked to the van, opened the door, and turned back to Jessica. "Perfect night for it, too."

"What do you mean?"

Father Greg smiled. "It's going to be a Christmas moon."

# 35

When Jessica got back to the Roundhouse, before she could get her coat off and sit down, her phone rang. The duty officer in the lobby of the Roundhouse told her that someone was on the way up to see her. A few minutes later a uniformed officer entered with Will Pedersen, the brick mason from the Manayunk crime scene.

This time Pedersen was dressed in a three-button blazer and jeans. His hair was neatly combed, and he wore tortoiseshell glasses.

He shook hands with both Jessica and Byrne.

"What can we do for you?" Jessica asked.

"Well, you had said that if I remembered anything else, I should get in touch."

"That's correct," Jessica said.

"I was thinking about that morning. The morning we met in Manayunk?"

"What about it?"

"Like I said, I've been down there a lot lately. I'm pretty familiar with all the buildings. The more I thought about it, the more I realized something was different."

"Different?" Jessica asked. "Different how?"

"Well, with the graffiti."

"The graffiti? On the warehouse?"

"Yes."

"How so?"

"Okay," Pedersen said. "I used to be a bit of a tagger, right? Ran with the skateboard boys in my teenage years." He seemed a bit reluctant to talk about this, shoving his hands deep into the pockets of his jeans.

"I think the statute of limitations may have run out on that," Jessica said.

Pedersen smiled. "Okay. I'm still kind of a fan though, you know? With all the murals and things around town, I'm always looking, taking pictures."

The Philadelphia Mural Arts Program had started in 1984 as a plan to eliminate destructive graffiti in the poorer neighborhoods. In its effort, the city reached out to graffiti writers in an attempt redirect their creative urges into making murals. Philadelphia had hundreds, if not thousands, of murals.

"Okay," Jessica said. "What does this have to do with the building on Flat Rock?"

"Well, you know how you see something every day? I mean, you see it, but you don't really look at it closely?"

"Sure."

"I was wondering," Pedersen said. "Did you take pictures of the south side of the building by any chance?"

Jessica sorted through the photographs on her desk. She found a picture of the south side of the warehouse. "What about it?"

Pedersen pointed to an area on the right side of the wall, next to a large red and blue gang tag. With the naked eye it looked like a small white smudge.

"See this here? That was not there two days before I met you guys."

"So you're saying it might have been painted the morning the body was put on the riverbank?" Byrne asked.

"Maybe. The only reason I noticed it was because it was white. It kind of stands out."

Jessica glanced at the photo. The picture had been taken with a digital camera, at a fairly high resolution. The print, however, was small. She would send her camera down to the AV Unit and have them make an enlargement from the original file.

"Do you think it might be important?" Pedersen asked.

"It might," Jessica said. "Thanks for bringing this to our attention."

"Sure."

"We'll give you a call if we need to speak to you again."

When Pedersen left, Jessica got on the phone to CSU. They would dispatch a tech to collect a paint sample from the building.

Twenty minutes later, an enlarged version of the JPEG file was printed and sitting on Jessica's desk. She and Byrne looked at it. The painted image on the wall was a larger, cruder version of the one found on Kristina Jakos's abdomen.

The killer had not only posed his victim on the bank of the river, but he had taken the time to tag the wall behind him with a symbol, a symbol meant to be seen.

Jessica had wondered if the telltale *gotcha* was in one of the crime-scene pictures.

Maybe it was.

WHILE WAITING FOR the lab report on the paint, Jessica's phone rang again. So much for the Christmas break. She wasn't even supposed to be there. Death goes on.

She punched the button, answered. "Homicide, Detective Balzano."

"Detective, this is PO Valentine, I work out of the Ninety-second."

Part of the Ninety-second District bordered the Schuylkill River. "What's up, Officer Valentine?"

"We're on the Strawberry Mansion Bridge right now. We found something you should see."

"Found something?"

"Yes, ma'am."

When you're in homicide, the call is usually about a some*body*, not a some*thing*. "What is it, Officer Valentine?"

Valentine hesitated a moment. It was telling. "Well, Sergeant Majette asked me to give you a call. He says you should get down here right away."

# 36

The Strawberry Mansion Bridge was built in 1897. It was one of the first steel bridges in the country, spanning the Schuylkill River between Strawberry Mansion and Fairmount Park.

This day, traffic was stopped at both ends. Jessica, Byrne, and Bontrager had to walk to the center of the bridge, where a pair of patrol officers met them.

Two boys, perhaps eleven or twelve years old, stood near the officers. The boys seemed a vibrating combination of fear and excitement.

On the north side of the bridge was something covered in a white plastic evidence sheet. Officer Lindsey Valentine approached Jessica. She was about twenty-four, bright-eyed, fit.

"What do we have?" Jessica asked.

Officer Valentine hesitated a moment. She may have worked out of the Ninety-second, but whatever was under the plastic had unnerved her a little. "Citizen called this in about a half hour ago. These two young men came across it while crossing the bridge."

Officer Valentine lifted the plastic. On the sidewalk was a pair of shoes. They were women's shoes, deep crimson in color, approximately size seven. Ordinary in all ways, except these red shoes had a pair of severed feet in them.

Jessica looked up, met Byrne's gaze.

"The boys found this?" Jessica asked.

"Yes, ma'am." Officer Valentine waved the boys over. The boys were white kids, just on the tip of hip-hop style. Mall rats with attitudes, but not right at this moment. Now they looked a little traumatized.

"We were just looking at them," the taller one said.

"Did you see who put them here?" Byrne asked.

"No."

"Did you touch them?"

"Uh-uh."

"Did you see anyone around them when you were walking up?" Byrne asked.

"No, sir," they said together, shaking their heads for emphasis. "We were here for like a minute or something and then a car stopped and told us to get away. They called the police after that."

Byrne glanced at Officer Valentine. "Who placed the call?"

Officer Valentine pointed to a new Chevrolet parked about twenty feet from the circle of crime-scene tape. A fortyish man in a business suit and topcoat stood next to it. Byrne held up a finger to him. The man nodded.

"Why did you stay here after the police were called?" Byrne asked the boys.

The two boys shrugged in unison.

Byrne turned to Officer Valentine. "Do we have their information?"

"Yes, sir."

"Okay," Byrne said. "You guys can go. We may want to talk to you again, though."

"What's going to happen to them?" the smaller boy asked, pointing to the body parts.

"What's going to *happen* to them?" Byrne asked.

"Yeah," the bigger one said. "Are you going to take them with you?"

"Yes," Byrne said. "We're going to take them with us."

"How come?"

"How *come*? Because this is evidence of a serious crime."

Both boys looked crestfallen. "Okay," said the smaller boy.

"Why?" Byrne asked. "Did you want to put them on eBay?"

He looked up. "Can you do that?"

Byrne pointed to the far side of the bridge. "Go home," he said. "Right now. Go home, or I swear to *God* I'll arrest your whole family."

The boys ran.

"Jesus," Byrne said. "Fucking *eBay*."

Jessica knew what he meant. She could not imagine herself at eleven years old, coming across a pair of severed feet on a bridge, and *not* freaking out. For these kids it was like an episode of *CSI*. Or some video game.

Byrne talked to the 911-caller while the frigid waters of the Schuylkill River flowed beneath. Jessica glanced at Officer Valentine. It was a strange moment, the two of them standing over what was certainly the severed remains of Kristina Jakos. Jessica recalled her own days in uniform, times when a detective would show up at a homicide she had secured. She remembered looking at the detective in those days with a small measure of envy and awe. She wondered if Officer Lindsey Valentine looked at her that way.

Jessica knelt down for a closer look. The shoes were low-heeled, round-toed, with a thin strap across the top, a wide toe-box. Jessica took a few pictures.

A canvass yielded the expected. Nobody had seen or heard anything. But one thing was obvious to the detectives. Something they did not need witness statements to tell them. These body parts had not been flung here randomly. They had been carefully placed.

\* \* \*

WITHIN AN HOUR they had the preliminary report back. To no one's surprise, blood tests presumptively indicated that the recovered body parts belonged to Kristina Jakos.

THERE IS A moment in all homicide investigations— investigations where you don't find the killer standing over the body, dripping knife or smoking gun in hand— when everything grinds to a halt. Calls don't come in, witnesses don't show, forensic results lag. On this day, at this time, it was just such a moment. Perhaps the fact that it was Christmas Eve had something to do with it. No one wanted to think about death. Detectives stared at computer screens, they tapped their pencils to some unheard beat, crime-scene photographs stared up from the desk: accusing, questioning, expecting, *waiting*.

It would be forty-eight hours before they could effectively question a sampling of people who took the Strawberry Mansion Bridge at approximately the time the remains were left there. The next day was Christmas Day and the usual traffic pattern would be different.

At the Roundhouse, Jessica gathered her things. She noticed that Josh Bontrager was still there, hard at work. He sat at one of the computer terminals, scrolling through arrest-history data.

"What are your Christmas plans, Josh?" Byrne asked.

Bontrager glanced up from his computer screen. "I'm going home tonight," he said. "I'm on duty tomorrow. New guy, and all."

"If you don't mind my asking, what *do* the Amish do for Christmas?"

"That depends on the group."

"Group?" Byrne asked. "There are different kinds of Amish?"

"Oh, sure. There's Old Order Amish, New Order Amish, Mennonite, Beachy Amish, Swiss Mennonites, Swartzentruber Amish."

"Are there parties?"

"Well, they don't put up lights, of course. But they do celebrate. It's a lot of fun," Bontrager said. "Plus they have second Christmas."

"Second Christmas?" Byrne asked.

"Well, it's really just the day after Christmas. They usually spend it visiting their neighbors, eating a lot. Sometimes they even have mulled wine."

Jessica smiled. "Mulled wine. I had no idea."

Bontrager blushed. "How you gonna keep 'em down on the farm?"

As Jessica made the rounds of the hapless souls on the next shift, relaying her holiday wishes, she turned at the door.

Josh Bontrager sat at a desk, looking at the photos of the horrific scene they'd found on the Strawberry Mansion Bridge earlier that day. Jessica thought she saw a slight trembling in the young man's hands.

Welcome to Homicide.

# 37

Moon's book is the most precious thing in his life. It is large and leather-bound, heavy, with gilded edges. It had belonged to his grandfather, and his father before that. Inside the front, on the title page, is the signature of the author.

*This is more valuable than anything.*

*Sometimes, late at night, Moon carefully opens the*

book, looking at the words and drawings by candle-light, savoring the fragrance of the old paper. It smells of his childhood. Now, as then, he is careful not to get the candle too close. He loves the way the golden edges wink in the soft yellow glow.

The first illustration is of a soldier climbing a great tree, his knapsack slung over his shoulder. How many times had Moon been that soldier, the strong young man in search of the tinderbox?

The next illustration is of Little Claus and Big Claus. Moon had been both men, many times.

The next drawing is of Little Ida's flowers. Between Memorial Day and Labor Day, Moon used to run through the flowers. Spring and summer were magic times.

Now, as he enters the great structure, he is filled with magic again.

The building stands above the river, a lost majesty, a forgotten ruin not far from the city. The wind moans across the wide expanse. Moon carries the dead girl to the window. She is heavy in his arms. He places her on the stone windowsill, kisses her icy lips.

As Moon goes about his business, the nightingale sings, complaining of the cold.

I know, little bird, Moon thinks.

I know.

Moon has a plan for this, too. Soon he will bring the Snow Man, and winter will be banished forever.

# 38

"I'll be in the city later," Padraig said. "I've got to stop at Macy's."

"What do you need from there?" Byrne asked. He was on his cell phone, not five blocks from the store. He was on call, but his tour had ended at noon. They had gotten the call from CSU on the paint used at the Flat Rock crime scene. Standard marine paint, available everywhere. The graffiti image of the moon—although an important development—had led nowhere. As yet. "I can get whatever you need, Da."

"I'm out of the scruffing lotion."

*My God,* Byrne thought. *Scruffing lotion.* His father was in his sixties, tough as oak plank, and was just now entering a phase of unbridled narcissism.

Ever since the previous Christmas, when Byrne's daughter Colleen had purchased her grandfather an array of Clinique facial products, Padraig Byrne had been obsessed with his skin. Then, one day, Colleen had written a note to Padraig saying that his skin looked great. Padraig had beamed, and from that moment, the Clinique ritual had become a mania, an orgy of sexagenarian vanity.

"I can get it for you," Byrne said. "You don't have to drive in."

"I don't mind. I want to see what else they have. I think they have a new M Lotion."

It was hard to believe he was speaking to Padraig Byrne. The same Padraig Byrne who had spent nearly forty years on the docks, a man who had once taken on a half dozen drunken Italian Mummers with only his fists and a gutful of Harp lager.

"Just because you don't care about your skin, doesn't mean that I have to look like a lizard in my autumn years," Padraig added.

*Autumn?* Byrne thought. He checked his face in the rearview mirror. Maybe he *could* take better care of his skin at that. On the other hand, he had to admit that the real reason he offered to stop at the store was that he really didn't want his father driving across town in the snow. He was getting overprotective, but he couldn't seem to help it. His silence won the argument. This time.

"Okay, you win," Padraig said. "Pick it up for me. But I want to stop by Killian's later, though. To say good-bye to the boys."

"You're not moving to California," Byrne said. "You can go back anytime."

In Padraig Byrne's eyes, moving to the Northeast was the equivalent of moving out of the country. It had taken the man five years to make the decision, and five more to make the first move.

"So you say."

"Okay. I'll pick you up in an hour," Byrne said.

"Don't forget my scruffing lotion."

*Christ,* Byrne thought as he clicked off his cell phone. *Scruffing lotion.*

KILLIAN'S WAS A rough and tumble bar near Pier 84, in the shadow of the Walt Whitman Bridge, a ninety-year-old institution that had survived a thousand donnybrooks, two fires, and a wrecking ball. Not to mention four generations of dockworkers.

A few hundred feet from the Delaware River, Killian's

was a bastion of the ILA, the International Longshore-man's Association. These men lived, ate, and breathed the river.

Kevin and Padraig Byrne entered, turning every head in the bar toward the door and the icy blast of wind it brought with it.

*"Paddy!"* they seemed to yell in unison. Byrne took a seat at the bar while his father made the rounds. The bar was half full. Padraig was in his element.

Byrne surveyed the gang. He knew most of them. The Murphy brothers—Ciaran and Luke—had worked side by side with Padraig Byrne for nearly forty years. Luke was tall and robust; Ciaran was short and thickset. Next to them were Teddy O'Hara, Dave Doyle, Danny Mc-Manus, Little Tim Reilly. If this hadn't been the unofficial home of ILA Local 1291, it could have been the meetinghouse of the Sons of Hibernia.

Byrne grabbed his beer, made his way over to the long table.

"So, what, you need a passport to go up there?" Luke asked Padraig.

"Yeah," Padraig said. "I hear they have armed checkpoints on Roosevelt. How else we gonna keep out the South Philly riffraff from the Northeast?"

"Funny, we look at it exactly the opposite. Seems to me you did too. Back in the day."

Padraig nodded. They were right. He had no argument for it. The Northeast was a foreign country. Byrne saw that look cross his father's face, a look he had seen a number of times over the past few months, the look that all but screamed *Am I doing the right thing?*

A few more of the boys showed up. Some brought houseplants with bright red bows on pots covered in bright green foil. This was the tough guy version of a housewarming gift, the greenery undoubtedly purchased by the distaff half of the ILA. It was turning into a

Christmas party/going-away party for Padraig Byrne. The juke played "Silent Night: A Christmas in Rome" by the Chieftains. The lager flowed.

An hour later Byrne glanced at his watch, slipped his coat on. As he was saying his good-byes, Danny McManus approached with a young man Byrne didn't know.

"Kevin," Danny said. "Ever meet my youngest son, Paulie?"

Paul McManus was slender, a little birdlike in his demeanor, wore rimless glasses. He was not at all like the mountain that was his father. Still, he looked strong enough.

"Never had the pleasure," Byrne said, extending a hand. "Nice to meet you."

"You too, sir," Paul said.

"So, are you working the docks like your dad?" Byrne asked.

"Yes, sir," Paul said.

Everyone at the nearby table exchanged a glance, a quick inspection of the ceiling, their fingernails, anything but Danny McManus's face.

"Paulie works at Boathouse Row," Danny finally said.

"Ah, okay," Byrne said. "What do you do down there?"

"Always something to do at Boathouse Row," Paulie said. "Scraping, painting, shoring up the docks."

Boathouse Row was a cluster of privately owned boathouses on the eastern bank of the Schuylkill River, in Fairmount Park, right near the art museum. They were home to the sculling clubs, and managed by the Schuylkill Navy, one of the oldest amateur athletic organizations in the country. They were also about the furthest thing imaginable from the Packer Avenue Terminal.

Was it river work? Technically. Was it working the river? Not in this pub.

"Well, you know what da Vinci said," Paulie offered, standing his ground.

More sideways glances. More cleared throats, shuffled feet. He was actually going to quote Leonardo da Vinci. In *Killian's*. Byrne had to give the kid credit.

"What did he say?" Byrne asked.

"In rivers, the water that you touch is the last of what has passed, and the first of that which comes," Paulie said. "Or something like that."

Everybody took a long, slow gulp from their bottle, no one wanting to be the first to say anything. Finally, Danny put an arm around his son. "He's a poet. What can you say?"

Three of the men at the table pushed their shot glasses, brimming with Jameson, over toward Paulie McManus. "Drink up, da Vinci," they said in unison.

They all laughed. Paulie drank.

A few moments later Byrne stood at the door, watching his father throw darts. Padraig Byrne was two games up on Luke Murphy. He was also up three lagers. Byrne wondered if his father should even be drinking at all these days. On the other hand, Byrne had never seen his father tipsy, let alone drunk.

The men formed a line on either side of the dartboard. Byrne imagined them all as young men in their twenties, just starting out with families, the notions of hard work and union loyalty and city pride a bright red pulse in their veins. They'd been coming to this place for more than forty years. Some even longer. Through every Phillies and Eagles and Flyers and Sixers season, through every mayor, through every municipal and private scandal, through all of their marriages and births and divorces and deaths. Killian's was a constant, and the lives and dreams and hopes of its denizens were, too.

His father threw a bull's-eye. Cheers and disbelief

erupted around the bar. Another round. And so it went for Paddy Byrne.

Byrne thought about his father's upcoming move. They had the truck scheduled for February 4. This move was the best thing for his father. It was quieter in the Northeast, slower. He knew that this was the beginning of a new life, but he could not shake that other feeling, the distinct and unsettling feeling that it was also the end of something.

# 39

The Devonshire Acres mental-health facility sat on a gentle slope in a small town in southeastern Pennsylvania. In its glory years, the huge fieldstone and mortar complex had been a spa and convalescent home for wealthy Main Line families. Now it was a state-subsidized long-term warehouse for lower income patients who required constant supervision.

Roland Hannah signed in, declining the escort. He knew his way around. He took the stairs to the second floor one at a time. He was in no hurry. The institutional-green hallways were ornamented with cheerless, time-faded Christmas decorations. Some looked as if they were from the 1940s or 1950s: jolly water-stained Santas, reindeer with their antlers bent and taped and repaired with long-yellowed Scotch tape. One wall held a message misspelled in individual letters made of cotton, construction paper, and silver glitter:

## HAPPY HODLIAYS!

Charles no longer came inside the facility.

ROLAND FOUND HER in the common room, near a window overlooking the rear grounds and the forest beyond. It had snowed for two days straight and a layer of white caressed the hills. Roland wondered what it looked like to her, through her young old eyes. He wondered what memories, if any, were triggered by the soft planes of virgin snow. Did she remember her first winter in the north? Did she remember snowflakes on her tongue? Snowmen?

Her skin was papery, fragrant, translucent. Her hair had long ago spent its gold.

There were four others in the room. Roland knew them all. They did not acknowledge him in any way. He crossed the room, removed his coat and gloves, put the present on the table. It was a robe and slippers, both lavender. Charles had meticulously wrapped and rewrapped the gift in festive foil paper featuring elves and workbenches and brightly colored tools.

Roland kissed her on the top of her head. She did not respond.

Outside the snow continued to fall—huge velvety flakes that lilted silently down. She watched, seeming to select an individual flake from the flurry, following it to the ledge, to the earth below, beyond.

They sat, not speaking. She had said only a few words in many years. The music in the background was Perry Como's "I'll Be Home for Christmas."

At six o'clock they brought her a tray. Creamed corn, breaded fish sticks, Tater Tots, along with a butter cookie with green and red sprinkles on a Christmas tree made of white icing. Roland watched as she arranged and rearranged her red plastic silverware from the outside in—fork, spoon, knife, then the reverse order. Three times. Always three times, until she had it right. Never two, never four, never more. Roland always wondered by what internal abacus this number had been determined.

"Merry Christmas," Roland said.

She looked up at him, eyes the palest blue. Behind them lived a universe of mystery.

Roland glanced at his watch. It was time to go.

Before he could stand up she took his hand in hers. Her fingers were carved ivory. Roland saw her lips tremble, and knew what was coming.

"Here are maidens, young and fair," she said. "Dancing in the summer air."

Roland felt the glaciers of his heart dislodge. He knew it was all Artemisia Hannah Waite remembered of her daughter Charlotte, and those terrible days in 1995.

"Like two spinning wheels at play," Roland answered.

His mother smiled, and finished the verse: "Pretty maidens dance away."

ROLAND FOUND CHARLES standing next to the van. A dusting of snow sat on his shoulders. In years past, Charles would look into Roland's eyes at this moment, searching for some sign that things had improved. Even to Charles, with his innate optimism, this was a practice long since dropped. Without a word, they slipped into the van.

After a brief prayer, they drove back to the city.

THEY ATE IN silence. When they were finished, Charles cleared the dishes. Roland could hear the television news in the office. A few moments later Charles poked his head around the corner.

"Come here and look at this," Charles said.

Roland walked into the small office. On the television screen was a shot of the parking lot at the Roundhouse, the police administration building on Race Street. Channel Six was doing a remote stand up. A reporter was following a woman across the parking lot.

The woman was young, dark-eyed, attractive. She carried herself with a great deal of poise and confidence. She wore a black leather coat and gloves. The name under her face on the screen said she was a detective. The reporter asked her questions. Charles turned up the volume on the television.

"—the work of one person?" the reporter asked.

"We can't rule that in or out," the detective said.

"Is it true that the woman was mutilated?"

"I can't comment on specifics related to the investigation."

"Is there anything you'd like to say to our viewers?"

"What we're asking for is help in finding the killer of Kristina Jakos. If you know something, even something that seems insignificant, please call the Homicide Unit of the PPD."

With this the woman turned and headed into the building.

*Kristina Jakos,* Roland thought. She was the woman they found murdered on the bank of the Schuylkill River in Manayunk. Roland had the news clipping on the corkboard next to his desk. He would read more about the case now. He grabbed a pen and wrote down the detective's name.

*Jessica Balzano.*

# 40

Sophie Balzano was clearly psychic when it came to Christmas presents. She didn't even need to shake the package. Like a miniature Carnac the Magnificent, she could place the gift against her forehead, and within seconds, by some little-girl magic, she seemed to be able to divine its contents. She clearly had a future in law enforcement. Or maybe Customs.

"This is shoes," she said.

She sat on the living-room floor, at the foot of the huge Christmas tree. Next to her sat her grandfather.

"I'm not telling," Peter Giovanni said.

Sophie then picked up one of the fairy-tale books Jessica had gotten from the library. She began to flip through it.

Jessica watched her daughter, thinking: *Find me a clue in there, sweetie.*

PETER GIOVANNI HAD spent nearly thirty years on the Philadelphia police force. He had been awarded many commendations, retiring with the rank of lieutenant.

Peter had lost his wife to breast cancer more than two decades earlier, and he had buried his only son, Michael, killed in Kuwait in 1991. Through it all he had identified himself as one thing, had one face that he presented to the world, one banner held high—that of policeman. And although he feared for his daughter every day, as any father would, his deepest sense of pride in life was the fact that his daughter was a homicide detective.

In his early sixties, Peter Giovanni was still active in the community, as well as in a number of police department charities. He was not a big man, but he carried a power that came from within. He still worked out a few times a week. He was still a clotheshorse, too. Today he wore an expensive black cashmere turtleneck and dove gray wool slacks. His shoes were Santoni loafers. With his ice gray hair, he looked like he had stepped off the pages of *GQ*.

He smoothed his granddaughter's hair, stood up, sat down next to Jessica on the sofa. Jessica was threading popcorn for a garland.

"What do you think of the tree?" he asked.

Every year, Peter and Vincent took Sophie on a drive to a Christmas-tree farm in the appropriately named Tabernacle, New Jersey, where they would cut down their own tree. Usually one of Sophie's choosing. Every year the tree seemed taller.

"Any bigger and we're going to have to move," Jessica said.

Peter smiled. "Hey. Sophie's getting bigger. The tree has to keep pace."

*Don't remind me,* Jessica thought.

Peter picked up a needle and thread, began to make his own popcorn garland. "Any leads on the case?" he asked.

Although Jessica was not investigating the Walt Brigham murder, and had three open files on her desk, she knew exactly what her father meant by "the case." Whenever a cop was killed, all police officers, active and retired, all across the country, took it personally.

"Nothing yet," Jessica said.

Peter shook his head. "Damn shame. There's a special place in hell for cop killers."

*Cop killer.* Jessica's gaze immediately went to Sophie, who was still camped by the tree, pondering a small box wrapped in red foil. Every time Jessica thought about the words "cop killer" she realized that both of this little girl's parents were targets every day of the week. Was it fair to Sophie? At times like these, in the warmth and safety of their home, she wasn't sure.

Jessica got up, stepped into the kitchen. Everything was under control. The gravy was simmering; the lasagna noodles were al dente, salad was made, wine was decanted. She took the ricotta out of the refrigerator.

The phone rang. She froze, hoping that it would only ring once, that the person on the other end would realize they had dialed the wrong number and hang up. A second passed. Then another.

*Yes.*

Then it rang again.

Jessica looked at her father. He looked back. They were both cops. It was Christmas Eve. They knew.

# 41

Byrne adjusted his tie for what might have been the twentieth time. He sipped his water, looked at his watch, smoothed the tablecloth. He wore a new suit, and he hadn't gotten comfortable in it yet. He fidgeted, buttoned, unbuttoned, rebuttoned, flattened the lapels.

He was sitting at a table at Striped Bass on Walnut Street, one of the tonier restaurants in Philadelphia, waiting for his date. But it wasn't just another date. For Kevin Byrne, it was *the* date. He was having Christmas Eve dinner with his daughter, Colleen. He had called in no fewer than four chits to wrangle the last-minute reservation.

He and Colleen had mutually agreed on this arrangement—dinner out—instead of trying to find a window of a few hours at his ex-wife's house to celebrate the holiday, a window that did not include Donna Sullivan Byrne's new boyfriend, or the awkwardness of Kevin Byrne trying to be a grown-up about the whole thing.

They agreed that they didn't need the tension. This was better.

Except for the fact that his daughter was late.

Byrne glanced around the restaurant, coming to the conclusion that he was the only civil servant in the room. Doctors, lawyers, investment bankers, a sprinkling of successful artist-types. He knew that taking Colleen here was overkill—she knew it too—but he wanted to make the evening special.

He took out his cell phone, checked it. Nothing. He was just about to send Colleen a text message when someone approached his table. Byrne looked up. It wasn't Colleen.

"Would you like to see the wine list?" the attentive waiter asked again.

"Sure," Byrne said. As if he would know what he was looking at. He had twice resisted ordering bourbon on the rocks. He didn't want to be sloppy this night. A minute later the waiter returned with the list. Byrne dutifully read it, the only thing registering—amid a sea of words like *Pinot, Cabernet, Vouvray,* and *Fume*—were the prices, all of them beyond his means.

He held the wine list up, figuring that if he put it down he would be pounced upon and forced to order a bottle.

Then he saw her. She wore a royal blue dress that brought infinity to her aquamarine eyes. Her hair was down around her shoulders, longer than he had seen it in a while, darker than it was in summer.

*My God*, Byrne thought. *She's a woman. She became a woman and I missed it.*

"I'm sorry I'm late," she signed before she was halfway across the room. People stared at her, for any number of reasons. Her elegant sign language, her posture and grace, her stunning looks.

Colleen Siobhan Byrne had been deaf since birth. It had only been in the past few years that both she and her father had become comfortable with her deafness. Whereas Colleen had never seen it as a handicap, it seemed she now understood that her father once had, and probably still did to a degree. A degree that was lessening by the year.

Byrne stood, gave his daughter a soul-replenishing hug.

"Merry Christmas, Dad," she signed.

"Merry Christmas, honey," he signed back.

"I couldn't get a cab."

Byrne waved a hand as if to say: *What? You think I was worried?*

She sat down. Within seconds her cell phone vibrated. She gave her father a sheepish grin, pulled out the phone, flipped it open. It was a text message. Byrne watched her read it, smile, blush. The message was clearly from a boy. Colleen sent a quick reply, put her phone away.

"Sorry," she signed.

Byrne wanted to ask his daughter two or three million questions. He stopped himself. He watched her delicately place her napkin on her lap, sip her water, peruse the menu. She had a woman's bearing, a woman's poise. There could be only one reason for this, Byrne thought, his heart shifting and cracking in his chest. Her child-hood was over.

And life would never be the same.

WHEN THEY FINISHED eating, it was that time. They both knew it. Colleen was full of teenage energy, prob-ably had a friend's Christmas party to attend. Plus she had to pack. She and her mother were going out of town for a week, visiting Donna's relatives for New Year's Eve.

"Did you get my card?" Colleen signed.

"I did. Thanks."

Byrne silently chastised himself for not sending out Christmas cards, especially to the one person who mat-tered. He'd even gotten a card from Jessica, slipped covertly into his briefcase. He saw Colleen sneak a glance at her watch. Before the moment became uncom-fortable, Byrne signed, "Can I ask you something?"

"Sure."

*Here goes,* Byrne thought. "What are your dreams?"

A flush, then a look of confusion, then acceptance. At least she didn't roll her eyes. "Is this going to be one of our talks?" she signed.

She smiled and Byrne's stomach flipped. She didn't have time to talk. She probably wouldn't have time for years to come. "No," he said, feeling his ears get hot. "I was just wondering."

A few minutes later she kissed him good-bye. She promised that they would have a heart-to-heart soon. He put her in a cab, returned to the table, ordered the bourbon. A double. Before it arrived, his cell phone rang.

It was Jessica.

"What's up?" he asked. But he knew that tone.

In response to his question, his partner uttered the

four worst words a homicide detective could hear on Christmas Eve.

"We've got a body."

# 42

The crime scene was once again on the bank of the Schuylkill River, this time adjacent to the Shawmont train station, near Upper Roxborough. The Shawmont station was one of the oldest stations in the United States. The trains no longer stopped there, and it had fallen into disrepair, but it was a frequent stop for railroad aficionados and purists, much photographed and rendered.

Just below the station, down a steep incline that angled toward the river, was the enormous derelict Shawmont waterworks, located on one of the last publicly owned riverfront parcels of land in the city.

The exterior of the mammoth pump house was overgrown with decades of scrub and vines and gnarled branches hanging from dead trees. In daylight it was an imposing relic of a time when the facility had taken water from the pool behind Flat Rock Dam and pumped it up to the Roxborough Reservoir. At night it was all but an urban mausoleum, a dark and forbidding haven for drug deals, clandestine unions of all sorts. The inside was gutted, stripped of anything even remotely of value. There was graffiti around the walls to a height of seven feet or so. A few ambitious taggers had written their sentiments at a height of perhaps fifteen feet on one wall.

The floor was an uneven topography of pebbled concrete, rusted iron, and sundry urban rubble.

As Jessica and Byrne approached the building, they could see the bright temporary lights illuminating the front of the building, the façade facing the river. A dozen officers, CSU techs, and detectives waited for them.

The dead woman sat in the window, legs crossed at the ankles, hands folded in her lap. Unlike Kristina Jakos, this victim did not appear to be mutilated in any way. At first, it looked as if she were praying, but closer inspection showed that her hands were cupped around an object.

Jessica stepped into the building. It was almost medieval in scale. Since the facility's closing, it had fallen into decay. A number of ideas had been floated regarding its future, not the least of which had been the possibility of turning it into a training facility for the Philadelphia Eagles. The cost of renovation would be enormous, though, and so far nothing had been done.

Jessica approached the victim, careful not to disturb any possible footprints, although there was no snow inside the building and collecting any thing usable was unlikely. She shone her light on the victim. This woman was in her late twenties or early thirties. She wore a long dress. It, too, seemed to be from another time, with its elasticized velvet bodice and fully shirred skirt. There was a nylon belt around her neck, knotted at the back. It appeared to be an exact duplicate of the one found around the neck of Kristina Jakos.

Jessica hugged the wall as she scanned the interior. The CSU techs would soon be setting up a grid. Before leaving, she took her Maglite, made a slow careful sweep of the walls. And saw it. About twenty feet to the right of the window, buried in a jumble of gang tags, was the graffiti of the white moon.

"Kevin."

Byrne stepped inside, followed the beam of light. He turned, found Jessica's eyes in the gloom. They had stood there before, as partners, at the threshold of a burgeoning evil, at a moment when something they thought they'd understood had become something bigger, something far more sinister, something that had redefined everything they'd believed about a case.

Standing outside, their breath formed vapor clouds in the night air. "ME's office won't be here for an hour or so," Byrne said.

"An hour?"

"Christmas in Philly," Byrne said. "Two other homicides already. They're stretched."

Byrne pointed to the victim's hands. "She's holding something."

Jessica looked closely. Something was in the woman's grasp. Jessica took a number of close-up pictures.

If they were to follow procedure to the letter, they would have to wait for the ME's office to pronounce the woman dead, and for a full set of photographs and perhaps video to be taken of the victim and the scene. But Philadelphia was not exactly following procedure this night—that bit about love thy neighbor came to mind, followed closely by that peace-on-earth business—and the detectives knew that the longer they waited, the more likely it was that precious information would be lost to the elements.

Byrne stepped closer, tried to gently pry apart the woman's fingers. Her fingertips responded to his touch. Full rigor had not set in.

At first glance it appeared that the victim had a ball of leaves or twigs in her cupped hands. In the harsh light it looked to be a dark brown material, definitely organic. Byrne stepped closer, set himself. He spread a large evidence bag on the woman's lap. Jessica tried to hold her Maglite steady. Byrne continued to pry apart the victim's grasp, slowly, one finger at a time. If the woman had scooped a ball of earth or compost from the ground during a struggle, it was possible that she had gotten important evidence from her killer lodged beneath her nails. There could even have been a piece of direct evidence in her hands—a button, a clasp, a piece of fabric. If something, such as hair or fiber or DNA evidence, could immediately point to an individual of interest, the sooner they could begin looking for him the better.

Little by little, Byrne pulled back the woman's dead fingers. When he finally had four fingers back on her right hand, they saw something they did not expect to see. In death this woman was not holding a fistful of earth or leaves or twigs. In death she held a small brown bird. In the light thrown by the emergency lamps it appeared to be a sparrow, or perhaps a wren.

Byrne gently closed the victim's fingers. They would place a clear plastic evidence bag around them to preserve every trace of evidence. This was far beyond their ability to assess or analyze in situ.

Then something totally unexpected happened. The bird wiggled out of the dead woman's grip and flew away. It darted around inside the huge, shadowed space of the waterworks, the beat of its flitting wings resonating off the icy stone walls, chirping either in protest or relief. Then it was gone.

"Son of a *bitch*," Byrne yelled. "*Fuck.*"

This was not good news for the team. They should have immediately bagged the corpse's hands and waited. The bird might have provided a host of forensic details, but even in its departure it yielded some information. It meant that the body could not have been there that long. The fact that the bird was still alive—perhaps preserved by the warmth of the cadaver—meant that the killer had posed this victim within the last few hours.

Jessica aimed her Maglite at the ground beneath the

window. A few of the bird's feathers remained. Byrne pointed them out to a CSU officer, who picked them up with a pair of forceps and placed them in an evidence bag.

They would now wait for the ME's office.

JESSICA WALKED TO the bank of the river, looked out, then back at the body. The figure was perched in the window, high above the gentle slope that ran to the road, then more steeply to the soft bank of the river.

*Another doll on a shelf,* Jessica thought.

Like Kristina Jakos, this victim faced the river. Like Kristina Jakos, she had a painting of the moon nearby. There was little doubt that there would be another painting on her body, an image of the moon rendered in semen and blood.

THE MEDIA SHOWED up just before midnight. They clustered at the top of the cutoff, near the train station, behind the crime-scene tape. It always amazed Jessica how fast they could get to a crime scene.

The story would make the morning editions of the paper.

# 43

The crime scene was locked down, sealed off from the city. The media had gone off to file their stories. CSU would process the evidence through the night, and far into the next day.

Jessica and Byrne stood near the river's edge. Neither could bring themselves to leave.

"You gonna be okay?" Jessica asked.

"Yeah." Byrne took a pint of bourbon out of his coat pocket. He toyed with the cap. Jessica saw it, said nothing. They were off duty.

After a full minute of silence, Byrne glanced over. "What?"

"You," she said. "You've got that look in your eye."

"What look?"

"The Andy Griffith look. The look that says you're thinking about turning in your papers and getting a sheriff's job in Mayberry."

"Meadville."

"See?"

"You cold?"

*Freezing my ass off,* Jessica thought. "Nah."

Byrne hit the bourbon, held it out. Jessica shook her head. He capped the bottle, held it.

"Years ago we used to drive out to my uncle's place in Jersey," he said. "I always knew when we were getting close because we would come upon this old cemetery. And by *old* I mean Civil War old. Maybe older. There was this small stone house by the gate, probably the caretaker's house, and in the front window was this sign that read: 'FREE FILL DIRT.' Ever see signs like that?"

Jessica had. She told him so. Byrne continued.

"When you're a kid, you never give stuff like that a second thought, you know? Year after year I saw that sign. It never moved, just faded in the sunlight. Every year, those blocky red letters got lighter and lighter. Then my uncle passed, my aunt moved back to the city, we stopped going out there.

"Years later, after my mother died, I went to her grave one day. Perfect summer afternoon. Blue sky, cloudless. I'm sitting there, telling her how things are going. A few plots down there was a fresh gravesite, right? And it suddenly hit me. I suddenly knew why that cemetery had free fill dirt. Why *all* cemeteries have free fill dirt. I thought about all those people who took them up on that offer over the years, filling their gardens, their potted plants, their window boxes. The cemeteries make space in the earth for the dead, and people take that dirt and grow things in it."

Jessica just looked at Byrne. The longer she knew the man, the more layers she saw. "That's, well, beautiful," she said, getting a little emotional, battling it. "I never would have thought of it that way."

"Yeah, well," Byrne said. "We Irish are all poets, you know." He uncapped the pint, took a swallow, capped it again. "And drinkers."

Jessica eased the bottle out of his hands. He didn't resist.

"Get some sleep, Kevin."

"I will. I just hate it when we're getting played and I can't put my finger on it."

"Me, too," Jessica said. She fished her keys out of her pocket, snuck another peek at her watch, then immediately chided herself about it. "You know, you ought to go running with me sometime."

"Running."

"Yeah," she said. "That's like walking, but faster."

"Ah, okay. It kind of rings a bell. I think I did it once when I was a kid."

"I may have a boxing match set up for the end of March, so I better start doing roadwork. We could run together. It does wonders, believe me. Clears the mind completely."

Byrne tried to suppress the laughter. "Jess. The only time I plan on running is when someone is chasing me. And I mean a big guy. With a knife."

The wind picked up. Jessica shivered, turned up her

collar. "I'm gonna go." There was a lot more she wanted to say, but there would be time. "You *sure* you're okay?"

"Never better."

*Right, partner,* she thought. She walked back to her car, slipped in, started it. As she pulled away she glanced at her rearview mirror, saw Byrne silhouetted against the lights on the other side of the river, now just another shadow in the night.

She looked at her watch. It was 1:15 AM.

It was Christmas Day.

# 44

Christmas morning broke clear and cold, bright with promise.

Pastor Roland Hannah and Deacon Charles Waite offered service at 7:00 AM. Roland's sermon was one of hope, of renewal. He spoke of The Cross and The Cradle. He quoted Matthew 2:1-12.

The baskets overflowed.

LATER, ROLAND AND Charles sat at the table in the basement beneath the church, a pot of cooling coffee between them. In an hour they would begin to prepare a Christmas ham dinner for upwards of one hundred homeless people. It would be served at their new facility on Second Street.

"Look at this," Charles said. He handed Roland the morning's *Inquirer*. There had been another murder.

Nothing special in Philadelphia, but this one had resonance. Deep resonance. This one had an echo that reverberated over the years.

A woman had been found in Shawmont. She had been discovered at the old waterworks near the train station, just on the eastern bank of the Schuylkill.

Roland's pulse raced. Two bodies found on the banks of the Schuylkill River in one week. Then there was the story in the previous day's paper, an article reporting that Detective Walter Brigham had been murdered. Roland and Charles knew all about Walter Brigham.

There was no denying the truth of it.

Charlotte and her friend had been found on the bank of the Wissahickon. They had been posed, just like these two women. Maybe, after all these years, it was not about girls. Maybe it was about the *water*.

Maybe this was a sign.

Charles dropped to his knees and prayed. His big shoulders shook. In moments he was whispering in tongues. Charles was a glossolalic, a true believer who, when overtaken by the spirit, would speak in what he believed to be God's idiom, an edification of one's self. To the casual observer, it might have sounded like so much gibberish. To the believer, to one moved to tongues, it was the language of Heaven.

Roland glanced back at the newspaper, closed his eyes. Soon, a divine calm descended upon him, and a voice inside gave query to his thoughts.

*Is it him?*

Roland touched the crucifix around his neck.

And knew the answer.

# PART THREE

# THE RIVER DARKNESS

# 45

"Why are we in here with the door closed, Sarge?" Park asked.

Tony Park was one of the few Korean-American detectives on the force. A family man in his late forties, a wizard on the computer, a skilled interrogator in the room, there was not a more practical, street-wise detective on the force than Anthony Kim Park. This time, his question was on the mind of everyone in the room.

The task force was four detectives strong. Kevin Byrne, Jessica Balzano, Joshua Bontrager, and Tony Park. Considering the enormous job of coordinating the forensic sections, collecting witness statements, conducting interviews, and all the other minutiae that made up a homicide investigation—a pair of *related* homicide investigations—the task force was meager. There simply was not enough manpower available.

"The door's closed for two reasons," Ike Buchanan said, "and I think you know the first one."

They all did. Task forces were played close to the vest these days, especially those given the challenge of hunting a compulsive killer. Mostly because a small group of men and women tasked with tracking down an individual had a way of drawing that individual to them, putting wives, children, friends, and family in jeopardy. It had happened to both Jessica and Byrne. It happened more than the general public knew.

"The second reason is, and I'm sorry to have to say this, is that things have had a way of making it into the media from this office lately. I don't want to start any rumors or any panic," Buchanan said. "Besides, as far as the city is concerned, we're not sure we have a compulsive out there. Right now, the media thinks we have two unsolved homicides that may or not be related. Let's see if we can keep it that way for a while."

It was always a delicate balance with the media. There were a lot of reasons not to give them too much information. Information had a way of rapidly becoming *dis*information. If the media ran with a story that a serial killer was walking the streets of Philadelphia, many things could result, most of them bad. Not the least of which was the possibility of a copycat killer taking the opportunity to get rid of a mother-in-law, husband, wife, boyfriend, boss. On the other hand, there had been a number of occasions when the newspapers and television stations had broadcast a suspect sketch for the PPD and within days—sometimes hours—they'd had their man.

As of this morning, the day after Christmas, the department had not yet released any specific details about the second victim.

"Where are we on the ID on the Shawmont victim?" Buchanan asked.

"Her name was Tara Grendel," Bontrager said. "She was identified through her DMV records. Her car was found half in, half out of a parking space at an indoor lot on Walnut. We're not sure if that was the abduction site or not, but it looks good for it."

"What was she doing in that garage? Did she work nearby?"

"She was an actress, working under the name Tara Lynn Greene. She had an audition the day she went missing."

"Where was the audition?"

"At the Walnut Street Theater," Bontrager said. He flipped back through his notes. "She left the theater alone at around 1 PM. Parking lot attendant said she walked in about ten after one, took the steps to the basement."

"Do they have surveillance cameras?"

"They do. But nothing is taped."

The maddening news was that there was another "moon" painting on Tara Grendel's abdomen. A DNA report was in the works to determine if there was a match to the blood and semen found on Kristina Jakos.

"We showed Tara's picture around Stiletto, and to Natalya Jakos," Byrne said. "Tara was not a dancer at the club. Natalya didn't recognize her. If she's connected to Kristina Jakos, it's not from her place of employment."

"What about Tara's family?"

"No family in town. Father deceased, mother living in Indiana," Bontrager said. "She's been notified. She's flying in tomorrow."

"What do we have on the crime scenes?" Buchanan asked.

"Not much," Byrne said. "No footprints, no tire tracks."

"And the clothes?" Buchanan asked.

The consensus now was that the killer was dressing his victims. "Both vintage dresses," Jessica said.

"We're talking thrift-store stuff?"

"Could be," Jessica said. They had a list of more than one hundred secondhand clothing and thrift stores. Unfortunately, the turnover in both product and personnel at such stores was quick, and none of the stores kept any detailed records of what came in and went out. It was going to take a lot of shoe leather and interviews to gather any information.

"Why these particular dresses?" Buchanan asked. "Are they from a play? A movie? A famous picture?"

"Working on it, Sarge."

"Walk me through it," Buchanan said.

Jessica went first. "Two victims, both white women in their twenties, both strangled, both left on the bank of the Schuylkill. Both victims had a drawing on their bodies, a detailed painting of the moon rendered in semen and blood. Both crime scenes had a similar drawing painted on a wall nearby. The first victim had her feet amputated. These body parts were recovered on the Strawberry Mansion Bridge."

Jessica flipped her notes back. "First victim was Kristina Jakos. Born in Odessa in the Ukraine, moved to the United States with her sister Natalya and brother Kostya. Parents deceased, no other relatives in the States. Until a few weeks ago Kristina lived with her sister in the Northeast. Kristina recently moved to North Lawrence with her roommate, one Sonja Kedrova, also from the Ukraine. Kostya Jakos is pulling a ten-year stretch in Graterford for aggravated assault. Kristina recently got a job at a Center City gentlemen's club called Stiletto, where she worked as an exotic dancer. On the night she went missing she was last seen at the All-City Launderette at approximately 11 PM."

"Do you think there's any connection to the brother?" Buchanan asked.

"Hard to say," Park said. "Kostya Jakos's victim was an elderly widow from Merion Station. Her son is in his sixties, no grandchildren in the area. It would be a pretty brutal payback if that was the case."

"What about something he stirred up inside?"

"He hasn't been a model prisoner, but nothing jumps over the wall as a motive to do this to his sister."

"Have we gotten DNA back on this blood-moon drawing on Jakos?" Buchanan asked.

"DNA on Kristina Jakos's drawing is in," Tony Park said. "The blood is not hers. The workup on the second victim is still out."

"Have we run it through CODIS?"

"Yes," Park said. The FBI Laboratory's Combined DNA Index System enabled federal, state, and local crime labs to exchange and compare DNA profiles electronically, thereby linking crimes to each other and to convicted offenders. "Nothing yet on that front."

"What about some crazy son of a bitch from the strip club?" Buchanan asked.

"I'm talking later today or tomorrow to some of the girls from the club who knew Kristina," Byrne said.

"What about this bird that was found at the Shawmont site?" Buchanan asked.

Jessica glanced at Byrne. *Found* was the word that stuck. No one had mentioned that the bird had flown away due to Byrne's prodding open the victim's hands.

"The feathers are at the lab," Tony Park said. "One of the techs is an avid birder, and he says he is not familiar with it. He's on it right now."

"Good," Buchanan said. "What else?"

"It looks like the killer used a carpenter's handsaw on the first victim," Jessica said. "Trace of sawdust was found in the wound. So, maybe a boatbuilder? Dock builder? Dock*worker*?"

"Kristina had been working on building sets for a Christmas play," Byrne said.

"Have we interviewed people she worked with at the church?"

"Yeah," Byrne said. "No one of interest."

"Any mutilation of the second victim?" Buchanan asked.

Jessica shook her head. "Body was intact."

At first they had entertained the possibility that their

killer was taking body parts as souvenirs. It looked less likely now.

"Any sexual angle?" Buchanan asked.

Jessica wasn't sure. "Well, despite the presence of the semen, there was no evidence of sexual assault."

"Similar murder weapon in both cases?" Buchanan asked.

"Identical," Byrne said. "Lab thinks it's the type of rope they use to separate the lanes in a swimming pool. However, they haven't found any trace of chlorine. They're running some more tests on the fibers now."

There were plenty of industries linked to the water trades in Philadelphia, a city that had two rivers to nurture and exploit. Sailing and powerboating on the Delaware. Sculling on the Schuylkill. Each year there were a number of events on both rivers. There was the Schuylkill Sojourn, a seven-day float up the entire length of the river. Then there was the Dad Vail Regatta, the largest collegiate regatta in the United States, with more than one thousand athletes taking part in the event, held the second week of May.

"The dump sites on the Schuylkill indicate that we are probably looking for someone with a pretty good working knowledge of the river," Jessica said.

Byrne thought of Paulie McManus, and his Leonardo da Vinci quote. *In rivers, the water that you touch is the last of what has passed and the first of that which comes.*

*What the hell was coming?* Byrne wondered.

"What about the sites themselves?" Buchanan asked. "Any significance?"

"Plenty of history in Manayunk. Same with Shawmont. So far, nothing has clicked."

Buchanan sat down, rubbed his hands over his eyes. "One singer, one dancer, both white and in their twenties. Both public abductions. There's a connection between these two victims, detectives. Find it."

There was a knock on the door. Byrne opened it. It was Nicci Malone.

"Got a minute, boss?" Nicci asked.

"Yeah," Buchanan said. Jessica thought she had never heard anyone sound quite so exhausted. Ike Buchanan was the link between the unit and the brass. If it happened on his watch, it came through him. He nodded to the four detectives. It was time to get back to work. They exited the office. Just as they were leaving, Nicci poked her head back through the doorway.

"There's someone downstairs to see you, Jess."

# 46

"I'm Detective Balzano."

The man waiting for Jessica in the lobby was in his mid-fifties—rust flannel shirt, tan Levi's, duck boots. He had thick fingers, bushy eyebrows, a complexion that complained of too many Philly Decembers.

"My name is Frank Pustelnik," he said, extending a callused hand. Jessica shook it. "I own a restaurant supply business on Flat Rock Road."

"What can I do for you, Mr. Pustelnik?"

"I've been reading about what happened at the old warehouse. And then of course I've seen all the activity over there." He held up a videocassette. "I have a surveillance camera on my lot. The lot that faces the building where . . . you know."

"That's a surveillance tape?"

"Yes."

"What's on it, exactly?" Jessica asked.

"I'm not really sure, but I think there's something you may want to see."

"When was the tape recorded?"

Frank Pustelnik handed Jessica the cassette. "It's from the day the body was found."

THEY STOOD BEHIND Mateo Fuentes in the editing bay of the AV Unit. Jessica, Byrne, and Frank Pustelnik.

Mateo popped the tape into a time-lapse VCR. He forwarded the tape. The images sped by. Most surveillance video machines recorded at a much slower speed than a regular VCR, so when they were played back on a consumer machine they were far too fast to watch.

The static night images rolled. Finally the picture got a little lighter.

"Right about there," Pustelnik said.

Mateo stopped the tape, hit PLAY. It was a high-angle shot. The time code indicated 7:00 AM.

In the far background was the parking lot of the crime-scene warehouse. The image was fuzzy, sparsely lighted. On the left side of the screen, near the top, was a small, light-colored blur near the area where the parking lot sloped down to the river. The image sent a shiver through Jessica. The blur was Kristina Jakos.

At the 7:07 AM mark, across the top of the screen, a car entered the parking lot. It moved right to left. It was impossible to tell the color, let alone the make or model. The car pulled around the back of the building. They lost sight of it. A few moments later a shadow lurched across the top of the screen. It appeared that someone was crossing the lot, heading toward the river, toward Kristina Jakos's body. Soon after, the dark shape blended into the darkness of the trees.

Then the shadow detached from the background, moved again. This time, quickly. Jessica deduced that whoever had driven in had crossed the lot, spotted Kristina Jakos's body, and then returned to his or her vehicle at a run. Seconds later, the car circled out from behind the building and sped for the exit onto Flat Rock Road. Then the surveillance video returned to its static status. Just the small light-colored smear near the river, the smudge that had once been a human life.

Mateo rewound the tape until the point just before the car drove away. He hit PLAY and let it run until they had a good angle on the rear of the automobile as it turned onto Flat Rock Road. He froze the image.

"Can you tell what kind of car that is?" Byrne asked Jessica. Her years in the Auto Unit made her the resident automobile expert. Although she didn't know some of the 2006 and 2007 models, she was good with luxury cars over the past decade. The Auto Unit dealt with a lot of stolen luxury cars.

"Looks like a BMW," Jessica said.

"Can we move in on that?" Byrne asked.

"Does *ursus americanus* defecate in its natural habitat?" Mateo asked.

Byrne glanced at Jessica, shrugged. Neither of them had any idea what Mateo was talking about. "I suppose it does," Byrne said. Sometimes you had to humor Officer Fuentes.

Mateo worked his dials. The image increased in size, but did not become significantly clearer. It was definitely the BMW logo on the car's trunk.

"Can you tell what model that is?" Byrne asked.

"It looks like a 525i," Jessica said.

"What about the plate?"

Mateo shifted the image, pulled back some. The

image was just a whitish gray rectangle of a smear, and there was only half of it at that.

"That's it?" Byrne asked.

Mateo glowered at him. "What do you think we do down here, Detective?"

"I've never been quite sure," Byrne said.

"You need to stand back to see it."

"How far back?" Byrne asked. "Camden?"

Mateo centered the image on the screen, zoomed in. Jessica and Byrne took a few steps back, squinted at the resulting image. Nothing. A few more steps. They were now out in the hallway.

"What do you think?" Jessica asked.

"I don't see anything," Byrne said.

They moved back as far as they could. The image on the screen was highly pixilated, but it was starting to take shape. It looked like the first two letters were HO.

HO.

HORNEE1, Jessica thought. She tossed a glance at Byrne, who said aloud what she was thinking:

"Son of a *bitch*."


# 47


David Hornstrom sat in one of the four interrogation rooms in the Homicide Unit. He had come in under his own power, and that was a good thing. If they had gone to pick him up for questioning an entirely different dynamic would have been in place.

Jessica and Byrne compared notes and strategies. They entered the small, battered space, which was not much bigger than a walk-in closet. Jessica sat, Byrne stood behind Hornstrom. Tony Park and Josh Bontrager observed through the two-way mirror.

"We just need to clear a few things up," Jessica said. This was standard cop-speak for *We don't want to have to chase you all over the city if it turns out you are our doer.*

"Couldn't we have done this at my office?" Hornstrom asked.

"Do you like to work out of your office, Mr. Hornstrom?" Byrne asked.

"Of course."

"So do we."

Hornstrom just stared, bested. After a few moments he crossed his legs, folded his hands in his lap. "Are you any closer to finding out what happened to that woman?" Conversational, now. This was standard creep-speak for *I have something to hide, but I firmly believe that I am smarter than you are.*

"I believe we are," Jessica said. "Thanks for asking."

Hornstrom nodded, as if he had just scored a point with the police. "We're all kind of freaked out down at the office."

"What do you mean?"

"Well, it's not every day that something like this happens. I mean, you guys run into it all the time. We're just a bunch of salesmen."

"Have you heard anything from your colleagues that might help with our investigation?"

"Not really."

Jessica looked daggers, waiting. "Would that be not really, or no?"

"Well, no. That was just a figure of speech."

"Ah, okay," Jessica said, thinking, *You're under arrest*

*for obstruction of justice. That's another figure of speech.* She flipped back through her notes. "You stated that you had not been back to the Manayunk property for a week prior to our first interview."

"That's correct."

"Were you in town that week?"

Hornstrom thought for a moment. "Yes."

Jessica slid a large manila envelope onto the table. For the moment she left it closed. "Are you familiar with the Pustelnik Restaurant Supply Company?"

"Sure," Hornstrom said. The color was starting to rise in his face. He leaned back slightly, putting a few extra inches between himself and Jessica. The first sign of defense.

"Well, it turns out they've had a theft problem there for quite some time," Jessica said. She undid the clasp on the envelope. Hornstrom didn't seem able to take his eyes off it. "A few months ago the owners installed surveillance cameras on all four sides of the building. Were you aware of that?"

Hornstrom shook his head. Jessica reached into the nine-by-twelve envelope, extracted a photograph, placed it on the scarred metal table.

"This is a still photograph taken from the surveillance tape," she said. "The camera was the one on the side facing the warehouse where Kristina Jakos was found. *Your* warehouse. It was taken the morning Kristina's body was discovered."

Hornstrom glanced casually at the photograph. "Okay."

"Would you take a closer look at it, please?"

Hornstrom picked up the photograph, scrutinized it. He swallowed hard. "I'm not sure what it is I'm supposed to be looking for." He put the photograph back down.

"Can you read the time stamp in the lower right-hand corner?" Jessica asked.

"Yes," Hornstrom said. "I see it. But I don't—"

"Can you see the automobile in the upper right-hand corner?"

Hornstrom squinted. "Not really," he said. Jessica could see the man's body language shift to an even more defensive posture. Arms crossed. Jaw muscles tightened. He began to tap his right foot. "I mean I can see *something*. I guess it could be a car."

"Maybe this will help," Jessica said. She took out another photograph, this one an enlargement of the automobile. It showed the left side of the trunk and a partial license plate. The BMW logo was somewhat clear. David Hornstrom paled immediately.

"That's not *my* car."

"That's the model you drive," Jessica said. "A black 525i."

"You can't be sure of that."

"Mr. Hornstrom, I spent three years in the Auto Unit. I can tell the difference between a 525i and a 530i in the dark."

"Yeah, but there are lots of these on the road."

"That's true," Jessica said. "But how many have that license plate?"

"To me it looks like HG. That's not necessarily HO."

"Don't you think we ran every black BMW 525i in Pennsylvania looking for registered plates that might be similar?" The truth was, they hadn't. But David Hornstrom didn't have to know that.

"This . . . this doesn't mean anything," Hornstrom said. "Anyone with Photoshop could have done this."

It was true. It would never stand up in court. The reason Jessica put it on the table was to rattle David Hornstrom. It was starting to work. On the other hand, he looked like a man about to ask for a lawyer. They needed to back off a little.

Byrne pulled out a chair, sat down. "How about astronomy?" he asked. "Are you into astronomy?"

The shift was abrupt. Hornstrom took a moment. "I'm sorry?"

"Astronomy," Byrne said. "I noticed you had a telescope in your office."

Hornstrom looked even more confused. *Now what?* "My telescope? What about it?"

"I've always wanted to get one. What kind is yours?"

It was the type of question David Hornstrom could probably have answered while in a coma. But here, in the Homicide Unit interrogation room, it didn't seem to come to him. Finally: "It's a Zhumell."

"A good one?"

"Pretty good. Far from top-of-the-line, though."

"What do you watch with it? The stars?"

"Sometimes."

"Ever gaze at the moon, David?"

The first thin beads of sweat opened on Hornstrom's forehead. He was either just about to admit something or shut down completely. Byrne downshifted. He reached into his briefcase, pulled out an audiocassette.

"We have the 911 call, Mr. Hornstrom," Byrne said. "And by that I mean, specifically, the 911 call that alerted the authorities to the fact that there was a dead body behind the warehouse on Flat Rock Road."

"Okay. But what does—"

"If we run some voice recognition tests on it, I have a distinct feeling it's going to match your voice." This was also unlikely, but it always sounded good.

"That's *crazy*," Hornstrom said.

"So, you're saying you did not place that call to 911 emergency?"

"No. I did not go back to the property, and I did not call 911."

Byrne held the younger man's gaze for an uncomfortable amount of time. Eventually Hornstrom looked away. Byrne set the tape on the table. "There's also some music on the 911 tape. Whoever placed that call forgot to turn off the music before they dialed. The music is faint, but it's there."

"I don't know what you're talking about."

Byrne reached over to the small boom box on the table, selected CD, hit PLAY. In a second, a song began to play. It was "I Want You" by Savage Garden. Hornstrom looked up in immediate recognition. He jumped to his feet.

"You had no right to go into my car! That is a clear violation of my civil rights!"

"What do you mean?" Byrne asked.

"You had no search warrant! That is my property!"

Byrne stared at Hornstrom until the man saw the wisdom of sitting down. Byrne then reached into his coat pocket. He pulled out a CD crystal case, and a small plastic bag from Coconuts Music. He also pulled out a receipt time-coded from one hour earlier. A receipt for Savage Garden's self-titled 1997 album.

"No one went into your car, Mr. Hornstrom," Jessica said.

Hornstrom looked at the bag, the CD case, the receipt. And knew. He had been played.

"Now, here's a suggestion," Jessica began. "Take it or leave it. At this moment, you are an important witness in a homicide investigation. The dividing line between witness and suspect—even at the best of times—is a thin one. Once you cross that line your life changes forever. Even if you turn out not to be the guy we're looking for, your name, in certain circles, is forever connected to words like 'murder investigation,' 'suspect,' 'person of interest.' Do you hear what I'm saying?"

A deep breath. On the exhale: "Yes."

"Good," Jessica said. "So, here you are, in a police station, with a critical choice to make. You can answer our questions honestly and we will get to the bottom of things. Or you can choose to play a dangerous game. Once you get a lawyer, we're done, the DA's office takes over and, let's face it, they're not the most flexible people in town. They make us look downright friendly."

The cards were dealt. Hornstrom appeared to weigh his options. "I'll tell you whatever you want to know."

Jessica held up the photograph of the car leaving the Manayunk parking lot. "This is you, isn't it?"

"Yes."

"You pulled into the parking lot that morning at approximately 7:07?"

"Yes."

"You saw Kristina Jakos's body, and you left?"

"Yes."

"Why didn't you call the police?"

"I . . . couldn't take the chance."

"What chance? What are you talking about?"

Hornstrom took a few moments. "We have a lot of important clients, okay? The market is very volatile now, and one hint of scandal could topple the whole thing. I panicked. I'm . . . I'm *sorry.*"

"Did you place the 911 call?"

"Yes," Hornstrom said.

"From an old cell phone?"

"Yes. I just changed carriers," he said. "But I *did call.* Doesn't that tell you something? Didn't I do the right thing?"

"So what you're saying is, you want some sort of commendation for doing the most basically decent thing imaginable? You find a dead woman on a riverbank and you think calling the police is some sort of noble act?"

Hornstrom buried his face in his hands.

"You lied to the police, Mr. Hornstrom," Jessica said. "This is something that is going to be with you for the rest of your life."

Hornstrom remained silent.

"Ever been to Shawmont?" Byrne asked.

Hornstrom looked up. "Shawmont? I guess I have. I mean I've driven *through* Shawmont. What does—"

"Ever been to a club called Stiletto?"

Pale as a sheet now. *Bingo*.

Hornstrom leaned back in his chair. It was clear that he was about to shut down.

"Am I under arrest?" Hornstrom asked.

Jessica was right. Time to slow down.

"We'll be back in a minute," Jessica said.

They stepped out of the room, closed the door. They entered the small alcove with the two-way mirror looking into the interrogation room. Tony Park and Josh Bontrager had been observing.

"What do you think?" Jessica asked Park.

"I'm not convinced," Park said. "I think he's just a player, a kid who found a body and saw his career going in the toilet. I say cut him loose. If we need him later, he might still like us enough to come in under his own power."

Park was right. Hornstrom didn't strike any of them as a stone killer.

"I'm going to take a ride up to the DA's office," Byrne said. "See if we can't get a little closer to Mr. HORNEE1."

They probably did not have enough to get a search warrant of David Hornstrom's house or vehicle yet, but it was worth a try. Kevin Byrne could be very persuasive. And David Hornstrom deserved to have the thumbscrews applied.

"Then I'm going to meet with some of the girls from Stiletto," Byrne added.

"Let me know if you need backup on that Stiletto detail," Tony Park said, smiling.

"I think I can handle it," Byrne said.

"I'm going to hole up with those library books for a few hours," Bontrager said.

"I'll get on the street and see if I can track down anything about these dresses," Jessica said. "Whoever our boy is, he had to get them somewhere."

# 48

*There lived a young woman named Anne Lisbeth. She was a beautiful girl, with gleaming teeth, shiny hair, and a pretty complexion. One day she had a child of her own, but her son was not very pretty, so he was sent to live with others.*

*Moon knows all about this.*

*While a laborer's wife brought up her child, Anne Lisbeth went to live at the count's castle, surrounded by silk and velvet. No breath was allowed to blow on her. No one was allowed to speak to her.*

*Moon watches Anne Lisbeth from the back of the room. She is as fair as the fable. She is surrounded by the past, by all that has lived before. In this room dwells the echo of many stories. It is a place of discarded things.*

*Moon knows about this, as well.*

*In the story, Anne Lisbeth lived for many years, be-*

*came a woman of respect and station. The people in her village called her Madame.*

*Moon's Anne Lisbeth will not live this long.*

*She will wear her dress today.*

# 49

There were about one hundred secondhand clothing and thrift-type stores in Philadelphia, Montgomery, Bucks, and Chester Counties, including those small boutiques that had sections devoted to consignment clothing.

Before she could plot her itinerary, Jessica got a call from Byrne. He had struck out on a search warrant for David Hornstrom. Plus, there was no manpower available to put a tail on the man. For the time being, the DA's office had decided not to move forward with a charge of obstruction. Byrne would keep the pressure on.

JESSICA BEGAN HER canvass on Market Street. The shops closest to Center City tended to be more expensive, specializing in consignment of designer clothes, or offering versions of whatever vintage style was popular du jour. Somehow, by the time Jessica reached the third store, she had picked up an adorable Pringle cardigan. She hadn't meant to. It had just happened.

She left her credit card and cash locked in her car after that. She was supposed to be conducting a homicide investigation, not building a wardrobe. She had with her photographs of both the dresses that had been found on the victims. So far, no one had recognized them.

The fifth store she visited was on South Street, tucked between a used record shop and a hoagie shack.

It was called TrueSew.

THE GIRL BEHIND the counter was about nineteen, blond and delicately pretty, fragile. The music was some kind of Euro trance, volume low. Jessica showed the girl her ID.

"What's your name?" Jessica asked.

"Sa'mantha," the girl said. "With an apostrophe."

"And where would I put that apostrophe?"

"After the first *a*."

Jessica wrote *Samantha*. "Got it. How long have you worked here?"

"About two months. Almost three."

"Good job?"

Sa'mantha shrugged. "It's okay. Except for when we have to go through the stuff that people bring in."

"What do you mean?"

"Well, some of it can be pretty skanky, right?"

"Skanky how?"

"Well, one time I actually found a moldy salami sandwich in the back pocket of a pair of overalls. I mean, okay, *one*, who puts a frickin' sandwich in their pocket? No Baggie, just the sandwich. And a *salami* sandwich at that."

"Yuck."

"Yuck squared. And, like, *two*, who doesn't even bother to *look* in the pockets of something before they sell it or donate it? Who would do that? Makes you wonder what else this guy donated, if you know what I mean. Can you imagine?"

Jessica could. She had seen her share.

"And another time we found like a dozen dead mice

at the bottom of this big box of clothes. Some of them were baby mice. I *freaked*. I don't think I slept for a week." Sa'mantha shuddered. "I may not sleep tonight. *So* glad I remembered that."

Jessica looked around the store. It looked totally disorganized. Clothes were piled on top of the circular racks. Some of the smaller items—shoes, hats, gloves, scarves—were still in cardboard boxes, scattered around the floor, prices written on the sides in black crayon. Jessica imagined that it was all part of a twenty-something Bohemian charm to which she no long subscribed. A pair of men browsed at the rear of the store.

"What sort of things do you sell here?" Jessica asked.

"All sorts," Sa'mantha said. "Vintage, Goth, jock, military. Some Riley."

"What's Riley?"

"Riley is a line. I think they're out of Hollywood. Or maybe that's just the buzz. They take vintage and recycled stuff and embellish it. Skirts, jackets, jeans. Not really my scene, but kinda cool. Mostly for women, but I've seen some kid's things."

"Embellish how?"

"Ruffles, embroidery, things like that. Pretty much one-of-a-kind merch."

"I'd like to show you some pictures," Jessica said. "Would that be okay?"

"Sure."

Jessica opened an envelope, produced photocopies of the dresses found on Kristina Jakos and Tara Grendel, along with a picture of David Hornstrom, the one taken for his Roundhouse visitor ID.

"Do you recognize this man?"

Sa'mantha looked at the photograph. "I don't think so," she said. "Sorry."

Jessica then put the photographs of the dresses on the

counter. "Have you sold anything like these to anyone recently?"

Sa'mantha scanned the pictures. She brought them into better light, took her time. "Not that I remember," she said. "These are pretty sweet dresses, though. Outside of the Riley line, most of the stuff we get in here is pretty basic. Levi's, Columbia Sportswear, old Nike and Adidas stuff. These dresses look like something out of like *Jane Eyre* or something."

"Who owns this store?"

"My brother. But he's not here right now."

"What's his name?"

"Danny."

"Any apostrophes?"

Sa'mantha smiled. "No," she said. "Just regular old Danny."

"How long has he owned the place?"

"Maybe two years. But my grandmother owned the place like forever before that. She still does, technically, I think. Loan-wise. She's the one you want to talk to. In fact, she'll be here later. She knows everything there is to know about vintage stuff."

*The receipt for getting older,* Jessica thought. She looked on the floor behind the counter, noticed a baby bounce chair. It had a toy bar across the front, one with brightly colored circus animals. Sa'mantha saw her looking at the chair.

"That's for my little boy," she said. "He's asleep in the back office now."

There was a sudden sadness to Sa'mantha's voice. It sounded like her situation was a legal thing, not necessarily a matter of the heart. Not Jessica's business, either.

The phone behind the counter rang. Sa'mantha answered. When she turned her back, Jessica noticed a pair of red and green streaks in her blond hair. Somehow, it

suited this young woman. After a few moments Sa'mantha
hung up.

"I like your hair," Jessica said.

"Thanks," Sa'mantha said. "Kind of my Christmas
groove. Probably time to change it."

Jessica gave Sa'mantha a pair of business cards.
"Would you ask your grandmother to call me?"

"Sure," she said. "She *loves* intrigue."

"I'll leave these photographs here, too. If you think of
anything else, feel free to get in touch."

"Okay."

When Jessica turned to leave, she noticed that the two
people who'd been at the back of the store had gone. No
one had passed her going to the front door.

"Do you have a back door here?" Jessica asked.

"Yeah," Sa'mantha said.

"You don't have a problem with shoplifting?"

Sa'mantha pointed to a small video monitor and VCR
under the counter. Jessica hadn't noticed them before. It
showed an angle on the hallway leading to the rear entrance. "This used to be a jewelry store, believe it or
not," Sa'mantha said. "They left the cameras and everything. I've been watching those guys the whole time we
were talking. Not to worry."

Jessica had to smile. Outflanked by a nineteen-year-
old. You never knew about people.

BY EARLY AFTERNOON Jessica had seen her share of Goth
kids, grunge kids, hip-hop kids, rock and rollers, and
homeless people, along with a contingent of Center City
secretaries and receptionists looking for that Versace
pearl in the oyster. She stopped at a small restaurant on
Third, grabbed a quick sandwich, called in. Among the
messages she had received was one from a thrift store on
Second Street. Somehow the information that the second victim had been dressed in a vintage outfit had

leaked to the press and it seemed that everyone who had ever even seen a thrift store was coming out of the woodwork.

The unfortunate possibility existed that their killer had purchased these items online, or had picked them up in a thrift store in Chicago, or Denver, or San Diego. Or maybe he'd simply had them in a steamer trunk for the past forty or fifty years.

She entered the tenth thrift store on her list, the Second Street location from which someone had called and left her a message. Jessica badged the young man at the register—a particularly alert looking kid in his early twenties. He had about him the wide-eyed, buzzy look of one two many Von Dutch energy drinks. Or maybe it was something a little more pharmaceutical. Even his spiky hair looked amped. She asked him if he had called the police, or knew who had. After looking everywhere but into Jessica's eyes, the young man said he knew nothing about it. Jessica wrote the call off as another crank. The oddball calls were starting to pile up on this case. After the Kristina Jakos story hit the papers and the Internet they had gotten calls from pirates, elves, fairies—even from the ghost of someone who had died at Valley Forge.

Jessica glanced around the long, narrow store. It was a clean, well-lit space. It smelled of a new coat of latex paint. In the front window was a step display of small appliances—toasters, blenders, coffeemakers, space heaters. Along the back wall were board games, vinyl LPs, a few framed art reproductions. To the right was furniture.

Jessica made her way down the aisles to the women's apparel. There were only five or six racks of clothing, but it all seemed to be clean and in decent shape, certainly organized, especially when compared to the inventory at TrueSew.

When Jessica had attended Temple University, and the ripped designer jeans fad had been in its first blossom, she had frequented the Salvation Army and secondhand stores looking for just the right pair. She had probably tried on hundreds. On a rack in the middle of the store she saw a pair of black Gap jeans for $3.99. The right size, too. She had to stop herself.

"Can I help you find anything?"

Jessica turned to see the man asking the question. It was more than a little odd. He sounded like he worked at Nordstrom or Saks. She was not used to getting waited on in a thrift store.

"My name is Detective Jessica Balzano." She showed the man her ID.

"Ah, yes." The man was tall, well groomed, soft-spoken, manicured. He seemed out of place in a second-hand shop. "I am the one who called." He extended his hand. "Welcome to the New Page Emporium. My name is Roland Hannah."

# 50

Byrne interviewed three dancers at Stiletto. As pleasant as the detail was, he had learned nothing, except that ex-otic dancers can be upward of six feet tall. None of the young ladies remembered anyone paying particular attention to Kristina Jakos.

Byrne decided to take another look at the Shawmont pump house.

\* \* \*

BEFORE HE GOT on Kelly Drive his cell phone rang. It was Tracy McGovern at the forensic lab.

"We got a match on those bird feathers," Tracy said.

Byrne winced when he thought about the bird. *God,* he hated fucking up. "What is it?"

"Ready for this?"

"That sounds like a loaded question, Tracy," Byrne said. "I'm not sure how to answer."

"The bird was a nightingale."

"A *nightingale*?" Byrne recalled the bird in the victim's grasp. It was a small, ordinary looking bird, nothing special. For some reason he'd thought a nightingale would be exotic looking.

"Yep. *Luscinia megarhynchos,* also known as the Rufous nightingale," Tracy said. "And here's the good part."

"Man, do I need a good part."

"Nightingales don't live in North America."

"That's the good part?"

"It is. Here's why. The nightingale is usually considered to be an English bird, but it can also be found in Spain, Portugal, Austria, and Africa. And here's the even *better* news. Not so much for the bird, mind you, but for us. Nightingales don't do very well in captivity. Ninety percent of those caught die within a month or so."

"Okay," Byrne said. "So how does one of them end up in the hands of a murder victim in Philly?"

"As well you may ask. Unless you bring one back from Europe yourself—and in this age of bird flu that would not be likely—there's only one way to get one."

"And how is that?"

"From a breeder of exotic birds. Nightingales have been known to survive in captivity if they're bred. Hand-raised, if you will."

"Please tell me there's a breeder in Philly."

"No, but there is one in Delaware. I called them, but they said they had not sold a nightingale, or bred one, in years. The owner said he would put together a list of breeders and importers and call back. I gave him your number."

"Good work, Tracy." Byrne clicked off, then called Jessica's voice mail, left her the information.

A freezing rain began to fall as he turned onto Kelly Drive, a cloudy gray mist that painted the road with a patina of ice. For Kevin Byrne, at that moment, it felt like the winter would never end, and there were three months to go.

*Nightingales.*

BY THE TIME Byrne reached the Shawmont waterworks, the freezing rain had turned into a full-blown ice storm. In the few feet from his car to the slick stone steps of the abandoned pump house he got fairly soaked.

Byrne stood in the huge open doorway, surveyed the main room of the waterworks. He was still stunned at the scale and sheer desolation of the building. He had lived in Philadelphia his entire life, but had never been there until this case. The site was so secluded—yet not too far from Center City—that he would bet many Philadelphians didn't even know it was there.

The wind swirled an eddy of rain into the building. Byrne stepped deeper into the gloom. He thought about the activity that had once taken place there, the commotion. A few generations of people had worked here, keeping the water flowing.

Byrne touched the stone sill where Tara Grendel had been found—

*—and sees the shadow of the killer, bathed in black, positioning the woman, facing her toward the river . . . hears the sound of the nightingale as he puts it into her hands, hands rapidly taking on rigor . . . sees the killer*

*stepping outside, glancing at the moon . . . hears the lilt of a nursery rhyme—*

—then stood back.

Byrne took a few moments, trying to shake off the images, trying to make sense of them. He had imagined the first few lines of a children's verse—it even seemed like a child's voice—but he could not understand the words. Something about maidens.

He walked the perimeter of the enormous space, training his Maglite on the pitted and rubbled floor. The crime-scene officers had taken detailed photographs, made scale drawings, combed it for evidence. They had found nothing significant. Byrne snapped off his flashlight. He decided to head back to the Roundhouse.

Before he stepped outside he was overcome by another sensation, a dark and forbidding awareness, the feeling that someone was watching him. He wheeled around, looking into the corners of the enormous room.

No one.

Byrne cocked his head, listened. Just the rain, the wind.

He stepped into the doorway, peered out. Through the thick gray mist, on the other side of the river, he saw a man standing on the riverbank, hands at his sides. The man seemed to be observing him. The figure was a few hundred feet away, and it was impossible to make out anything specific, except that a man in a dark coat was standing there, in a winter ice storm, and he was *watching* Byrne.

Byrne stepped back into the building, out of sight, waited a few moments. He poked his head around the corner. The man was still there, standing motionless, studying the monstrous building on the eastern bank of the Schuylkill. For a second the small figure faded into and out of the landscape, lost in a sheet of water.

Byrne receded into the darkness of the pump house.

He got on his cell phone, called the unit. In seconds he told Nick Palladino to get down to the location, on the western bank of the Schuylkill, across from the Shawmont pump house, and bring the cavalry. If they were wrong, they were wrong. They would apologize to the man and all go about their day.

But Byrne somehow knew he wasn't wrong. The feeling was that strong.

"Hang on a second, Nick."

Byrne kept the telephone connection open, waited a few moments, trying to calculate which bridge was nearest to his location, which bridge would get him to the other side of the Schuylkill fastest. He crossed the floor space, waited a moment in the huge arch, sprinted to his car, just as someone stepped out of a high portico on the north side of the building, just a few feet away, directly into his path. Byrne didn't look at the man's face. For the moment he couldn't take his eyes off the small caliber weapon in the man's hand. A weapon pointed at Byrne's stomach.

The man holding the gun was Matthew Clarke.

"What are you doing?" Byrne screamed. *"Get the fuck out of my way!"*

Clarke did not move. Byrne could smell the alcohol on the man's breath. He could also see the gun shaking in the man's hand. Never a good combination.

"You're going to come with me," Clarke said.

Over Clarke's shoulder, through the thick haze of rain, Byrne could see the figure of a man still standing on the far riverbank. Byrne tried to mind-print the image. It was impossible. The man could be five eight or six feet. Twenty or fifty.

"Give me the gun, Mr. Clarke," Byrne said. "You're obstructing an investigation. This is very serious."

The wind picked up, whipping off the river, bringing a mass of sleet with it. "I want you to take out your weapon, really slowly, and put it on the ground," Clarke said.

"I can't do that."

Clarke cocked the pistol. His hand began to shake. "You do what I tell you."

Byrne saw the rage in the man's eyes, the heat of madness. The detective slowly unbuttoned his coat, reached inside, removed his weapon with two fingers. He then ejected the magazine, threw it over his shoulder, into the river. He placed the gun on the ground. He was not about to leave behind a loaded weapon.

"Let's go." Clarke pointed toward his car, which was parked near the train depot. "We're going to take a ride."

"Mr. Clarke," Byrne said, searching for the right tone of voice. He calculated his chances of making a move to disarm Clarke. Never good odds under the best of circumstances. "You don't want to do this."

"I said, let's *go*."

Clarke put the gun to Byrne's right temple. Byrne closed his eyes. *Colleen,* he thought. *Colleen.*

"We're going to take a ride," Clarke said. "You and me. If you don't get in my car, I will kill you right here."

Byrne opened his eyes, turned his head. Across the river, the man was gone.

"Mr. Clarke, this is the end of your life," Byrne said. "You have no idea the world of shit you've just stepped into."

"Don't say another word. Not one. Do you hear me?"

Byrne nodded.

Clarke stepped behind Byrne, put the gun's barrel against the small of his back. "Let's go," he said once more. They walked to the car. "Do you know where we're heading?"

Byrne did. But he needed Clarke to say it out loud. "No," he said.

"We're going to the Crystal Diner," Clarke replied. "We're going to the place where you killed my wife."

They reached the car. They slipped inside at the same moment—Byrne into the driver's seat, Clarke directly behind him.

"Nice and slow," Clarke said. "Drive."

Byrne started the car, put on the wipers, the defrosters. His hair and face and clothes were soaked, his pulse was thrumming in his ears.

He wiped the rain from his eyes, and then headed toward the city.

# 51

Jessica Balzano and Roland Hannah sat in the small back room of the thrift shop. The walls bore a number of Christian posters, a Christian calendar, framed inspirational sayings in needlepoint, pictures drawn by children. In one corner was an orderly pile of painting supplies—cans, rollers, pans, drop cloths. The walls in the back room were a pastel yellow.

Roland Hannah was lanky, light-haired, trim. He wore faded jeans, worn Reeboks, and a white sweatshirt with a slogan on the front, printed in black letters:

LORD, IF YOU CAN'T MAKE ME SKINNY, MAKE ALL MY FRIENDS FAT.

There were flecks of paint on his hands.

"Can I offer you a coffee or tea? A soda perhaps?" he asked.

"I'm fine, thanks," Jessica said.

Roland sat down at the table, across from Jessica. He folded his hands, knitted his fingers together. "How can I help you?"

Jessica opened her notebook, clicked a pen. "You said that you called the police."

"That's correct."

"Can I ask why?"

"Well, I read the account of these terrible murders," Roland said. "The detail of the vintage clothing caught my eye. I just figured I might be able to help."

"How so?"

"I've been at this quite a while, Detective Balzano," he said. "Although this store has only recently opened, I have served the community and the Lord in some capacity for many years. And as far as the ministry thrift shops in Philadelphia are concerned, I know just about everyone. I know a number of the Christian ministers in New Jersey and Delaware also. I figured I might be able to facilitate introductions, things like that."

"How long have you been at this location?"

"We just opened our doors here about ten days ago," Roland said.

"Have you gotten a lot of customers?"

"Yes," Roland said. "The good word is spreading."

"Do you know many of the people who come here to shop?"

"Quite a few," he said. "The location has been printed in our church bulletin for some time now. Some of the alternative papers here have even included us in their listing sections. On the day we opened we had balloons for the children, along with cake and punch for all."

"What sort of things do the customers buy mostly?"

"Depends on their ages, of course. The married couples tend to look at the furniture and children's clothes. Young people, such as yourself, tend to head right for the jeans and denim jackets. They always think there'll be the Juicy Couture or Diesel or Vera Wang article of clothing buried amid the Sears and JCPenney's. I can tell you that it rarely happens. Most of the designer items are snatched up before they reach our shelves, I'm afraid."

Jessica looked closely at the man. If she had to guess, she would say he was a few years younger than she was. "Young people such as me?"

"Well, yes."

"How old do you think I am?"

Roland scrutinized her, hand on chin. "I'd say twenty-five or twenty-six."

Roland Hannah was her new best friend. "Can I show you some photographs?"

"Certainly," he said.

Jessica took out the pictures of the two dresses. She put them on the table. "Have you ever seen these dresses before?"

Roland Hannah looked closely at the pictures. Soon, recognition seemed to dawn on his face. "Yes," he said. "I think I've seen these dresses."

After a frustrating day of dead ends, the words almost didn't register. "You sold these dresses?"

"I'm not sure. I may have. I think I remember unpacking them and placing them on display."

Jessica's pulse galloped. It was that feeling all investigators get when the first solid clue falls from the sky. She wanted to call Byrne. She checked the impulse. "How long ago was this?"

Roland thought for a moment. "Let's see. We've been open for maybe ten days or so, like I said. So I'd reckon it was about two weeks ago that I would have put them on the rack. I think we had them when we opened. So, about two weeks."

"Do you know the name David Hornstrom?"

"David Hornstrom?" Roland asked. "I'm afraid I don't."

"Do you recall who might have bought the dresses?"

"I'm not sure I remember. But if I saw some photographs, I might be able to tell you. Pictures might jog my memory. Do the police still do that?"

"Do what?"

"Have people look through mug shots? Or is that something they only do on TV?"

"No, we do a lot of that," Jessica said. "Would you be willing to come down to the Roundhouse right now?"

"Of course," Roland said. "Anything I can do to help."

# 52

The traffic on Eighteenth Street was snarled. Cars were slipping and sliding. The temperature was dropping rapidly and the sleet was relentless.

A million thoughts raced through Kevin Byrne's mind. He thought about the other times in his career when he had faced a gun. He wasn't getting any better at it. His stomach was tied in steel knots.

"You don't want to do this, Mr. Clarke," Byrne said again. "There's still time to call this off."

Clarke remained silent. Byrne glanced into the rearview mirror. Clarke had the thousand-yard stare in place.

"You don't get it," Clarke finally said.

"I *do* get it."

"No, you don't. How could you? Have you ever lost someone you love to violence?"

Byrne had not. But he had come close once. He had almost lost everything once when his daughter had been in the hands of a killer. He had nearly crossed the threshold of sanity himself that dark day.

"Pull over," Clarke said.

Byrne eased the car to the curb. He put it in park, kept it running. The only sound was the click and clack of the windshield wipers keeping time with Byrne's hammering heart.

"What now?" Byrne asked.

"We're going to go into the diner, and we are going to end this. For you and me."

Byrne glanced at the diner. Through the mist of freezing rain, the lights sparkled and shimmered. The front window had been replaced already. The floor had been bleached clean. It was as if nothing had occurred in there. Except it had. And that was the reason they were back.

"It doesn't have to end this way," Byrne said. "If you put down the weapon, there's still a chance of getting your life back."

"You mean I can just walk away like this never happened?"

"No," Byrne said. "I'm not going to insult you by telling you that. But you can get help."

Byrne glanced again in the rearview. And saw it.

There were now two small red dots of light on Clarke's chest.

Byrne closed his eyes for the moment. This was the best of news, the worst of news. He had kept the phone open the whole time, ever since Clarke had confronted him at the pump house. Obviously, Nick Palladino had called SWAT, and they had deployed at the diner. For the second time in about a week. Byrne glanced up the street. He spotted SWAT officers positioned at the mouth of the alley next to the diner.

This could all end suddenly, violently. Byrne wanted the former, but not the latter. He was fair at negotiation tactics, but far from an expert. Rule number one. Remain calm. No one has to die. "I'm going to tell you something," Byrne said. "And I want you to listen carefully. Do you understand?"

Silence. The man was about to blow.

"Mr. Clarke?"

"What?"

"I need to tell you something. But first you must do exactly as I say. You must sit absolutely still."

"What are you talking about?"

"Have you noticed that there is no traffic?"

Clarke looked out the window. A block away, a pair of sector cars had blocked Eighteenth Street.

"Why are they doing that?" Clarke asked.

"I'll tell you all about it in a second. But first I want you to look down, very slowly. Just tilt your head. No sudden moves. Look down at your chest, Mr. Clarke."

Clarke did as Byrne suggested. "What is *this*?" he asked.

"This is the end of things, Mr. Clarke. Those are laser sights. They are coming from the rifles of two SWAT officers."

"Why are they on *me*?"

*Oh God,* Byrne thought. *This was far worse than he imagined. Matthew Clarke was beyond recall.*

"Again, do not move your body," Byrne said. "Just your eyes. I want you to look at my hands now, Mr. Clarke." Byrne had both hands on the steering wheel, at the ten o'clock and two o'clock positions. "Can you see my hands?"

"Your hands? What about them?"

"See how they're gripping the wheel?" Byrne asked.

"Yes."

"If I so much as lift the index finger on my right hand, they will pull the trigger. They will take the shot," Byrne said, hoping it rang true. "Remember what happened to Anton Krotz in the diner?"

Byrne could hear Matthew Clarke begin to sob. "Yes."

"That was one shooter. This is two."

"I . . . I don't care. I'll shoot you first."

"You'll never get the shot off. If *I* move, it's over. One single millimeter. It's over."

Byrne watched Clarke in the rearview. He was about to unhinge any second.

"You've got children, Mr. Clarke," Byrne said. "Think of them. You don't want to leave them this legacy."

Clarke shook his head, rapidly, side to side. "They're not going to let me go today, are they?"

"No," Byrne said. "But from the moment you lower the gun, your life will begin to get better. You're not like Anton Krotz, Matt. You're not like him."

Clarke's shoulders began to shake. "Laura."

Byrne let it play for a few moments. "Matt?"

Clarke looked up, his face streaked with tears. Byrne had never seen a man so close to the edge.

"They're not going to wait much longer," Byrne said. "Help me help you."

Then, in Clarke's reddened eyes, Byrne saw it. The crack in the man's resolve. Clarke lowered his weapon. Instantly a shadow crossed the left side of the car, obscured by the pall of freezing rain that streaked the windows. Byrne glanced over. It was Nick Palladino. He had a shotgun leveled at Matthew Clarke's head.

*"Put the weapon on the floor, and your hands above your head!"* Nick shouted. *"Do it now!"*

Clarke didn't move. Nick racked the shotgun.

*"Now!"*

After an agonizingly long second, Matthew Clarke complied. In the next second the door was thrown open and Clarke was pulled from the car, thrown roughly to the street, instantly surrounded by police officers.

A few moments later, as Matthew Clarke lay face-down in the middle of Eighteenth Street in the winter rain, his arms out to his sides, a SWAT officer aimed his rifle at the man's head. A uniformed officer approached, put a knee to Clarke's back, roughly pulled his wrists together and handcuffed him.

Byrne thought about the overwhelming power of grief, the unyielding grip of madness that must have led Matthew Clarke to this moment.

The officers yanked Clarke to his feet. Before they stuffed him into the back of a nearby sector car, he looked at Byrne.

Whoever Clarke had been a few weeks earlier, the person who had presented himself to the world in the guise of Matthew Clarke—husband, father, citizen—no longer existed. When Byrne stared into the man's eyes, he did not detect even a flicker of life. Instead, he saw a man disintegrated, and where a soul should have been there now burned the cold blue flame of madness.

# 53

Jessica found Byrne in the back room at the diner, a towel around his neck, a steaming cup of coffee in his hand. The rain had turned everything to ice, and the whole city was moving at a crawl. She had been back at the Roundhouse going through mug books with Roland Hannah when the officer-needs-assistance call had come in. All but a handful of detectives had rushed out the door. Whenever a cop was in distress the entire available force headed in their direction. When Jessica pulled up to the diner there had to have been ten sector cars on Eighteenth Street.

Jessica crossed the diner, Byrne stood. They embraced. It wasn't something you were supposed to do, but she couldn't care less. When the call went out, she was convinced she would never see him again. If that ever happened, a piece of her would most certainly have died with him.

They broke the embrace, looked around the diner a little awkwardly. They sat down.

"You okay?" Jessica asked.

Byrne nodded. Jessica wasn't so sure.

"Where did this start?" she asked.

"Up in Shawmont. At the waterworks."

"He followed you up there?"

Byrne nodded. "He must have."

Jessica thought about it. At any given time, any detective

on the force might be the subject of a stalker—current investigations, old investigations, crazy people you put away years ago getting out of prison. She thought about Walt Brigham's body on the side of the road. Anything could happen at any time.

"He was going to do it right where his wife was killed," Byrne said. "Me first, then himself."

"Jesus."

"Yeah, well. There's more."

Jessica couldn't imagine what he meant. "What do you mean, *more?*"

Byrne sipped his coffee. "I saw him."

"You saw him? You saw who?"

"Our doer."

"*What?* What are you talking about?"

"At the Shawmont site. He was across the river, just watching me."

"How do you know it was him?"

Byrne stared into his coffee for a moment. "The way you know anything in this job. It was him."

"Did you get a good look at him?"

Byrne shook his head. "No. He was on the other side of the river. In the rain."

"What did he do?"

"He didn't do anything. I think he wanted to come back to the scene, and figured the other side of the river would be safe."

Jessica considered this. It was common enough, coming back like that.

"That's why I called Nick to begin with," Byrne said. "If I hadn't . . ."

Jessica knew what he meant. If he hadn't called it in he might be lying on the floor in the Crystal Diner, ringed by a pool of blood.

"Did we hear from the bird breeders in Delaware yet?" Byrne asked, clearly attempting to shift the focus.

"Nothing yet," Jessica said. "I was thinking we should look into subscription lists to bird breeding magazines. There can't be that many subscribers in—"

"Tony's already on it," Byrne said.

Jessica should have known. Even in the middle of all this Byrne was thinking. He sipped his coffee, turned to her, half smiled. "And how was *your* day?" he asked.

Jessica smiled back. She hoped it looked genuine. "Far less adventurous, thank God." She related the morning and afternoon at the thrift stores, about meeting Roland Hannah. "I've got him looking at mugs right now. He operates a church thrift store. He might have sold our boy the dresses."

Byrne drained his coffee, stood. "I've got to get out of here," he said. "I mean, I like this place, but not this much."

"The boss wants you to go home."

"I'm fine," Byrne said.

"You sure?"

Byrne didn't answer. A few moments later a uniformed officer crossed the diner, handed Byrne his weapon. Byrne could tell from its heft that the magazine had been replaced. When Nick Palladino had listened to Byrne and Matthew Clarke on Byrne's open cell-phone line, he had dispatched a sector car to the Shawmont site to retrieve the weapon. Philly didn't need another gun on the street.

"Where's our Amish detective?" Byrne asked Jessica.

"Josh is working the bookstores, seeing if anybody remembers selling books on bird breeding, exotic birds, and the like."

"He's all right," Byrne said.

Jessica didn't know what to say. Coming from Kevin Byrne, this was high praise.

"What are you going to do now?" Jessica asked.

"Well, I *am* going to go home, but just to take a hot

shower and change clothes. Then I'm going to hit the streets. Maybe somebody else saw this guy standing on the other side of the river. Or saw his car pull over."

"Want some help?" she asked.

"No, I'm good. You stick with the rope and the bird breeders. I'll call you in an hour."

# 54

Byrne took Hollow Road down to the river. He passed beneath the expressway, parked the car, got out. The hot shower had done him some good, but unless the man for whom they were looking was still standing there, on the bank of the river, hands behind his back, waiting to be cuffed, this was going to be a shitty day. But then every day you had a gun pointed at you was a shitty day.

The rain had let up, but the ice remained. It all but covered the city. Byrne made his way carefully down the slope to the edge of the river. He stood between two barren trees, directly across from the pump house, the hum of the cars on the expressway behind him. He looked at the pump house. Even from this distance, the structure was imposing.

He stood in the exact spot where the man who had been watching him had stood. He thanked God that the man in question was not a sniper. Byrne imagined someone with a scope rifle standing there, leaning on the tree for balance. He could have picked Byrne off with ease.

He looked at the ground in the immediate area. No

cigarette butts, no convenient glossy candy wrappers to dust for prints.

Byrne crouched down on the riverbank. The flowing water was just inches away. He leaned forward, touched a finger to the freezing current and—

—*saw a man carrying Tara Grendel up to the pump house . . . a featureless man staring at the moon . . . a length of blue and white rope in his hands . . . heard the sound of a small boat slapping against stone . . . saw two flowers, one white, one red, and—*

—pulled his hand back, as if the water had been on fire. The images were getting stronger, clearer, more unnerving.

*In rivers, the water that you touch is the last of what has passed and the first of that which comes.*

Something was coming.

*Two flowers.*

A few seconds later his cell phone rang. Byrne stood, flipped open the phone, answered. It was Jessica.

"There's another victim," she said.

Byrne glanced down, at the dark intractable water of the Schuylkill. He knew, but asked anyway. "On the river?"

"Yeah, partner," she said. "On the river."

# 55

They met on the bank of the Schuylkill River, near the oil refineries in the Southwest. The crime scene was partially hidden from both the river and the nearby bridge.

The acrid smell of effluent from the refineries filled the air, their lungs.

The primary detectives on the case were Ted Campos and Bobby Lauria. These two had been partners forever. The old cliché about finishing each other's sentences was true, but it went beyond that with Ted and Bobby. One time they had even gone shopping separately and bought the same tie. Once they found out, of course, they never wore the ties. They weren't too crazy about the story being told, for that matter. It was all a little too *Brokeback Mountain* for the likes of a pair of old-school tough guys like Bobby Lauria and Ted Campos.

Byrne, Jessica, and Josh Bontrager pulled up to find a pair of sector cars, about fifty yards apart, sealing the road. The scene was far south of the first two victims, nearly at the confluence point where the Schuylkill met the Delaware, in the shadow of the Platt Bridge.

Ted Campos met the three detectives at the side of the road. Byrne introduced him to Josh Bontrager. A CSU van was on scene, as well as Tom Weyrich from the ME's office.

"What do we have, Ted?" Byrne asked.

"We have a female DOA," Campos said.

"Strangled?" Jessica asked.

"Looks like it." He pointed toward the river.

The body was lying on the riverbank, near the base of a dying maple tree. When Jessica saw the body, her heart sank. It was something she had feared might happen, and now it had. "Oh no."

The corpse was that of a child. No more than thirteen or so years old. Her slight shoulders were twisted at an unnatural angle, her torso was covered with leaves and trash. She too wore a long vintage dress. Around her neck was what looked to be an identical nylon belt.

Tom Weyrich stood next to the body, dictating notes.

"Who found her?" Byrne asked.

"Security guard," Campos said. "Came down for a smoke. Guy's a fucking wreck."

"When?"

"About an hour ago. But Tom thinks this woman has been out here a while."

The word shocked everyone. "Woman?" Jessica asked.

Campos nodded. "I thought the same thing," he said. "And she's been dead for some time. There's a good deal of decay."

Tom Weyrich approached them. He pulled off his latex gloves, slipped on his leather ones.

"That's not a child?" Jessica asked. She was stunned. The victim could not have been much taller than four feet.

"No," Weyrich said. "She's small, but mature. She was probably about forty."

"So, how long do you think she's been out here?" Byrne asked.

"I'm guessing a week or so. No way to tell here."

"This happened before the Shawmont killing?"

"Oh, yeah," Weyrich said.

Two officers from the Crime Scene Unit emerged from the van and began to make their way to the riverbank. Josh Bontrager followed.

Jessica and Byrne watched the team set up a crime scene and perimeter. Until further notice this was not their case, nor was it even officially related to the two murders they were investigating.

"Detectives," Josh Bontrager called out to them.

Campos, Lauria, Jessica, and Byrne all made their way down to the riverbank. Bontrager was standing in an area about fifteen feet from the body, just slightly up-river.

"Look." Bontrager pointed to an area behind the scrub of low bushes. In the ground was an item so incongruous in this setting that Jessica had to get right up to it to make sure that what she *thought* she was looking at was indeed what she *was* looking at. It was a lily. A red plastic lily stuck into the snow. On the tree next to it, about three feet from the ground, was a painted white moon.

Jessica took a pair of photographs. She then stood back and let the CSU photographer document the whole scene. Sometimes the context of an item at a crime scene was as important as the item itself. The where of something sometimes superseded the what.

*A lily.*

Jessica glanced at Byrne. He seemed to be riveted by the red flower. She then looked at the body. The woman was so petite that it was easy to see how she could have been mistaken for a child. Jessica could see that the victim's dress was too large, and had been unevenly hemmed. The woman's arms and legs were intact. No amputations visible. Her hands were open. She held no bird.

"Does this sync with your boy?" Campos asked.

"Yeah," Byrne said.

"Same MO with the belt?"

Byrne nodded.

"Want the case?" Campos half smiled, but was also half serious.

Byrne didn't answer. It wasn't up to him. There was a good chance that these cases were going to be grouped into a much larger task force soon, one that involved the FBI and other federal agencies. There was a compulsive killer on a rampage, and this woman may have been his first victim. For some reason this freak was obsessed with vintage costumes and the Schuylkill, and they hadn't the slightest clue who he was, or where he was going to strike next. Or if he already *had*. There could be ten bodies between where they were standing and the Manayunk crime scene.

"This guy is not going to stop until he makes his point, is he?" Byrne asked.

"Doesn't look like it," Campos said.

"The river is a hundred fucking miles long."

"One hundred twenty-*eight* fucking miles long," Campos replied. "Give or take."

*One hundred twenty-eight miles,* Jessica thought. Much of it shielded from roads and expressways, bounded by trees and shrubs, a river that snaked through maybe a half dozen counties into the heart of southeast Pennsylvania.

One hundred twenty-eight miles of killing ground.

# 56

It was her third cigarette of the day. Her *third*. Three wasn't bad. Three was like not smoking at all, right? Back when she was using she'd been up to two packs. Three was like she had already quit. Or whatever.

Who was she·kidding? She knew she wasn't going to quit for real until her life was in order. Sometime around her seventieth birthday.

Sa'mantha Fanning opened the back door, peeked into the store. Empty. She listened. Baby Jamie was quiet. She closed the door, pulled her coat tightly around her. *Man,* it was cold. She hated having to come outside to smoke, but at least she wasn't one of those gargoyles you saw on Broad Street, standing in front of their buildings, hunched against the wall, sucking away on a butt. That was the reason she never smoked in front of the store, even though it was a lot easier to keep an eye on things from there. She refused to look like some criminal. Still, it was colder than a pocketful of penguin shit out here.

She thought about her plans for New Year's Eve, or rather her nonplans. It would just be her and Jamie, maybe a bottle of wine. Such was the life of a single mother. A single broke mother. A single barely *employed* broke mother whose ex-boyfriend and father of her child was a lazy-ass pipehead who had yet to give her one friggin' dime in child support. She was nineteen and her life story was already written.

She opened the door again, just to give a listen, and almost jumped out of her skin. A man stood right in the doorway. He had been alone in the store, all by himself. He could have stolen anything. She was definitely going to get fired, family or no.

"Man," she said. "You scared the *crap* outta me."

"I'm sorry," he said.

He was well dressed, had a nice face. He was not her typical customer.

"My name is Detective Byrne," he said. "I'm with the Philadelphia Police Department. The homicide division."

"Oh, okay," she said.

"I was wondering if you might have a few minutes to talk."

"Sure. No problem," she said. "But I did already speak with a . . ."

"Detective Balzano?"

"Right. Detective Balzano. She had on this great leather coat."

"That's her." He gestured to the inside of the store. "Would you like to go inside where it's a little warmer?"

She held up her cigarette. "I can't smoke in there. Ironic, huh?"

"I'm not sure what you mean."

"I mean half the stuff in there already smells pretty funky," she said. "Is it okay if we talk out here?"

"Sure," the man replied. He stepped through the doorway, closed the door. "I just have a few more questions. I promise not to keep you too long."

She almost laughed. *Keep me from what?* "I've got nowhere to be," she said. "Fire away."

"Actually, I have only one question."

"Okay."

"I was wondering about your son."

The word caught her off guard. What did Jamie have to do with anything? "My son?"

"Yes. I was wondering why you are going to put him out. Is it because he isn't pretty?"

At first she thought the man was making a joke—albeit a joke she didn't get. But he wasn't smiling. "I'm not sure what you're talking about," she said.

"The count's son is not nearly as fair as you think."

She looked into his eyes. He seemed to look right through her. Something was wrong here. Something was *way* wrong. And she was all by herself. "Do you think I might, like, see some identification or something?" she asked.

"No." The man stepped toward her. He unbuttoned his coat. "That won't be possible."

Sa'mantha Fanning took a few steps backward. A few steps were all she had. Her back was already against the bricks. "Have . . . have we met before?" she asked.

"Yes, we have, Anne Lisbeth," the man said. "Once upon a time."

# 57

Jessica sat at her desk, worn out, the events of the day—the discovery of the third victim, coupled with the near miss with Kevin—having all but drained her.

Plus, the only thing worse than fighting Philly traffic was fighting Philly traffic on ice. It was physically exhausting. Her arms felt like she had gone ten rounds; her neck was stiff. On the way back to the Roundhouse she had narrowly avoided three accidents.

Roland Hannah had spent almost two hours with a book of mug shots. Jessica had also given him a sheet with five more recent photos, one of which was the visitor ID photograph of David Hornstrom. He had not recognized anyone.

The investigation into the murder of the victim found in the Southwest would soon be turned over to the task force, and new files would soon pile up on her desk.

Three victims. Three women strangled, left on a riverbank, all of them dressed in vintage dresses. One had been horribly mutilated. One had held a rare bird in her grasp. One had been found with a red plastic lily nearby.

Jessica turned to the evidence of the nightingale. There were three companies in New York, New Jersey, and Delaware that bred exotic birds. She decided not to wait for a call back. She picked up the phone. She got basically the same information from all three firms. She was told that with sufficient knowledge, and the proper conditions, a person could breed a nightingale. They gave her a list of books and publications. She hung up the phone, each time feeling she was at the foothills of a huge mountain of knowledge she did not have the energy to climb.

She got up to get a cup of coffee. Her phone rang. She answered, punched the button.

"Homicide, Balzano."

"Detective, my name is Ingrid Fanning."

It was the voice of an older woman. Jessica didn't recognize the name. "What can I do for you ma'am?"

"I'm the co-owner of TrueSew. My granddaughter spoke to you earlier."

"Oh, right, yes," Jessica said. The woman was talking about Sa'mantha.

"I've been looking at the photographs you left," Ingrid said. "The photographs of the dresses?"

"What about them?"

"Well, for one thing, these are not vintage dresses."

"They're not?"

"No," she said. "These are *reproductions* of vintage dresses. I would put the originals at around the second half of the nineteenth century. Closer to the end. Perhaps 1875 or so. Definitely a late Victorian silhouette."

Jessica wrote down the information. "How do you know they are reproductions?"

"A few reasons. One, much of the detailing is missing. They don't appear to be very well made. And two, if these were original, and in this kind of shape, they would sell for three to four thousand dollars each. Believe me, they would not be on the rack at a thrift store."

"But reproductions might be?" Jessica asked.

"Oh, sure. There are a lot of reasons to reproduce clothing like this."

"For instance?"

"For instance someone might be producing a play or a film. Someone might be re-creating a particular event at a museum, perhaps. We get calls all the time from local theater groups. Not for anything like these dresses, mind you, but rather for more recent period clothing. Lots of calls for 1950s and 1960s stuff these days."

"Has clothing like this ever passed through your store?"

"A few times. But what these dresses are is costuming, not vintage."

Jessica considered the fact that she had been looking in the wrong places. She should have concentrated on theatrical supply. She would begin now.

"I appreciate the call," Jessica said.

"It's quite all right," the woman replied.

"Say thanks to Sa'mantha for me."

"Well, my granddaughter's not here. When I came in the store was locked and my great-grandson was in his crib in the office."

"Is everything all right?"

"I'm sure it is," she said. "She probably ran out to the bank or something."

Jessica hadn't thought Sa'mantha the type to up and leave her son alone. On the other hand, she didn't really know the young woman at all. "Thanks again for calling," she said. "If you think of anything else, please give us a ring."

"I will."

Jessica thought about the date. The late 1800s. What was the reason? Was the killer obsessed with that time period? She made notes. She would look up important dates and events in Philadelphia around that time. Perhaps their psycho was fixated on some incident that took place on the river in that era.

BYRNE SPENT THE late afternoon doing background checks on everyone even remotely connected with Stiletto—bartenders, parking attendants, night cleaners, delivery people. Although they were not the most savory lot, none of them had anything on their records to indicate the kind of violence unleashed in the river killings.

He walked over to Jessica's desk, sat down.

"Guess who came up blank?" Byrne asked.

"Who?"

"Alasdair Blackburn," Byrne said. "Unlike his father, he has no record. And the odd thing is that he was born here. Chester County."

This was a little surprising to Jessica. "He sure gives the impression he's from the old country. 'Aye' and all that."

"Exactly my point."

"What do you want to do?" she asked.

"I think we should take a ride to his house. See if we can catch him out of his element."

"Let's go." Before Jessica could grab her coat her phone rang. She answered. It was Ingrid Fanning again.

"Yes, ma'am," Jessica said. "Did you remember something else?"

It wasn't something else Ingrid Fanning had remembered. It was something else alto*gether*. Jessica listened for a few moments, a little incredulous, and said, "We'll be there in ten minutes." She hung up the phone.

"What's up?" Byrne asked.

Jessica took a moment. She needed it to process what she'd just heard. "That was Ingrid Fanning," she said. She gave Byrne a brief recap of her earlier conversation with the woman.

"Does she have something for us?"

"I'm not sure," Jessica said. "She seems to think someone has her granddaughter."

"What do you mean?" Byrne asked. He was on his feet now. "Who has her granddaughter?"

Jessica took another moment before responding. It wasn't nearly enough time. "Somebody named Detective Byrne."

# 58

Ingrid Fanning was a tough seventy—thin, wiry, vigorous, dangerous in her youth. Her cloud of white hair was tied into a ponytail. She wore a long blue wool skirt and cream cashmere turtleneck. The store was empty. Jessica noticed that the music had changed to Celtic. She also noticed that Ingrid Fanning's hands were shaking.

Jessica, Byrne, and Ingrid stood behind the counter. Beneath the counter was an older model Panasonic VHS machine and a small black-and-white monitor.

"After I called you the first time I began to straighten up a bit behind here, and I noticed that the videotape had stopped," Ingrid said. "It's an old machine. It's always doing that. I rewound it some, and I accidentally hit PLAY instead of RECORD. I saw this."

Ingrid played the tape. When the high-angle image appeared on the screen it showed an empty hallway leading to the back of the store. Unlike most surveillance systems, this was nothing very sophisticated, just an ordinary VHS cassette machine, set on SLP. It probably provided six hours of real-time coverage. There was also audio. The view of the empty hallway was underscored by the faint sounds of traffic passing on South Street, the occasional car horn, the same music Jessica recalled from her visit.

After a minute or so a figure walked up the hallway, peering briefly through a doorway to the right. Jessica immediately recognized the woman as Sa'mantha Fanning.

"That's my granddaughter," Ingrid said. Her voice was trembling. "The room on the right is where Jamie was."

Byrne glanced at Jessica, shrugged. *Jamie?*

Jessica pointed to the baby in the crib behind the counter. The baby was fine, fast asleep. Byrne nodded.

"She would go out back to smoke a cigarette," Ingrid continued. She dabbed at her eyes with a handkerchief. Whatever was coming was not good, Jessica thought. "She told me she quit, but I knew."

On the tape, Sa'mantha continued down the hallway to the door at the end. She opened it, allowing a wedge of gray daylight to spill down the corridor. She closed it behind her. The hallway remained empty, silent. The door stayed closed for forty-five seconds or so. It then opened about a foot. Sa'mantha poked her head in, listening. She closed the door once more.

The image remained static for thirty more seconds. Then the camera shook slightly, and changed positions, as if someone had tilted the lens downward. Now all they could see was the bottom half of the door, and the last few feet of the hallway. A few seconds later they heard footsteps, saw a figure. It appeared to be a man, but it was impossible to tell. The viewpoint showed the back of a dark coat from the waist down. They saw him reach into his pocket, retrieve a light-colored rope.

An icy hand grabbed Jessica's heart.

*Was this their killer?*

The man put the rope back into his coat pocket. A few moments later the door opened wide. It appeared that Sa'mantha was checking on her son again. She was a step lower than the level of the store, visible only from the neck down. She appeared startled to see someone standing there. She said something that was garbled on the tape. The man spoke in response.

"Could you play that again?" Jessica asked.

Ingrid Fanning hit REWIND, STOP, PLAY. Byrne turned up the volume on the monitor. On tape, the door opened again. A few moments later the man said, *"My name is Detective Byrne."*

Jessica saw Kevin Byrne's fists clench, his jaw tighten.

Shortly after, the man stepped through the doorway, closed the door behind him. There were twenty or thirty seconds of agonizing silence. Just the sound of the passing traffic and the thump of the music.

Then they heard a scream.

Jessica and Byrne both looked at Ingrid Fanning. "Is there anything else on the tape?" Jessica asked.

Ingrid shook her head, dabbed at her eyes. "They never came back in."

Jessica and Byrne walked down the hallway. Jessica looked at the camera. It was still pointed downward. They opened the door, stepped through. Behind the shop was a small area, perhaps eight by ten feet, bordered by a wooden fence at the back. The fence had a gate that opened onto an alley that cut behind the buildings. Byrne called in a request for officers to begin a canvass of the area. They would dust the camera and the door, but neither detective believed they would find fingerprints belonging to anyone other than an employee of TrueSew.

Jessica tried to construct a scenario in her mind in which Sa'mantha had not been drawn into this madness. She could not.

The killer had visited the store, perhaps looking for a Victorian dress.

The killer knew the name of the detective who was chasing him.

And now he had Sa'mantha Fanning.

# 59

Anne Lisbeth sits in the boat, wearing her dress—a midnight blue. She has stopped struggling against the ropes.

It is time.

Moon pushes the boat down the tunnel that leads to the main canal—the ØSTTUNNELEN, as his grandmother used to call it. He dashes out of the boathouse, past the Elfin Hill, past the Old Church Bell, all the way to the schoolhouse. He loves to watch the boats.

Soon he sees Anne Lisbeth's boat come into view, floating past the Tinder Box, then beneath the Great Belt Bridge. He recalls the days when the boats passed by all day—yellow and red and green and blue.

The Snow Man's house is empty now.

It will soon be occupied.

Moon stands with the rope in his hands. He waits at the end of the last canal, by the little schoolhouse, surveying the village. So much to do, so many repairs to make. He wishes his grandfather were there. He recalls those cold mornings, the smell of the old wooden toolbox, the damp sawdust, the way his grandfather would hum "I Danmark er jeg fodt," the glorious aroma of his pipe.

Anne Lisbeth will now take her place on the river, and they all will come. Soon. But not before the last two stories.

First, Moon will bring the Snow Man.

Then he will meet his princess.

# 60

The Crime Scene Unit had fingerprinted the third victim at the scene and was rushing the prints through processing. So far the tiny woman found in the Southwest had not been identified. Josh Bontrager worked the missing-person angle. Tony Park was walking the plastic lily through the lab.

The woman also had the same "moon" drawing on her stomach. The DNA reports on the semen and blood found on the first two victims had concluded that the samples were identical. No one expected a different result this time. It was being fast-tracked nonetheless.

A pair of techs at the document section of the crime lab had now been exclusively assigned to the case to track down the origin of the moon drawing.

The Philadelphia field office of the FBI had been contacted regarding the abduction of Sa'mantha Fanning. They were analyzing the tape and processing the scene. For the time being, the case was out of the hands of the PPD. Everyone expected the case to become a homicide. As always, everyone hoped they were wrong.

"Where are we on the fairy-tale angle?" Buchanan asked. It was just after six o'clock. Everyone was exhausted, hungry, ill-tempered. Lives were being put on hold, plans cancelled. Some holiday season. They were waiting on the preliminary report from the medical examiner's office. Jessica and Byrne were among the handful of detectives in the duty room. "Working on it," Jessica said.

"You might want to look into this," Buchanan said.

He handed Jessica a section of a page from that morning's *Inquirer*. It was a brief article about a man named Trevor Bridgwood. Bridgwood was a traveling storyteller and troubadour, the article said. Whatever that was.

Buchanan had given them more than a suggestion, it seemed. He had dug up the lead, and they *would* follow up.

"We're on it, Sarge," Byrne said.

THEY MET IN a hotel room at the Sofitel on Seventeenth Street. Later that evening, Trevor Bridgwood was doing a reading and signing at Joseph Fox Bookshop, an independent bookstore on Sansom Street.

*There must be money in the fairy-tale business,* Jessica thought. The Sofitel was far from cheap.

Trevor Bridgwood was in his early thirties, slender and graceful, decorous. He had a sharp nose and a receding hairline, a theatrical manner.

"This is all rather new to me," he said. "More than a little unnerving, I might add."

"We're just looking for some information," Jessica said. "We appreciate you meeting with us on such short notice."

"I hope I can assist."

"Can I ask what it is you do exactly?" Jessica asked.

"I am a storyteller," Bridgwood replied. "I spend nine or ten months of the year on the road. I appear all over the world, performing in the United States, Great Britain, Australia, Canada. Anywhere English is spoken."

"In front of live audiences?"

"Mostly. But I also perform on radio and television."

"And your main focus is fairy tales?"

"Fairy tales, folk tales, fables."

"What can you tell us about them?" Byrne asked.

Bridgwood stood, walked to the window. He moved like a dancer. "There's an awful lot to know," he said. "It's an old form of storytelling, encompassing many different styles and traditions."

"Just the primer then, I guess," Byrne said.

"We can begin with 'Cupid and Psyche,' if you wish, which was written around A.D. 150 or so."

"Maybe something a little more recent," Byrne said.

"Of course." Bridgwood smiled. "There are many touchstones in between Apuleius and *Edward Scissorhands*."

"Such as?" Byrne asked.

"Where to begin. Well, Charles Perrault's *Histoires ou Contes du temps passé* was important. That collection contained 'Cinderella,' 'The Sleeping Beauty,' 'Little Red Riding Hood,' and others."

"When was this?" Jessica asked.

"It was 1697, or thereabouts," Bridgwood said. "Then of course in the early 1800s the Brothers Grimm published two volumes of collected stories titled *Kinder und Hausmärchen*. These are some of the best known fairy tales, of course—'The Pied Piper of Hamelin,' 'Tom Thumb,' 'Rapunzel,' 'Rumpelstiltskin.' "

Jessica took the best notes she could. Her German and French were sorely lacking.

"After that, Hans Christian Andersen published his *Fairy Tales Told for Children* in 1835. Ten years later two men named Asbjornsen and Moe released a collection called *Norwegian Folk Tales,* from which we read 'The Three Billy Goats Gruff' and others.

"Arguably, as we approach the twentieth century, there are really no major new works or new collections to be found. Much of it is retelling of classics as we move into Humperdinck's opera of *Hansel and Gretel.* Then Disney released *Snow White and the Seven Dwarfs* in 1937, the form was revived, and it has flourished ever since."

"Flourished?" Byrne asked. "Flourished how?"

"Ballet, theater, television, movies. Even the film *Shrek* owes the form. And, to a certain extent, *The Lord of the Rings*. Tolkien himself published 'On Fairy Stories,' an essay on the subject that he expanded from a lecture he gave in 1939. It is still widely read and discussed in college-level fairy-tale studies."

Byrne looked at Jessica, back at Bridgwood. "There are college courses in this?" she asked.

"Oh yes." Bridgwood smiled, a little sadly. He crossed the room, sat at the desk. "You probably have the notion that fairy tales are rather sweet little morality tales for children."

"I guess I do," Byrne said.

"Some are. Many are much darker than that. In fact, a book called *The Uses of Enchantment* by Bruno Bettelheim explored the psychology of fairy tales and children. It won the National Book Award.

"There are, of course, many other important figures. You asked for an overview, and that's what I'm giving you."

"If you could sum up what they all have in common, it might make it easier for us," Byrne said. "What is the common thread?"

"Essentially, a fairy tale is a story that arises out of myth and legend. Written tales probably grew out of the oral folk-tale tradition. They tend to involve the mysterious or supernatural, they tend not to be tied to any specific moment in history. Hence the phrase 'once upon a time.' "

"Are they tied to any religion?" Byrne asked.

"Not usually," Bridgwood said. "They can be quite spiritual, however. They usually involve a humble hero, a perilous quest, a vile villain. Folks are usually all good or all bad in fairy tales. Many times the conflict is resolved by using, to some extent, magic. But this is terribly broad. *Terribly* broad."

Bridgwood sounded apologetic now, like a man who had shortchanged an entire field of academic study.

"I don't want to leave you with the impression that fairy tales are all alike," he added. "Nothing could be further from the truth."

"Can you think of any specific stories or collections that focus on the moon as its subject?" Jessica asked.

Bridgwood thought for a few moments. "One that springs to mind is a rather long story that is really a series of very short sketches. It is a narrative that tells of a young painter and the moon."

Jessica flashed on the "paintings" found on their victims. "What happens in the stories?" she asked.

"Well, this painter is very lonely, you see." Bridgwood suddenly became quite animated. It appeared that he was shifting into a theatrical mode—better posture, hand gestures, lively tone. "He lives in a small town and has no friends. One night he is sitting in his window and the moon comes to him. They talk for a while. Before long the moon makes the painter a promise that every night he will return and tell the painter what he has witnessed all over the world. In this way, the painter, without leaving his home, could imagine these scenes, render them to canvas, and perhaps become famous. Or maybe just make a few friends. It is a marvelous story."

"You say the moon comes to him every night?" Jessica asked.

"Yes."

"For how long?"

"The moon comes thirty-two times."

*Thirty-two times,* Jessica thought. "And this was a Grimms' tale?" she asked.

"No, this was written by Hans Christian Andersen. The story is called 'What the Moon Saw.'"

"And when did Hans Christian Andersen live?" she asked.

"From 1805 to 1875," Bridgwood said.

*I would put the originals at around the second half of the nineteenth century,* Ingrid Fanning had said about the dresses. *Closer to the end. Perhaps 1875 or so.*

Bridgwood reached into a suitcase on the table. He extracted a leather-bound book. "This is not by any means the complete works of Andersen, nor despite its weathered appearance, is it particularly valuable. You are welcome to borrow it." He slipped a card into the book. "Return it to this address whenever you are finished. Take as long as you like."

"That would be helpful," Jessica said. "We'll get it back to you as soon as possible."

"Now, if you'll excuse me."

Jessica and Byrne stood, slipped on their coats.

"I'm sorry I have to rush," Bridgwood said. "I have a performance in twenty minutes. Can't keep the little wizards and princesses waiting."

"Of course," Byrne said. "We thank you for your time."

At this, Bridgwood crossed the room, reached into a closet, pulled out a very old-looking black tuxedo. He hung it on the back of the door.

Byrne asked, "Is there anything else you can think of that might help us?"

"Only this: To understand magic, you have to believe." Bridgwood slid into the old tuxedo coat. Suddenly he was a denizen of the late nineteenth century—slender, aristocratic, somewhat peculiar. Trevor Bridgwood turned, winked. "At least a little bit."

# 61

It was all in Trevor Bridgwood's book. And the knowledge was horrifying.

"The Red Shoes" was a fable about a girl named Karen, a dancer who has her feet amputated.

"The Nightingale" was about a bird that captivated an emperor with its song.

"Thumbelina" was about a tiny woman who lived on a lily pad.

Detectives Kevin Byrne and Jessica Balzano, along with four other detectives, stood speechless in the suddenly quiet duty room, looking at pen and ink illustrations from a children's book, the realization of what they were facing a raging stream beneath their thoughts. The anger in the air was palpable. The feeling of frustration was worse.

Someone was killing the citizens of Philadelphia in a series of murders based on the stories of Hans Christian Andersen. The killer had struck three times that they knew of, and now there was a good chance that he had Sa'mantha Fanning. Which fable would she be? Where was he going to place her on the river? Would they be able to find her in time?

All these questions paled in the light of one other gruesome fact contained between the covers of the book they had borrowed from Trevor Bridgwood.

Hans Christian Andersen wrote nearly two hundred stories.

# 62

The details surrounding the strangulation murders of the three victims found along the banks of the Schuylkill River had leaked, and every newspaper in the city, the region, and the state was carrying the story of a compulsive killer in Philadelphia. The headlines, as expected, were lurid.

*A Fairy Tale Murderer in Philadelphia?*

*A Fabled Killer?*

*Who is the Schuylkiller?*

*Hansel and Regrettable?* trumpeted the *Record*, a tabloid rag of the lowest order.

The usually jaded Philadelphia media were off and running. There were news crews up and down the Schuylkill River, doing stand-up shots on the bridges, on the banks. A news helicopter had flown the entire length of the river, taking footage as it did so. The bookstores and libraries could not keep books on Hans Christian Andersen on the shelves, nor the works of the Brothers Grimm and Mother Goose. It was close enough for the sensationalists.

Calls were coming into the department every few minutes about ogres and monsters and trolls following children throughout the city. One woman called and said she had seen a man in a wolf costume in Fairmount Park. A sector car followed up and found it to be true.

The man was currently in the drunk tank at the Round-house.

By the morning of December 30 there were a total of five detectives and six crime-scene officers assigned to investigate the crimes.

Sa'mantha Fanning had not yet been found.

There were no suspects.

# 63

At just after three o'clock on December 30 Ike Buchanan stepped out of his office, got Jessica's attention. She had been collating rope suppliers, trying to track down retail outlets that carried the specific brand of swim lane rope. Trace evidence of the rope had been found on the third victim. The bad news was that, in this day and age of Internet shopping, you could buy just about anything without face-to-face contact. The good news was that Internet shopping generally required a credit card or Pay-Pal. That was Jessica's next line of inquiry.

Nick Palladino and Tony Park were off to Norristown to interview people at the Centre Theater, looking into anyone there who might have been connected to Tara Grendel. Kevin Byrne and Josh Bontrager were canvassing the area near where the third victim had been found.

"Can I see you a minute?" Buchanan asked.

Jessica welcomed the break. She stepped into his office. Buchanan motioned for her to close the door. She did.

"What's up, boss?"

"I'm pulling you off the multiple. Just for a few days."

The statement took her by surprise, to say the least. No, it was more like a hook to the gut. It was almost as if he had said she was *fired*. He hadn't, of course, but she had never been pulled from an investigation before. She didn't like it. She didn't know a cop who did.

"Why?"

"Because I'm putting Eric on that gang hit. He's got the contacts, it's his old patch, and he speaks the language."

There had been a triple homicide the day before, a Latino couple and their ten-year-old son had been killed, execution-style, while sleeping in their beds. The theory was that it was gang retaliation, and Eric Chavez, before joining the Homicide Unit, had worked Antigang.

"So you want me to—"

"Work the Walt Brigham case," Buchanan said. "You'll be partnered with Nicci."

Jessica felt a strange mixture of emotions. She had worked one detail with Nicci, and she looked forward to the chance of working with her again, but Kevin Byrne was her partner, and they had a bond that transcended gender and age and time on the job.

Buchanan held out a notebook. Jessica took it from him. "These are Eric's notes on the case. It should get you up to speed. He said to call him if you had any questions."

"Thanks, Sarge," Jessica said. "Does Kevin know?"

"I just talked to him."

Jessica wondered why her cell phone hadn't yet rung. "Is he partnering up?" As soon as she said it, she identified the feeling spiking through her: jealousy. If Byrne picked up another partner, even on a temporary basis, it would feel like she was being cheated on.

*What are you, in high school, Jess?* she thought. *He's*

*not your boyfriend, he's your partner. Get a freakin'
grip.*

"Kevin, Josh, Tony, and Nick will work the cases.
We're stretched to the limit here."

It was true. From a peak of 7,000 police officers three
years earlier, the PPD was down to 6,400, the lowest it
had been since the mid-nineties. And it got worse from
there. Around 600 officers were currently listed as injured and not reporting for work, or were on restricted
desk duty. Special plainclothes teams in each district were
being switched back to uniformed patrol, boosting the
police profile in some neighborhoods. Recently, the commissioner had announced the formation of the Strategic
Intervention Tactical Enforcement Mobile Unit, an elite
forty-six-officer anticrime team to patrol the city's most
dangerous areas. For the last three months every
nonessential officer at the Roundhouse had been put
back on the street. It was a bad time for Philly's cops, and
sometimes a detective's assignments, and their focus,
shifted at a moment's notice.

"How long?" Jessica asked.

"Just for a few days."

"I have calls out, boss."

"I understand. If you have a few spare minutes, or if
something breaks, follow it. But for now, our plate is
full. And we simply don't have the warm bodies. Work
with Nicci."

Jessica understood the pressure to solve a cop killing.
If the criminals were getting bolder and bolder these
days—and there was little debate about that—they
would go off the chart if they thought they could exe-
cute a cop on the street and not feel the heat.

"Hey, partner." Jessica turned. It was Nicci Malone.
She liked Nicci a lot, but it sounded . . . funny. No. It
sounded *wrong.* But, like any other job, you go where

the boss puts you, and right now she was partnered with the only other female homicide detective in Philly.

"Hey." It was all Jessica could muster. She was certain that Nicci read it.

"Ready to roll?" Nicci asked.

"Let's do it."

# 64

Jessica and Nicci drove down Eighth Street. It had begun to rain again. Byrne still hadn't called.

"Bring me up to speed," Jessica said, a little shell-shocked. She was used to working more than one case at a time—the truth was that most homicide detectives worked three and four at a time—but she still found it a little difficult to shift gears, to take on the mind-set of a new perpetrator. And a new partner. Earlier in the day she was thinking about a psychopath who was placing bodies along a riverbank. Her mind was filled with ti-tles of Hans Christian Andersen stories—"The Little Mermaid," "The Princess and the Pea," "The Ugly Duckling"—wondering which, if any, might be next. Now she was chasing a cop killer.

"Well, I think one thing is obvious," Nicci said. "Walt Brigham wasn't a victim of some botched robbery. You don't douse someone with gasoline and set them on fire to get their wallet."

"So you think it was someone Walt Brigham put away?"

"I think that's a good bet. We ran his arrests and convictions for the past fifteen years. Unfortunately, no firebugs in the group."

"Anyone recently released from prison?"

"Not in the last six months. And I don't see whoever did this waiting that long to get to the guy he blamed for putting them away, do you?"

No, Jessica thought. There was a high level of passion—insane as that passion might be—in what was done to Walt Brigham. "What about someone involved in his last case?" she asked.

"Doubt it. His last official case was a domestic. Wife bashed her husband with a crowbar. He's dead, she's in prison."

Jessica knew what this meant. Because there were no eyewitnesses to Walt Brigham's murder, and there was a dearth of forensics, they would have to begin at the beginning—everybody Walt Brigham had arrested, convicted, even ruffled, starting with his last case and moving backward. That narrowed the suspect pool down a few thousand.

"So, we're off to Records?"

"I have a few more ideas before we bunker up with the paperwork," Nicci said.

"Hit me."

"I spoke with Walt Brigham's widow. She said Walt kept a storage locker. If this was something personal—as in, nothing directly to do with the job—there might be something in there."

"Anything to keep my face out of a file cabinet," Jessica said. "How do we get in?"

Nicci held up a single key on a key ring, smiled. "I stopped by Marjorie Brigham's house this morning."

THE EASY MAX Storage on Mifflin Street was a large, U-shaped, two-story facility that housed more than a hundred units of varying sizes. Some were heated, most were not. Unfortunately, Walt Brigham had not sprung for one of the heated units. It was like walking into a meat locker.

The space was about eight feet by ten feet, stacked nearly to the ceiling with cardboard boxes. The good news was that Walt Brigham was an organized man. All the boxes were of the same type and size—the kind you buy flat at office-supply stores—and most were labeled and dated.

They started at the back. There were three boxes dedicated to nothing but Christmas and birthday cards. Many of the cards were from Walt's children, and as Jessica went through them she saw the years of their lives pass and, as the children got older, their grammar and penmanship improve. The teenage years were easy to spot, with just simple signatures of their names, not the gushy sentiments of childhood, as glittery handmade cards yielded to Hallmark. Another box contained only maps and travel brochures. It seemed that Walt and Marjorie Brigham were summer RV people, taking trips to Wisconsin, Florida, Ohio, and Kentucky.

At the bottom of the box was on old piece of yellowed notebook paper. On it was a list that contained a dozen girls' names—Melissa, Arlene, Rita, Elizabeth, Cynthia among them. They were all crossed out, except for the last one. The last name on the list was Roberta. Walt Brigham's oldest daughter's name was Roberta. Jessica realized what she was holding in her hand. It was a list of possible names for a young couple's first child. She gently returned it to the box.

While Nicci looked through a few boxes of letters and household documents, Jessica sifted through a box of photographs. Weddings, birthday parties, graduations, police functions. Like always, whenever faced with rooting through the personal effects of a victim, you wanted to accrue as much information as possible, while at the same time preserving some degree of the victim's privacy.

More boxes produced more photographs and mementos, all meticulously dated and catalogued. An incredibly young Walt Brigham at the police academy, a handsome Walt Brigham on his wedding day, dressed in a rather striking navy blue tuxedo. Pictures of Walt in uniform, Walt with his kids in Fairmount Park, Walt and Marjorie Brigham squinting at the camera on a beach somewhere, maybe Wildwood, their faces a deep pink that portended a painful sunburn that night.

What was she gleaning from all this? What she already suspected. Walt Brigham was no renegade cop. He was a family man who collected and cherished the touchstones of his life. Neither Jessica nor Nicci found anything to indicate why someone had so viciously taken his life.

They continued to look through the boxes of memories, interlopers in the forest of the dead.

# 65

The third victim found on the bank of the Schuylkill River was named Lisette Simon. She'd been forty-one, had lived with her husband in Upper Darby, had no children. She worked for a county mental-health facility in North Philadelphia.

Lisette Simon was just under forty-eight inches tall. Her husband Ruben was an attorney with a storefront legal firm in the Northeast. They would be interviewing him that afternoon.

Nick Palladino and Tony Park had returned from Norristown. No one at the Centre Theater had noticed anyone paying particular attention to Tara Grendel.

Despite the circulation and publication of her picture in all local and state media—broadcast and print alike— there was still no trace of Sa'mantha Fanning.

THE WHITEBOARD WAS covered with photographs, notes, memos, a mosaic of disparate clues and blind alleys.

Byrne stood in front of it, as frustrated as he was impatient.

He needed his partner.

They all knew that the Brigham case was going to get political. The department needed movement on the case, and they needed it now. The City of Philadelphia could not have its high-profile police officers at risk.

There was no denying that Jessica was one of the best detectives in the unit. Byrne did not know Nicci Malone that well, but she had a good reputation, and a ton of street cred, coming out of North detectives.

Two women. In a department as politically sensitive as the PPD, having two female detectives working a case in this bright a spotlight was smart.

Besides, Byrne thought, it might take some of the media attention away from the fact that there was a compulsive killer walking the streets.

THERE WAS NOW full agreement that the pathology of the river killings was rooted in the stories of Hans Christian Andersen. But how were the victims being selected?

Chronologically Lisette Simon had been the first victim. She had been left on the bank of the Schuylkill in the Southwest.

The second victim had been Kristina Jakos, placed on

the bank of the Schuylkill in Manayunk. The victim's amputated feet were found on the Strawberry Mansion Bridge, which spans the river.

Victim number three was Tara Grendel, abducted from a Center City parking garage, murdered, then left on the bank of the Schuylkill, in Shawmont.

Was the killer leading them upriver?

Byrne marked the three crime scenes on a map. There was a long stretch of the river between the Southwest scene and the Manayunk scene, the two sites they believed represented the first two murders chronologically.

"Why the long stretch of river between dump sites?" Bontrager asked, reading Byrne's thoughts.

Byrne ran his hand along the crooked length of the river. "Well, we can't be sure there *isn't* a body in here somewhere. But my guess is that there aren't too many places to pull over and do what he had to do without being seen. Nobody really looks at the area beneath the Platt Bridge. The Flat Rock Road scene is shielded from the expressway and the road. The Shawmont pump house is totally secluded."

It was true. As the river passed through the city, its banks were visible from many vantage points. Especially on Kelly Drive. Nearly all year that stretch was frequented by joggers, rowers, cyclists. There were places to pull over, but the road was rarely deserted. There was always traffic.

"So he was looking for privacy," Bontrager said.

"Exactly," Byrne said. "And enough time."

Bontrager sat at a computer, maneuvered his way over to Google Maps. The farther the river got from the city, the more secluded were its banks.

Byrne studied the satellite map. If the killer was leading them upriver, the question remained: To where? The distance between the Shawmont pump station and the headwaters of the Schuylkill River had to be nearly one hundred miles. There were lots of places to hide a body and not be seen.

And how was he choosing his victims? Tara had been an actress. Kristina had been a dancer. There was a connection there. Both had been performers. Entertainers. But the connection ended with Lisette. Lisette was a mental-health professional.

Age?

Tara had been twenty-eight. Kristina had been twenty-four. Lisette had been forty-one. Too much of a range.

*Thumbelina. The Red Shoes. The Nightingale.*

Nothing tied the women together. Nothing on the surface, at least. Except the fables.

The scant information on Sa'mantha Fanning did not lead them in any obvious direction. She was nineteen years old, unmarried, had a six-month-old son named Jamie. The boy's father was a loser named Joel Radnor. He had a short sheet—a few drug possession charges, one simple assault, nothing else. He had been in Los Angeles for the past month.

"What if our guy is some kind of stage-door Johnny?" Bontrager asked.

It had crossed Byrne's mind, even if he knew the theater angle was a long shot. These victims had not been chosen because they'd been acquainted with each other. They had not been selected because they'd frequented the same clinic, or church, or social club. They'd been chosen because they had fit the killer's terribly warped story. They had answered a body type, a visage, a countenance that satisfied an ideal.

"Do we know if Lisette Simon did any kind of theater?" Byrne asked.

Bontrager got to his feet. "I'll find out." He left the duty room as Tony Park entered with a thicket of computer printouts in hand.

"This is everyone who Lisette Simon worked with at the mental-health clinic in the past six months," Park said.

"How many names are in there?" Byrne asked.

"Four hundred sixty-six."

"Jesus Christ."

"He's the only one *not* in there."

"Let's see if we can't whittle that down to males eighteen to fifty for starters."

"You got it."

An hour later they had the list reduced to a manageable ninety-seven names. They began the mind-numbing task of running a variety of checks—PDCH, PCIC, NCIC—on each of them.

Josh Bontrager spoke to Ruben Simon. Ruben's late wife, Lisette, had never been involved with the theater.

# 66

The temperature had dropped a few more degrees and the storage locker was even more like a refrigerator. Jessica's fingers were turning blue. As awkward as it made it to work with paper, she put her leather gloves on.

The last box she looked in had some water damage. It contained a single accordion folder. Inside were damp photocopies of files taken from the murder books of victims over the past twelve years or so. Jessica opened the folder to the most recent section.

Inside were two eight by ten black-and-white photographs, both of the same stone building, one shot from a few hundred feet away, one much closer. The photos were curled with water damage and had DUPLICATE stamped across the upper right. They were not official PPD photographs. The structure in the photograph appeared to be a farmhouse; the long shot revealed that it sat on a gently sloping hill, with a line of snow-covered trees in the background.

"Have you run across any other pictures of this house?" Jessica asked.

Nicci looked closely at the photographs. "No. Haven't seen it."

Jessica flipped one of the pictures over. On the back was a series of five numbers, the last two of which were obscured by water damage. The first three numbers appeared to be 195. A zip code, maybe? "Do you know where the 195 zip code is?" she asked.

"195," Nicci said. "Berks County, maybe?"

"That's what I was thinking."

"Whereabouts in Berks?"

"No idea."

Nicci's pager went off. She unclipped it, read the message. "It's the boss," she said. "You have your phone with you?"

"You don't have a phone?"

"Don't ask," Nicci said. "I've lost three in the last six months. They're gonna start docking me."

"With me it's pagers," Jessica said.

"We'll make a good team."

Jessica handed Nicci her cell phone. Nicci stepped out of the storage locker to make the call.

Jessica glanced back at one of the photographs, the one showing a closer view of the farmhouse. She flipped it over. On the back were three letters, nothing else.

*ADC.*

*What does that mean?* Jessica wondered. *Aid to*

*Dependent Children? American Dental Council? Art Director's Club?*

Sometimes Jessica hated the way cops thought. She'd been guilty of it herself in the past, the abbreviated notes you wrote to yourself in a case file, with the intention of fleshing them out at a later date. Detectives' notebooks always went into evidence, and the thought that a case might hang on something you wrote in a hurry at a red light while balancing a cheeseburger and a cup of coffee in the other hand was always a challenge.

But, when Walt Brigham had made these notes, he had no idea another detective would one day be reading and trying to make sense of them—a detective investigating his homicide.

Jessica flipped over the first photograph again. Just those five numbers. The numbers 195 followed by what might have been a 72 or a 78. Perhaps 18.

Did the farmhouse have something to do with Walt's murder? It was dated a few days before his death.

*Gee thanks, Walt,* Jessica thought. *You go and get yourself killed and you leave the investigating detectives a Sudoku puzzle to figure out.*

195.

ADC.

Nicci stepped back in, handed Jessica her phone.

"That was the lab," she said. "We struck out on Walt's car."

*Square one, forensically speaking,* Jessica thought.

"But they told me to tell you that the lab ran some further tests on the blood found on your multiples," Nicci added.

"What about it?"

"They said the blood is old."

"Old?" Jessica asked. "What do you mean, old?"

"Old as in whoever it belonged to has probably been dead a long time."

# 67

Roland wrestled with the devil. And while it was a daily occurrence for a man of faith such as himself, today the devil had him in a headlock.

He had looked at all the photos at the police station, hoping for a sign. He had seen so much evil in those eyes, so many blackened souls. All of them spoke to him of their deeds. None had spoken of Charlotte.

But it could not be coincidence. Charlotte had been found on the bank of the Wissahickon, posed as if she had been some doll in a story.

And now the river killings.

Roland knew that the police would eventually catch up with Charles and him. He had been blessed all these years, blessed with his stealth, his righteous heart, his endurance.

He would receive a sign. He was sure of it.

The good Lord knew that time was of the essence.

"I'VE NEVER BEEN able to go back down there."

Elijah Paulson was telling the harrowing tale of the time he had been assaulted while walking home from the Reading Terminal Market.

"Maybe one day, with the Lord's blessing, I will be able to. But not now," Elijah Paulson said. "Not for a good long while."

This day the victim's group had only four participants.

Sadie Pierce, as always. Old Elijah Paulson. A young woman named Bess Schrantz, a North Philly waitress whose sister had been brutally assaulted. And Sean. He sat outside the group, as he often did, listening. But this day there seemed to be something churning beneath his surface.

When Elijah Paulson sat down, Roland turned to Sean. Perhaps at last this was the day that Sean was ready to tell his story. A hush fell upon the room. Roland nodded. After a minute or so of fidgeting, Sean stood, began.

"My father left us when I was small. When I was growing up it was just my mother, my sister, and myself. My mother worked at a mill. We didn't have a lot, but we got by. We had each other."

The members of the group nodded. No one here was well off.

"One summer day we went to this small amusement park. My sister loved to feed the pigeons and the squirrels. She loved the water, the trees. She was gentle that way."

As Roland listened, he could not bring himself to look at Charles.

"That afternoon she wandered off, and we couldn't find her," Sean continued. "We looked everywhere. Then it got dark. Later that night they found her in the woods. She . . . she had been killed."

A murmur skirted the room. Words of sympathy, sorrow. Roland found that his hands were trembling. *Sean's story was nearly his own.*

"When did this happen, Brother Sean?" Roland asked.

After taking a moment to compose himself, Sean said, "This was in 1995."

\* \* \*

TWENTY MINUTES LATER the meeting wrapped with a prayer and a blessing. The faithful filed out.

"Bless you," Roland said to all of them at the door. "See you on Sunday." The last person through was Sean. "Do you have a few moments, Brother Sean?"

"Sure, Pastor."

Roland closed the door, stood in front of the young man. A few long moments later, he asked, "Do you know what an important day this has been for you?"

Sean nodded. It was clear that his emotions were not far from the surface. Roland took Sean in an embrace. Sean sobbed softly. When the tears ran their course, they broke the embrace. Charles crossed the room, handed Sean a box of tissues, retreated.

"Can you tell me more about what happened?" Roland asked.

Sean bowed his head for a moment. When he looked up, he glanced around the room and leaned forward, as if to share a secret. "We always knew who did it, but they never could find any evidence. The police, I mean."

"I see."

"Well, it was the sheriff's office that did the investigating. They said they never found enough evidence to arrest anyone."

"Where are you from exactly?"

"It was near a little village called Odense."

"Odense?" Roland asked. "Like the town in Denmark?"

Sean shrugged.

"Does this person still live there?" Roland asked. "The person you suspected?"

"Oh, yes," Sean said. "I can give you the address. Or I can even show you, if you like."

"That would be good," Roland said.

Sean looked at his watch. "I have to work today," he said. "But I can go tomorrow."

Roland glanced at Charles. Charles left the room. "That will be fine."

Roland walked Sean toward the door, his arm around the young man's shoulders.

"Did I do the right thing in telling you, Pastor?" Sean asked.

"Oh my, yes," Roland said, opening the door. "It was the right thing to do." He held the young man in another deep embrace. He found that Sean was shaking. "I'll take care of everything."

"Okay," Sean said. "Tomorrow then?"

"Yes," Roland replied. "Tomorrow."

# 68

In his dream they have no faces. In his dream they stand in front of him, statuary, statu*esque,* unmoving. In his dream he cannot see their eyes, but nevertheless knows they are looking at him, accusing him, demanding justice. Their silhouettes cascade into the fog, one after the other, a grim, unflinching still-life army of the dead.

He knows their names. He recalls the position of their bodies. He remembers their smells, the way their flesh felt beneath his touch, the way their waxy skin, in death, did not respond.

But he cannot see their faces.

And yet their names echo in his dream-chamber of remembrance. Lisette Simon, Kristina Jakos, Tara Grendel.

He hears a woman crying softly. It is Sa'mantha Fanning, and there is nothing he can do to help her. He sees her walking down the hallway. He follows, but with every step the corridor grows, lengthens, darkens. He opens the door at the end, but she is gone. In her place is a man carved of shadows. He draws his weapon, levels, aims, fires.

Smoke.

KEVIN BYRNE WOKE with a start, his heart pounding in his chest. He glanced at the clock. It was 3:50 AM. He looked around his bedroom. Empty. No specters, no ghosts, no shambling parade of corpses.

Just the dream-sound of water, just the knowledge that all of them, all the faceless dead in the world, were standing in the river.

# 69

On the morning of the last day of the year the sun was bone pale. The weather forecast predicted a snowstorm.

Jessica was off duty, but her mind was not. Her thoughts jumped from Walt Brigham to the three women found on the banks of the river to Sa'mantha Fanning. Sa'mantha had still not been found. The department did not hold out much hope that she was still alive.

Vincent was on duty; Sophie was bundled off to her

grandfather's house for New Year's Eve. Jessica had the place to herself. She could do whatever she wanted.

So why was she sitting in her kitchen, nursing her fourth cup of coffee, thinking about the dead?

At just after eight o'clock there was a knock at her door. It was Nicci Malone.

"Hey," Jessica said, more than a little surprised. "Come on in."

Nicci stepped inside. "*Man,* it's cold."

"Coffee?"

"Oh, yeah."

THEY SAT AT the dining room table. Nicci had brought a number of files.

"There's something here you should see," Nicci said. She was pumped.

She opened a large envelope, took out a few photocopied pages. They were pages from Walt Brigham's notebook. Not his official detective's book, but a second, personal notebook. The last entry regarded the Annemarie DiCillo case, dated two days before Walt's murder. The notations were in Walt's now familiar cryptic hand.

Nicci had also signed out the DiCillo PPD homicide case file. Jessica scanned it.

Byrne had told Jessica about the case, but seeing the details made her sick. Two little girls at their birthday party in Fairmount Park in 1995. Annemarie DiCillo and Charlotte Waite. They had walked into the forest, and never walked out. How many times had Jessica taken her own daughter to the park? How many times had she taken her eyes off Sophie just for a second?

Jessica looked at the crime-scene photographs. The girls were found near the base of a pine tree. Close-up photographs showed what appeared to be a makeshift nest built around them.

There were a few dozen witness statements from families that were in the park that day. No one seemed to have seen anything. The little girls were there one minute, and the next they were gone. Police were called at about 7 PM that evening, and a tender-age search was conducted, involving two officers and dogs from the K-9 unit. At 3 AM the next morning the girls were found near the bank of the Wissahickon Creek.

Over the next few years there were periodic entries into the file, mostly from Walt Brigham, some from his partner John Longo. Each of the entries was similar. Nothing new.

"Look." Nicci took out the photographs of the farmhouse, flipped them over. On the back of one picture was the partial zip code. On the other were the three letters ADC. Nicci pointed to a timeline in Walt Brigham's notes. Among the many bits of shorthand were the same letters: ADC.

*ADC was Annemarie DiCillo.*

A jolt of electricity shot through Jessica. The farmhouse had something to do with Annemarie's murder. And Annemarie's murder had something to do with Walt Brigham's death.

"Walt was getting close." Jessica said. "He was murdered because he was closing in on the killer."

"Bingo."

Jessica considered the evidence and the theory. Nicci was probably right. "What do you want to do?" she asked.

Nicci tapped the picture of the farmhouse. "I want to take a ride to Berks County. Maybe we can find this house."

Jessica was on her feet in an instant. "I'll go with you."

"Aren't you off duty?"

Jessica laughed. "What's off duty?"

"It's New Year's Eve."

"As long as I'm home and in my husband's arms by midnight, I'm good."

At just after 9 AM on December 31, Detectives Jessica Balzano and Nicolette Malone of the Philadelphia Police Department's Homicide Division got on the Schuylkill Expressway. They headed to Berks County, Pennsylvania.

They headed upriver.

PART FOUR

# WHAT THE
# MOON SAW

# 70

You stand where the waters meet, at the confluence of two great rivers. The winter sun is low in a salt-colored sky. You choose a path, follow the smaller river north, winding among lyrical names and historic places—Bartram's Garden, Point Breeze, Grays Ferry. You float past sullen row houses, past the majesty of the city, past Boathouse Row and the Museum of Art, past the train yards, the East Park Reservoir, and the Strawberry Mansion Bridge. You slide northwest, whispering in your wake ancient incantations—Miquon, Conshohocken, Wissahickon. You leave the city now, and hover among the phantoms of Valley Forge, Phoenixville, Spring City. The Schuylkill snakes into history, the nation's remembrance. Yet still, it is the hidden river.

You soon bid farewell to the river main, entering a haven of silence, a thin, meandering tributary heading southwest. The waterway narrows, widens, narrows again, a twisting tangle of rock and shale and water willow.

Suddenly, from the silted winter mist appears a handful of buildings. A huge trellis spans the canal, once grand, now fallen into neglect and disrepair, its bright colors dour and flaked and dry.

You see an old structure, at one time a proud boathouse. The fragrance of marine paint and varnish still lives in the air. You enter a room. It is a tidy place, a place of deep shadow and sharp angles.

*In this room you find a workbench. On the bench is an old, but sharp, saw. Next to it, a coil of blue and white rope.*

*You see a dress laid out on a daybed, waiting. It is a beautiful gown, pale strawberry in color, shirred to the waist. A dress for a princess.*

*You continue, winding through a maze of narrow canals. You hear the echo of laughter, the lap of waves against small brightly colored boats. You smell the aroma of carnival foods—elephant ears, cotton candy, the glorious tang of sauerbraten on fresh seeded rolls. You hear the lilt of the calliope.*

*And farther on, farther still, until all is silent again. Now it is a place of darkness. A place where graves chill the earth.*

*It is here that Moon will meet you.*

*He knows you are coming.*

# 71

Throughout southeastern Pennsylvania there were small towns and villages scattered among the farms, most with just a handful of commercial enterprises, a pair of churches, a small school. In addition to growing cities like Lancaster and Reading there were bucolic villages like Oley and Exeter, hamlets virtually untouched by time.

As they passed through Valley Forge, Jessica realized how much of her state she had not experienced. As

much as she hated to admit it, she had been twenty-six
before she had actually seen the Liberty Bell up close.
She imagined it was like that for a lot of people who
lived near history.

THERE WERE MORE than thirty zip codes in Berks
County. The area covered by the 195 zip code prefix
covered a large area at the southeastern end of the
county.

Jessica and Nicci took a few back roads and began to
ask about the farmhouse. They had debated involving
local law enforcement in their quest, but things like that
at times entailed red tape, jurisdictional issues. They
kept it open, available as an option, but decided to do it
on their own for the time being.

They inquired at small shops, gas stations, the occasional roadside stands. They stopped at a church on
White Bear Road. People were pleasant enough, but no
one seemed to recognize the farmhouse, or have any
idea where it was located.

At noon the detectives took a road heading south
through Robeson Township. A few wrong turns put
them on a rough two-lane that wound through the
woods. Fifteen minutes later they came upon an auto
body and collision shop.

The fields surrounding the enterprise were a necropo-
lis of corroded vehicle shells—fenders and doors, long
rusted bumpers, engine blocks, aluminum truck caps.
To the right was an outbuilding; a sulking corrugated
shed pitching at about a forty-five degree angle to the
ground. Everything was overgrown, neglected, covered
with gray snow and grime. If it hadn't been for the lights
in the windows—including a struggling neon sign adver-
tising *Mopar*—the building would have looked derelict.

Jessica and Nicci pulled into the parking lot, itself
populated with broken-down cars, vans, trucks. There

was an RV on blocks. Jessica wondered if that was where the proprietor lived. A sign above the entrance to the garage read:

DOUBLE K AUTO / TWICE THE VALUE

An ancient, disinterested mastiff, chained to a pole, gave a cursory *woof* as they approached the main building.

JESSICA AND NICCI entered. The three-bay garage was jammed with automotive debris. A greasy radio on the counter played Tim McGraw. The place smelled like WD40, grape candy, and old lunch meat.

The bell on the door announced them, and after a few seconds two men approached. They were twins in their early thirties. They wore matching grimy blue overalls, had disheveled blond hair, blackened hands. Their name tags read KYLE and KEITH.

Hence the *Double K,* Jessica suspected.

"Hi," Nicci said.

Neither man answered. Instead, they slowly ran their eyes over Nicci, then Jessica. Nicci plowed ahead. She showed her ID, introduced herself. "We're with the Philadelphia Police Department."

Both men pulled faces, mugging, mocking. They remained silent.

"We'd like a few minutes of your time," Nicci added.

Kyle smiled a big yellow grin. "I've got all day for you, darlin'."

*Here we go,* Jessica thought.

"We're looking for a house that might be located around here," Nicci said, unfazed. "I'd like to show you a few pictures."

"Oooo," Keith said. "We like pitchers. Us country folk need pitchers cuzz'n we cain't *read*."

Kyle snorted laughter.

"Are they *dirty* pitchers?" he added.

The two brothers bumped grimy fists.

Nicci just stared for a moment, unblinking. She took a deep breath, regrouped, began again. "If you could just take a look at these, we'd really appreciate it. Then we'll be on our way." She held up a photograph. The two men glanced at it, went back to ogling.

"Yeah," said Kyle. "That's my house. We could take a ride up there now if you like."

Nicci glanced at Jessica, back at the brothers. Up came the Philly. "You've got a mouth on you, you know that?"

Kyle laughed. "Oh, you got that right," he said. "Ask any girl in town." He ran his tongue over his lips. "Why don't you come here and find out for yourself?"

"Maybe I will," Nicci said. "Maybe I'll slap it into the next fuckin' county." Nicci took a step toward them. Jessica put a hand on Nicci's arm, held tight.

"Guys? *Guys?*" Jessica said. "We thank you for your time. We really do appreciate it." She held up one of her business cards. "You've seen the picture. If you think of something, please give us a call." She put her card on the counter.

Kyle looked at Keith, back at Jessica. "Oh I can think of something. Hell, I can think of a *lot* of things."

Jessica looked at Nicci. She could almost see the steam coming out of her ears. After a moment, she felt the tension in Nicci's arm ease. They turned to leave.

"Is your home number on the card?" one of them yelled.

Another hyena laugh.

Jessica and Nicci reached the car, slipped inside. "Remember that kid in *Deliverance*?" Nicci asked. "The one who played the banjo?"

Jessica buckled up. "What about him?"

"Looks like he had twins."

Jessica laughed. "Where to?"

They both looked down the road. The snow gently fell. The hills were covered with a silken duvet of white.

Nicci glanced at the map on the seat, tapped south. "I think we should go this way," she said. "And I think it's time to change tactics."

AT AROUND ONE they arrived at a family-style restaurant called Doug's Den. The exterior was a deep brown rough siding, the roof a gambrel style. The parking lot held four vehicles.

As Jessica and Nicci approached the door, it began to snow in earnest.

THEY ENTERED THE restaurant. Two older men, a pair of locals instantly identifiable by their John Deere caps and worn-looking down vests, held down the far end of the bar.

The man wiping the countertop was fifty—big shoulders and hands, just starting to go thick in the middle. He wore a lime green sweater vest over a crisp white shirt, black Dockers.

"Afternoon," he said, brightening a bit at the notion of two young women entering the establishment.

"How ya doin'?" Nicci asked.

"Good," he said. "What can I get for you ladies?" He was soft-spoken, affable.

Nicci gave the man a sideways glance, the one you give someone when you think you recognize them. Or want them to *think* you do. "You used to be on the job, didn't you?" she asked.

The man smiled. "You can tell?"

Nicci winked. "It's in the eyes."

The man tossed the bar rag under the counter, sucked in his gut an inch. "I was a state trooper. Nineteen years."

Nicci went into coquette mode, as if he had just said he was Ashley Wilkes. "You were a *statie*? What barracks?"

"Erie," he said. "Troop E. Lawrence Park."

"Oh, I *love* Erie," Nicci said. "Were you born there?"

"Not far away. In Titusville."

"When did you put in your papers?"

The man looked at the ceiling, calculating. "Well, let's see." He paled slightly. "Wow."

"What?"

"I just realized that it was almost ten years ago."

Jessica would bet the man knew exactly how long it had been, probably down to the hour and minute. Nicci reached out, touched him lightly on the back of his right hand. Jessica marveled. It was like watching Maria Callas warm up for a performance of *Madame Butterfly*.

"I bet you could still fit into that uniform," Nicci said.

In went the gut another inch. He was kind of cute in his big, small-town-boy way. "Oh, I don't know about that."

Jessica couldn't help thinking that, whatever this guy had done for the state he had *definitely* not been an investigator. If he couldn't see through this line of crap, he couldn't have found Shaquille O'Neal in a day-care center. Or maybe he just wanted to hear it. Jessica saw this sort of reaction in her father all the time these days.

"Doug Prentiss," he said, extending his hand. Handshakes and introductions all around. Nicci told him they were Philly PD, but not homicide.

Of course, they'd known most of this information about Doug before they'd set foot in his establishment. Like lawyers, cops liked to have the answer to a question before it was asked. The shiny Ford pickup parked closest to the door had a license plate that read DOUG1, and a sticker in the back window that read STATE TROOPERS DO IT ON THE SIDE OF THE ROAD.

"I imagine you're on duty," Doug said, ready to serve. If Nicci had asked, he probably would have painted her house. "Can I get you a cup of coffee? Just brewed."

"That would be great, Doug," Nicci said. Jessica nodded.

"Two coffees, coming up."

Doug was off like a shot. He soon returned with two steaming mugs of coffee, along with a bowl of individually packaged creamers on ice.

"Are you out here on official business?" Doug asked.

"Yes, we are," Nicci said.

"If there's anything I can do to help, just ask."

"I can't tell you how happy I am to hear that, Doug," Nicci said. She sipped from her cup. "Good coffee."

Doug puffed a little chest. "What's the job?"

Nicci took out a nine by twelve envelope, opened it. She extracted the photograph of the farmhouse, slid it across the bar. "We're trying to locate this place, but we're not having too much luck. We're fairly certain it's in this zip code. Does it look familiar to you?"

Doug put on a pair of bifocals, picked up the photograph. After looking at it carefully he said, "I don't recognize this place, but if it's anywhere in this area I know who would."

"Who is that?"

"A woman named Nadine Palmer. She and her nephew run the little arts-and-crafts store down the road," Doug said, clearly pleased to be back in the saddle again, even if it was just for a few minutes. "She's a heck of a painter. So's her nephew."

# 72

The Art Ark was a small weather-beaten store at the end of the block, on the one and only main street in the small town. The display in the window was a cleverly arranged collage of brushes, paints, canvases, water-color pads, along with the expected silo-and-barn land-scapes of local farms, produced by local artists, painted by people most likely instructed by—or related to—the proprietor.

A bell over the door announced Jessica and Nicci's entrance. They were greeted by the aroma of potpourri, linseed oil, and a subtle undercurrent of cat.

The woman behind the counter was in her early six-ties. Her hair was pulled into a bun and held in place by an elaborately carved wooden pick. If they were not in Pennsylvania, Jessica would have placed the woman at a Nantucket art fair. Maybe that was the idea.

"Afternoon," the woman said.

Jessica introduced herself and Nicci as police officers. "Doug Prentiss referred us to you," she said.

"Good-looking man that Doug Prentiss."

"Yes he is," Jessica said. "He said you might be able to help us."

"Do what I can," she replied. "Name's Nadine Palmer, by the way."

Nadine's words promised cooperation, even though her body language had tightened up a little when she'd heard the word "police." It was to be expected. Jessica brought out the photograph of the farmhouse. "Doug said you might know where this house was."

Before Nadine looked at the photograph she asked, "Might I see some ID?"

"Absolutely," Jessica said. She pulled her badge, flipped it open. Nadine took it from her, scrutinized it.

"Must be exciting work," she said, handing the ID back.

"Sometimes," Jessica replied.

Nadine picked up the photograph. "Oh, sure," she said. "I know the place."

"Is it far from here?" Nicci asked.

"Not too far."

"Do you know who lives there?" Jessica asked.

"Don't think anyone lives there now." She took a step toward the back of the store, yelled, "Ben?"

"Yeah?" came a voice from the basement.

"Can you bring up the watercolor that's leaning up against the freezer?"

"The small one?"

"Yes."

"Sure thing," he replied.

A few seconds later a young man came up the steps carrying a framed watercolor. He was in his early to mid-twenties, right out of central casting for small-town Pennsylvania. He had a shock of wheat-colored hair that fell into his eyes. He wore a navy blue cardigan, white T-shirt, and jeans. He was almost feminine in his features.

"This is my nephew, Ben Sharp," Nadine said. She went on to introduce Jessica and Nicci and explain who they were.

Ben handed his aunt the tastefully framed and matted watercolor. Nadine put it onto an easel next to the counter. The painting, realistically rendered, was almost an exact duplicate of the photo.

"Who painted this?" Jessica asked.

"Yours truly," Nadine said. "I snuck out there one Saturday in June. A long, *long* time ago."

"It's beautiful," Jessica said.

"It's for sale." Nadine winked. From the back room came the sound of a teakettle whistling. "If you'll excuse me a second." She walked out of the room.

Ben Sharp looked between his two visitors, shoved his hands deep into his pockets, rocked on his heels for a moment. "So, you guys are up from Philly?" he asked.

"That's right," Jessica said.

"And you're detectives?"

"Right again."

"Wow."

Jessica glanced at her watch. It was past two. If they were going to track down this house, they had better get going. She then noticed a display of paintbrushes on the counter behind Ben. She pointed to it.

"What can you tell me about these brushes?" she asked.

"Just about anything you'd like to know," Ben said.

"Are they all pretty much the same?" she asked.

"No, ma'am. First of all, they come in different grades—master, studio, academic. All the way down to economy, although you really don't want to paint with economy. They're more for the hobbyist. I use the studio, but that's because I get a discount. I'm not as good as Aunt Nadine, but I'm coming along."

At this, Nadine reentered the shop with a tray bearing a steaming pot of tea. "Do you have time for a cup of tea?" she asked.

"I'm afraid we don't," Jessica said. "But thanks." She turned to Ben, held up the photograph of the farmhouse. "Are you familiar with this house?"

"Sure," Ben said.

"How far away is it?"

"Maybe ten minutes or so. It's kind of hard to find. If you like, I can show you where it is."

"That would be very helpful," Jessica said.

Ben Sharp beamed. Then his expression darkened. "Is that okay, Aunt Nadine?"

"Of course," she said. "Not exactly turning away customers, it being New Year's Eve and all. I should probably just close up and pop the Cold Duck."

Ben ran into the back room, returned wearing a parka. "I'll bring my van around, meet you out front."

While they waited, Jessica glanced around the shop. It had that small-town atmosphere that she found appealing of late. Maybe that was what she was looking for now that Sophie was getting older. She wondered what the schools were like around here. She wondered if there *were* schools around here.

Nicci nudged her, dissolving her daydream. It was time to go.

"Thanks for your time," Jessica said to Nadine.

"Anytime," Nadine said. She came around the counter, walked them to the door. It was then that Jessica noticed the wooden box near the radiator; the box contained a cat and four or five newborn kittens.

"Couldn't interest you in a kitten or two, could I?" Nadine asked with a hopeful smile.

"No thanks," Jessica said.

As she opened the door and stepped into the snowy Currier & Ives afternoon, Jessica glanced back at the nursing cat.

Everyone was having babies.

# 73

The house was much more than ten minutes away. They drove on roundabout roads, and deep into the woods, as the snow continued to fall. A few times they encountered white-out conditions and had to stop. After about twenty minutes, they came to a curve in the road, and a private lane that all but disappeared into the trees.

Ben pulled over, waved them up alongside his van. He rolled down his window. "There's a few different ways in, but this is probably the easiest. Just follow me."

He turned onto the snow-drifted track. Jessica and Nicci followed. Soon they came into a clearing, and merged with what was probably the long driveway leading to the house.

As they approached the structure, cresting a brief rise, Jessica held up the photograph. It had been taken from the other side of the hill, but even from this distance there was no mistaking it. They had found the house that Walt Brigham had photographed.

The driveway ended in a turnaround, fifty feet from the building. There were no other vehicles in sight.

As they exited the car, the first thing Jessica noticed was not the remoteness of the house, or even the rather picturesque winter setting. It was the silence. She could almost hear the snow hitting the ground.

Jessica had been raised in South Philly, had attended Temple University, had spent all her life within a few miles of the city. These days, when she answered a homicide call in Philly she was greeted by car horns, buses, loud music. Sometimes, by the shouts of angry citizens. This was idyllic by comparison.

Ben Sharp got out of his van, left it idling. He slipped on a pair of wool gloves. "I don't think anyone lives here anymore."

"Did you know who lived here before?" Nicci asked.

"No," he said. "Sorry."

Jessica glanced at the house. There were two windows in the front, staring out like sinister eyes. There were no lights. "How did you know about this place?" she asked.

"We used to come here when we were kids. It was pretty spooky then."

"Kinda spooky *now*," Nicci said.

"There used to be a couple of big dogs on the property."

"They ran loose?" Jessica asked.

"Oh, yeah," Ben said, smiling. "That was the challenge."

Jessica looked around the grounds, around the area near the porch. There were no chains, no water bowls, no paw prints in the snow. "And this was how long ago?"

"Oh, a *long* time ago," Ben said. "Fifteen years."

*Good,* Jessica thought. When she'd been in uniform she'd done her time with big dogs. Every cop did.

"Well, we'll let you get back to the shop," Nicci said.

"Do you want me to wait for you?" Ben asked. "Show you the way back?"

"I think we can take it from here," Jessica said. "We appreciate your help."

Ben looked a little disappointed; perhaps because he felt like he might be part of a police investigation team now. "No problem."

"And say thanks again to Nadine for us."

"I will."

A few moments later Ben slipped into his van, backed

into the turnaround, and headed toward the road. In seconds his vehicle disappeared into the pines.

Jessica looked at Nicci. They both glanced toward the house.

It was still there.

THE PORCH WAS stone; the front door was solid oak, formidable. On it was a rusted iron knocker. It looked older than the house.

Nicci knocked with her fist. Nothing. Jessica put an ear to the door. Silence. Nicci knocked one more time, this time using the knocker, the sound echoing for a moment on the old stone porch. No response.

The window to the right of the front door was thick with years of grunge. Jessica rubbed away some of the grime, cupped her hands to the glass. All she saw was the layer of grime on the inside. It was completely opaque. She couldn't even tell if there were curtains or blinds behind the glass. The same was true of the window to the left of the door.

"So, what do you want to do?" Jessica asked.

Nicci looked toward the road, back at the house. She glanced at her watch. "What I *want* to do is get into a hot bubble bath with a glass of Pinot Noir. But here we are in Butter Churn, PA."

"Should we call the sheriff's office?"

Nicci smiled. Jessica didn't know the woman all that well, but she knew the smile. Every detective had that smile in their arsenal. "Not just yet."

Nicci reached out, tried the doorknob. Locked tight. "Let me see if there's another way in," Nicci said. She jumped off the porch, headed around the side of the house.

For the first time that day, Jessica wondered if they weren't wasting their time. There really wasn't a single piece of direct evidence that linked Walt Brigham's murder to this house.

Jessica pulled out her cell phone. She decided that she'd better call Vincent. She looked at the LCD readout. No bars. No signal. She put her phone away.

A few seconds later, Nicci returned. "I found an open door."

"Where?" Jessica asked.

"Around back. It leads to the root cellar, I think. Maybe a storm cellar."

"It was open?"

"Kinda."

Jessica followed Nicci around the building. The land behind the structure led to a valley, which in turn led to the woods beyond. As they rounded the rear of the building, Jessica's sense of isolation grew. She had thought for a moment there that she might like to live somewhere like this, away from the noise, the pollution, the crime. Now she wasn't so sure.

They reached the entrance to the root cellar, a pair of heavy wooden doors built into the ground. It was crossbeamed with a four-by-four. They lifted the cross beam, set it aside, pulled open the doors.

Immediately the smell of mildew and wood rot reached their noses. There was a hint of something else, something animal.

"And they say police work isn't glamorous," Jessica said.

Nicci looked at Jessica. "Well?"

"After you, Auntie Em."

Nicci clicked on her Maglite. *"Philly PD!"* she yelled into the black hole. No answer. She glanced back at Jessica, fully jazzed. "I love this *job*."

Nicci took the lead. Jessica followed.

As more snowstorm clouds gathered over southeastern Pennsylvania, the two detectives descended into the frigid darkness of the cellar.

# 74

Roland felt the warm sun on his face. He heard the slap of the league ball against leather, smelled the deep redolence of neat's-foot oil. There wasn't a single cloud in the sky.

He was fifteen.

There had been ten of them that day, eleven including Charles. It was late April. They'd each had their favorite baseball player—Lenny Dykstra, Bobby Munoz, Kevin Jordan, and the retired Mike Schmidt among them. Half of them wore some homemade version of Mike Schmidt's jersey.

They had played a pickup game in a field near Lincoln Drive, sneaking onto a ball diamond just a few hundred yards from the creek.

Roland looked over to the trees. He saw his stepsister Charlotte there, along with her friend Annemarie. Most of the time the two girls drove him and his friends crazy. Mostly they prattled and squeaked about nothing in the world that could possibly matter. But not always, not Charlotte. Charlotte was a special girl, as special as her twin brother Charles. Like Charles, her eyes were a robin's-egg blue that shamed the springtime sky.

Charlotte and Annemarie. The two were inseparable. That day they stood in their sundresses, shimmering in the dazzling light. Charlotte wore lavender ribbons. It was a birthday party for them—they had been born on the same day, exactly two hours apart, Annemarie being the older of the two. They had met in the park when they were six, and now they had to have their party there.

At six o'clock they all heard the thunder, shortly followed by their mothers calling for them.

Roland had walked away. He picked up his mitt, and simply walked away, leaving Charlotte behind. He had left her for the devil that day, and since that day the devil had owned his soul.

To Roland, as with many people in the ministry, the devil was not an abstract. It was a real being, and could manifest itself in many forms.

He thought of the intervening years. He thought of how young he was when he opened the mission. He thought of Julianne Weber, about how she had been brutalized by a man named Joseph Barber, how Julianne's mother had come to him. He had spoken to little Julianne. He thought about how he had confronted Joseph Barber in that North Philly hovel, the look in Barber's eyes when the man knew he had come to earthly judgment, how the wrath of the Lord was imminent.

*Thirteen knives,* Roland thought. *The devil's number.*

Joseph Barber. Basil Spencer. Edgar Luna.

So many others.

Had they been innocent? No. Perhaps they had not been directly responsible for what had happened to Charlotte, but they had been the devil's minions.

"There it is." Sean pulled the vehicle to the side of the road. There was a sign amid the trees, next to a narrow snowbound lane. Sean got out of the van, cleaned the fresh snow from the sign.

### WELCOME TO ODENSE

Roland lowered his window.

"There's a wooden one-lane bridge a few hundred

yards in," Sean said. "I remember that it used to be in pretty bad shape. Might not even be *there* anymore. I think I should go take a look before we drive in."

"Thank you, Brother Sean," Roland said.

Sean pulled his wool cap tighter, knotted his scarf. "I'll be right back."

He walked down the lane—slow going in the calf-deep snow—and within moments disappeared into the storm.

Roland glanced at Charles.

Charles was wringing his hands, rocking in his seat. Roland put a hand on Charles's big shoulder. It would not be long now.

Soon they would come face-to-face with Charlotte's killer.

# 75

Byrne looked at the contents of the envelope—a handful of photographs, each with a notation scrawled along the bottom in ballpoint pen—but had no idea what any of it meant. He glanced again at the envelope itself. It was addressed to him, c/o the Police Department. Hand lettered, blocky style, black ink, no return, Philly postmark.

Byrne was at a desk in the duty room at the Roundhouse. The room was all but deserted. Anyone with anything to do on New Year's Eve was out getting ready to do it.

There were six photographs: small Polaroid prints.

Written along the bottom of each print was a series of numbers. The numbers looked familiar—they appeared to be those of PPD case files. It was the pictures themselves he could not understand. They were not official department photos.

One was a snapshot of a small lavender plush toy. It looked like a bear. Another was a picture of a girl's barrette, also lavender. Yet another was a photograph of a small pair of socks. It was hard to tell the exact color, due to the slight overexposure of the print, but they looked to be lavender as well. There were three more photos, all of unrecognized objects that were each a shade of lavender.

Byrne scrutinized each photograph again. They were mostly close-ups, so there was little context. Three of the objects were on carpeting, two on a hardwood floor, one on what appeared to be concrete. Byrne was writing down the numbers as Josh Bontrager came in, holding his coat.

"Just wanted to say Happy New Year, Kevin." Bontrager crossed the room, shook Byrne's hand. Josh Bontrager was a hand-shaker. In the past week or so, Byrne had probably shaken the young man's hand thirty times.

"Same to you, Josh."

"We'll catch this guy next year. You'll see."

It was a little bit of country wit, Byrne supposed, but it came from the right place. "No doubt." Byrne picked up the sheet with the case numbers on it. "Could you do me a favor before you leave?"

"Sure."

"Could you get these files for me?"

Bontrager put down his coat. "I'm on it."

Byrne turned back to the photographs. Each showed a lavender item, he saw again. A girl's item. A barrette, a bear, a pair of socks with a small ribbon at the top.

What did it mean? Did the photos represent six vic-

tims? Were they killed because of the color lavender?
Was it the signature of a serial killer?

Byrne glanced out the window. The storm was picking
up. Soon the city would come to a halt. For the most
part, police welcomed snowstorms. They tended to slow
things down, smooth out arguments that often led to as-
saults, to homicides.

He looked back at the pictures in his hand. Whatever
they represented had already happened. The fact that a
child was involved—probably a young girl—did not
bode well.

Byrne got up from his desk, walked through the corri-
dors to the elevators, and waited for Josh.

# 76

The cellar was dank and musty. It was made up of one
large room and three smaller ones. In the main section
were a few wooden boxes stacked in one corner, a large
steamer trunk. The other rooms were mostly empty.
One had a boarded-up coal chute and bin. One had a
long rotted shelving unit. On it were a few old one-
gallon green glass jars, a pair of broken jugs. Tacked
above were cracked leather bridles, along with an old
leg-hold trap.

The steamer trunk was not padlocked, but the broad
latch seemed to be rusted shut. Jessica found an iron bar
nearby. She swung the bar. Three hits later, and the latch
sprung. She and Nicci opened the trunk.

Across the top was an old bed sheet. They pulled it away. Beneath that were layers of magazines: *Life, Look, Woman's Home Companion, Collier's.* The smell of mildewed paper and moth cakes drifted up. Nicci shifted some of the magazines.

Beneath them was a leather binder, perhaps nine by twelve inches, veined and covered with a thin green layer of mold. Jessica opened it. There were only a handful of pages.

Jessica flipped to the first two pages. On the left was a yellowed news clipping from the *Inquirer,* a news item from April 1995, an article concerning the murder of two young girls in Fairmount Park. Annemarie DiCillo and Charlotte Waite. The illustration on the right was a crude pen and ink drawing of a pair of white swans in a nest.

Jessica's pulse began to race. Walt Brigham had been right. This house—or more accurately the occupants of this house—had something to do with the murder of Annemarie and Charlotte. Walt had been closing in on the killer. He had been getting close and the killer had followed him into the park that night, to the precise spot the little girls had been murdered, and burned him to death.

Jessica considered the potent irony of it all.

In death, Walt Brigham had led them to his killer's house.

In death, Walt Brigham might get his revenge.

# 77

The six case files were homicides. Each one of the victims had been male, all of them between the ages of twenty-five and fifty. Three of the men had been stabbed to death—one of them with a pair of garden shears. Two of the men had been bludgeoned, one run over by a large vehicle, possibly a van. All of them had been from Philadelphia. Four had been white, one black, one Asian. Three had been married, two divorced, one single.

What they all had in common was that they had all been suspected, to some degree, of violence against young girls. All six were dead. And, it appeared, at the scene of their murders there had been some sort of lavender item. Socks, a barrette, plush toys.

There wasn't a single suspect in any of the cases.

"Are these files tied to our killer?" Bontrager asked.

Byrne had almost forgotten that Josh Bontrager was still in the room. The kid was quiet that way. Maybe it was out of respect. "I'm not sure," Byrne said.

"Do you want me to hang around, maybe follow up on some of them?"

"No," Byrne said. "It's New Year's Eve. Go have a good time."

After a few moments, Bontrager grabbed his coat and walked toward the door.

"Josh," Byrne said.

Bontrager turned around, expectant. "Yeah?"

Byrne pointed to the files. "Thanks."

"Sure." Bontrager held up two of the books by Hans Christian Andersen. "I'm going to read these tonight. I figure that if he's going to do this again, a clue might be in here."

*Some New Year's Eve,* Byrne thought. *Reading fairy tales.* "Good work."

"I thought I'd call you if I came up with something. Is that okay?"

"Absolutely," Byrne said. The kid was starting to remind Byrne of himself when he'd been new to the unit. An Amish version, but still similar. Byrne got up, put on his coat. "Hang on. I'll walk you down."

"Cool," Bontrager said. "Where are you headed?"

In the case files, Byrne had looked at the investigating officers on each of the homicides. On all cases it had been Walter J. Brigham and John Longo. Byrne had looked up Longo. He had retired in 2001, and now lived in the Northeast.

Byrne hit the button on the elevator. "I think I'll take a ride to the Northeast."


JOHN LONGO LIVED in a well-tended town house in Torresdale. Byrne was greeted by Longo's wife Denise, a slender, attractive woman in her early forties. She brought Byrne down to the basement workshop, a look of skepticism and slight suspicion behind her warm smile.

The walls were covered with plaques and photos, half devoted to Longo in various locations, wearing various police gear. The other half were family pictures—weddings in a park, Atlantic City, somewhere tropical.

Longo looked a few years older than his official PPD photograph, his dark hair now confettied with gray, but he was still trim and athletic. A few inches shorter than Byrne, a few years younger, Longo looked like he could still run down a suspect if he had to.

After the standard who-do-you-know, who-have-you-worked-with dance, they finally got to the reason for Byrne's visit. Something about Longo's responses told Byrne that Longo had in some way expected this day to come.

The six photographs were laid out on the workbench, a surface otherwise devoted to making wooden bird-houses.

"Where did you get these?" Longo asked.

"Honest answer?" Byrne asked.

Longo nodded.

"I thought you sent them."

"No." Longo looked at the envelope, inside and out, flipped it over. "It wasn't me. In fact, I was hoping to go the rest of my life without ever seeing anything like this again."

Byrne understood. There was plenty he himself didn't want to ever see again. "How long were you on the job?"

"Eighteen years," Longo said. "Half a career for some guys. Way too long for others." He studied one of the photographs closely. "I remember this. There have been many nights when I wished I didn't."

The photograph was the one depicting the small plush bear.

"That was taken at a crime scene?" Byrne asked.

"Yes." Longo crossed the room, opened a cabinet, pulled out a bottle of Glenfiddich. He held up the bottle, and raised an eyebrow questioningly. Byrne nodded. Longo poured them both a drink, handed a glass to Byrne.

"It was the last case I worked," Longo said.

"This was North Philly, right?" Byrne knew all this. He just needed it to sync.

"Badlands. We were on this prick. Hard. For *months*. Name was Joseph Barber. Had him in for questioning twice for a series of rapes of young girls, couldn't hold him. Then he did it again. Got a tip he was holed up in an old drug house near Fifth and Cambria." Longo drained his drink. "He was dead when we got there. Thirteen knives in his body."

"Thirteen?"

"Yeah." Longo cleared his throat. This was not easy for him. He poured himself another drink. "Steak knives. Cheap. The kind you might get at a flea market. Untraceable."

"Was the case ever closed?" Byrne knew the answer to this, too. He wanted to keep Longo talking.

"Not to my knowledge."

"Did you follow it?"

"I didn't want to. Walt stuck with it for a while. He tried to make a case that Joseph Barber was killed by some sort of vigilante. Never got any traction." Longo pointed to the photograph on the workbench. "I looked at that lavender bear on the floor, and knew I was finished. I've never looked back."

"Any idea who the bear belonged to?" Byrne asked.

Longo shook his head. "When the evidence was cleared and the property released, I showed it to the little girl's parents."

"These were the parents of Barber's last victim?"

"Yeah. They said they had never seen it before. Like I said, Barber was a serial child rapist. I didn't want to think how and where he might have gotten it."

"What was Barber's last victim's name?"

"Julianne." Longo's voice cracked. Byrne arranged a few tools on the bench, waited. "Julianne Weber."

"Did you ever follow up?"

He nodded. "A few years ago I drove by their house, parked across the street. I saw Julianne as she left for school. She looked okay—at least, to the world she looked okay—but I could see that sadness in her every step."

Byrne could see that this conversation was nearing a

close. He gathered the photos, his coat and gloves. "I'm sorry about Walt. He was a good man."

"He was the job," Longo said. "I couldn't make it to the party. I didn't even—" The emotion took over for a few moments. "I was in San Diego. My daughter had a little girl. My first grandchild."

"Congratulations," Byrne said. As soon as the word left his lips—although heartfelt—it sounded empty. Longo drained his glass. Byrne followed suit, stood, slipped on his coat.

"This is the part where people usually say 'If there's anything else I can do, please don't hesitate to call,' " Longo said. "Right?"

"I guess it is," Byrne replied.

"Do me a favor."

"Sure."

"Hesitate."

Byrne smiled. "Okay."

As Byrne turned to leave, Longo put a hand on his arm. "There is something else."

"Okay."

"Walt said I was probably seeing things at the time, but I was convinced."

Byrne folded his hands, waited.

"The pattern of the knives," Longo said. "The wounds on Joseph Barber's chest."

"What about them?"

"I wasn't sure until I saw the postmortem photos. But I'm positive the wounds spelled out a *C*."

"The letter *C*?"

Longo nodded, poured himself another drink. He sat down at his workbench. The conversation was now officially over.

Byrne thanked him again. On the way up, he saw that Denise Longo had been standing at the top of the stairs.

She saw him to the door. She was much cooler to him than she had been when he'd arrived.

While his car was warming up, Byrne looked at the photograph. There was probably going to be a lavender-bear sort of case in his future, probably his near future. He wondered if he, like John Longo, would have the courage to walk away.

# 78

Jessica searched every inch of the trunk, flipped through every magazine. There was nothing else. She found a few yellowed recipes, a few *McCall's* patterns. She found a box of small paper-wrapped demitasse cups. The newspaper wrapping was dated March 22, 1950. She turned back to the portfolio.

Tucked into the back of the binder was a page bearing a number of horrific drawings—hangings, mutilations, disembowelings, dismemberments—childlike in their scrawl, extremely disturbing in their content.

Jessica turned back to the first page, the news article on the murder of Annemarie DiCillo and Charlotte Waite. Nicci read it too.

"Okay," Nicci said. "I'm calling this in. We need cops out here. Walt Brigham liked whoever lived here for the Annemarie DiCillo case, and it looks as though he was right. God knows what else we're going to find in this place."

Jessica handed Nicci her phone. A few moments later,

after trying and not getting a signal in the cellar, Nicci walked up the stairs and outside.

Jessica turned back to the boxes.

*Who had lived here?* she wondered. *Where is that person now?* In a small town like this, if the person was still anywhere in the area, people would surely know. Jessica sifted through the boxes in the corner. There were more old newspapers, some in a language she couldn't identify, perhaps Dutch or Danish. There were moldy board games, rotting in their long-mildewed boxes. Nothing else mentioned the Annemarie DiCillo case.

She opened yet another box, this one not as timeworn as the others. Inside were newspapers and magazines of a more recent vintage. On top was a year's worth of *Amusement Today,* a newsletter-style magazine that appeared to be a trade publication devoted to the amusement-park industry. Jessica flipped over an issue. She found an address label. *M Damgaard.*

*Is this Walt Brigham's killer?* Jessica tore off the label, shoved it in her pocket.

She had been hauling boxes toward the door when a noise stopped her in her tracks. At first it sounded as if it might just be the settling of dry timbers, creaking in the wind. She heard it again, the sound of old, thirsty wood.

"Nicci?"

Nothing.

Jessica was just about to head up the stairs when she heard the sound of rapidly approaching footsteps. *Running* footsteps, muffled by the snow. She then heard what might have been a struggle, or maybe it was Nicci struggling to carry something. Then another sound. Her name?

*Did Nicci just call her?*

"Nicci?" Jessica asked.

Silence.

"Did you make contact with—"

Jessica never finished her question. At that moment

the heavy cellar doors slammed shut, the sound of the timbers resounding loudly in the cold stone confines of the cellar.

Then Jessica heard something far more ominous.

The huge doors were being secured with the cross-beam.

From the outside.

# 79

Byrne paced the parking lot at the Roundhouse. He didn't feel the cold. He thought about John Longo and his story.

*He tried to make a case that Barber was killed by some sort of vigilante. Never got any traction.*

Whoever had sent Byrne the photographs—and it was probably Walt Brigham—was trying to make that same argument. Why else would every item in the photographs be lavender? It must be some sort of calling card the vigilante left, a personal touch from someone who had taken it upon himself to eliminate men who had committed violence against girls and young women.

Someone had killed these suspects before the police could make a case against them.

Before leaving the Northeast, Byrne had put in a call to Records. He had requested that they pull every unsolved homicide for the past ten years. He had also asked for a cross reference with the search term "lavender."

Byrne thought about Longo, ensconced in his basement, making birdhouses, of all things. To the outside world, Longo looked content. But Byrne could see the ghost. If he looked closely at his own face in the mirror—something he did less and less these days—he would probably see it in himself.

The town of Meadville was starting to look good.

Byrne shifted gears, thought about the case. *His* case. The river killings. He knew he had to tear it all down and build it back up from the beginning. He had encountered psychos of this sort before, murderers who took their cue from something we all saw and took for granted every day.

Lisette Simon was first. Or at least they thought so. A forty-one-year-old woman who worked in a mental-health-care facility. Maybe the killer started there. Maybe he met Lisette, worked with her, made some discovery that triggered this rampage.

Compulsive killers start close to home.

*The name of the killer is in that computer readout.*

Before Byrne could head back into the Roundhouse, he sensed a presence nearby.

"Kevin."

Byrne spun around. It was Vincent Balzano. He and Byrne had worked a detail a few years earlier. He had, of course, seen Vincent at any number of police functions with Jessica. Byrne liked him. What he knew about Vincent on the job was that he was a little unorthodox, had placed himself in jeopardy more than once to save a fellow officer, and was fairly hotheaded. Not all that different from Byrne himself.

"Hey, Vince," Byrne said.

"You talk to Jess today?"

"No," Byrne said. "What's up?"

"She left a message for me this morning. I've been on the street all day. I just picked up the messages an hour ago."

"You worried?"

Vincent looked at the Roundhouse, then back at Byrne. "Yeah. I am."

"What did her message say?"

"She said she and Nicci Malone were headed up to Berks County," Vincent said. "Jess was off duty. And now I can't get hold of her. Do you have any idea where in Berks?"

"No," Byrne said. "You try her cell?"

"Yeah," he said. "I get her voice mail." Vincent turned away for a moment, then back. "What's she *doing* up in Berks? Is she working your multiple?"

Byrne shook his head. "She's working Walt Brigham's case."

"Walt Brigham's case? What's up there?"

"I'm not sure."

"What's the last thing she logged?"

"Let's go see."

BACK IN THE duty room of the Homicide Unit, Byrne pulled the binder of Walt Brigham's murder. He flipped to the most recent entry. "This is from last night," he said.

The file contained photocopies of two photographs, both sides—black-and-white pictures of an old stone farmhouse. They were duplicates. On the back of one was five numbers, two obscured by what looked like water damage. Beneath that, written in red pen, in a cursive style known well to both men as belonging to Jessica, was the following:

*195- / Berks County / N of French Creek?*

"You think this is where she went?" Vincent asked.

"I don't know," Byrne said. "But if her voice mail message said that she was heading to Berks with Nicci, there's a good chance."

Vincent pulled out his cell, tried Jessica again. Nothing. For a moment, it appeared that Vincent was going to throw the phone through the window. The *closed* window. Byrne knew the feeling.

Vincent pocketed his cell phone, headed for the door.

"Where are you going?" Byrne asked.

"I'm going up there."

Byrne took the pictures of the farmhouse, put the binder away. "I'm going with you."

"You don't have to."

Byrne stared. "How do you figure that?"

Vincent hesitated for a moment, nodded. "Let's go."

They reached Vincent's car—a fully restored 1970 Cutlass S—at nearly a run. Byrne was out of breath by the time he slipped into the passenger seat. Vincent Balzano was in far better shape.

Vincent decked a blue light on the dash. By the time they reached the Schuylkill Expressway they were traveling at eighty miles per hour.

# 80

The darkness was nearly complete. Just a thin sliver of cold daylight came between the crack in the storm-cellar doors.

Jessica called out a few times, listened. Silence. Empty, country silence.

She put her shoulder to the nearly horizontal doors and pushed.

Nothing.

She angled her body for maximum leverage and tried again. Again the doors did not move. Jessica looked between the two doors. She saw a dark strip across the center, which meant that the four-by-four crossbeam was in place. Obviously, the door had not closed on its own.

Someone was out there. Someone had slid the crossbeam across the doors.

*Where was Nicci?*

Jessica looked around the cellar. Against one wall were an old rake and a short-handled shovel. She grabbed the rake, tried to slip the handle between the doors. It did not fit.

She stepped into the other room, was hit by the thick smell of mold and mice. She found nothing. No tools, no levers, no hammers or saws. And the Maglite was starting to fade. Against the far wall, an inside wall, was a pair of ruby curtains. She wondered if they led to another room.

She tore down the curtains. In the corner was a ladder, secured to the stone wall by bolts and a pair of brackets. She banged her flashlight against her palm, got a few more lumens of yellow light from it. She ran the beam up to the cobwebbed ceiling. There, cut into the ceiling, was an access door. It looked as if it had not been used in many years. Jessica gauged that she was now near the center of the house. She wiped some of the soot from the ladder, then tested the first rung. It creaked beneath her weight, but held. She put the Maglite between her teeth, and started up the ladder. She pushed against the wood access door, and was rewarded with a faceful of black dust.

*"Fuck!"*

Jessica stepped back onto the floor, wiped the soot from her eyes, spit a few times. She took off her coat, draped it over her head and shoulders. She started back up the ladder again. For a second it felt as if one of the rungs was going to give. It cracked slightly. She shifted her feet and her weight to the sides of the rungs, braced herself. This time when she pushed on the ceiling door, she turned her head. The wood budged. It wasn't nailed shut, and there was nothing heavy on top of it.

She tried one more time, this time using all her strength. The access door gave way. As Jessica slowly pushed it up, she was greeted by thin afternoon light. She pushed the door fully and it toppled over onto the floor of the room above. Although the air in the house was thick and stale, she welcomed it. She took a few deep breaths.

She took the coat from her head, slipped it back on. She looked up to the beamed ceiling of the old farmhouse. She calculated that she would emerge into a small pantry off the kitchen. She stopped, listened. Just the sound of the wind. She pocketed the Maglite, drew her weapon, and continued up the ladder.

Seconds later Jessica stepped through the opening and into the house, glad to be out of the oppressive confines of the damp cellar. She slowly turned 360 degrees. What she saw nearly took her breath away. She had not just entered an old farmhouse.

She had entered another century.

# 81

Byrne and Vincent made Berks County in record time, courtesy of Vincent's muscle car and his ability to maneuver through expressway traffic in what was becoming a full-blown snowstorm. After getting their bearings concerning the general boundaries of the 195 zip code area, they found themselves in Robeson Township.

They took a two-lane road south. Houses were spread out here, none of them resembling the isolated-looking old farmhouse they sought. After a few minutes of trolling the road, they came upon a man shoveling snow near the street.

The man, perhaps in his late sixties, was shoveling out the apron of his driveway, a driveway that looked more than fifty feet long.

Vincent pulled over on the other side of the street, rolled his window down. Within seconds there was snow in the car.

"Hi," Vincent said.

The man looked up from his chore. It looked like he was wearing every item of clothing he'd ever owned—three coats, two hats, three pairs of gloves. His scarves were knitted, homemade, rainbow colored. He was bearded; his gray hair was in a braid. Former flower child. "Afternoon, young man."

"You didn't shovel that whole thing did you?"

The man laughed. "No, my two grandsons did. They never finish anything though."

Vincent showed him the picture of the farmhouse. "Are you familiar with this place?"

The man moved slowly across the road. He stared at the picture, giving the task its full due. "No. Sorry."

"Did you happen to see two other police detectives come by today? Two women in a Ford Taurus?"

"No, sir," the man said. "Can't say that I did. I'd remember that."

Vincent thought for a moment. He pointed to the crossroad ahead. "Anything up this way?"

"Only thing up there is Double K Auto," he said. "If someone was lost or looking for directions, I imagine they might have pulled in there."

"Thank you sir," Vincent said.

"You are welcome young man. Peace."

"Don't work too hard on this," Vincent called to him, putting the car in gear. "It's only snow. It will be gone by spring."

The man laughed again. "It's a thankless job," he said, walking back across the road. "But I've got karma to spare."

DOUBLE K AUTO was a ramshackle, corrugated steel building set back from the road. Derelict cars and auto parts dotted the landscape for a quarter mile in all directions. It looked like a snow-covered topiary of alien beings.

Vincent and Byrne entered the establishment at just after five o'clock.

Inside, at the back of a large grimy lobby, a man stood near the counter, reading *Hustler*. He made no attempt to hide it or put it away in the face of potential customers. He was in his thirties, greasy blond hair, filthy garage overalls. His nametag read KYLE.

"How ya doin'?" Vincent offered.

Cool reception. Closer to cold. The man didn't say a word.

"I'm good, too," Vincent said. "Thanks for asking." He held up his badge. "I was wondering if—"

"Can't help you."

Vincent froze, badge high. He glanced at Byrne, back to Kyle. He held this position for a few moments, then continued.

"I was wondering if two other police officers might have stopped here earlier today. Two female detectives from Philadelphia."

"Can't help you," the man repeated, going back to his magazine.

Vincent took a series of short, quick breaths, like someone preparing to lift a great weight. He took a step forward, put his badge away, flipped back the hem of his coat.

"You're saying that two police officers from Philadelphia did *not* stop here earlier in the day. Is that correct?"

Kyle screwed up his face, as if he were slightly retarded. "I'm dowwy. Do you hab a heawing pwobwem?"

Vincent flicked a glance at Byrne. He knew that Byrne wasn't too keen on jokes at the expense of the hearing impaired. Byrne kept his cool.

"One last time, while we're still friends," Vincent said. "Did two female detectives from Philadelphia stop here today, looking for a farmhouse? Yes or no?"

"Don't know nothin' about it, sport," Kyle said. "Have a nice night."

Vincent laughed, which at the moment was actually scarier than his growl. He ran a hand through his hair, over his jaw. He looked around the lobby area. His eyes landed on something that caught his interest.

"Kevin," he said.

"What?"

Vincent pointed to a nearby trash can. Byrne looked.

There, on top of a pair a greasy Mopar boxes, sat a business card with the familiar badge logo—raised black type, white card stock. It belonged to Detective Jessica Balzano, Philadelphia Police Department, Homicide Division.

Vincent spun on his heels. Kyle was still standing by the counter, watching. But his magazine was now on the floor. When Kyle realized they weren't leaving he made a move to reach beneath the counter.

At that moment, Kevin Byrne saw something incredible.

Vincent Balzano ran across the room, leapt over the counter, and grabbed the blond man by the throat, slamming him back into a display rack. Oil filters, air filters, and spark plugs flew.

All of this seemed to take place in under a second. Vincent was a blur.

In one smooth move, with his left hand wrapped tightly around Kyle's throat, Vincent drew his weapon and aimed it at a dirt-streaked curtain hanging in the doorway to what was probably a back room. The fabric looked as if it had at one time been a shower curtain, although Byrne doubted that Kyle was too familiar with that concept. The point was, someone was standing behind the curtain. Byrne had seen him too.

"Step out here," Vincent yelled.

Nothing. No movement. Vincent pointed his weapon at the ceiling. He fired a round. The blast was ear-shattering. He pointed the gun back at the curtain.

*"Now!"*

A few seconds later a man stepped out of the back room, hands out to his sides. He was Kyle's identical twin. His nametag read KEITH.

"Detective?" Vincent asked.

"I'm on him," Byrne replied. He looked at Keith, which was enough. The man was petrified. There was no need for Byrne to draw his weapon. Yet.

Vincent turned his attention fully to Kyle. "Now, you've got about two fuckin' seconds to start talking, Jethro." He put his weapon to Kyle's forehead. "No. Make that one second."

"I don't know what you're—"

"Look into my eyes and tell me I'm not crazy." Vincent tightened his grip on Kyle's throat. The man was turning olive green. "Go ahead."

All things considered, choking a man while expecting him to talk was probably not the best interrogation technique. But right about now Vincent Balzano was not considering all things. Just one.

Vincent shifted his weight and brought Kyle down to the concrete, slamming the air from his lungs. He put a knee into the man's groin.

"I see your lips moving, but I'm not hearing anything." Vincent eased off on the man's throat. Slightly. "Talk. Now."

"They . . . they were here," Kyle said.

"When?"

"About noon."

"Where did they go?"

"I . . . I don't know."

Vincent pressed the barrel of his weapon into Kyle's left eye.

"Wait! I really don't know I don't know I don't know!"

Vincent took a deep calming breath. It didn't seem to help. "When they left, which way did they go?"

"South," Kyle managed.

"What's down there?"

"Doug's. Maybe they went there."

"What the fuck is *Doug's*?"

"Duh-diner."

Vincent withdrew his weapon. "Thuh-thanks, Kyle."

Five minutes later the two detectives drove south. But not before they had searched every square inch of Double K Auto. There were no other signs that Jessica and Nicci had spent time there.

# 82

Roland could wait no longer. He pulled on his gloves, his knit cap. He did not look forward to walking blindly through the woods in a snowstorm, but he had no choice. He glanced at the fuel gauge. The van had been running, heater on, since they had stopped. They were down to less than one-eighth of a tank.

"Wait here," Roland said. "I'm going to look for Sean. I won't be long."

Charles studied him with deep fear in his eyes. Roland had seen it many times before. He took his hand.

"I will be back," he said. "I promise."

Roland stepped out of the van, shut the door. A sheet of snow slid from the top of the vehicle, dusting his shoulders. He brushed himself off, glanced through the window, waved to Charles. Charles waved back.

Roland made his way down the lane.

THE TREES SEEMED to close ranks. Roland had been walking for nearly five minutes. He did not find the bridge Sean had spoken of, or much else. He turned around a few times, adrift in the miasma of snow. He'd lost his bearings.

"Sean?" he said.

Silence. Just the empty white forest.

*"Sean!"*

There was no reply. The sound was muffled by the falling snow, deadened by the trees, swallowed by the dusk. Roland decided to head back. He was not dressed properly for this, and this was not his world. He would return to the van, and wait there for Sean. He glanced down. The blowing snow had all but obscured his *own* footprints. He turned, walked as quickly as he could in the direction from which he had come. Or so he believed.

As he trudged back, the wind suddenly picked up. Roland turned his back to the gust, covered his face with his scarf, waited out the blast. When it ebbed, he looked up and saw through a narrow clearing in the trees. There was a stone farmhouse, and in the distance, perhaps a quarter mile beyond, a large trellis and what looked like a tableau of amusement-park displays.

*My eyes must be playing tricks,* he thought.

Roland turned toward the house and suddenly sensed

noise and movement to his left—a snapping sound, soft, unlike branches underfoot, more like fabric rippling in the wind. Roland wheeled around. He saw nothing. Then he heard another sound, this time closer. He shone his light through the trees and caught a dark silhouette shifting side to side in the illumination, something partially obscured by the pines twenty yards ahead. In the falling snow it was impossible to tell what it was.

Was it an animal? A sign of some sort?

*A person?*

As Roland slowly approached, the object came into focus. It was not a person, or a sign. It was Sean's coat. Sean's coat was hanging from a tree, powdered with fresh snow. His scarf and gloves lay at the base.

Sean was nowhere to be seen.

"Oh my," Roland said. "Oh Lord, no."

Roland hesitated for a few moments, then picked up Sean's coat, shook off the snow. At first he thought the coat had been hanging from a broken branch. It had not. Roland looked more closely. The coat was hanging from a small pocketknife stabbed into the bark of the tree. Beneath the coat, there was something carved—something round, about six inches in diameter. Roland trained his flashlight on the carving.

It was the face of the moon. It was freshly cut.

Roland began to shiver. And it had nothing to do with the frigid weather.

"It is so delightfully cold," a voice whispered, riding on the wind.

A shadow moved in the near dark, then it was gone, dissolved into the insistent flurry. "Who's *there*?" Roland asked.

"I am Moon," came the whisper, now behind him.

*"Who?"* Roland's voice sounded thin and scared. It shamed him.

"And you are the Snow Man."

Roland heard the rush of footsteps. It was too late. He began to pray.

In a blizzard of white, Roland Hannah's world went black.

# 83

Jessica hugged the wall, her weapon held out in front of her. She was in a short hallway between the kitchen and living room of the farmhouse. Adrenaline raced through her system.

She had cleared the kitchen in short order. The room had a single wooden table, two chairs. Stained floral wallpaper over white chair rails. The cabinets were empty. There was an old cast-iron stove, probably idle for years. A thick layer of dust covered everything. It was like being in a museum that time had forgotten.

As she moved down the hall toward the front room, Jessica listened for any indication of another human presence. All she heard was the thud of her own pulse in her ears. She wished she had worn a Kevlar vest, wished she had backup. She had neither. Someone had deliberately trapped her in the basement. She had to assume that Nicci was hurt, or being held against her will.

Jessica sidled up to the corner, silently counted to three, then peered into the front room.

The ceiling was more than ten feet, and there was a large stone fireplace against the far wall. The floors were old plank. The walls, long given over to mold, had at one time been painted with a calcimine wash. There was a single medallion-back sofa in the center of the room, a sun-bleached green velvet, Victorian in style. Next to it sat a round tabouret table. On it was a leather book. This room was not dusty. This room was still being used.

Drawing closer, she saw a slight depression at the right side of the sofa, the end near the table. Whoever came here sat at that end, perhaps reading the book. Jessica glanced up. There were no ceiling fixtures, either electrical or candled.

Jessica scanned the corners of the space, sweat lacing her back despite the cold. She made her way over to the fireplace, put a hand to the stone. Cold. But in the grate were remnants of a partially burned newspaper. She fished out a corner, looked at it. It was dated three days earlier. Someone had been here recently.

Off the living room was a small bedroom. She peeked inside. There was a double-bed frame with a mattress, sheets and blanket pulled taut. A small table for a nightstand; on it was an antique man's comb and a delicate woman's hairbrush. She looked beneath the bed, then edged over to the closet, took a deep breath, and threw open the door.

Inside were two items. A man's dark suit, and a long cream-colored dress, both looking to be from another time. They hung on red velvet hangers.

Jessica holstered her weapon, stepped back into the living room, tried the front door. Locked. She could see scrapings along the keyhole, bright metal amid the rusted iron. A key was needed. She could also see why she had been unable to see through the windows from the outside. They were covered with old butcher paper. A closer look showed her that the windows were secured with dozens of rusted screws. They had not been opened in years.

Jessica crossed the plank floor to the couch, her footsteps creaking in the wide-open space. She picked up the book on the end table. Her breath caught.

*The Stories of Hans Christian Andersen.*

Time slowed, stopped.

*It was all related. All of it.*

Annemarie and Charlotte. Walt Brigham. The river killings—Lisette Simon, Kristina Jakos, Tara Grendel. There was one person responsible for it all, and she was in his house.

Jessica opened the book. Each story had an illustration, and each illustration was rendered in the same style as the painting found on the victims' bodies, the moon paintings of semen and blood.

Throughout the book were news articles, bookmarking various stories. One of the articles was dated a year earlier, the story of two men found dead in a barn in Mohrsville, Pennsylvania. The police said they had been drowned, then tied into burlap bags. The illustration was of a man holding a large boy and a small boy in his outstretched hands.

The next article was from eight months ago, the account of an elderly woman who had been strangled and found stuffed into an oak barrel on her property in Shoemakersville. The illustration was of a kindly woman holding cakes and pies and cookies. The words *Aunt Millie* were scrawled across the illustration in an innocent hand.

The next pages were articles about missing people—men, women, children—each accompanied by a delicate drawing, each depicting the stories of Hans Christian Andersen. "Little Claus and Big Claus." "Auntie Toothache." "The Flying Trunk." "The Snow Queen."

At the back of the book was a *Daily News* article about the murder of Detective Walter Brigham. Next to it was an illustration of a tin soldier.

Jessica felt the nausea rise. She held a death book, an anthology of murder.

Also inserted in the book's pages was a faded color brochure that showed a pair of happy-looking children in a small, brightly colored boat. The pamphlet looked to be from the 1940s. In front of the children was a large display set into a hillside. It was a twenty-foot tall book. In the center of the display was a young woman dressed as the Little Mermaid. At the top of the page, in cheerful red letters, it read:

*Welcome to StoryBook River: A World of Enchantment!*

At the very end of the book, Jessica found a short news article. It was dated fourteen years earlier.

ODENSE, Pennsylvania (AP)—After nearly six decades, a small theme park in southeast Pennsylvania will close for good when its summer season ends. The family that owns StoryBook River says it does not plan to redevelop the property. Proprietor Elise Damgaard says her husband Frederik, who immigrated to the United States from Denmark as a young man, opened StoryBook River as a park for children. The park itself was patterned after the Danish city of Odense, birthplace of Hans Christian Andersen, whose stories and fables were the basis for many of the attractions.

Beneath the article was the clipped headline from an obituary:

### ELISE M. DAMGAARD, RAN AMUSEMENT PARK.

Jessica looked around for something with which she could break the windows. She picked up the end table. It had a marble top, some heft. Before she could cross the room she heard paper rustling. No. Something softer. She felt a breeze, making the cold air even colder for a second. Then she saw it: the small brown bird landed on the couch next to her. She had no doubt in her mind. It was a nightingale.

"You are my Ice Maiden."

It was a man's voice, a voice she knew, but could not immediately place. Before Jessica could turn and draw her weapon, the man yanked the table from her grasp. He swung it at her head, slamming it into her temple with a force that brought with it a universe of stars.

The next thing Jessica knew she was on the living room's wet, cold floor. She felt icy water against her face. It was melting snow. A man's hiking boots stood inches from her face. She rolled onto her side, the light fading. Her attacker grabbed her by the feet and pulled her across the floor.

Seconds later, before she fell unconscious, the man began to sing.

*"Here are maidens, young and fair . . ."*

# 84

The snow was unremitting. At times Byrne and Vincent had to pull over to let a squall pass. What lights they saw—the occasional house, the occasional commercial enterprise—seemed to come and go in the fog of white.

Vincent's Cutlass was built for the open road, not the snow-covered country lane. At times they drove five miles an hour, wipers on high, headlights illuminating no more than ten feet ahead of them.

They passed through small town after small town. At

six o'clock they realized it might be hopeless. Vincent angled to the side of the road, pulled out his cell phone. He tried Jessica again. He got her voice mail.

He glanced at Byrne, Byrne at him.

"What do we do?" Vincent asked.

Byrne pointed out the driver's side window. Vincent turned, looked.

The sign seemed to appear out of nowhere.

DOUG'S DEN.

THERE WERE ONLY two couples in the restaurant, along with a pair of middle-aged waitresses. The interior was standard home-style small-town décor—red and white checked tablecloths, vinyl-covered chairs, a ceiling spider-webbed with white Christmas minilights. A fire burned in a stone fireplace. Vincent showed his ID to one of the waitresses.

"We're looking for two women," Vincent said. "Police officers. They may have stopped here today."

The waitress looked at the two detectives with well-worn country skepticism.

"Can I see that ID again?"

Vincent took a deep breath, handed the wallet to her. She scrutinized it for what seemed like thirty seconds, handed it back.

"Yes. They were here," she said.

Byrne noticed that Vincent had that look. The impatient look. *The Double K Auto look.* Byrne hoped Vincent wasn't about to start body-slamming sixty-year-old waitresses.

"About what time?" Byrne asked.

"Maybe one o'clock or so. They spoke to the owner. Mr. Prentiss."

"Is Mr. Prentiss here now?"

"No," the waitress said. "I'm afraid he stepped out for a bit."

Vincent checked his watch. "Do you know where these two women went from here?" he asked.

"Well, I know where they said they were *heading*," she said. "There's a small art-supply store at the end of this street. It's closed now, though."

Byrne looked at Vincent. Vincent's eyes said: *No it isn't.*

And then he was out the door, once again a blur.

# 85

Jessica was cold and damp. Her head felt as if it were full of broken glass. Her temple throbbed.

At first it felt as if she might be in a boxing ring. She'd been knocked down a few times in sparring, and the first sensation had always been one of falling. Not to the canvas—through space. Then the pain.

She was not in the ring. It was too cold.

She opened her eyes, felt the ground around her. Wet earth, pine needles, leaves. She sat up, a little too quickly. The world spun out of balance. She lowered herself onto an elbow. After a minute or so, she looked around.

She was in the forest. There was even an inch or so of snow that had accumulated upon her.

*How long have I been out here? How did I get here?*

She looked around. There were no footprints. The heavy snow had blanketed everything. Jessica gave herself a quick once-over. Nothing broken, nothing seemed fractured.

The temperature was dropping; the snow was falling harder.

Jessica stood up, steadied herself against a tree, did a quick accounting.

No cell phone. No weapon. No partner.

*Nicci.*

AT SIX-THIRTY IT stopped snowing. But it had gotten fully dark, and Jessica had no way of knowing direction. She was far from an outdoor expert to begin with, but what little she knew she could not use.

The forest was dense. Every so often she clicked on her dying Maglite, hoping to gain some sort of bearing. She didn't want to use up what little battery life she had. She didn't know how long she would be out here.

She lost her footing a few times on icy rocks hidden beneath the snow, repeatedly tumbling to the ground. She decided to walk from barren tree to barren tree, holding on to low branches. It made her progress slower, but she did not need to twist an ankle or worse.

After something like thirty minutes, Jessica stopped. She thought she heard . . . a stream? Yes, it was the sound of water trickling. But where was it coming from? She determined that it was coming from over a slight rise to her right. She slowly negotiated the incline, saw it. A narrow brook snaked its way through the woods. She was no expert on waterways, but the fact that it was moving meant something. Didn't it?

She would follow it. She didn't know if it was leading her deeper into the forest, or closer to civilization. Either way, she was certain of one thing. She had to move. If she stayed in one place, dressed as she was, she would not survive the night. She flashed on the image of Kristina Jakos's frozen skin.

She pulled her coat close to her body, and followed the stream.

# 86

The gallery was called the Art Ark. There were no lights on in the store, but there was a light in the window on the second floor. Vincent pounded hard on the door. After a while a woman's voice, coming from behind the drawn curtain on the door, said, "We're closed."

"We're the police," Vincent said. "We need to talk to you."

The curtain pulled to the side a few inches. "You don't work for Sheriff Toomey," the woman said. "I'm going to call him."

"We're with the Philadelphia PD, ma'am," Byrne said, stepping between Vincent and the door. They were about a second or two away from Vincent knocking the door down, along with what sounded like an elderly woman behind it. Byrne held up his badge. A flashlight shone through the glass. A few seconds later, lights came on inside the store.

"THEY WERE HERE this afternoon," Nadine Palmer said. In her sixties, she wore a red terry cloth robe and Birkenstocks. She had offered them both coffee, which they declined. The TV was on in the corner of the store, another showing of *It's a Wonderful Life*.

"They had a picture of a farmhouse," Nadine said. "Said they were looking for it. My nephew Ben took them up there."

"Is this the house?" Byrne asked, showing her the picture.

"That's the one."

"Is your nephew here now?"

"No. It's New Year's *Eve*, young man. He's with his friends."

"Can you tell us how to get there?" Vincent asked. He was pacing, tapping his fingers on the counter, all but vibrating.

The woman looked at them both a little skeptically. "Lots of interest in that old farmhouse of late. Is there something going on I should know about?"

"Ma'am, it's extremely important we get up to that house right now," Byrne said.

The woman took another few seconds, just for country effect. Then she pulled out a sketchpad and uncapped a pen.

While she drew the map, Byrne glanced at the television in the corner. The movie had been interrupted by a news bulletin on WFMZ, Channel 69. When Byrne saw the subject of the report his heart sank. It was about a murdered woman. A murdered woman who'd just been found on the bank of the Schuylkill River.

"Could you turn that up, please?" Byrne asked.

Nadine turned up the volume.

"—the young woman has been identified as Sa'mantha Fanning of Philadelphia. She had been the subject of an intensive search by local and federal authorities. Her body was found on the eastern bank of the Schuylkill River, near Leesport. More details as we have them."

Byrne knew they were not far from the crime scene, but there was nothing they could do from here. They were way out of their jurisdiction. He called Ike Buchanan at home. Ike would contact the district attorney of Berks County.

Byrne took the map from Nadine Palmer. "We appreciate this. Thank you very much."

"Hope it helps," Nadine said.

Vincent was already out the door. As Byrne turned to leave, a rack of postcards caught his eye, postcards depicting displays of fairy-tale characters—life-size exhibits with what looked like real people in costumes.

*Thumbelina. The Little Mermaid. The Princess and the Pea.*

"What are these?" Byrne asked.

"Those are vintage postcards," Nadine said.

"This was a real place?"

"Oh, sure. It used to be a sort of theme park. Kinda big in the 1940s and 1950s. Pennsylvania had a lot of them in those days."

"Is it still open?"

"No, sorry to say. In fact, they're tearing it down in a few weeks. It hasn't been open in years. I thought you knew about it."

"What do you mean?"

"The farmhouse you're looking for?"

"What about it?"

"StoryBook River is about a quarter mile away. It's been in the Damgaard family for years."

The name slammed into his brain. Byrne ran out of the store, jumped into the car.

As Vincent sped off, Byrne took out the computer printout Tony Park had compiled, the list of patients from the county mental-health clinic. In seconds, he found what he was looking for.

One of Lisette Simon's patients was a man named Marius Damgaard.

Detective Kevin Byrne understood. It was all part of the same evil, an evil that had begun on a bright spring day in April 1995. A day when two little girls had wandered into the forest.

And now Jessica Balzano and Nicci Malone were caught in the fable.

# 87

There's a darkness that lived in southeastern Pennsylvania's woods, a pitch-blackness that seemed to consume every trace of light around it.

Jessica edged along the bank of the running stream, the only sound the flow of the black water. The going was excruciatingly slow. She used her Maglite sparingly. The thin beam illuminated the plump snowflakes falling around her.

She had picked up a branch earlier, and was using it to probe ahead of herself in the darkness, not unlike a blind person on a city sidewalk.

She continued onward, flicking the branch, toeing the frozen ground with each step. She came to a huge obstacle in her path.

Directly ahead was an enormous deadfall of trees. If she were to continue along the stream, she would have to make it over the top. She was wearing leather-soled shoes. Not exactly designed for hiking or climbing.

She found the shortest route, began to scale the tangle of roots and branches. It was covered with snow, with ice beneath that. More than once Jessica slipped, falling backward, scraping her knees and elbows. Her hands felt like they were frozen solid.

After three more attempts, she managed to hold her footing. She made her way to the top, then tumbled down the other side, crashing onto a pile of broken branches and pine needles.

She sat there for a few moments, exhausted, fighting tears. She clicked on the Maglite. It was almost dead. Her muscles ached, her head was throbbing. She frisked herself again, looking for something, anything—gum, mint, breath freshener. She found something in her inside pocket. She was sure it was a tic tac. Some dinner. When she maneuvered it out, she found it was far better than a Tic Tac. It was a Tylenol caplet. She sometimes took a few of the pain relievers with her on the job, and this one must have been a leftover from a previous headache, or hangover. Regardless, she popped it in her mouth, wiggled it down her throat. It probably wouldn't do much for the freight train roaring through her head, but it was a small bead of sanity, a touchstone of a life that seemed a million miles away.

She was in the middle of the forest, it was pitch-black, she had no food or shelter. Jessica thought about Vincent and Sophie. Right about now Vincent was probably climbing the walls. They had made a pact a long time ago—based on the inherent danger of the their jobs— that they would not let dinnertime pass without a phone call. No matter what. Never. If either of them didn't call, something was wrong.

Something was most assuredly wrong here.

Jessica stood up, wincing at the array of pains and aches and scrapes. She tried to get control of her emotions. Then she saw it. A light in the near distance. It was faint, flickering, but clearly manmade, a tiny pin dot of illumination in the huge black picture of night. It might be candles or oil lamps, perhaps a kerosene heater. Regardless, it represented life. It represented *warmth*. Jessica wanted to cry out, but decided against it. The light was too far away, and she had no idea if there were animals nearby. She did not need that kind of attention now.

She could not tell if the light was coming from a house, or even from a structure of any sort. She could not hear the sounds of a nearby road, so it probably wasn't a commercial enterprise, or a vehicle. Maybe it was a small campfire. People camped in Pennsylvania year-round.

Jessica gauged the distance between her and the light, probably no more than a half mile. But it was a half mile she could not see. There could be just about anything in that distance. Rocks, culverts, ditches.

Bears.

But at least she now had a direction.

Jessica took a few shaky steps forward, and headed toward the light.

# 88

Roland was floating. His arms and legs were bound with strong rope. The moon was high, the snow had stopped, the clouds had lifted. In the light reflected from the luminous white earth he saw many things. He was floating down a narrow canal. On either side were large skeletal structures. He saw a display of a huge story-book, open at the center. He saw a display of stone toad-stools. One exhibit looked like the decayed façade of a Norse castle.

The boat was smaller than a dinghy. Roland soon re-alized he was not the only passenger. Someone was sitting directly behind him. Roland struggled to turn around, but he could not move.

"What do you want from me?" Roland asked.

The voice came in a soft whisper, inches from his ear. "I want you to stop the winter."

*What is he talking about?*

"How . . . how can I do that? How can I stop the winter?"

There was a long silence, just the sound of the wooden boat tapping the icy stone walls of the canal as it moved through the maze.

"I know who you are," came the voice. "I know what you've been doing. I've known all along."

A black dread descended upon Roland. Moments later the boat stopped in front of a derelict display to Roland's right. The exhibit contained large snowflakes made of moldering pine, a rusted iron stove with a long neck and tarnished brass knobs. Leaning against the stove were a broom handle and oven scraper. In the middle of the display was a throne made of sticks and twigs. Roland could see the green of the recently snapped branches. The throne was new.

Roland struggled against the ropes, against the nylon belt around his neck. The Lord had abandoned him. He had sought the devil so long, only for it to end like this.

The man stepped around him, to the front of the boat. Roland looked into his eyes. He saw the reflection of Charlotte's face.

Sometimes it's the devil you know.

Beneath the quicksilver moon, the devil leaned forward, gleaming knife in hand, and cut out Roland Hannah's eyes.

# 89

It seemed to take forever. Jessica had fallen only once—slipping on an icy patch on what seemed like a paved path.

The lights she had observed from the stream came from a one-story house. It was still a good distance away, but Jessica saw that she was now in a complex of dilapidated buildings, built around a maze of narrow canals.

Some of the buildings looked like shops in a small Scandinavian village. Others were made to resemble seaport structures. As she wove her way along the banks of the canals, moving deeper into the complex, there were more buildings, more dioramas. All were decrepit, time-worn, broken.

Jessica knew where she was. She had entered the theme park. She had entered StoryBook River.

She found herself a hundred feet away from a building that might have been a re-creation of a Danish schoolhouse.

Inside was candlelight. Bright candlelight. Shadows flickered and danced.

She instinctively went for her weapon, but her holster was empty. She crept closer to the building. In front of her was the widest canal she had yet seen. It led to a boathouse. To her left, thirty or forty feet away, was a small footbridge spanning the canal. At one end of the bridge was a statue holding a lighted kerosene lamp. It cast an eerie copper glow on the night.

As she got closer to the bridge, she realized the figure on it was not a statue at all. It was a man. A man standing on the overpass, staring at the sky.

When Jessica stepped within a few feet of the bridge her heart skipped a beat.

The man was Joshua Bontrager.

And his hands were covered with blood.

# 90

Byrne and Vincent followed the winding road deep into the forest. At times it was merely one lane wide, iced over. Twice they had to cross shaky bridges. A mile or so into the woods they found a gated path leading farther east. Nadine Palmer's handdrawn map didn't show a gate.

"I'm going to try her one more time." Vincent's cell phone was on a dashboard mount. He reached out, hit a number. In a second, the speaker offered the ringing tone. Once. Twice.

And then the phone was answered. It was Jessica's voice mail, but it sounded different. A long hiss, then static. Then breathing.

"Jess," Vincent said.

Silence. Just the low murmur of electronic noise. Byrne looked at the LCD screen. The connection was still open.

*"Jess."*

Nothing. Then a rustling sound. Then, faintly, a voice. A *man's* voice.

*"Here are maidens, young and fair."*

"What?" Vincent asked.

*"Dancing in the summer air."*

"Who the fuck is this?"

*"Like two spinning wheels at play."*

"Answer me!"

*"Pretty maidens dance away."*

As Byrne listened, the skin on his arms began to dimple. He looked at Vincent. The man's expression was blank, impenetrable.

Then the connection broke.

Vincent hit the speed dial. The phone rang again. The same voice mail. He clicked off.

"What the fuck is happening?"

"I don't know," Byrne said. "But it's your move, Vince."

Vincent buried his face in his hands for a second, then looked up. "Let's go find her."

Byrne got out of the car at the gate. It was chained shut with a huge coil of rusted iron chain, padlocked with an old lock. It appeared not to have been disturbed in a long time. Both sides of the road leading deeper into the forest fell off to deep, frozen culverts. They'd never be able to drive around. The vehicle's headlights cut the darkness to a distance of only fifty feet, then the light was choked by the blackness.

Vincent got out of the car, went into the trunk, and retrieved a shotgun. He racked it, shut the trunk. He reached back into the car, cut the headlights and the engine, grabbed the keys. The darkness was now complete; the night, silent.

They stood, two Philadelphia police officers, in the middle of rural Pennsylvania.

Without a word, they started up the trail.

# 91

"It could only have been one place," Bontrager said. "I read the stories, I put it together. It could have only been here. StoryBook River. I should have thought of it before. As soon as it hit me, I got on the road. I was going to call the boss, but I thought it might be a long shot, and it's New Year's Eve."

Josh Bontrager was standing at the center of the footbridge now. Jessica tried to process it all. At that moment, she didn't know what to believe, or who to trust.

"You knew about this place?" Jessica asked.

"I grew up not too far from here. I mean, we weren't allowed to come here, but we all knew about it. My grandmother used to sell some of our preserves to the owners."

"Josh." Jessica gestured to his hands. "Whose blood is that?"

"A man I found."

"A man?"

"Down by the first canal," Josh said. "It's . . . it's pretty bad."

"You found *who*?" Jessica asked. "What are you talking about?"

"He's in one of the exhibits." Bontrager looked at the ground for a moment. Jessica didn't know how to read it. He looked up. "I'll show you."

They walked back across the footbridge. The canals snaked through trees, winding toward the forest, back again. They trod on the narrow stone edges. Bontrager kept his flashlight trained on the ground. After a few minutes they came to one of the displays. There was a stove, a pair of large wooden snowflakes, a stone replica of a sleeping dog. Bontrager shone his flashlight on a figure in the middle of the display, sitting on a throne of sticks. The figure had its head wrapped in red cloth.

The sign above the display read THE SNOW MAN.

"I know this story," Bontrager said. "It's about a snowman who longs to be by a stove."

Jessica stepped closer to the figure. She gently pulled off the wrappings. Dark blood, nearly black in the illumination from the flashlight, dripped into the snow.

The man was bound and gagged. Blood poured from his eyes. Or, more accurately, from their empty sockets. In their place were black triangles.

"My God," Jessica said.

"What?" Bontrager asked. "You know him?"

Jessica steadied herself. The man was Roland Hannah.

"Did you check his vitals?" she asked.

Bontrager looked at the ground. "No, I . . ." Bontrager began. "No, ma'am."

"It's all right, Josh." She stepped forward, felt for a pulse. After a few seconds she found it. He was still alive.

"Call the sheriff's office," Jessica said.

"Already did," Bontrager said. "They're on the way."

"You have your weapon?"

Bontrager nodded, removed his Glock from his holster. He handed it to Jessica. "I don't know what's going on in that building over there." Jessica pointed to the schoolhouse. "But whatever it is we have to stop it."

"Okay." Bontrager's voice sounded a lot less confident than his answer.

"You all right?" Jessica popped the weapon's magazine. Full. She slammed it home, chambered a round.

"Good to go," Bontrager said.

"Keep the light low."

Bontrager took the lead, stooping and keeping his Maglite close to the ground. They were no more than one hundred feet from the schoolhouse. As they wound their way back through the trees, Jessica tried to get a handle on the layout. The small structure had no porch or balconies. There was one door, and two windows in the front. Its sides were obscured by trees. Beneath one of the windows was a small pile of bricks.

When Jessica saw the bricks, she knew. It had been nagging her for days, and now she finally understood.

*His hands.*

*His hands were too soft.*

Jessica peered in the front window. Through the lace curtains she saw the one-room interior. A small stage was at the rear. There were a few wooden chairs scattered about the space, but no other furniture.

There were candles everywhere, including an ornate chandelier suspended from the ceiling.

On stage was a coffin in which Jessica saw the form of a woman. The woman was dressed in a strawberry pink gown. Jessica could not see if she was breathing or not.

A man walked onto the stage, dressed in a dark formal tailcoat, and white wing tip shirt. His vest was red paisley, and his tie a black silk puff. A watch chain looped his vest pockets. A Victorian top hat sat on a nearby table.

He stood over the woman in the elaborately carved coffin, studying her. There was a rope in his hands, a line that looped up to the ceiling. Jessica followed the rope with her gaze. It was difficult to see through the grimy window, but when she made it out, it gave her deep chills. Above the woman hung a large crossbow aimed at her heart. Loaded into the prod was a long steel arrow.

The bow was drawn and was connected to the rope that looped through an eyelet in a beam and then back down.

Jessica stayed low, moving to the clearer window on the left. When she peered through, the scene was unobscured. She almost wished it were not.

The woman in the coffin was Nicci Malone.

# 92

Byrne and Vincent crested the hill overlooking the theme park. The moonlight cast a clear blue light over the valley, and they got a good overview of the park's layout. Canals snaked through the desolate trees. Around each turn, sometimes back to back, were displays and backdrops reaching fifteen to twenty feet in the air. Some looked like giant books, others like ornate storefronts.

The air smelled of earth and compost and rotting flesh.

Only one building had light. A small structure, no more than twenty by twenty feet, near the end of the main canal. From where they stood they saw shadows in the light. They also spotted two people peering into the windows.

Byrne spied a path leading down. It was mostly snow-covered, but there were markers on either side. He pointed it out to Vincent.

A few moments later they headed into the valley, into StoryBook River.

# 93

Jessica opened the door and stepped into the building. She held her weapon at her side, pointing it away from the man on the stage. She was immediately struck by the overpowering smell of dead flowers. The coffin was brimming with them. Daisies, lilies of the valley, roses, gladiolas. The smell was deep and sweetly cloying. She almost gagged.

The peculiarly dressed man onstage immediately turned to greet her.

"Welcome to StoryBook River," he said.

Although his hair was combed straight back, with a razorlike parting on the right side, Jessica recognized him immediately. It was Will Pedersen. Or the young man who had said he was Will Pedersen. The brick mason they had questioned the morning Kristina Jakos's body was found. The man who had come to the Roundhouse—Jessica's own *shop*—and told them of the moon paintings.

They'd had him, and he had walked away. Anger twisted Jessica's stomach. She needed to calm herself. "Thank you," she answered.

"Is it cold out there?"

Jessica nodded. "Very."

"Well, you're welcome to stay here as long as you like." He turned to a large Victrola to his right. "Do you like music?"

Jessica had been here before, at the border of such madness. She would play his game, for the moment. "I love music."

Holding the rope tautly in one hand, he turned the crank with the other, lifted the arm, placed it on an old 78 rpm record. A scratchy rendition of a waltz began, performed on a calliope.

"This is 'The Snow Waltz,'" he said. "It is my absolute favorite."

Jessica closed the door. She glanced around the room. "So, your name isn't Will Pedersen is it?"

"No. I apologize for that. I really don't like to lie."

The idea had needled her for days, but there had been no reason to chase it down. *Will Pedersen's hands were too soft for him to be a brick mason.*

"Will Pedersen is a name I borrowed from a very famous man," he said. "Lieutenant Vilhelm Pedersen illustrated some of Hans Christian Andersen's books. He was truly a great artist."

Jessica glanced at Nicci. She still couldn't tell if she was breathing. "It was clever of you to use that name," she said.

He smiled broadly. "I had to think quickly! I didn't know you were going to talk to me that day."

"What *is* your name?"

He thought on this. Jessica noticed that he appeared taller than the last time they had met, broader through the shoulders. She looked into his dark and penetrating eyes.

"I have been known by many names," he finally replied. "Sean, for one. Sean is a variation of John. Just like Hans."

"But what is your real name?" Jessica asked. "That is, if you don't mind me asking."

"I don't mind. My birth name is Marius Damgaard."

"May I call you Marius?"

He waved a hand. "Please call me Moon."

"Moon," Jessica echoed. She shuddered.

"And please put down the gun." Moon pulled the rope tight. "Put it on the floor, and kick it away from you." Jessica looked at the crossbow. The steel arrow was aimed at Nicci's heart.

"Now, please," Moon added.

Jessica lowered her weapon to the floor. She kicked it away.

"I'm sorry about before, at my grandmother's house," he said.

Jessica nodded. Her head throbbed. She had to *think*. The sound of the calliope made it difficult. "I understand."

Jessica stole another glance at Nicci. No movement.

"When you came to the police station, was that just to taunt us?" Jessica asked.

Moon looked hurt. "No, ma'am. I was simply afraid you would miss it."

"The moon drawing on the wall?"

"Yes, ma'am."

Moon circled the table, smoothing Nicci's gown. Jessica watched his hands. Nicci did not respond to his touch.

"May I ask you a question?" Jessica asked.

"Of course."

Jessica searched for the right tone. "Why? Why have you done all this?"

Moon stopped, his head down. Jessica thought he hadn't heard. Then he looked up, his expression sunny once more.

"To bring the people back, of course. Back to StoryBook River. They're going to tear it all down. Did you know that?"

Jessica found no reason to lie. "Yes."

"You never came here as a child, did you?" he asked.

"No," Jessica said.

"Imagine. This was a magical place where children came. *Families* came. Memorial Day through Labor Day. Every year, year after year."

As he spoke, Moon slightly loosened his grip on the rope. Jessica glanced at Nicci Malone, saw her chest rise and fall.

*If you want to understand magic, you have to believe.*

"And who is this?" Jessica gestured toward Nicci. She hoped this man was too far gone to know she was just playing his game. He was.

"This is Ida," he said. "She will help me bury the flowers."

Although Jessica had read "Little Ida's Flowers" as a child, she could not remember the story's details. "Why are you going to bury the flowers?"

Moon looked vexed for a moment. Jessica was losing him. His fingers caressed the rope. Then he said, slowly, "So that next summer they will bloom more beautifully than ever."

Jessica took a small step to her left. Moon did not notice. "Why do you need the crossbow? I can help you bury the flowers if you like."

"That is kind of you. But in the story, James and Adolphus had crossbows. They could not afford guns."

"I'd like to hear about your grandfather." Jessica edged to her left. Again it went unnoticed. "If you'd like to tell me."

Tears immediately rimmed Moon's eyes. He looked away from Jessica, perhaps in embarrassment. He wiped away the tears, then looked back. "He was a great man. He designed and built StoryBook River with his own hands. All the amusements, all the displays. He was from Denmark, you know, just like Hans Christian Andersen. He was from a small village called Sonder-Oske. Near Aalborg. In fact, this is his father's suit." He gestured to his costume. He stood straighter, as if at attention. "Do you like it?"

"I do. It's very becoming."

The man who called himself Moon smiled. "His name was Frederik. Do you know what that name means?"

"No," Jessica said.

"It means peaceful ruler. That's what my grandfather was. He ruled this peaceful little kingdom."

Jessica glanced past him. There were two windows at the back of the room, one on either side of the stage. Josh Bontrager was working his way around the building to the right. It was her hope that she could distract the man long enough to get him to drop the rope for a moment. She glanced to the window on the right. She didn't see Josh.

"Do you know what Damgaard means?" he asked.

"No." Jessica took another small stride to her left. Moon followed her with his gaze this time, angling himself slightly away from the window.

"In Danish, Damgaard means 'the farmstead by the pond.'"

Jessica needed to keep him talking. "That's pretty," she said. "Have you actually ever been to Denmark?"

Moon's face lit up. He blushed. "Gosh, no. I've only been out of Pennsylvania once."

*To get the nightingales,* Jessica thought.

"When I was small, StoryBook River was already on hard times, you see," he said. "There were all these other places, big noisy ugly places where families went instead. It was bad for my grandmother." He tightened the rope. "She was a hard woman, but she loved me." He gestured to Nicci Malone. "This was her mother's dress."

"It's lovely."

A shadow by the window.

"When I went to the bad place, after the swans, my

grandmother came to see me every weekend. She took the train."

"You mean the swans in Fairmount Park? In 1995?"

"Yes."

Jessica saw the outline of a shoulder in the window. Josh was there.

Moon placed a few more dead flowers in the coffin, gently arranging them. "My grandmother died, you know."

"I read it in the paper. I'm sorry."

"Thank you."

"The tin soldier was close," he said. "He was *very* close."

In addition to the river killings, the man standing in front of her had burned Walt Brigham to death. Jessica flashed on the immolated corpse in the park.

"He was smart," Moon added. "He would have stopped the story before it was over."

"What about Roland Hannah?" Jessica asked.

Moon raised his eyes slowly to meet hers. His gaze seemed to bore right through her. "The Snow Man? There is much about him you do not know."

Jessica moved farther to her left, drawing Moon's eyes from Josh. Josh was now fewer than five linear feet from where Nicci was. If Jessica could just get the man to drop the rope for a second . . .

"I believe people will come back here," Jessica said.

"Do you think so?" He reached over, started the record again. The sound of the steam whistles once more filled the room.

"Absolutely," she said. "People are curious."

Moon went distant again. "I didn't know my great-grandfather. But he was a seafaring man. One time, my grandfather told me a story about him, about how, as a young man, he was out at sea and saw a mermaid. I knew it wasn't true. I'd read it in a book. He also told me that he helped the Danish people build a place called Solvang in California. Do you know that place?"

Jessica had never heard of it. "No."

"It's a genuine Danish village. I'd like to go there someday."

"Maybe you will." Another step to the left. Moon looked up quickly.

"Where are you going, tin soldier?"

Jessica stole a glance at the window. Josh had a large rock in his hands.

"Nowhere," she answered.

Jessica could see Moon's expression shift from affable host to utter madness and rage. He pulled the rope taut. The mechanism of the crossbow groaned above Nicci Malone's prone body.

# 94

Byrne sighted down his pistol. Inside the candlelit room, the man onstage stood behind a coffin. A coffin with Nicci Malone in it. A large crossbow aimed a steel arrow at her heart.

The man was Will Pedersen. He had a white flower in his lapel.

*The white flower*, Natalya Jakos had said.

*Take the shot.*

Seconds earlier Byrne and Vincent had approached the front of the schoolhouse. Jessica was inside, trying to negotiate with the lunatic on the stage. She was working her way to the left.

Did she know that Byrne and Vincent were there? Was she maneuvering out of the way to give them a clear shot?

Byrne raised the barrel of his weapon slightly, allowing for the distortion of the path of the bullet as it passed through the glass. He wasn't sure how the slug would be affected. He sighted down the barrel.

He saw Anton Krotz.

*The white flower.*

He saw the knife at Laura Clarke's throat.

*Take the shot.*

Byrne saw the man lift his arms, the rope. He was going to trigger the crossbow mechanism.

Byrne couldn't wait. Not this time.

He fired.

# 95

Marius Damgaard pulled the rope as a gunshot thundered through the room. At the same instant, Josh Bontrager slammed the rock through the window, smashing the pane into a shower of crystalline glass. Damgaard staggered back, blood now blossoming on his crisp white shirt. Bontrager gained his footing on the icy shards, then lunged across the room, onto the stage, toward the coffin. Damgaard reeled, fell backward, his full weight on the rope. The crossbow mechanism triggered as Damgaard disappeared through the shattered window, leaving a slick scarlet trail on the floor, the wall, the windowsill.

As the steel arrow launched, Josh Bontrager reached Nicci Malone. The projectile slammed into his right thigh, passing through it and into Nicci's flesh. Bontrager shrieked in agony as a great burst of his blood shot across the room.

A moment later, the front door crashed in.

Jessica dove for her weapon, rolled on the floor, aimed. Somehow Kevin Byrne and Vincent were standing in front of her. She scrambled to her feet.

The three detectives dashed over to the stage. Nicci was still alive. The arrowhead had cut into her right shoulder, but the wound did not look serious. Josh's injury looked far worse. The razor sharp arrow had sliced deeply into his leg. It may have hit an artery.

Byrne tore off his coat, his shirt. He and Vincent lifted Bontrager, tied a tight tourniquet around his upper leg. Bontrager screamed in pain.

Vincent turned to his wife, held her. "Are you okay?"

"Yes," Jessica said. "Josh called for backup. The sheriff's office is on the way."

Byrne looked through the shattered window. A dry canal ran behind the building. Damgaard was gone.

"I've got this." Jessica applied pressure to Josh Bontrager's wound. "Go after him," she said.

"Are you sure?" Vincent asked.

"I'm sure. *Go.*"

Byrne slipped his coat back on. Vincent grabbed his shotgun.

They ran out the door into the black night.

# 96

Moon is bleeding. He makes his way to the entrance to StoryBook River, winding his way through the darkness. He cannot see very well, but he knows every turn of the canals, every stone, every display. His breathing is wet and labored, his pace is slow.

He stops for a moment, reaches into his pocket, retrieves his matches. He remembers the story of the little match seller. Barefoot, and with no coat, she found herself alone on New Year's Eve. It was very cold. As the evening grew late, the little girl struck match after match for warmth.

In each flare she saw a vision.

Moon lights a match. In the flame he envisions the beautiful swans, shimmering in the springtime sun. He strikes another. This time he sees Thumbelina, her tiny form on the lily pad. The third match is the nightingale. He remembers her song. The next is Karen, graceful in her red shoes. Then Anne Lisbeth. Match after match glows brightly in the night. Moon sees each face, recalls each story.

He has just a few matches left.

Perhaps, like the little match seller, he will light them all at once. When the girl in the story did that, her grandmother came down and lifted her to heaven.

Moon hears a sound, turns. There is a man standing by the bank of the main canal, just a few feet away. He is not a big man, but he is broad-shouldered, strong *looking. He throws a length of rope over the crossbeam of the huge trellis spanning the Østtunnelen canal.*

Moon knows the story is ending.

He strikes the matches, begins to recite.

*"Here are maidens, young and fair."*

One by one the match heads ignite.

*"Dancing in the summer air."*

A warm radiance fills the world.

*"Like two spinning wheels at play."*

Moon drops the matches to the ground. The man steps forward, ties Moon's hands behind him. Moments later Moon feels the soft rope coil around his neck, sees the gleaming knife in the man's hand.

*"Pretty maidens dance away."*

Moon is swept from his feet, high into the air, moving skyward, heavenward. Below him he sees the beaming faces of the swans, of Anne Lisbeth, of Thumbelina, of Karen, of all the others. He sees the canals, the displays, the wonder that is StoryBook River.

The man disappears into the forest.

On the ground the matchlight flares brightly, burns for a moment, then grows dim.

For Moon, there is now only darkness.

# 97

Byrne and Vincent searched the grounds directly adjacent to the schoolhouse, flashlights held over weapons, finding nothing. The tracks leading around the north side of the structure had been Josh Bontrager's. They dead-ended at the window.

They walked along the banks of the narrow canals that snaked through the trees, their Maglites cutting thin beams through the utter gloom of the night.

After the second turn of the canal they saw the footprints. And blood. Byrne caught Vincent's eye. They would search on separate sides of the six-foot-wide channel.

Vincent crossed the arching footbridge, Byrne stayed on the near side. They hunted through the turning tributaries of the canals. They came upon the decayed displays, all decorated with fading signs:

THE LITTLE MERMAID. THE FLYING TRUNK. THE STORY OF THE WIND. THE OLD STREETLAMP. Real skeletons sat on the displays. Rotting clothes swaddled the figures.

Minutes later, they came to the end of the canals. Damgaard was nowhere in sight. The trellis that spanned the main canal near the entrance was fifty feet away. Beyond that, the world. Damgaard was gone.

"Don't move," came a voice directly behind them.

Byrne heard the rack of a shotgun.

"Put the weapons down nice and slow."

"We're Philly PD," Vincent said.

"I'm not in the habit of repeating myself, young man. Put the weapons on the ground *now*."

Byrne understood. It was the Berks County sheriff's department. He glanced to his right. Deputies moved through the trees, their flashlights slicing the darkness. Byrne wanted to protest—every second they delayed was one more second Marius Damgaard had to get away—but they had no choice. Byrne and Vincent complied. They put their weapons on the ground, then their hands on their heads, interlaced their fingers.

"One at a time," came the voice. "Slowly. Let's see some ID."

Byrne reached into his coat, produced his badge. Vincent followed suit.

"Okay," the man said.

Byrne and Vincent spun around, retrieved their weapons. Behind them stood Sheriff Jacob Toomey and a pair of younger deputies. Jake Toomey was a grizzled fifty, thick neck, country crew cut. His deputies were both 180 pounds of deep-fried adrenaline. Serial killers didn't come to this part of the world that often.

Moments later a county EMS crew ran past, heading to the schoolhouse.

"This all has to do with the Damgaard boy?" Toomey asked.

Byrne laid out the evidence quickly and succinctly.

Toomey looked out over the theme park, then at the ground. *"Shit."*

"Sheriff Toomey." A call came from the other side of the canals, near the park's entrance. The group of men followed the voice, reaching the mouth of the canal. Then they saw it.

A body swung from the center bar of the trellis that spanned the entrance. Above the body, was the once festive legend:

## S ORY OOK RIV R

Half a dozen flashlights illuminated Marius Damgaard's corpse. His hands were tied behind his back. His feet were just a few feet over the water. He was hanging by a blue and white rope. Byrne also saw a pair of footprints leading off into the forest. Sheriff Toomey dispatched a pair of deputies to follow. Shotguns in their hands, they disappeared into the woods.

Marius Damgaard was dead. When Byrne and the others trained their flashlights on the body, they also saw that he had not only been hanged, he had been gutted. A long gaping wound ran from throat to stomach. Entrails dangled, steaming in the frigid night air.

Minutes later, the two deputies returned empty-handed. They met their boss's stare, shook their heads. Whoever had been here, at the site of Marius Damgaard's execution, was gone.

Byrne looked at Vincent Balzano. Vincent turned on his heels and ran back to the schoolhouse.

It was over. Except for the steady dripping from Marius Damgaard's mutilated corpse.

The sound of blood becoming the river.

# 98

Two days after the uncovering of the horrors in Odense, Pennsylvania, the media had all but set up permanent residence in the small rural community. This was international news. Berks County was not ready for the unwanted attention.

Josh Bontrager endured six hours of surgery. He was in stable condition at the Reading Hospital and Medical Center. Nicci Malone had been treated and released.

The initial FBI reports indicated that Marius Damgaard had murdered at least nine people. No forensic evidence had yet been found that tied him directly to the murders of Annemarie DiCillo and Charlotte Waite.

Damgaard had been committed to a mental-health facility in upstate New York for nearly eight years, from the ages of eleven to nineteen. He was released after his grandmother had been taken ill. Within weeks after Elise Damgaard died, his killings resumed.

A thorough search of the house and grounds turned up a number of gruesome finds. Not the least of which was that Marius Damgaard had kept a vial of his grandfather's blood beneath his bed. DNA tests matched it to the "moon" drawings on the victims. The semen belonged to Marius Damgaard himself.

Damgaard had masqueraded as Will Pedersen, and also as a young man named Sean at Roland Hannah's ministry. He had been counseled at the county mental-health facility where Lisette Simon worked. He had visited TrueSew many times, choosing Sa'mantha Fanning as his ideal Anne Lisbeth.

When Marius Damgaard learned that the StoryBook River property—a thousand-acre area Frederik Damgaard had incorporated as a township called Odense in the 1930s—had been condemned and seized for back taxes, and that it was scheduled for demolition, he felt his universe began to crumble. He decided to lead the world back to his beloved StoryBook River, making a trail of death and horror as directions.

ON JANUARY 3, Jessica and Byrne stood near the mouth of the canals that snaked through the theme park. The sun was out; the day portended a false spring. In daylight, it looked drastically different. Despite the rotting timbers and crumbling stonework, Jessica could see how it had once been a place where families had come to enjoy its unique atmosphere. She had seen vintage brochures. It was somewhere she might have brought her daughter.

Now it was a freak show, a place of death that would draw people from all over the world. Perhaps Marius Damgaard would get his wish. The entire complex was a crime scene, and would remain so for a long time to come.

Were there other bodies to be found? Other horrors to discover?

Time would tell.

They had sorted through the hundreds of papers and files—city, state, county, and now federal. One witness statement stuck out for both Jessica and Byrne, a statement unlikely ever to be fully understood. A resident of Pine Tree Lane, one of the access roads leading to the entrance to StoryBook River, had seen a vehicle that night, an idling vehicle just on the shoulder of the road. Jessica and Byrne had visited the spot. It was less than a hundred yards from the trellis where Marius Damgaard had been found hanging and eviscerated. The FBI had taken footwear impressions leading to and from the entrance. The footprints were made by a very popular brand of men's rubber overshoe, available everywhere.

The witness said the idling vehicle was an expensive looking green SUV with yellow fog lamps and extensive detailing.

The witness did not get a license plate.

OUTSIDE THE MOVIE *Witness,* Jessica had never seen so many Amish people in her life. It seemed that the entire Amish population of Berks County had come to Reading. They milled about the lobby of the hospital. The older folks brooded, prayed, observed, shooed the children away from the candy and soda vending machines.

When Jessica introduced herself, they all shook her hand. It seemed that Josh Bontrager had come by it honestly.

"YOU SAVED MY life," Nicci said.

Jessica and Nicci Malone stood at the foot of Josh Bontrager's hospital bed. His room was filled with flowers.

The razor-sharp arrow had slashed Nicci's right shoulder. Her arm was in a sling. The doctors said she would be IOD—injured on duty—for about a month.

Bontrager smiled. "All in a day," he said.

His color had returned; his smile had never left. He sat up in bed, surrounded by about a hundred different cheeses, breads, jars of preserves, and sausages, all wrapped in wax paper. Homemade get-well cards abounded.

"When you get better, I'm buying you the best dinner in Philly," Nicci said.

Bontrager stroked his chin, apparently considering his options. *"Le Bec Fin?"*

"Yeah. Okay. *Le Bec Fin*. You're on," Nicci said.

Jessica knew that *Le Bec* would set Nicci back a few hundred. Small price to pay.

"But you better be careful," Bontrager added.

"What do you mean?"

"Well, you know what they say."

"No, I don't," Nicci said. "What *do* they say, Josh?"

Bontrager winked at her and Jessica. "Once you go Amish, you never go back."

# 99

Byrne sat on a bench outside the courtroom. He had testified countless times in his career—grand juries, preliminary hearings, murder trials. Most of the time he had known exactly what he was going to say, but not this time.

He entered the courtroom, taking a seat in the first row. Matthew Clarke looked about half the size he had been the last time Byrne had seen him. This was not uncommon. Clarke had been holding a gun and guns made people appear bigger. Now the man was craven and small.

Byrne took the stand. The ADA led him through the events of the week leading up to the incident where Clarke took him hostage.

"Is there anything you'd like to add?" the ADA finally asked.

Byrne looked into Matthew Clarke's eyes. He had seen so many criminals in his time, so many men who had no regard for anyone's property or human life.

Matthew Clarke did not belong in jail. He needed help.

"Yes," Byrne said, "there is."

THE AIR OUTSIDE the courthouse had warmed since morning. The weather in Philadelphia was incredibly fickle, but somehow it was nearing forty-two degrees.

As Byrne exited the building he looked up and saw Jessica approaching.

"Sorry I couldn't make it," she said.

"No problem."

"How'd it go?"

"I don't know." Byrne shoved his hands into his coat pockets. "I really don't." They fell silent.

Jessica watched him for a while, wondering what was going through his mind. She knew him well, and knew that the matter of Matthew Clarke would weigh heavily on his heart.

"Well, I'm heading home." Jessica knew when the walls went up with her partner. She also knew there would eventually come a day when Byrne would talk about it. They had all the time in the world. "Need a ride?"

Byrne looked at the sky. "I think I'm going to walk for a while."

"Uh-oh."

"What?"

"You start walking, the next thing you know you'll be running."

Byrne smiled. "You never know."

Byrne turned up his collar, descended the steps.

"See you tomorrow," Jessica said.

Kevin Byrne didn't answer.

PADRAIG BYRNE STOOD in the front room of his new home. The boxes were stacked everywhere. His favorite chair was positioned across from his new 42-inch plasma television, a housewarming gift from his son.

Byrne walked into the room, a pair of glasses in hand, glasses containing two inches of Jameson each. He handed one to his father.

They stood, strangers in a strange place. They had never been in a moment like this before. Padraig Byrne had just left the only house in which he had ever lived. The house into which he had carried his bride, raised his son.

They lifted their glasses.

"*Dia duit,*" Byrne said.

"*Dia is Muire duit.*"

They clinked glasses, downed the whiskey.

"You going to be okay?" Byrne asked.

"I'm *fine,*" Padraig said. "Don't you worry about me."

"Right, Da."

Ten minutes later, as Byrne was pulling out of the driveway, he glanced up to see his father standing in the doorway. Padraig looked a little smaller in this place, a little farther away.

Byrne wanted to freeze the moment in his mind. He didn't know what tomorrow would bring, how much time they would have together. But he knew that, for the moment, for the foreseeable future, everything was okay.

He hoped his father felt the same way.

BYRNE RETURNED THE moving van, retrieved his car. He got off the expressway and headed down to the Schuylkill. He got out, stood at the riverbank.

He closed his eyes, reliving the moment when he pulled the trigger in that house of madness. Had he hesitated? He honestly couldn't remember. Regardless, he had taken the shot, and that was what mattered.

Byrne opened his eyes. He watched the river, contemplated the secrets of a thousand years as it flowed silently past him; the tears of desecrated saints, the blood of broken angels.

The river never tells.

He got back into his car, reached the entrance to the expressway. He looked at the green and white signs. One led back to the city. One led west, toward Harrisburg, Pittsburgh, and points northwest.

Including Meadville.

Detective Kevin Francis Byrne took a deep breath.

And made his choice.

# 100

There was purity in his darkness, a clarity underscored by the serene weight of permanence. There were moments of relief, as if it had all happened—all of it, from the moment he first stepped onto that damp field, to the day he first turned the key in the door of that ramshackle row house in Kensington, to the stinking breath of Joseph Barber as he bid good-bye to this mortal coil—to lead him to this black, seamless world.

But darkness was not darkness to the Lord.

Every morning they came to his cell and led Roland Hannah to the small chapel, where he would hold service. At first he did not want to leave his cell. But soon he realized that this was just a diversion, a stopover on his road to salvation and glory.

He would be in this place the rest of his life. There had been no trial. They had asked Roland what he had done, and he had told them. He would not lie.

But the Lord came here too. In fact, the Lord was here this very day. And in this place were many sinners, many men in need of correction.

Pastor Roland Hannah would deal with them all.

# 101

Jessica arrived at the Devonshire Acres facility at just after four o'clock on February 5. The imposing fieldstone complex was set atop a gently rolling hill. A few outbuildings dotted the landscape.

Jessica came to the facility to speak with Roland Hannah's mother, Artemisia Waite. Or to try to. Her boss had left it up to her whether or not to conduct the interview, to put a period at the end of the report, the story that began on a bright spring day in April 1995, a day when two little girls went to the park for a birthday picnic, the day when a long litany of horrors began.

Roland Hannah had pled out, and was serving eighteen life sentences, no parole. Kevin Byrne, along with a retired detective named John Longo, had helped compile the state's case against the man, much of it based on Walt Brigham's notes and files.

It was unknown whether Roland Hannah's stepbrother Charles had been involved in the vigilante murders, or whether he had been with Roland that night in Odense. If he had, one mystery remained: How had Charles Waite gotten back to Philly? He could not drive. It was the court-appointed psychologist's opinion that the man functioned at the level of a bright nine-year-old.

Jessica stood in the parking lot, next to her car, her mind swirling with questions. She sensed a presence approaching. She was surprised to see it was Richie DiCillo.

"Detective," Richie said. It was almost as if he had been expecting her.

"Richie. Good to see you."

"Happy New Year."

"Same to you," Jessica said. "What brings you all the way out here?"

"Just following up on something." He said it with the sort of finality Jessica recognized in all veteran cops. There would be no more questions about it.

"How's your father?" Richie asked.

"He's good," Jessica said. "Thanks for asking."

Richie glanced at the complex of buildings, back. The moment drew out. "So, how long have you been on the job now? If you don't mind me asking."

"I don't mind at all," Jessica said, smiling. "It's not like you're asking my age. It's been more than ten years."

"Ten years." Richie mugged, nodded. "I've been at it almost thirty. Flies by, doesn't it?"

"It does. You don't think it will, but it seems like just yesterday I put on the blues and hit the street for the first time."

It was all subtext, and they both knew it. Nobody saw through or created bullshit better than cops. Richie rocked on his heels, glanced at his watch. "Well, I've got bad guys waiting to be caught," he said. "Good seeing you."

"Same here." Jessica wanted to add a great deal to that. She wanted to say something about Annemarie, about how sorry she was. She wanted to say how she understood that there was a hole in his heart that would never be filled, no matter how much time passed, no matter how a story ended.

Richie got out his car keys, turned to go. He hesitated for a moment, as if he had something to say, but had no idea how to say it. He glanced at the main building of the facility. When he looked back at Jessica, she thought she saw something in the man's eyes she had never seen before, not in a lifer, not in a man who had seen as much as Richie DiCillo had seen.

She saw peace.

"Sometimes," Richie began, "justice is done."

Jessica understood. And the understanding was a cold dagger in her chest. She probably should have let it lie, but she was her father's daughter. "Didn't someone once say that we get justice in the next world, but in this world we have the law?"

Richie smiled. Before he turned and walked across the parking lot, Jessica glanced at his overshoes. They looked new.

*Sometimes justice is done.*

A minute later Jessica saw Richie pull out of the parking lot. He waved one last time. She waved back.

As he drove away, Jessica found she was not all that surprised to find that Detective Richard DiCillo drove a large green SUV, an SUV with yellow fog lamps and extensive detailing.

Jessica looked at the main building. On the second floor were a series of small windows. In the window she spotted two people watching her. It was too far away to make out their features, but there was something about the tilt of their heads, the set of the shoulders, that told her she was being observed.

Jessica thought about StoryBook River, about that heart of madness.

Had Richie DiCillo been the one who tied Marius Damgaard's hands behind him and hanged him? Had Richie driven Charles Waite back to Philadelphia?

Jessica decided that she just might take another ride to Berks County. Maybe justice had not yet been done.

FOUR HOURS LATER she found herself in her kitchen. Vincent was in the basement with two of his brothers watching a Flyers game. Dishes were in the dishwasher. Leftovers were put away. She had a glass of Montepulciano working. Sophie sat in the living room, watching a DVD of *The Little Mermaid*.

Jessica walked into the living room, sat next to her daughter. "Tired, sweetie?"

Sophie shook her head and yawned. "No."

Jessica held Sophie close. Her daughter had that little-girl bubble-bath smell. Her hair was a bouquet of flowers. "Time for bed anyway."

"Okay."

Later, with her daughter snuggled under the covers, Jessica kissed Sophie on the forehead, reached over to turn out the light.

"Mom?"

"What, sweetie?"

Sophie rummaged under the quilt. She pulled out a book by Hans Christian Andersen, one of the tomes Jessica had checked out of the library.

"Read me a story?" Sophie asked.

Jessica took the book from her daughter, opened it, glanced at the illustration on the title page. It was a woodcut illustration of the moon.

Jessica closed the book, flipped off the light.

"Not tonight, honey."

TWO AM.

Jessica sat on the edge of the bed. She had felt the stirrings inside her for a few days. Not the certainty, but the possibility of the possibility, a feeling once removed from hope, twice from disappointment.

She turned to look at Vincent. Dead to the world. God only knew what galaxies he conquered in his dreams.

Jessica glanced out the window, at the full moon high in the night sky.

Just moments later she heard the egg timer ding in the bathroom. Poetic, she thought. *Egg timer.* She got up, scuffed her way across the bedroom.

She flipped on the light, looked at the two ounces of white plastic sitting on the vanity. She was scared of the *yes*. Scared of the *no*.

*Babies*.

Detective Jessica Balzano—a woman who strapped on a weapon and faced danger every day of her life— trembled slightly as she stepped into the bathroom, and closed the door.

# EPILOGUE

There was music. A piano song. Bright yellow daffodils smiled from the window boxes. The common room was nearly empty. It would soon fill up.

The decorations on the walls were bunnies and ducks and Easter eggs.

At five thirty they brought dinner. Tonight it was Salisbury steak and mashed potatoes. There was also a cup of applesauce.

Charles looked out the window, at the long shadows growing in the forest. It was springtime, the air was fresh. The world smelled like green apples. Soon it would be April. April meant danger.

Charles knew there was still peril in the forest, a darkness that swallowed the light. He knew that girls should not venture into the woods. His twin sister Charlotte had ventured into the woods.

He took his mother's hand.

It was up to him, now that Roland was gone. There was so much evil out there. Ever since he had come to live at Devonshire Acres he had watched the shadows take human form. And at night he heard their whispers. He heard the rustling of leaves, the swirling of the wind.

He put his arm around his mother. She smiled. They would be safe now. As long as they stayed together,

they would be safe from the bad things in the forest.
Safe from those who would do them harm.

*Safe*, Charles Waite thought.

Ever after.

# ACKNOWLEDGMENTS

There are no fables without magic. My deepest thanks to Meg Ruley, Jane Berkey, Peggy Gordijn, Don Cleary, and all at the Jane Rotrosen Agency; thanks as always to my fabulous editor, Linda Marrow, as well as Dana Isaacson, Gina Centrello, Libby McGuire, Kim Hovey, Rachel Kind, Dan Mallory, and the great team at Ballantine Books; thanks again to Nikola Scott, Kate Elton, Cassie Chadderton, Louisa Gibbs, Emma Rose, and the brilliant group at Random House UK.

A cheer (yo) for the Philly crew: Mike Driscoll and the gang at Finnigan's Wake (and Ashburner Inn), as well as Patrick Ghegan, Jan Klincewicz, Karen Mauch, Joe Drabyak, Joe Brennan, Halley Spencer (Mr. Wonderful), and Vita DeBellis.

For their expertise, thanks to the Honorable Seamus McCaffery, Detective Michele Kelly, Sgt. Gregory Masi, Sgt. Joanne Beres, Detective Edward Rocks, Detective Timothy Bass, and the men and women of the Philadelphia Police Department; thanks to J. Harry Isaacson, MD; thanks to Crystal Seitz, Linda Wrobel, and the gracious folks at the Reading & Berks County Visitors Bureau for the coffee and maps; thanks to DJC and DRM for the wine and patience.

Once again, I'd like to thank the city and people of Philadelphia for indulging my imagination.

READ ON FOR A PREVIEW OF
RICHARD MONTANARI'S
CHILLING NEW NOVEL

# BADLANDS

AVAILABLE IN HARDCOVER
FROM BALLANTINE BOOKS
IN SEPTEMBER 2008

In the darkness, in the deep violet folds of night, he hears whispers: low, plaintive sounds that dart and shudder and scratch behind the wainscoting, the cornice, the parched and wormy wood lath. At first the words seem foreign, as if uttered in another language, but as dusk inches toward dawn he comes to recognize every voice—every pitch, tone, and timbre—as a mother would her child on a crowded playground.

Some nights he hears a solitary scream rage beneath the floorboards, stalking him from room to room, down the grand staircase, across the foyer, through the kitchen and pantry, into the consecrated silence of the cellar. There, below ground, entombed by a thousand centuries of bone and fur, he accepts the gravity of his sins. Perhaps it is the dampness itself that accuses, icy droplets on stone shimmering like tears on a brocade bodice.

As memories flower, he recalls Elise Beausoleil, the girl from Chicago. He recalls her proud manner and capable hands, the way she bargained in those final seconds, as if she were still the prettiest girl at the prom. A Dickensian waif in her high boots and belted coat, Elise Beausoleil liked to read. Jane Austen was her favorite, she said, although she considered Charlotte Brontë a close second. He found a yellowed copy of Villette in her purse. He kept Elise in the library.

In time he recalls Monica Renzi, her thick limbs and

body hair, the frisson of exhilaration as he enthusiastically raised his hand like one of her contemptuous classmates when she asked why. The daughter of a Scranton shopkeeper, Monica liked to dress in red; shy and wordstruck and virginal. Monica once told him that he reminded her of a young banker in one of those old movies she had watched with her grandmother on Saturday nights. Monica's room was the solarium.

He recalls the thrill of the chase, the bitter coffees consumed in rail stations and bus terminals, the heat and noise and dust of amusement parks and Home Days and county fairs, the frigid mornings in the car. He recalls the excitement of driving through the city, his quarry so delicately in hand, the puzzle enticingly engaged.

In that gauzy cleave between shade and light, in that gray confessional of dawn, he remembers it all.

EACH MORNING the house falls silent. Dust settles, shadows depart, voices still.

On this morning he showers and dresses and breakfasts, steps through the front door onto the porch. Daffodils near the sidewalk fence greet him, brazen blondes spiriting through the cold sod. A breeze carries the first breath of spring.

Behind him looms a sprawling Victorian house, a lady of long-faded finery. Her back gardens and side yards are overgrown, her stone paths tufted, her gutters dense with verdigris. She is the very museum of his existence, a house crafted at a time when dwellings of such distinction and character were given names, names that would enter the consciousness of the landscape, the soul of the city, the lore of the region.

In this mad place where walls move and stairways lead nowhere, where closets give onto clandestine workshops and portraits solemnly observe each other in the midday silence, he knows every corridor, every hinge, every sill, sash, and dentil.

This place is called Faerwood. In each of its rooms there dwells a restive soul. In each soul, a secret.

HE STANDS in the center of the crowded shopping mall, taking in the aromas: the food court and its myriad riches; the department store with its lotions and powders and cloying toilettes; the salt of young women. He surveys the overweight couples in their twenties, urging the laden pram. He laments the invisible elderly.

At ten minutes to nine he slips into a narrow store. It is garishly lit, stocked floor to ceiling with ceramic figurines and rayon roses. Small, shiny balloons dance in the overheated air. An entire wall is devoted to greeting cards.

There is only one other patron in the store. He has been following her all evening, has seen the sadness in her eyes, the weight on her shoulders, the fatigue in her stride.

She is the Drowning Girl.

He eases next to her, selects a few cards from the glittering array, chuckles softly at each, returns them to the rack. He glances around. No one is watching.

It is time.

"You look a little confused," he says.

She glances up. She is tall and thin, magnificently pale. Her ash blond hair is pinned in a messy fashion, held in place by white plastic barrettes. Her neck is carven ivory. She wears a lilac backpack.

She doesn't respond. He has scared her.

Walk away.

"There are too many choices!" she says animatedly, but not without caution. He expects this. He is, after all, an unknown piece on her game board of strangers. She giggles, chews on a fingernail. Adorable. She is about seventeen. The best age.

"Tell me the occasion," he says. "Maybe I can help."

A flash of distrust now—cat paws on an oven door. She peers around the room, at the publicness of it all. "Well," she begins, "my boyfriend is . . ."

Silence.

He begs the conversation forward. "He's what?"

She doesn't want to say, then she does. "Okay . . . he's not exactly my boyfriend, right? But he's cheating on me." She tucks a filament of hair behind an ear. "Well, not exactly cheating. Not yet." She turns to leave, turns back. "Okay, he asked out my best friend, Courtney. The slut." She reddens, a sheer crimson pall on her flawless skin. "I can't believe I'm telling you this."

He is dressed casually this evening: faded jeans, black linen blazer, loafers, a little extra gel in his hair, a silver ankh around his neck, eyeglasses of a modern style. He looks young enough. Besides, he has the sort of bearing that invites faith. It always has. "The cad," he says.

Wrong word? No. She smiles. Seventeen going on thirty.

"More like a jerk. A total jerk." Another nervous giggle.

He leans away from her, increasing the distance by mere inches. Important inches. She relaxes. She has decided he is no threat. Like one of her cool teachers.

"Do you think dark humor is appropriate for the occasion?"

She considers this. "Probably," she says. "Maybe. I don't know. I guess."

"Does he make you laugh?"

Boyfriends—boys who become boyfriends—usually do. Even the ones who cheat on achingly beautiful seventeen-year-old girls.

"Yeah. He's kinda funny. Sometimes." She looks up,

making deep eye contact. This moment all but splinters his heart. "But not lately."

"I was looking at this one," he says. "I think it might be just the right sentiment." He lifts a card from the rack, considers it for a moment, hands it over. It is a bit risqué. His hesitation speaks of his respect for the age difference, the fact that they've just met.

She takes the card, opens it, reads the greeting. A moment later she laughs, covering her mouth. A tiny snort escapes. She blushes, embarrassed.

In this instant her image blurs, as it always has, like a face obscured by rain on a shattered windshield.

"This is, like, totally perfect," she says. "Totally. Thanks."

He watches as she glances at the vacant cashier, then at the video camera. She turns her back to the camera, stuffs the card into her bag, looks at him, a smile on her face. If there was a purer love, he could not imagine it.

"I need another card, too," she says. "But I'm not sure you can help me with that one."

"You'd be surprised what I can do."

"It's for my parents." She cocks a hip. Another blush veils her pretty face, then quickly disappears. "It's because I've—"

He holds up a hand, stopping her. It is better this way. "I understand."

"You do?"

"Yes."

"What do you mean?"

He smiles. "I was once your age."

She parts her lips to answer, but instead remains silent.

"It all works out in the end," he adds. "You'll see. It always does."

She looks away for a second. It is as if she has made some sort of decision in this moment, as though a great weight has been lifted from her shoulders. She glances back at him, smiles sadly, and says: "Thanks."

Instead of responding, he just gazes at her with great fondness. The overhead lights cast golden highlights in her hair. In an instant, it comes to him.

He will keep her in the pantry.

TEN MINUTES later he follows her, unseen, into the parking lot, conscious of the shadow, the light, the carbon blue chiaroscuro of the evening. It has begun to rain, a light drizzle that does not threaten a downpour.

He watches as she crosses the avenue, steps into a shelter. Soon after, she boards the bus, a shuttle to the train station.

He slips a CD into the player. In seconds the sounds of "Vedrai, Carino" fill the car. It regales his soul—once again, exalting this moment, as only Mozart can.

He follows the bus into the city, his heart ablaze, the hunt renewed.

She is Emma Bovary. She is Elizabeth Bennet. She is Cassiopeia and Cosette.

She is his.